Praise for the nove~~l~~
bestselling auth~~or~~

"Macomber is a skilled storyt~~eller~~"

"Debbie Macomber demonstrates her impressive skills with characterization and her flair for humor."
—*RT Book Reviews*

"Whether [Debbie Macomber] is writing lighthearted romps or more serious relationship books, her novels are always engaging stories that accurately capture the foibles of real-life men and women with warmth and humor."
—*Milwaukee Journal Sentinel*

"Debbie Macomber tells women's stories in a way no one else does."
—*BookPage*

"Macomber...is no stranger to the *New York Times* beseller list. She knows how to please her audience."
—*Oregon Statesman Journal*

Praise for the novels of bestselling author Sheila Roberts

"Sweet, affecting, and emotionally charged, this multi-threaded story highlights the complex relationships between mothers and daughters, and while more women's fiction than pure romance, this is sure to appeal to fans of both genres."
—*Library Journal* on *A Wedding on Primrose Street*

"Whenever I start a Sheila Roberts book, I know that I won't be able to stop until the very last page. *A Wedding on Primrose Street* is no exception.... It's like going home and visiting with old friends."
—*Fresh Fiction*

"*The Lodge on Holly Road* is the ultimate in feel-good family drama and heart-melting romance."
—*USA TODAY*

"Homing in on issues many readers can identify with, Roberts's women search for solutions to a common challenge with humor..."
—*Publishers Weekly*

DEBBIE MACOMBER

SHEILA ROBERTS

Wedding Dreams

MIRA

ISBN-13: 978-0-7783-1903-0

Recycling programs for this product may not exist in your area.

Wedding Dreams

Copyright © 2016 by Harlequin Books S.A.

The publisher acknowledges the copyright holders of the individual works as follows:

First Comes Marriage
Copyright © 1991 by Debbie Macomber

Sweet Dreams on Center Street
First published in 2012 by MIRA Books under the title
Better Than Chocolate
Copyright © 2012 by Sheila Rabe
This edition published August 2016

For questions and comments about the quality of this book, please contact us at CustomerService@Harlequin.com.

www.MIRABooks.com

Printed in U.S.A.

CONTENTS

FIRST COMES MARRIAGE

Debbie Macomber

Also by Debbie Macomber

Blossom Street

The Shop on Blossom Street
A Good Yarn
Susannah's Garden
Back on Blossom Street
Twenty Wishes
Summer on Blossom Street
Hannah's List
The Knitting Diaries
  ("The Twenty-First Wish")
A Turn in the Road

Cedar Cove

16 Lighthouse Road
204 Rosewood Lane
311 Pelican Court
44 Cranberry Point
50 Harbor Street
6 Rainier Drive
74 Seaside Avenue
8 Sandpiper Way
92 Pacific Boulevard
1022 Evergreen Place
Christmas in Cedar Cove
  (*5-B Poppy Lane* and
  A Cedar Cove Christmas)
1105 Yakima Street
1225 Christmas Tree Lane

Dakota Series

Dakota Born
Dakota Home
Always Dakota
Buffalo Valley

The Manning Family

The Manning Sisters
  (*The Cowboy's Lady* and
  The Sheriff Takes a Wife)

The Manning Brides
  (*Marriage of Inconvenience* and
  Stand-In Wife)
The Manning Grooms
  (*Bride on the Loose* and
  Same Time, Next Year)

Christmas Books

A Gift to Last
On a Snowy Night
Home for the Holidays
Glad Tidings
Christmas Wishes
Small Town Christmas
When Christmas Comes
  (now retitled *Trading
  Christmas*)
*There's Something About
  Christmas*
Christmas Letters
The Perfect Christmas
Choir of Angels
  (*Shirley, Goodness and Mercy*,
  Those Christmas Angels and
  Where Angels Go)
Call Me Mrs. Miracle

Heart of Texas

VOLUME 1
  (*Lonesome Cowboy* and
  Texas Two-Step)
VOLUME 2
  (*Caroline's Child* and
  Dr. Texas)
VOLUME 3
  (*Nell's Cowboy* and
  Lone Star Baby)
Promise, Texas
Return to Promise

To Anna and Anton Adler,
Russian immigrants and my loving grandparents.
Thank you for the wonderful heritage you gave me.

One

"You must be Zachary Thomas," Janine said breathlessly as she whirled into the office. "Sorry I'm late, but I got hung up in traffic on Fourth Avenue. I didn't realize they'd torn up the whole street." Still a little winded, she unfastened her coat, tossed it over the back of the visitor's chair and threw herself down, facing the large executive desk.

The man on the other side blinked twice as though he didn't know quite what to think.

"I'm Janine Hartman." She drew in a deep breath. "Gramps said if he wasn't back from his appointment, I should introduce myself."

"Yes," Zachary said after a moment of strained silence. "But he didn't tell me you'd be wearing—"

"Oh, the bandanna dress," Janine said, smoothing one hand over her lap. The dress had been constructed of red and blue bandannas; it featured a knee-length zigzag hemline and closely hugged her hips. "It was a gift. And since I'm meeting the girl who made it later, I thought I should wear it."

"And the necklace?"

Janine toyed with the colored Christmas-tree lights strung between large beads on a bootlace that dangled from her neck. "It's a bit outrageous, isn't it? That was a gift, too. I think it's kind of cute, don't you? Pamela is so clever."

"Pamela?"

"A teenager from the Friendship Club."

"I…see," Zach said.

"I do volunteer work there and the two of us hit it off as soon as we met. Pam's mother doesn't live in the area and she's at that awkward age and needs a friend. For some reason she took a liking to me, which was fine because I think she's wonderful."

"I see," he said again.

Janine doubted he did.

"The necklace is *different* I'll grant you," Zach was saying—which wasn't admitting to much. His dark eyes narrowed as he studied it.

Now that she'd met Zachary Thomas, Janine could understand why her grandfather was so impressed with him—if appearances were anything to judge by. In his well-tailored suit, he was the very picture of a high-powered executive, crisp, formal and in control. He was younger than she'd assumed, possibly in his early thirties, but it was difficult to tell. His facial features were attractive enough, but he wasn't strikingly handsome. Still, she found herself fascinated by the strength of character she saw in the uneven planes of his face. His dark hair was cut military short. His jaw was strong, his cheekbones high and his mouth full. That was the way she'd describe him physically, but there was apparently much more to this man than met the eye. At least, her grandfather was convinced of it.

Several months earlier Anton Hartman had merged his well-established business-supply firm with the fast-expanding company owned by Zachary Thomas. Together the two men had quickly dominated the market.

For weeks now, Gramps had wanted Janine to meet Zachary. His name had popped up in every conversation, no matter what they were discussing. To say her grandfather thought highly of his partner was an understatement.

"Gramps has spoken...well of you," she said next.

A hint of a smile—just the merest suggestion—touched his mouth, giving her the impression that he didn't smile often. "Your grandfather has one of the keenest business minds in the country."

"He's incredible, isn't he?"

Zachary's nod betrayed no hesitation.

There was a polite knock on the door and a tall middle-aged woman wearing a navy-blue pin-striped suit stepped into the room. "Mr. Hartman phoned," she announced primly. "He's been delayed and asked that you meet him at the restaurant."

Zach's lean dark face tightened briefly before he cast Janine an uneasy glance. "Did he say when he was going to get there?"

"I'm sorry, Mr. Thomas, but he didn't."

Janine looked at her watch. She was supposed to meet Pam at three. If they were delayed much longer, she'd be late.

She scowled at Zach's apparent reluctance to entertain her in Gramp's absence. "Maybe it would be best if we rescheduled for another day," she offered brightly. She wasn't any happier about the prospect of waiting in a restaurant, just the two of them, than he was. "Gramps is held up, I'm meeting Pam, and you're obviously a busy man."

An uncomfortable silence followed her remark. "Is it your habit not to show up when your grandfather's expecting you?" he asked sharply.

Janine bristled. "Of course not." She swallowed the words to defend herself. Her suggestion hadn't been unreasonable and he had no right to insinuate that she was inconsiderate and rude.

"Then I feel we should meet your grandfather at the restaurant as he requested," he finished stiffly.

"By all means," she said, forcing a smile. She stood and reached for her coat, watching Zach from the corner of her eye. He didn't like her. That realization had a peculiar effect on Janine. She felt disappointed and a little sad. Zach hadn't said much, and actually there hadn't been time for a real conversation, but she'd sensed his attitude almost from the first. He thought of her as spoiled and frivolous, probably because he knew she didn't hold a responsible job and loved to travel. Part of her longed to explain that there were good reasons she'd chosen the lifestyle she had. But from the looks he was sending her, it would be a waste of breath.

Besides, it was more important to maintain the peace, however strained, for Gramps's sake. She'd have enjoyed getting to know Zach, perhaps even becoming friends, but that didn't seem likely.

That morning, before Gramps had left the house, he'd been as excited as a little boy about their luncheon date. He'd come down the stairs whistling when he'd joined her for breakfast, his blue eyes sparkling. When she'd refused the use of the limousine, he'd spent the next fifteen minutes giving her detailed directions, as though she'd never driven in downtown Seattle.

Almost as an afterthought, he'd mentioned that he had a morning meeting with an important client. If he hadn't returned by the time she arrived, she was to go directly to Zach's office, introduce herself and wait for him there.

Shrugging into a raincoat, Zachary moved toward the door. "Are you ready?"

She nodded, burying her hands in her pockets.

Thankfully the restaurant her grandfather had chosen was close by. Without further discussion, they began to walk the few short blocks, although Janine had trouble matching her stride with Zach's much longer one.

Struggling to keep up with him, Janine studied Zachary Thomas, trying to determine exactly what disturbed her about the man. His height was a good example. He wasn't tall—under six feet, she guessed—and since she was almost five-eight there wasn't more than a few inches' difference between them. Why, then, did he make her feel much shorter?

He must have sensed her scrutiny because he turned and glared at her. Janine gave him a feeble smile, and felt the color rise in her cheeks. Zach's dismissive glance did nothing to boost her ego. She wasn't vain, but Janine knew she was attractive. Over the years, plenty of men had told her so, including Brian, the man who'd broken her heart. But she could have warts on her nose for all the notice Zachary Thomas gave her.

If he found the bandanna dress disconcerting, he was probably put off by her hairstyle as well. She wore it short, neatly trimmed in the back with extra-long bangs slanted across her forehead. For years Janine had kept her hair shoulder-length, parted in the middle. One afternoon a few weeks earlier, for no particular reason, she'd decided to have it cut. She was in the mood for something radical and the style she now sported seemed more appropriate to the pages of a fashion magazine. Pam had been crazy about the change, insisting she looked "phenomenal." Janine wasn't convinced. Her one comfort was that, given time, her hair would grow back.

Janine suspected Zach had characterized her as flamboyant, if not downright flashy. She, in turn, would describe him as austere and disciplined, perhaps solitary. Her grandfather saw all that, she knew, and a good deal more.

"Mr. Hartman is waiting for you," the maître d' informed them when they entered the plush waterfront restaurant. He led them across the thick carpet to a high semicircular booth upholstered in blue velvet.

"Janine, Zach." Anton Hartman smiled broadly as they approached. The years had been kind to her grandfather. His bearing was still straight and confident, although his hair had grown completely white. His deep blue eyes, only a little faded, were filled with warmth and wisdom. "I apologize for the inconvenience."

"It wasn't any problem," Zach answered for both of them before Janine could respond—as if he'd expected her to complain!

Ignoring him, Janine removed her coat and kissed her grandfather's leathery cheek.

"Janine," he began, then gasped. "Where did you get that…dress?"

"Do you like it?" She threw out her arms and whirled around once to give him the full effect. "I know it's a bit unconventional, but I didn't think you'd mind."

Gramps's gaze flickered to Zach, then back to her. "On anyone else it would be scandalous, but on you, my dear, it's a work of art."

"Honestly, Gramps," she said, laughing softly. "You never could lie very well." She slid into the booth next to her grandfather, forcing him into the center, between her and Zach. Gramps looked a bit disgruntled, but after her turbulent first encounter with Zach, she preferred to keep her distance. For that matter, he didn't seem all that eager to be close to her, either.

She glanced at him and noted, almost smugly, that he was already studying the menu. No doubt he found ordinary conversation a waste of time. Janine picked up her own menu. She was famished. At breakfast she'd only had time for coffee and a single piece of toast, and she had every intention of making up for it now.

When the waiter came to take their order, Janine asked for the seafood entrée and soup *and* salad. She'd decide about dessert later, she said. Once he'd left, Gramps leaned toward Zach. "Janine never has to worry about her weight." He made this sound as if it was a subject of profound and personal interest to them both. "Her grandmother was the same way. How my Anna could eat, and she never gained an ounce. Janine's just like her."

"Gramps," Janine whispered under her breath. "I'm sure Zach couldn't care less how much I weigh."

"Nonsense," Gramps said, gently patting her hand. "I hope you two had the chance to introduce yourselves."

"Oh, yes," Janine returned automatically.

"Your granddaughter is everything you claimed," Zachary said, but the inflection in his voice implied something completely different to Janine than it did to her grandfather. She guessed that to Anton, he seemed courteous and complimentary. But he was telling Janine he'd found her to be the spoiled darling he'd long suspected. He didn't openly dislike her, but he wasn't too impressed with her, either.

Unfortunately, that was probably due to more than just the dress and the lightbulb necklace.

Janine watched for her grandfather's reaction to Zach's words and she knew she was right when his gaze warmed and he nodded, obviously pleased by his partner's assessment. Zachary Thomas was clever, Janine had to grant him that much.

"How did the meeting with Anderson go?" Zach asked.

For a moment her grandfather stared at him blankly.

"Oh, Anderson… Fine, fine. Everything went just as I'd hoped." Then he cleared his throat and carefully spread the linen napkin across his lap. "As you both know," he said, "I've been wanting the two of you to meet for some time now. Janine is the joy of my life. She's kept me young and brought me much happiness over the years. I fear that, without her, I would have turned into a bitter old man."

His look was so full of tenderness that Janine had to lower her eyes and swallow back a rush of tears. Gramps had been her salvation, too. He'd taken her in after the sudden deaths of her parents, raised her with a gentle hand and loved her enough to allow her to be herself. It must've been difficult for him to have a six-year-old girl unexpectedly thrust into his life, but he'd never complained.

"My only son died far too young," Anton said slowly, painfully.

"I'm sorry," Zachary murmured.

The genuine compassion Janine heard in his voice surprised her. And it definitely pleased her. Zach's respect and affection for her grandfather won her immediate approval—even if the man didn't seem likely to ever feel anything so positive toward *her*.

"For many years I mourned the loss of my son and his wife," Anton continued, his voice gaining strength. "I've worked all my life, built an empire that stretches across these fifty states, and in the process have become a wealthy man."

Janine studied her grandfather closely. He was rarely this serious. He wasn't one to list his accomplishments, and she wondered at his strange mood.

"When Zach brought his business into the area, I saw in him a rare gift, one that comes along seldom in this life. It's said that there are men who make things happen, those who watch things happen and those who wonder what happened. Zachary is a man who makes things happen. In many ways, the two of us are alike. That's one of the primary reasons I decided to approach him with a proposal to merge our companies."

"I'm honored that you should think so, sir."

"Sir," Anton repeated softly and chuckled. He raised his hand, motioning for the waiter. "You haven't called me that in six months, and there's no reason to start again now."

The waiter returned with a bottle of expensive champagne. Soon glasses were poured and set before them.

"Now," Anton continued, "as I said earlier, I have the two people I love most in this world together with me for the first time, and I don't mind telling you, it feels good." He raised his glass. "To happiness."

"Happiness," Janine echoed, sipping her champagne.

Her eyes met Zach's above the crystal flute and she saw a glint of admiration. If she were dining on it, she'd starve—to quote a favorite expression of her grandfather's—but it was just enough for her to know that he'd think more kindly of her because of her love for Anton.

Her grandfather chuckled and whispered something in his native tongue, a German dialect from the old country. Over the years she'd picked up a smattering of the language, but when she'd repeated a few phrases to a college German professor, he'd barely recognized the words. Gramps paused and his smile lingered on Janine, then went to Zach. Whatever Gramps was muttering appeared to please him. His blue eyes fairly twinkled with delight.

"And now," he said, setting his glass aside, "I have an important announcement to make."

He turned to Janine and his face softened with affection. "I feel as though I've been an impossible burden to you, child, what with running this company." He shook his head. "Never in all my dreams did I expect to accumulate so much in a single lifetime. I've stayed in the business far longer than I should. It's time for me to retire and do a little traveling."

"It's past time," Janine said. For years, she'd been urging her grandfather to lessen his heavy work schedule. He'd often spoken of revisiting his birthplace and the surrounding countries. He talked at length of cousins and friends he'd left behind in the small German settlement. It was located in what was now part of Russia.

"This is where Zachary comes into the picture," Anton explained. "I know myself all too well. Full retirement would be impossible for me. If I stopped working, I'd shrivel up and die. That's just the way I am," he said simply.

Neither Janine nor Zachary disputed his words.

"I'll never be able to keep my fingers out of the business, yet I want to enjoy my travels. I couldn't do that if I was fretting about what was going on at the office." He paused as if he expected one of them to contradict him. "I believe I've come upon a solution. As of this afternoon, Zachary, I'm handing the reins to you. You will assume my position as chairman of the board. I realize this is sooner than we discussed, but the time is right and I hope you'll agree."

"But, Anton—"

"Gramps—"

Anton held up his hand. "I've thought about this long and hard," he said confidently. "I find Zach's honesty unquestionable, his loyalty certain and his intelligence keen. He's shrewd, perceptive and insightful. I can think of no better man, and there's no better time."

Janine noticed that Zach seemed uncomfortable with the praise. "Thank you," was all he said.

"A share of this company will belong to you someday, Janine," Anton said next. "Do you have any objections to this appointment?"

She opened her mouth, but nothing came out. Of course she approved. What else could she do? "Whatever you decide is fine with me."

Anton turned his attention to the other man. "Zachary, do you accept?"

Although their acquaintance had been brief, Janine knew instinctively that it took a lot to fluster this man. But her grandfather had managed to do so.

Zachary continued to stare at him as though he couldn't quite believe what he was hearing. But when he spoke, his voice was well modulated, revealing little emotion. "I'm honored."

"For the next few months, we'll be working closely together, much as we have in the past, but with a difference. No longer will I be showing you the ropes. I'll be handing them to you."

The first course of their lunch arrived, and after that, the conversation flowed smoothly. Her grandfather made sure of it. He was jubilant and entertaining, witty and charming. It would have been impossible not to be affected by his good humor.

When they'd finished the meal, Zachary looked at his watch. "I'm sorry to leave so soon, but I have an appointment."

Janine took a last sip of her coffee. "I should be leaving, too." She reached for her purse and coat, then slid out of the booth, waiting for her grandfather to join her.

"If neither of you objects, I'm going to linger over my coffee," Anton said, nodding toward his steaming cup.

"Of course." Janine leaned over to kiss him goodbye.

Zachary walked out to the street with her. Before he left, he shook her hand. "It's been a pleasure, Ms. Hartman."

"You're sure?" she teased, unable to stop herself.

"Yes." His eyes held hers and he smiled. She walked away feeling oddly excited about their meeting. Zach wasn't an easy person to know, but she suspected he was everything her grandfather claimed and more.

Gramps's mood remained cheerful when he got home later that evening. Janine was in the library sipping herbal tea with her feet tucked under her as she watched the local news.

Sitting in the wingback leather chair next to her, Gramps crossed his legs and chose one of his Havana cigars. Janine shook her head affectionately as he lit it; she loved her grandfather dearly and wished he'd stop smoking, though she no longer bothered to express that wish. He was the kind of man who did exactly as he chose, got exactly what he wanted. He was obviously pleased with the way their luncheon had gone, and she wondered briefly if Zach had said anything about her afterward. Somehow she doubted it.

"Well," he said after a moment, "What do you think of Zachary Thomas?" He blew a steady stream of smoke at the ceiling while he awaited her answer.

All afternoon, Janine had prepared herself for his question. Several complicated answers had presented themselves, clever replies that would sidestep her true feelings, but she used none of them now. Her grandfather expected the truth, and it was her duty to give it to him.

"I'm not sure. He's a very…reserved man, isn't he?"

Anton chuckled. "Yes, he is, but I've never known you to walk away from a challenge. The boy's a little rough around the edges, but on the inside, he's pure gold."

Janine hadn't thought of Zach in those terms—a challenge. Frankly, she doubted there'd be much reason for her to have any future contact with him. Gramps and Zach would be working closely together, but she had almost nothing to do with the business.

"I've earned his trust, but it took time," Gramps was saying now.

"I'm glad you've decided to retire," she said absently, half listening to the weather report.

"Zachary will change," her grandfather added.

He had her full attention now. "Gramps," she said patiently, holding in a laugh. "Why should he? He's achieved considerable financial success. Everything's looking good for him. What possible reason could there be for him to change?"

Anton stood and poured himself a liberal dose of brandy, swirling it slowly in the bottom of the snifter. "You're going to change him," he said after a thoughtful moment.

"Me?" Janine laughed outright. "*I'm* going to change Zachary Thomas?" she repeated in wide-eyed disbelief. That would be the day!

"Before you argue with me, and I can see that's what you're dying to do, I have a story I want to tell you. A rather sad one as it happens."

Janine picked up the remote control and snapped off the television. She'd often listened to her grandfather's parables. "So tell me."

"It's about a boy, born on the wrong side of the tracks

to an alcoholic father and a weak mother. He never had much of a chance in life. His father was abusive enough for the state to remove the lad and his younger sister. He was barely eight and subjected to a long series of foster homes, but he refused to be separated from his sister. He'd promised her he'd always take care of her.

"Once, there wasn't any alternative and the two were sent to separate homes. Beside himself with worry for his sister, the young boy ran away. The authorities were in a panic, but three days later, he turned up two hundred miles away at the home where they'd placed Beth Ann."

"He probably felt responsible for her."

"Yes. Which made matters much worse when she drowned in a swimming accident. He was twelve at the time."

"Oh, no." A pain squeezed Janine's heart at the agony the boy had suffered.

"He blamed himself, of course," Anton said softly.

"The poor kid."

"This lad never seemed to belong to anyone after that," Gramps said, staring into his brandy. "He never quite fit in, but that wasn't entirely his fault." He paused to take another puff of his cigar. "His mother died a month after his sister. They were the only ones who'd ever truly loved him. He lost contact with his father, which was probably for the best. So his family was gone and no one seemed to want this troubled, hurting boy."

"Did he turn into a juvenile delinquent?" It made sense to Janine that he would; she'd dealt with a number of troubled teenagers through her volunteer work and was familiar with the tragic patterns that so often evolved in cases like this.

"No, I can't say he did." Gramps dismissed her question with a shake of his head, more interested in continuing his tale than getting sidetracked by her questions. "He drifted through adolescence without an anchor and without ever being allowed to enjoy those formative years."

"Gramps—"

He raised his hand to stop her. "When he was eighteen, he joined the military. He did well, which isn't surprising, considering his intelligence and the fact that he had little regard for his own well-being. There was no one to mourn if he died. Because of his courage, he advanced quickly, volunteering for the riskiest assignments. He traveled all over the world to some of the most dangerous political hot spots. His duties were often top secret. There's no telling how far he might have gone had he chosen to remain in the armed services, but for some reason, he resigned. No one understood why. I suspect he wanted to start his life over. This was when he opened a business-supply company. Within a year, he had my attention. His methods were aggressive and creative. I couldn't help admiring the way he handled himself and the company. Within five years, he'd become one of my most serious rivals. I saw a strength in him that age had stolen from me. We met. We talked. As a result of these talks we joined forces."

"Obviously you're telling me about Zachary's life."

Anton grinned and slowly sipped his brandy. "You noticed his remoteness quickly. I thought knowing all this would help you. Zach's never had the security that a caring home and family provide. He's never really experienced love, except what he shared with his sister, Beth Ann. His life has been a long progression of painful experiences. By sheer force of will, he's managed to overcome every obstacle placed in his path. I realize

Zachary Thomas isn't going to win any Mr. Personality contests, but by heaven, he's earned my respect."

Janine had rarely heard such emotion in her grandfather's voice. "Zach told you all this?"

Anton's laughter echoed through the room. "You're joking, aren't you? Zach has never spoken of his past to me. I doubt that he has to anyone."

"You had him investigated?"

Gramps puffed on his cigar before answering. "It was necessary, although I'd guessed early on that his life hadn't been a bed of roses."

"It's all very sad, isn't it?"

"You're going to be very good for him, my dear."

Janine blinked. "Me?"

"Yes, you. You're going to teach him to laugh and enjoy life. But most important, you're going to teach him about love."

She hesitated, uncertain of her grandfather's meaning. "I don't think I understand. I realize Zach and I will probably see each other now and then since he's assuming your responsibilities with the company, but I don't see how I could have any great impact on his life."

Gramps smiled, a slow lazy smile that curved the corners of his mouth. "That's where you're wrong, my dear. You're going to play a very big role in Zach's life, and he in yours."

Janine was still confused. "Perhaps I missed something this afternoon. I thought you made Zach the chairman of the board."

"I did." A lazy swirl of smoke circled his head.

"I don't understand where I come into the picture."

"I don't suppose you do," he said softly. "You see, Janine, I've chosen Zachary to be your husband."

Two

For a stunned moment, Janine said nothing. "You're teasing, aren't you, Gramps?"

"No," he said, lighting a second cigar. He paused to stare at the glowing tip, his eyes filled with mischief—and with something else, less easily defined. "I'm serious."

"But…" Janine's thoughts were so jumbled she couldn't make sense of them herself, let alone convey her feelings to her grandfather.

"I've been giving the matter serious consideration for some time now. Zach's perfect for you and you're the ideal complement to him. You're going to have beautiful blond-haired children."

"But…" Janine discovered she was absolutely speechless. One minute she was listening to a touching story, and the next her grandfather was telling her about the husband he'd arranged for her—and even the color of her children's hair.

"Once you think about it," Gramps said confidently, "I'm sure you'll agree with me. Zach is a fine young man, and he'll make you an excellent husband."

"You… Zach talked…agreed?" The words stumbled over the end of her tongue.

"Do you mean have I suggested this arrangement to Zach?" Gramps asked. "Heavens, no. At least not yet." He chuckled as if he found the thought amusing. "Zach wouldn't appreciate my blatant interference in his personal affairs. With him, I'll need to be far more subtle. To be honest, I considered making this marriage part of my handing over the chairmanship, but after thinking it through, I changed my mind. Zach would never have agreed. There are other ways, I decided, better ways. But I don't want you to worry about it. That's between Zach and me."

"I...see." At this point, Janine wasn't sure *what* she saw, other than one determined old man caught between two worlds. In certain respects, the old ways continued to dominate his thinking, but his success in America allowed him to appreciate more modern outlooks.

Gramps inhaled deeply on his cigar, his blue eyes twinkling. "Now, I realize you probably find the idea of an arranged marriage slightly unorthodox, but you'll get used to it. I've made a fine choice for you, and I know you're smart enough to recognize that."

"Gramps, I don't think you fully understand what you're suggesting," she said, trying to gather her scattered wits, hoping she could explain the ridiculousness of this whole scheme without offending him.

"But I do, my child."

"In this country and in this age," she continued slowly, "men and women choose their own mates. We fall in love and then marry."

Gramps frowned. "Sadly, that doesn't work," he muttered.

"What do you mean, it doesn't work?" she cried, losing her patience. "It's been like this for years and years!"

"Look at the divorce rate. I read in the paper recently that almost fifty percent of all marriages in this country fail. In the old country, there was no divorce. Parents decided whom a son or daughter would marry, and their decision was accepted without question. First comes marriage, and then comes love."

"Gramps," Janine said softly, wanting to reason this out with him. Her grandfather was a logical man; surely, if she explained it properly, he'd understand. "Things are done differently now. First comes love, then comes marriage."

"What do you young people know about love?"

"A good deal, as it happens," she returned, lying smoothly. Her first venture into love had ended with a broken heart and a shattered ego, but she'd told Gramps little if anything about Brian.

"Pfft!" he spat. "What could you possibly know of love?"

"I realize," she said, thinking fast, "that your father arranged your marriage to Grandma, but that was years ago, and in America such customs don't exist. You and I live *here* now, in the land of the free. The land of opportunity."

Gramps gazed down into his brandy for a long moment, lost in thought. Janine doubted he'd even heard her.

"I'll never forget the first time I saw my Anna," he said in a faraway voice. "She was sixteen and her hair was long and blond and fell in braids to her waist. My father spoke to her father and while they were talking, Anna and I sat at opposite ends of the room, too shy to look at each other. I wondered if she thought I was handsome. To me, she was the most beautiful girl in the world. Even now, after all these years, I can remember how my heart beat with excitement when I saw her. I knew—"

"But, Gramps, that was nearly sixty years ago! Marriages aren't decided by families anymore. A man and a woman discover each other without a father introducing them. Maybe the old ways were better back then, but it's simply not like that now." Gramps continued to stare into his glass, lost in a world long since enveloped by the passage of time.

"The next day, Anna's parents visited our farm and again our two fathers spoke. I tried to pretend I wasn't concerned, determined to accept whatever our families decided. But when I saw our fathers shake hands and slap each other on the back, I knew Anna would soon be mine."

"You loved her before you were married, didn't you?" Janine asked softly, hoping to prove her point.

"No," he returned flatly, without hesitation. "How could I love her when I'd only seen her twice before the wedding? We hadn't said more than a handful of words to each other. Love wasn't necessary for us to find happiness. Love came later, after we arrived in America."

"Wasn't it unusual for a marriage to be arranged even then? It wasn't *that* long ago." There had to be some point for her to contend, Janine mused.

"Perhaps it was unusual in other parts of the world, but not in Vibiskgrad. We were a small farming community. Our world had been ravaged by war and hate. We clung to each other, holding on to our own traditions and rituals. Soon our lives became impossible and we were forced to flee our homes."

"As I said before, I can understand how an arranged marriage—back then—might be the best for everyone involved. But I can't see it working in this day and age. I'm sorry to disappoint you, Gramps, but I'm not willing to accept Zachary Thomas as my husband, and I'm sure he'd be equally unwilling to marry me."

Briefly Gramps's face tensed with a rare display of

disappointment and indignation, then quickly relaxed. Janine had seldom questioned his authority and had never openly defied him.

"I suppose this is a shock to you, isn't it?" he said.

If it astonished *her,* she couldn't wait to hear what Zachary Thomas thought! They'd only met once, but he hadn't disguised his opinion of her. He wouldn't take kindly to Gramps's plan of an arranged marriage—especially to a woman he viewed as spoiled and overindulged.

"All I'm asking is that you consider this, Janine," Gramps said. "Promise me you'll at least do that. Don't reject marriage to Zach simply because you think it's old-fashioned."

"Oh, Gramps…" Janine hated to refuse him anything. "It isn't just me. What about Zach? What about *his* plans? What if he—"

Gramps dismissed her questions with an abrupt shrug. "How often do I ask something of you?" he persisted.

Now he was going to use guilt. "Not often," she agreed, frowning at him for using unfair tactics.

"Then consider Zach for your husband!" His eyes brightened. "The two of you will have such beautiful children. A grandfather knows these things."

"I promise I'll think about it." But it wouldn't do any good! However, discretion was a virtue Janine was nurturing, and there'd never been a better time to employ it than now.

Gramps didn't mention Zach Thomas or even hint at the subject of her marrying his business partner again until the following evening. They'd just sat down to dinner, prepared to sample Mrs. McCormick's delicious fare, when Gramps looked anxiously at Janine. "So?" he asked breathlessly.

From the moment he'd walked into the house that afternoon, Gramps's mood had been light and humorous. Grinning, he handed her the platter of thinly sliced marinated and grilled flank steak. It happened to be one of Janine's favorite meals. "So?" he repeated, smiling at her. "What did you decide?"

Janine helped herself to a crisp dinner roll, buttering it slowly as her thoughts chased each other in frantic circles. "Nothing."

His smile collapsed into a frown. "You promised me you'd consider marrying Zach. I gave you more time than Anna's father gave her."

"You have to know now?"

"Now!"

"But, Gramps, a simple yes or no isn't an appropriate response to something as complex as this. You're asking me to decide on a lifelong commitment in less than twenty-four hours." She was stalling for time, and Gramps had probably guessed as much. Frankly, she didn't know what to tell him. She couldn't, wouldn't, marry Zach—even if he was willing to marry her—but she hated disappointing her grandfather.

"What's so difficult? Either you marry him or not!"

"I don't understand why you've decided to match me up with Zach Thomas," she cried. "What's wrong with Peter?" She'd been dating the other man casually for the last few months. Her heart was too bruised after what had happened with Brian for her to date anyone seriously.

"You're in love with that whitewashed weakling?"

Janine signed loudly, regretting the fact that she'd introduced Peter into their conversation. "He's very nice."

"So is chocolate mousse!" Gramps muttered. "Peter Donahue would make you a terrible husband. I'm shocked you'd even think about marrying him."

"I hadn't actually thought about him in those terms," she said. Peter was witty and fun, but Gramps was right; they weren't suited as husband and wife.

"I thank the good Lord you've been given some sense."

Janine took a deep breath and finally asked a question that had been nagging at her all afternoon. "Did— did you arrange my father's marriage?"

Gramps lowered his eyes, but not before he could disguise the pain there. "No. He fell in love with Patrice while he was in college. I knew the match wasn't a good one, but Anna reminded me that this was America and young people fell in love by themselves. She convinced me they didn't need a father's guiding hand the way we did in the old country."

"Do you think he would've listened if you'd wanted to arrange a marriage?"

Her grandfather hesitated, and his hand tightened on his water glass. "I don't know, but I'd like to believe he would have."

"Instead he married my mother."

Neither spoke for a long moment. Janine remembered little of her parents, only bits and pieces of memory, mostly unconnected. What she did recall were terrible fights and accusations, a house filled with strife. She could remember hiding under her bed when the shouting started, pressing her hands to her ears. It was her father who used to find her, who comforted her. Always her father. Her memory included almost nothing of her mother. Even pictures didn't jar her recollection, although Janine had spent hour upon hour looking at photographs, hoping to remember *something*. But the woman who'd given birth to her had remained a stranger to her in life and in death.

"You're the only consolation I have from Steven's marriage," Anton said hoarsely. "At least I had you after Steven and Patrice died."

"Oh, Gramps. I love you so much and I hate to disappoint you, but I can't marry Zach and I can't see him agreeing to marry me."

Her grandfather was silent after that, apparently mulling over her words as he finished his dinner. "I suppose I seem like a feeble old man, still trying to live the old ways."

"Gramps, no, I don't think that at all."

He planted his elbows squarely on the table and linked his fingers, gazing at her. His brow was puckered in a contemplative frown. "Perhaps it would help if you told me what you want in a husband."

She hesitated, then glanced away, avoiding eye contact. Once she'd been so certain of what she wanted. "To be perfectly honest, I'm not sure. Romance, I suppose."

"Romance." Gramps rolled the word off his tongue as though he was tasting an expensive wine.

"Yes," she said with a nod of her head, gaining confidence.

"And what exactly is romance?"

"Well…" Now that she'd been called upon to define it, Janine couldn't quite put that magical feeling into words. "It's…it's an awareness that comes from the heart."

"The heart," her grandfather repeated, smacking his palm against his chest.

"Romance is the knowledge that a man would rather die than live his life without me," she said, warming to the subject.

"You want him to die?"

"No, just to be willing."

Gramps frowned. "I don't think I understand."

"Romance is forbidden trysts on lonely Scottish moors," she added, thinking of an historical romance she'd read as a teenager.

"There aren't any moors in the Seattle area."

"Don't distract me," she said, smiling, her thoughts gaining momentum. "Romance is desperate passion."

He snorted. "That sounds more like hormones to me."

"Gramps, please!"

"How can I understand when all you say is ridiculous things? You want romance. First you claim it's a feeling in the heart, then you say it's some kind of passion."

"It's more than that. It's walking hand in hand along the beach at twilight and gazing into each other's eyes. It's speaking of love without ever having to say the words." She paused, feeling a little foolish at getting so carried away. "I don't know if I can adequately describe it."

"That's because you haven't experienced it."

"Maybe not," she agreed reluctantly. "But I will someday."

"With Zach," he said with complete assurance and a wide grin.

Janine didn't bother to argue. Gramps was being obstinate and arguing with him was pointless. The only recourse she had was time itself. Soon enough he'd realize that neither she nor Zach was going to fall in with his scheme. Then, and only then, would he drop the subject.

A week passed and Gramps hadn't said another word about arranging a marriage between her and Zachary Thomas. It was a cold windy March evening and the rain was coming down in torrents. Janine loved nights like this and was curled up in her favorite chair with a mystery novel when the doorbell chimed. Gramps had gone out for the evening and she wasn't expecting anyone.

She turned on the porch light and looked out the peephole to discover Zach standing there, a briefcase in his hand. His shoulders were hunched against the pelting rain.

"Zach," she said in surprise, throwing open the door.

"Hello, Janine," he said politely, stepping inside. "Is your grandfather here?"

"No." She held the book against her chest, her heart pounding hard. "He went out."

Zach frowned, clearly confused. "He asked me to stop by. There were some business matters he wanted to discuss. Did he say when he'd be home?"

"No, but I'm sure if he asked you over, it'll be soon. Would you care to wait for him?"

"Please."

She took his raincoat, then led him into the library where she'd been reading. A fire was burning, and its warmth hugged the room. The three-story house, situated in Seattle's Mt. Baker district, was a typical turn-of-the-century home with high ceilings and spacious rooms. The third floor had once housed several servants. Charles was their only live-in help now, and his quarters had always been an apartment over the carriage house. He worked exclusively for Gramps, driving the limousine. Mrs. McCormick arrived early in the mornings and was responsible for housekeeping and meal preparation.

"Can I get you something to drink?" she asked, once he was comfortably seated.

"Coffee, if you have it."

"I made a fresh pot about twenty minutes ago."

Janine brought him a cup from the kitchen, then sat across from Zach, wondering what, if anything, she should say about Gramps and his idea of an arranged marriage.

She doubted that Gramps had broached the subject yet. Otherwise he wouldn't be sitting there so calmly sipping coffee. He'd be outraged and infuriated, and studying him now, she concluded that he wasn't even slightly ruffled. It was on the tip of her tongue to warn him about what was coming, but she decided against it. Better that he learn the same way she had.

Lacing her fingers together, she smiled, feeling awkward and a little gauche. "It's nice to see you again."

"You, too. I'll admit I'm a bit disappointed, though."

"You are?"

"On the drive over, I was trying to guess what you'd be wearing this time. A dress made from bread sacks? A blouse constructed out of men's socks?"

She muttered under her breath, annoyed by his teasing. He had the uncanny ability to make her feel fifteen all over again. So much for any possibility that they'd ever be compatible. And Gramps seemed to think he knew them both so well.

"I'll admit that an Irish cable-knit sweater and jeans are a pleasant surprise," he said.

A flicker of admiration sparked in his dark eyes, something that had been missing the first time they met.

In that instant, Janine knew.

She went stock-still, almost dizzy with the realization. Not only had Gramps approached Zach, but they'd apparently reached some sort of agreement. Otherwise Zach would never have been this friendly, this openly appreciative. Nor would he arrive unannounced when

Gramps had specifically stated that he'd be gone for the evening.

They were obviously plotting against her. Well, she had no intention of putting up with it. None. If Zach and Gramps thought they could lure her into marriage, they had a real shock coming.

Squaring her shoulders, she slid to the edge of her chair. "So you gave in to the pressure," she said, shooting him a scalding look. Unable to stay seated, she jumped to her feet and started pacing, rubbing her palms together as she cornered her thoughts. "Gramps got to you, didn't he?"

"I beg your pardon?" Zach stared up at her, his eyes curious.

"And you agreed?" She threw up her hands and groaned, "I don't believe it, I simply don't believe it. I thought better of you than this."

"What don't you believe?"

"Of all the men I've met over the years, I would've sworn you were the type who'd refuse to be bought. I'm disappointed in you, Zach."

He remained calm and unperturbed, which infuriated her more than anything he could have said or done.

"I haven't got the slightest idea what you're talking about," was all he said.

"Oh, sure, play the innocent," she snapped. She was so incensed that she continued to pace. Standing still was impossible.

In response, Zach merely glanced at his watch and drank his coffee. "Does your grandfather know you suffer from these bouts of hysteria?"

"Funny, Zach, very funny."

He exhaled an exaggerated sigh. "All right, I'll take

the bait. What makes you think I've been bought? And what exactly am I getting in exchange?"

"Technically you're not getting anything, and I want that understood this very minute, because *I* refuse to be sold." Arms akimbo, she turned to glare down at him with the full force of her disdain. "What did he offer you? The entire company? Lots of money?"

Zach shrugged. "He's offered me nothing."

"Nothing," she repeated slowly, feeling unreasonably insulted. "He was just going to *give* me away." That was enough to deflate the billowing sails of her pride. Stunned, she sat down again. "I thought the bride's family was supposed to supply some kind of dowry. Gramps didn't even offer you money?"

"Dowry?" Zach repeated the word as if he'd never heard it before.

"Gramps's family received a cow and ten chickens from my grandmother's family," she said, as if that explained everything. "But apparently I'm not even worth a single hen."

Zach set his coffee aside and sat straight in his chair. "I think we'd better begin this conversation again. I'm afraid I lost you back there when you said something about cracking under pressure. Perhaps you should enlighten me about what I'm supposed to have done."

Janine just glared at him.

"Humor me."

"All right, if you insist. It's obvious that Gramps talked to you about the marriage."

"Marriage," he echoed in a shocked voice. His face went blank. "To whom?"

"Me, of course."

Zach flung himself out of the chair, bolting to his feet. "To you?"

"Don't look so horrified! My ego's taken about all it can for one evening. I'm not exactly the Wicked Witch of the West, you know. Some men would be more than happy to marry me." Not Brian, and certainly not Peter, but she felt it was important that Zach think she was sought after.

"Marriage between us is…would be impossible. It's completely out of the question. I don't ever plan to marry—I have no use for a wife or family."

"Tell that to Gramps."

"I have every intention of doing so." His face tightened and Janine guessed her grandfather was due for an earful when he got home. "What makes that crazy old man think he can order people's lives like this?" he asked angrily.

"His own marriage was arranged for him. Trust me, Zach, I argued until I was exhausted, but Gramps hasn't given up his old-country beliefs and he thinks the two of us—now this is really ridiculous—are perfect for each other."

"If you weren't serious, I'd find this highly amusing."

Janine noticed that he seemed rather pale. "I appear to have jumped to the wrong conclusion earlier. I apologize for that but, well, I thought… I assumed Gramps had spoken to you already and you'd agreed."

"Was that when you started mumbling about a cow and a few chickens?"

She nodded and her long bangs fell over her eyes. Absently she pushed them aside. "For a moment there, I thought Gramps was offering me to you gratis. I know it's silly, but I felt insulted by that."

For the first time since they'd entered into this conversation, Zach's face softened and he granted her a faint smile. "Your grandfather loves you, no question."

"I know." Feeling self-conscious, she threaded her fingers through her hair. "I've used every argument I could come up with. I explained the importance of romance and told him how vital it is for men and women to fall in love with the person of their choice. However, he refused to accept any of it."

"He wouldn't listen to you?"

"He listened," she replied, feeling defeated, "but he disputed everything I said. Gramps says the modern version of love and marriage is a complete failure. With the divorce rate what it is, I'm afraid I don't have much of an argument."

"That's true enough," Zach said, looking frustrated.

"I told him men and women fall in love and then decide to get married, but Gramps insists it's better if marriage comes first."

Zach rubbed a hand over his face. "Now that I think about it, your grandfather's been introducing you into every conversation, telling me how wonderful you are."

Janine gasped softly. "He's done the same to me about you. He started weeks before we even met."

Pressing his lips together, Zach nodded. "A lot of things are beginning to make sense."

"What should we do?" Janine wondered aloud. "It's perfectly obvious that we'll have to agree on a plan of action. I hate to disappoint Gramps, but I'm not willing to be married off like…like…" Words failed her.

"Especially to me."

Although his low words were devoid of emotion, Janine recognized the pain behind his statement. Knowing what she did about his past, the fact that he'd experienced only brief patches of love in his life and little or no approval tugged at her heart.

"I didn't mean it to sound like that," she insisted. "My

grandfather wouldn't have chosen you if he didn't think you were pretty special. He prides himself on his ability to judge character, and he's always been impressed with you."

"Let's not kid ourselves, Janine," Zach returned, his voice hardening. "You're an uptown girl. We're totally unsuited."

"I agree with you there, but not for the reasons you assume. From the minute I stepped into your office, you made it clear that you thought of me as some kind of snob. I'm not, but I refuse to waste my breath arguing with you."

"Fine."

"Instead of hurling insults at each other," she suggested, crossing her arms in a show of indignation, "why don't we come up with a plan to deal with Gramps's preposterous idea?"

"That isn't necessary," he countered. "I want no part of it."

"And you think I do?"

Zach said nothing.

Janine expelled her breath loudly. "It seems to me the solution is for one of us to marry someone else. That would quickly put an end to this whole thing."

"I already told you I have no intention of marrying," he said emphatically. "You're the one who insinuated you had plenty of men hanging around just waiting for you to say 'I do.'"

"None that I'd consider marrying, for heaven's sake," she grumbled. "Besides, I'm not currently in love with anyone."

Zach laughed, if the sound that came from his throat could be called a laugh. "Then find a man who's current.

If you fall in and out of love that easily, surely there's got to be at least one prospect on the horizon."

"There isn't. *You're* going to have to come up with someone! Why don't you go out there and sweep some sweet young thing off her feet," she muttered sarcastically.

"I'm not willing to sacrifice my life so you can get off scot-free." His words were low and furious.

"But it's perfectly all right for *me* to sabotage mine? That makes a lot of sense."

"Okay," he said after a tense moment. He paused, shaking his head. "That idea's obviously not going to work. I guess we'll have to come up with something better."

"Okay, then." Janine gestured toward him. "It's your turn."

He glared at her, seeming to dislike her even more. In all honesty, Janine wasn't too pleased with the way she was behaving, either. She'd been sarcastic and needlessly rude, but then, Zach had driven her to it. He could be the most unpleasant man.

Still, Janine was about to say something conciliatory when the sound of the front door opening distracted her. Her gaze flew to Zach and he nodded, reassuring her that he'd handle the situation.

They'd returned to their chairs and were seated by the time Gramps appeared in the library doorway.

"Zach, I'm sorry for the delay. I'm glad to see Janine entertained you." Her grandfather smiled brightly as if to tell her he approved and hoped she'd taken advantage of this hour alone with Zach.

"We did manage to have a stimulating conversation," Zach said, his eyes briefly meeting Janine's.

"Good. Good."

Zach stood and reached for his briefcase. "There were some figures you wanted to go over with me?"

"Yes." Looking satisfied with himself, Gramps led the way out of the room. Zach followed him, with a glance back at Janine that said he'd get in touch with her later.

Later turned out to be almost a week. She was puttering around outside, trimming back the rosebushes and deciding where to plant the geraniums this year, when Mrs. McCormick came to tell her she was wanted on the phone.

"Hello," Janine said cheerfully.

"We need to talk," Zach said without preamble.

"Why?" she demanded. If he was going to keep her hanging for six anxious days, then she wasn't going to give the impression that she was thrilled to hear from him.

"Your grandfather laid his cards on the table this afternoon. I thought you might be interested in hearing what he's offering me to take you off his hands."

Three

"All right," Janine said, bracing herself. "What's he offering you? Huge bonuses?"

"No," Zach said quickly.

"Cash? I want to know exactly how much."

"He didn't offer me money."

Janine frowned. "What then?"

"I think we should meet and talk about it."

If her grandfather had openly approached Zach with the arranged-marriage idea, Janine knew darn well that Gramps would've made it worth Zach's while. Despite his claims to the contrary, it wouldn't have surprised Janine to discover that the newly appointed chairman of the board of Hartman-Thomas Business Supply had taken the bait.

"You want us to meet?" she repeated in a faltering voice.

"There's a restaurant on University Way—Italian 642. Have you heard of it?"

"No, but I'll find it."

"Meet me there at seven." Zach paused, then added, "And listen, it might not be a good idea to tell your grandfather that we're getting together. He might misunderstand."

"I won't say anything," she promised.

Zach hesitated once more. "We have a lot to discuss."

Janine's heartbeat accelerated, and she felt the perspiration break out on her forehead. "Zach," she began, "you haven't changed your mind, have you? I mean, you're not actually considering this ridiculous idea of his? You can't... We agreed, remember?" She swiped at her forehead with the back of her free hand as she waited for him to answer.

"There's nothing to worry about," he finally said.

Replacing the receiver, Janine had the sudden horrible sensation of being completely at her grandfather's mercy. He was an unshakably stubborn man who almost always got what he wanted. Faced with a mountain, Anton Hartman either climbed it, tunneled through it or forged a path around it; failing such active alternatives, he settled down in the foothills and waited for the mountain to dissolve. He claimed he won a majority of his battles by simply displaying patience. Janine called it not knowing when to pack up and go home.

She knew her grandfather's methods, but then so did Zach. She hoped Anton's candidate for her husband would at least be able to withstand a few bribes, however tempting. Apparently he did, because he'd told her she had nothing to worry about. On the other hand, he sounded downright eager to discuss the subject with her.

"He *says* he never wants to get married," she muttered aloud in an effort to reassure herself. Indeed, Zachary Thomas was the last man who'd be humming "The Wedding March"—especially when someone else was directing the band.

Janine was waiting in the library, coat draped over her arm, when her grandfather got home at six-thirty. He kissed her dutifully on the cheek and reached for the evening paper, scanning the headlines as he settled into his big leather chair.

"Zach called," she said without thinking. She hadn't intended to mention that to Gramps.

Anton nodded. "I thought he might. You meeting him for dinner?"

"Dinner? Zach and me?" she squeaked. "No, of course not! Why would you even think I'd agree to a dinner date with…him?" Darn, she'd nearly forgotten her promise to keep their meeting a secret. She detested lying to her grandfather, but there was no help for it.

"But you are dining out?"

"Yes." She couldn't very well deny that, dressed as she was and carrying her coat.

"Then you're seeing Peter Donahue again?"

"No. Not exactly," Janine said uncomfortably, "I'm meeting a…friend."

"I see." The corners of Gramps's mouth quirked into a knowing smile.

Janine could feel the telltale heat saturating her face. She was a terrible liar and always had been. Gramps knew as surely as if she'd spelled it out that she was meeting Zach. And when she told Zach she'd let it slip, he'd be furious with her, and rightly so.

"What did Zach want?"

"What makes you think he wanted anything?" Janine asked fervently. Her heart was thundering as she edged toward the door. The sooner she escaped, the better.

"You just said Zach phoned."

"Oh. Yes, he did, earlier, but it wasn't important. Something about…something." Brilliant! She rushed out of the house before Gramps could question her further. What a fool she was. She'd blurted out the very thing she'd wanted to keep secret.

By the time Janine located the Italian restaurant in the University district and found a parking place, she was ten minutes late.

Zach was sitting in a booth in the farthest corner of

the room. He frowned when he saw her and glanced at his watch, just so she'd know she'd kept him waiting.

Ignoring his disgruntled look, Janine slid onto the polished wooden bench, removed her coat and casually announced, "Gramps knows."

Zach's frown deepened. "What are you talking about?"

"He knows I'm having dinner with you," she explained. "The minute he walked in the door, I told him you'd called—I just wasn't thinking—and when he asked why, I told him it had to do with *something*. I'm sure you'll be able to make up an excuse when he asks you later."

"I thought we agreed not to say anything about our meeting."

"I know," she said, feeling guiltier than ever. "But Gramps asked if I was going out with Peter and he just looked so smug when I told him I wasn't." At Zach's sudden movement, she burst out, "Well, what was I supposed to do?"

He grunted, which wasn't much of an answer.

"If I wasn't going out with Peter, I'd have to come up with another man on the spot, and although I'm clever, I don't think *that* fast." She was breathless with frustration when she'd finished.

"Who's Peter?"

"This guy I've been seeing off and on for the past few months."

"And you're in love with him?"

"No, I'm not." Doubtless Zach would suggest she simply marry Peter and put an end to all of this annoyance.

Zach reached abruptly for the menu. "Let's order, and while we're eating we can go over what we need to discuss."

"All right," Janine said, grateful to leave the topic of her blunder. Besides, seven was later than she normally dined, and she was famished.

The waitress appeared then, and even as she filled Janine's water glass, her appreciative gaze never strayed from Zach. Once more Janine was struck by the knowledge that although he wasn't handsome in the traditional sense, he seemed to generate a good deal of female interest.

"I'll have the clam spaghetti," Janine said loudly, eyeing the attractive waitress, who seemed to be forgetting why she was there. The woman was obviously far more interested in studying Zach than in taking their order.

"I'll have the same," Zach said, smiling briefly at the waitress as he handed her his menu. "Now, what were you saying?" he asked, returning his attention to Janine.

"As I recall, you were the one who insisted we meet. Just tell me what my grandfather said and be done with it." No doubt the offer had been generous; otherwise Zach wouldn't have suggested this dinner.

Zach's hand closed around the water glass. "Anton called me into his office to ask me a series of leading questions."

"Such as?"

Zach shrugged. "What I thought of you and—"

"How'd you answer him?"

Zach took a deep breath. "I said I found you attractive, energetic, witty, a bit eccentric—"

"A bandanna dress and a string of Christmas-tree lights doesn't make me eccentric," Janine said, her voice rising despite herself.

"If the Christmas-tree lights are draped around your neck it does."

They were attracting attention, and after a few curious stares, Zach leaned closer and said, "If you're going to argue with everything I say, we'll be here all night."

"I'm sure our waitress would enjoy that," Janine snapped, then immediately regretted it. She sounded downright *jealous*—which, of course, was ridiculous.

"What are you talking about?"

"Never mind."

"Shall we return to the conversation between your grandfather and me?"

"Please," she said, properly chastised.

"Anton spent quite a long time telling me about your volunteer work at the Friendship Club and your various other community activities."

"And I'll bet his report was so glowing, I rank right up there with Joan of Arc and Florence Nightingale."

Zach grinned. "Something like that, but then he added that although you were constantly busy, he felt your life lacked contentment and purpose."

Janine could see it coming, as clearly as if she were standing on a track and a freight train was heading toward her. "Let me guess. He probably said I needed something meaningful in my life—like a husband and children."

"Exactly." Zach nodded, his grin barely restrained. "In his opinion, marriage is the only thing that will fulfill you as a woman."

Janine groaned and sagged against the back of her seat. It was worse than she thought. And to her chagrin, Zach actually seemed amused.

"You wouldn't look so smug if he said marriage was the only thing that would fulfill you as a *man*," she muttered. "Honestly, Zach, do I look like I'm wasting away from lack of purpose?" She gestured dramatically with her hands. "I'm happy, I'm busy…in fact I'm completely delighted with my life." It wasn't until she'd finished that she realized she was clenching her teeth.

"Don't take it so personally."

Janine rolled her eyes, wondering what his reaction would be if he was on the receiving end of this discussion.

"In case you didn't know it, Anton's a terrible chauvinist," he remarked, still smiling. "An old-fashioned word, perhaps, for an old-fashioned man."

"That's true, but he *is* my grandfather," she said. "And he's so charming, it's easy to forgive him."

Zach picked up his wineglass and gazed at it thoughtfully. "What I can't figure out is why he's so keen on marrying you off now. Why not last year? Or next year?"

"Heavens, I don't know. I suppose he thinks it's time. My biological clock's ticking away and the noise is probably keeping him awake at night. By age twenty-four, most of the women from the old country had four or five children."

"He certainly seems intent on the idea of seeing you married soon."

"Tell me about it!" Janine cried. "I'd bet cold cash that when he brought up the subject he said you were the only suitable man he'd found for me."

"Anton also said you have a generous heart, and that he feared some fast-talker would show up one day and you'd fall for him."

"Really?" she asked weakly. Her heart stopped, then jolted to life again. Anton's scenario sounded exactly like her disastrous romance with Brian. She sighed deeply. "So then he told you he wants me to marry someone he respects, someone he loves like a son. A man of discretion and wisdom and honor. A man he trusts enough to merge companies with."

Zach arched his brows. "You know your grandfather well."

"I can just imagine what came next," Janine added scathingly and her stomach tensed at her grandfather's insidious cleverness. Zach wasn't someone who could be bought, at least not with offers of money or prestige. Instead, Gramps had used a far more subtle form of inducement. He'd addressed Zach's pride, complimented his achievements, flattered him. To hear Gramps tell it, Zachary Thomas was the only man alive capable of taking on the task of becoming Janine's husband.

"What did you tell him?" she asked, her voice low.

"I told him no way."

Janine blinked back surprise mingled with a fair amount of indignation. "Just like that? Couldn't you at least have mulled it over?" Zach was staring at her as though he thought someone should rush over and take her temperature. "Forget I said that," she mumbled, fussing with her napkin in order to avoid meeting his eyes.

"I didn't want to encourage him."

"That was wise." Janine picked up her water glass and downed half the contents.

"To your grandfather's credit, he seemed to accept my answer."

"Don't count on it," Janine warned.

"Don't worry, I know him, too. He isn't going to give up easily. That's the reason I suggested you and I meet to talk about this. If we keep in touch, we can anticipate Anton's strategy."

"Good idea."

Their salads arrived and Janine frowned when the waitress tossed Zach another suggestive glance. "So," she began in a conversational tone once the woman had left, "Gramps was smart enough not to offer you a large incentive if you went along with his scheme."

"I didn't say that."

She stabbed viciously at her salad. "I hadn't expected him to stoop that low. Exactly what tactics did he use?"

"He said something about family members having use of the limousine."

Janine's fork made a clanging sound as it hit the side of her salad bowl. "He offered you the limousine if you married me? That's all?"

"Not even that," Zach explained, not bothering to disguise his amusement, "only the *use* of it."

"Why…why, that's insulting." She crammed some salad into her mouth and chewed the crisp lettuce as though it were leather.

"I considered it a step above the cow and ten chickens you suggested the first time we discussed this."

"Where he came from, a cow and ten chickens were worth a lot more than you seem to realize," Janine exclaimed, and immediately regretted raising her voice, because half the patrons in the restaurant turned to stare. She smiled blandly at those around her, then slouched forward over her salad.

She reached for a bread stick, broke it in half and glared at it. "The use of the limo," she repeated, indignant.

"Don't look so upset." He grinned. "I might have accepted."

Zach was deriving far too much pleasure from this to suit her. "Your attitude isn't helping any," she said, frowning righteously.

"I apologize."

But he didn't act the least bit apologetic. When she'd first met Zach, Janine had assumed he was a man who rarely smiled, yet in the short time they'd spent together today, he'd practically been laughing outright.

The waitress brought their entrées, but when Janine took her first bite, she realized that even the pretense of eating was more than she could manage. She felt too wretched. Tears sprang to her eyes, which embarrassed her even more, although she struggled to hide them.

"What's wrong?" Zach surprised her by asking.

Eyes averted, Janine shook her head, while she attempted to swallow. "Gramps believes I'm a poor judge of character," she finally said. And she was. Brian had proved it to her, but Gramps didn't know about Brian. "I feel like a failure."

"He didn't mean any of it," Zach said gently.

"But couldn't he have come up with something a little more flattering?"

"He needed an excuse to marry you off, otherwise his suggestion would have sounded crazy." Zach hesitated. "You know, the more we discuss this, the more ludicrous the whole thing seems." He chuckled softly and leaned forward to set his elbows on the table. "Who would've believed he'd come up with the idea of the two of us marrying?"

"Thank you very much," Janine muttered. He sat there shredding her ego and apparently found the process just short of hilarious.

"Don't let it get to you. You're not interested in me as a husband, anyway."

"You're right about that—you're the last person I'd ever consider marrying," she lashed out, then regretted her reaction when she saw his face tighten.

"That's what I thought." He attacked his spaghetti as though the clams were scampering around his plate.

The tension between them mounted. When the waitress arrived to remove their plates, Janine had barely touched her meal. Zach hadn't eaten much, either.

After paying for their dinner, Zach walked her to her car, offering no further comment. As far as Janine was concerned, their meeting hadn't been at all productive. She felt certain that Zach was everything Gramps claimed—incisive, intelligent, intuitive. But that was at the office. As a potential husband and wife, they were completely ill-suited.

"Do you still want me to keep in touch?" she asked when she'd unlocked her car door. They stood awkwardly together in the street, and Janine realized they hardly knew what to say to each other.

"I suppose we should, since neither of us is interested in falling in with this plan of his," Zach said. "We need to set our differences aside and work together, otherwise we might unknowingly play into his hands."

"I won't be swayed and you won't, either." Janine found the thought oddly disappointing.

"If and when I do marry," Zach informed her, "which I sincerely doubt, I'll choose my own bride."

It went without saying that Janine was nothing like the woman he'd want to spend his life with.

"If and when *I* marry, I'll choose my own husband," she said, sounding equally firm. And it certainly wouldn't be a man her grandfather had chosen.

"I don't know if I like boys or not," thirteen-year-old Pam Hudson admitted over a cheeseburger and French fries. "They can be so dumb."

It'd been a week since Janine's dinner with Zach, and she was surprised that the teenager's assessment of the opposite sex should so closely match her own.

"I'm not even sure I like Charlie anymore," Pam said

as she stirred her catsup with a French fry. Idly she smeared it around the edges of her plate in a haphazard pattern. "I used to be so crazy about him, remember?"

Janine smiled indulgently. "Every other word was Charlie this and Charlie that."

"He can be okay, though. Remember when he brought me that long-stemmed rose and left it on my porch?"

"I remember." Janine's mind flashed to the afternoon she'd met Zach. As they left the restaurant, he'd smiled at her. It wasn't much as smiles went, but for some reason, she couldn't seem to forget how he'd held her gaze, his dark eyes gentle, as he murmured polite nonsense. Funny how little things about this man tended to pop up in her mind at the strangest moments.

"But last week," Pam continued, "Charlie was playing basketball with the guys, and when I walked by, he pretended he didn't even know me."

"That hurt, didn't it?"

"Yeah, it did," Pam confessed. "And after I bought a T-shirt for him, too."

"Does he wear it?"

A gratified smile lit the girl's eyes. "All the time."

"By the way, I like how you're doing your hair."

Pam beamed. "I want it to look more like yours."

Actually, the style suited Pam far better than it did her, Janine thought. The sides were cut close to the head, but the long bangs flopped with a life of their own—at least on Janine they did. Lately she'd taken to pinning them back.

"How are things at home?" Janine asked, watching the girl carefully. Pam's father, Jerry Hudson, was divorced and had custody of his daughter. Pam's mother worked on the East Coast. With no family in the area, Jerry felt that his daughter needed a woman's influence.

He'd contacted the Friendship Club about the same time Janine had applied to be a volunteer. Since Jerry worked odd hours as a short-order cook, she'd met him only once. He seemed a decent sort, working hard to make a good life for himself and his daughter.

Pam was a marvelous kid, Janine mused, and she possessed exceptional creative talent. Even before her father could afford to buy her a sewing machine, Pam had been designing and making clothes for her Barbie dolls. Janine's bandanna dress was one of the first projects she'd completed on her new machine. Pam had made several others since; they were popular with her friends, and she was ecstatic about the success of her ideas.

"I think I might forgive Charlie," she went on to say, her look contemplative. "I mean, he was with the guys and everything."

"It's not cool to let his friends know he's got a girl-friend, huh?"

"Yeah, I guess...."

Janine wasn't feeling nearly as forgiving toward Zach. He'd talked about their keeping in touch, but hadn't called her since. She didn't believe for an instant that Gramps had given up on his marriage campaign, but he'd apparently decided to let the matter rest. The pressure was off, yet Janine kept expecting some word from Zach. The least he could do was call, she grumbled to herself, although she made no attempt to analyze the reasons for her disappointment.

"Maybe Charlie isn't so bad, after all," Pam murmured, then added wisely, "This is an awkward age for boys, especially in their relationships with girls."

"Say," Janine teased, "who's supposed to be the adult here, anyway? That's my line."

"Oh, sorry,"

Smiling, Janine stole a French fry from Pam's plate and popped it into her mouth.

"So when are you leaving for Scotland?" Pam wanted to know.

"Next week."

"How long are you going to be gone?"

"Ten days." The trip was an unexpected gift from her grandfather. One night shortly after she'd met Zach for dinner, Gramps had handed her a packet with airline tickets and hotel reservations. When she'd asked why, his reply had been vague, even cryptic—something about her needing to get away. Since she'd always dreamed of visiting Scotland, she'd leapt at the chance.

It wasn't until she'd driven Pam home that Janine thought she should let Zach know she was going to be out of the country. It probably wasn't important, but he'd made such a point of saying they should keep in touch....

Janine planned her visit to the office carefully, making sure Gramps would be occupied elsewhere. Since she'd been shopping for her trip, she was carrying several department and clothing store bags. She was doing this for a reason. She wanted her visit to appear unplanned, as if in the course of a busy day, she'd suddenly remembered their agreement. She felt that dropping in would seem more spontaneous than simply calling.

"Hello," she said to Zach's efficient secretary, smiling cheerfully. "Is Mr. Thomas available? I'll only need a moment of his time."

The older woman clearly disapproved of this intrusion, but although she pursed her lips, she didn't verbalize her objection. She pushed the intercom button and Janine felt a tingle of awareness at the sound of Zach's strong masculine voice.

"This is a pleasant surprise," he said, standing as Janine breezed into the room.

She set her bags on the floor and with an exaggerated sigh, eased herself into the chair opposite his desk and crossed her legs. "I'm sorry to drop in unannounced," she said casually, "but I have some news."

"No problem." His gaze fell to the bags heaped on the floor. "Looks like you had a busy afternoon."

"I was shopping."

"So I see. Any special reason?"

"It's my trousseau." Melodramatically, she pressed the back of her hand against her forehead. "I can't take the pressure anymore. I've come to tell you I told my grandfather to go ahead and arrange the wedding. Someday, somehow, we'll learn to love each other."

"This isn't amusing. Now what's so important that it can't—"

"Mr. Thomas," his secretary said crisply over the intercom, "Mr. Hartman is here to see you."

Janine's eyes widened in panic as her startled gaze flew to Zach, who looked equally alarmed. It would be the worst possible thing for Gramps to discover Janine alone with Zach in his office. She hated to think how he'd interpret that.

"Just a minute," Zach said, reading the hysteria in her eyes. She marveled at how composed he sounded. He pointed toward a closed door and ushered her into a small room—or a large closet—that was practically a home away from home. A bar, refrigerator, microwave, sink and other conveniences were neatly arranged inside. No sooner was the door slammed shut behind her than it was jerked open again and three large shopping bags were tossed in.

Janine felt utterly ridiculous. She kept as still as she

could, afraid to turn on the light and almost afraid to breathe for fear of being discovered.

With her ear against the door, she tried to listen to the conversation, hoping to discover just how long Gramps intended to plant himself in Zach's office.

Unfortunately, she could barely hear a thing. She risked opening the door a crack; a quick glance revealed that both men were facing away from her. That explained why she couldn't understand their conversation.

It was then that Janine spotted her purse. Strangling a gasp, she eased the door shut and staggered away from it. She covered her mouth as she took deep breaths. When she found the courage to edge open the door and peek again, she saw that all her grandfather had to do was glance downward.

If he shuffled his feet, his shoe would catch on the strap and he'd drag it out of the office with him.

Zach turned away from the window, and for the first time Janine could hear and see him clearly.

"I'll take care of that right away," he said evenly. He was so calm, so composed, as though he often kept women hidden in his closet. He must have noticed Janine's purse because he frowned and his gaze flew accusingly toward her.

Well, for heaven's sake, she hadn't purposely left it there for Gramps to trip over! He wasn't even supposed to be in the building. That very morning, he'd told her he was lunching at the Athletic Club with his longtime friend, Burt Coleman. Whenever Gramps ate lunch with his cronies, he spent the afternoon playing pinochle. Apparently he'd changed his habits, just so her hair would turn prematurely gray.

Several tortured minutes passed before Zach escorted Gramps to the door. The instant it was shut, Janine stepped into the office, blinking against the brightness after her wait in the dark. "My purse," she said in a strangled voice. "Do you think he saw it?"

"It would be a miracle if he didn't. Of all the stupid things to do!"

"I didn't purposely leave it out here!"

"I'm not talking about that," Zach growled. "I'm referring to your coming here in the first place. Are you crazy? You couldn't have called?"

"I…had something to tell you and I was in the neighborhood." So much for her suave, sophisticated facade. Zach was right, of course; she *could* have told him just as easily by phone.

He looked furious. "For the life of me I can't think of a solitary thing that's so important you'd do anything this foolish. If your grandfather saw the two of us together, he'd immediately jump to the wrong conclusion. Until this afternoon, everything's been peaceful. Anton hasn't mentioned your name once and, frankly, I appreciated that."

His words stung. "I… I won't make the mistake of coming again—ever," she vowed, trying to sound dignified and aloof. She gathered her purse and her bags as quickly as possible and hurried out of the office, not caring who saw her leave, including Gramps.

"Janine, you never did say why you came." Zach had followed her to the elevator.

Janine stared at the light above the elevator that indicated the floor number, as though it was a message of the utmost importance. Her hold on the bags was precarious and something was dragging against her feet, but she couldn't have cared less. "I'm sorry to have imposed on your valuable time. Now that I think about it, it wasn't even important."

"Janine," he coaxed, apparently regretting his earlier outburst. "I shouldn't have yelled."

"Yes, I know," she said smoothly. The elevator opened and with as little ceremony as possible, she slipped inside. It wasn't until she was over the threshold that she realized her purse strap was tangled around her feet.

So much for a dignified exit.

Four

"The castle of Cawdor was built in the fifteenth century and to this day remains the seat of the earl of Cawdor," the guide intoned as Janine and several other sightseers toured the famous landmark. "In William Shakespeare's *Macbeth,* the castle plays an important role. Macbeth becomes the thane of Cawdor...."

For the first few days of Janine's visit to Scotland, she'd been content to explore on her own. The tours, however, helped fill in the bits and pieces of history she might otherwise have missed.

The castle of Cawdor was in northeastern Scotland. The next day, she planned to rent a car and take a meandering route toward Edinburgh, the political heart of Scotland. From what she'd read, Edinburgh Castle was an ancient fortress, built on a huge rock, that dominated the city's skyline. Gramps had booked reservations for her at an inn on the outskirts of town.

The Bonnie Inn, with its red-tiled roof and black-trimmed gables, had all the charm she'd expected, and more. Janine's room offered more character than comfort, but she felt its welcome as if she were visiting an old friend. A vase filled with fresh flowers and dainty jars of bath salts awaited her.

Eager to explore, she strolled outside to investigate the extensive garden. There was a chill in the April air and she tucked her hands in her pockets, watching with amusement as the partridges fed on the lush green lawn.

"Janine?"

At the sound of her name, she turned, and to her astonishment discovered Zach standing not more than ten feet away. "What are you doing here?" she demanded.

"Me? I was about to ask you the same question."

"I'm on vacation. Gramps gave me the trip as a gift."

"I'm here on business," Zach explained, and his brow furrowed in a suspicious frown.

Janine was doing her own share of frowning. "This is all rather convenient, don't you think?"

Zach took immediate offense. "You don't believe I planned this, do you?"

"No," she agreed reluctantly.

Zach continued to stand there, stiff and wary. "I had absolutely nothing to do with this," he said.

"If you hadn't been so rude to me the last time we met," she felt obliged to inform him, with a righteous tilt to her chin, "you'd have known well in advance that Gramps was sending me here, and we could have avoided this unpleasant shock."

"If you hadn't been in such an all-fired hurry to leave my office, you'd have discovered I was traveling here myself."

"Oh, that's perfect! Go ahead and blame me for everything," she shrieked. "As I recall, you were furious at my being anywhere near your precious office."

"All right, I'll admit I might have handled the situation poorly," Zach said, and the muscles in his jaw hardened. "But as you'll also recall, I did apologize."

"Sure you did," she said, "after you'd trampled all over my ego. I've never felt like more of a fool in my life."

"You?" Zach shouted. "It may surprise you to know that I don't make a habit of hiding women in my office."

"Do you think I enjoyed being stuffed in that...closet like a bag of dirty laundry?"

"What was I supposed to do? Hide you under my desk?"

"It might've been better than a pitch-black closet."

"If you're so keen on casting blame, let me remind you I wasn't the one who left my purse in full view of your grandfather," Zach said. "I did everything but perform card tricks to draw his attention away from it."

"You make it sound like I'm at fault," Janine snapped.

"I'm not the one who popped in unexpectedly. If you had a job like everyone else—"

"If I had a job," she broke in, outraged. "You mean all the volunteer work I do doesn't count? Apparently the thirty hours a week I put in mean nothing. Sure, I've got a degree. Sure, I could probably have my pick of a dozen different jobs, but why take employment away from someone who really needs it when so many worthwhile organizations are hurting for volunteers?" She was breathless by the time she finished, and so angry she could feel the heat radiating from her face.

She refused to tolerate Zach's offensive insinuations any longer. From the moment they'd met, Zach had clearly viewed her as spoiled and frivolous, without a brain in her head. And it seemed that nothing had altered his opinion.

"Listen, I didn't mean—"

"It's obvious to me," she said bluntly, "that you and I are never going to agree on anything." She was so furious she couldn't keep her anger in check. "The best thing for us to do is completely ignore each other. It's obvious that you don't want anything to do with me and, frankly, I feel the same way about you. So, good day,

Mr. Thomas." With that she walked away, her head high and her pride intact.

For the very first time with this man, she'd been able to make a grand exit. It should have felt good. But it didn't.

An hour later, after Janine had taken the tourist bus into Edinburgh, she was still brooding over her latest encounter with Zachary Thomas. If there was any humor at all in this situation, it had to be the fact that her usually sage grandfather could possibly believe she and Zach were in any way suited.

Determined to put the man out of her mind, Janine wandered down Princes Street, which was packed with shoppers, troupes of actors giving impromptu performances and strolling musicians. Her mood couldn't help but be influenced by the festive flavor, and she soon found herself smiling despite the unpleasant confrontation with her grandfather's business partner.

Several of the men who passed her in the street were dressed in kilts, and Janine felt as if she'd stepped into another time, another world. The air swirled with bagpipe music. The city itself seemed gray and gloomy, a dull background for the colorful sights and sounds, the excitement of ages past.

It was as Janine walked out of a dress shop that she bumped into Zach a second time. He stopped, his eyes registering surprise and what looked to Janine like a hint of regret—as though confronting her twice in the same day was enough to try anyone's patience.

"I know what you're thinking," he said, pinning her with his dark intense gaze.

"And I'm equally confident that you don't." She held her packages close and edged against the shop window to avoid hindering other pedestrians on the crowded sidewalk.

"I came here to do some shopping," Zach said gruffly. "I wasn't following you."

"You can rest assured I wasn't following *you*."

"Fine," he said.

"Fine," she repeated.

But neither of them moved for several nerve-racking seconds. Janine assumed Zach was going to say something else. Perhaps she secretly hoped he would. If they couldn't be friends, Janine would've preferred they remain allies. They should be uniting their forces instead of battling each other. Without a word, Zach gestured abruptly and wheeled around to join the stream of people hurrying down the sidewalk.

A half hour later, with more packages added to her collection, Janine strolled into a fabric store, wanting to purchase a sizable length of wool as a gift for Pam. She ran her fingertips along several thick bolts of material, marveling at the bold colors. The wool felt soft, but when she lifted a corner with her palm, she was surprised by how heavy it was.

"Each clan has its own tartan," the white-haired lady in the shop explained. Janine enjoyed listening to her voice, with its enthusiastic warmth and distinct Scottish burr. "Some of the best-known tartans come in three patterns that are to be worn for different occasions— everyday, dress and battle."

Intrigued, Janine watched as the congenial woman walked around the table to remove a blue-and-green plaid. Janine had already seen that pattern several times. The shop owner said that tourists were often interested in this particular tartan, called Black Watch, because it was assigned to no particular clan. In choosing Black

Watch, they weren't aligning themselves with any one clan, but showing total impartiality.

Pleased, Janine purchased several yards of the fabric.

Walking down the narrow street, she was shuffling her packages in her arms when she caught sight of Zach watching a troupe of musicians. She started to move away, then for no reason she could name, paused to study him. Her impression of him really hadn't changed since that first afternoon. She still thought Zach Thomas opinionated, unreasonable and...fine, she was willing to admit it, attractive. *Very* attractive, in a sort of rough-hewn way. He lacked the polish, the superficial sophistication of a man like Brian, but he had a vigor that seemed thoroughly masculine. He also had the uncanny ability to set her teeth on edge with a single look. No other man could irritate her so quickly.

The musicians began a lively song and Zach laughed unselfconsciously. His rich husky tenor was smooth and relaxed as it drifted across the street toward her. Janine knew she should've left then, but she couldn't. Despite everything, she was intrigued.

Zach must have felt her scrutiny because he suddenly turned and their eyes locked before Janine could look away. The color rose to her cheeks and for a long moment, neither moved. Neither smiled.

It was in Janine's mind to cross the street, swallow her pride and put an end to this pointless antagonism. During the past several weeks her pride had become familiar fare; serving it up once more shouldn't be all that difficult.

She was entertaining that thought when a bus drove past her belching a thick cloud of black smoke, momentarily blocking her view of Zach. When the bus had passed, Janine noticed that he'd returned his attention to the musicians.

Disheartened, she headed in the opposite direction. She hadn't gone more than a block when she heard him call her name.

She stopped and waited for him to join her. With an inquiring lift of one eyebrow, he reached for some of her packages. She nodded, repressing a shiver of excitement as his hand brushed hers. Shifting his burden, he slowed his steps to match Janine's. Then he spoke. "We need to talk."

"I don't see how we can. Every time you open your mouth you say something insulting and offensive."

Only a few minutes earlier, Janine had been hoping to put an end to this foolish antagonism, yet here she was provoking an argument, acting just as unreasonable as she accused him of being. She stopped midstep, disgusted with herself. "I shouldn't have said that. I don't know what it is about us, but we seem to have a hard time being civil to each other."

"It might be the shock of finding each other here."

"Which brings up another subject," Janine added fervently. "If Gramps was going to arrange for us to meet, why send us halfway around the world to do it?"

"I used to think I knew your grandfather," Zach murmured. "But lately, I'm beginning to wonder. I haven't got a clue why he chose Scotland."

"He came to me with the tickets, reminding me it'd been almost a year since I'd traveled anywhere," Janine said. "He told me it was high time I took a vacation, that I needed to get away for a while. And I bought it hook, line and sinker."

"You?" Zach cried, shaking his head, clearly troubled. "Your grandfather sent me here on a wild-goose chase. Yes, there were contacts to make, but this was a trip any of our junior executives could've handled. It wasn't until I arrived at the inn and found you booked there that I realized what he was up to."

"If we hadn't been so distracted trying to figure out who was to blame for that fiasco at your office, we might've been able to prevent this. At least, we'd have guessed what Gramps was doing."

"Exactly," Zach said. "Forewarned is forearmed. Obviously, we have to put aside our differences and stay in communication. That's the key. Communication."

"Absolutely," Janine agreed, with a nod of her head.

"But letting him throw us together like this is only going to lead to trouble."

What kind of trouble, he didn't say, but Janine could guess all too easily. "I agree with you."

"The less time we spend together, the better." He paused when he noticed that she was standing in front of the bus stop.

"If we allow Gramps to throw us together, it'll just encourage him," she said. "We've got to be very firm about this, before things get completely out of hand."

"You're right." Without asking, he took the rest of the packages from her arms, adding them to the bags and parcels he already carried. "I rented a car. I don't suppose you'd accept a ride back to the inn?"

"Please." Janine was grateful for the offer. They'd started off badly, each blaming the other, but fortunately their relationship was beginning to improve. That relieved her. She'd much rather have Zachary for a friend than an enemy.

They spoke very little on the twenty-mile ride back to the Bonnie Inn. After an initial exchange of what sights they'd seen and what they'd purchased, there didn't seem to be much to say. They remained awkward and a little uneasy with each other. And Janine was all too aware of how intimate the confines of the small rented car were. Her shoulder and her thigh were within scant inches of brushing against Zach, something she was determined to ignore.

The one time Janine chanced a look in his direction, she saw how intent his features were, as if he was driving a dangerous, twisting course instead of a straight, well-maintained road with light traffic. His mouth was compressed, bracketed by deep grooves, and his dark eyes had narrowed. He glanced away from the road long enough for their eyes to meet. Janine smiled and quickly looked down, embarrassed that he'd caught her studying him so closely. She wished she could sort out her feelings, analyze all her contradictory emotions in a logical manner. She was attracted to Zach, but not in the same way she'd been attracted to Brian. Although Zach infuriated her, she admired him. Respected him. But he didn't send her senses whirling mindlessly, as Brian had. Then again, she didn't think of him as a brother, either. Her only conclusion was that her feelings for Zach were more confusing than ever.

After thanking him for the ride and collecting her parcels, she left Zach in the lobby and tiredly climbed the stairs to her room. She soaked in a hot scented bath, then changed into a blue-and-gold plaid kilt she'd bought that afternoon. With it, she wore a thin white sweater under her navy-blue blazer. She tied a navy scarf at her neck, pleased with the effect. A little blush, a dab of eye shadow and she was finished, by now more than ready for something to eat.

Zach was waiting to be seated in the dining room when she came downstairs. He wore a thick hand-knit sweater over black dress slacks and made such a virile sight she found it difficult not to stare.

The hostess greeted them with a warm smile. "Dinner for two?"

Janine reacted first, flustered and a little embarrassed. "We're not together," she said. "This gentleman was here before me." Anything else would negate the agreement they'd made earlier.

Zach frowned as he followed the hostess to a table set against the wall, close to the massive stone fireplace. The hostess returned and directed Janine to a table against the same wall, so close to Zach that she could practically read the menu over his shoulder. She was reading her own menu when Zach spoke. "Don't you think we're both being a little silly?"

"Yes," she admitted. "But earlier today we agreed that being thrown together like this could lead to trouble."

"I honestly don't think it would hurt either of us to have dinner together, do you?"

"No… I don't think it would." They'd spend the entire meal talking across the tables to each other, anyway.

He stood up, grinning. "May I join you?"

"Please." She couldn't help responding with a smile.

He pulled out the other chair, his gaze appreciative. "Those colors look good on you."

"Thanks." She had to admit he looked good—darkly vibrant and masculine—himself. She was about to return his compliment when it dawned on her how senselessly they were challenging fate.

"It's happening already," she whispered, leaning toward him in order to avoid being overheard.

"What?" Zach glanced around as though he expected ghostly clansmen to emerge from behind the drapes.

"You're telling me how good I look in blue and I was

about to tell you how nice *you* look and we're smiling at each other and forming a mutual admiration society. Next thing you know, we'll be married."

"That's ridiculous!"

"Sure, you say that now, but I can see a real problem here."

"Does this mean you want me to go back to my table and eat alone?"

"Of course not. I just think it would be best if we limited the compliments. All right?"

"I'll never say anything nice about you again."

Janine smiled. "Thank you."

"You might want to watch that, as well," he warned with a roguish grin. "If we're too formal and polite with each other, that could lead us straight to the jewelers. Before we know what's happening, we'll be choosing wedding bands."

Janine's lips quivered with a barely restrained smile. "I hadn't thought about that." They glanced at each other and before either could hold it in, they were laughing, attracting the attention of everyone in the dining room. As abruptly as they'd started, they stopped, burying their faces in the menus.

After they'd ordered, Janine shared her theory with Zach, a theory that had come to her on their drive back to the inn. "I think I know why Gramps arranged for us to meet in Scotland."

"I'm dying to hear this."

"Actually, I'm afraid I'm the one responsible." She heaved a sigh of remorse. Every part of her seemed aware of Zach, which was exactly what she didn't want. She sighed again. "When Gramps first mentioned the idea of an arranged marriage, I tried to make him understand that love wasn't something one ordered like…

like dinner from a menu. He genuinely didn't seem to grasp what I was saying and asked me what a woman needed to fall in love."

"And you told him a trip to Scotland?" Zach's eyes sparkled with the question.

"Of course not. I told him a woman needed romance."

Zach leaned forward. "I hate to appear dense, but I seem to have missed something."

Pretending to be annoyed with him, Janine explained, "Well, Gramps asked me to define romance…"

"I'd be interested in learning that myself." Zach wiped the edges of his mouth with his napkin. Janine suspected he did it to cover a growing need to smile.

"It isn't all that easy to explain, you know," Janine said. "And remember this was off the top of my head. I told Gramps romance was forbidden trysts on Scottish moors."

"With an enemy clan chieftain?"

"No, with the man I loved."

"What else did you tell him?"

"I don't remember exactly. I think I said something about a moonlight stroll on the beach, and…and desperate passion."

"I wonder how he'll arrange that?"

"I don't think I want to find out," Janine murmured. Considering how seriously Gramps had taken her impromptu definition, she almost dreaded the thought of what he might do next.

When they'd finished, their plates were removed by the attentive waiter and their coffee served. To complicate her feelings, she was actually a little sad their dinner was about to end.

They left the dining room, and Zach escorted her up the stairs. "Thank you for being willing to take a risk and share dinner with me," he said, his voice deadpan. "I enjoyed it, despite the, uh, danger."

"I did, too," Janine said softly. More than she cared to admit. Against her better judgment, her mind spun with possible ways to delay their parting, but she decided against each one, not wanting to tempt fate any more than she already had.

Zach walked her to her room, pausing outside her door. Janine found herself searching for the right words. She longed to tell him she'd enjoyed spending the evening with him, talking and laughing together, but she didn't know how to say it without sounding like a woman in love.

Zach appeared to be having the same problem. He raised one hand as though to touch her face, then apparently changed his mind, dropping his hand abruptly. She felt strangely disappointed.

"Good night," he said curtly, stepping back.

"Good night," she echoed, turning to walk into her room. She closed the door and leaned against it, feeling unsettled but at a loss to understand why.

After ten restless minutes she ventured out again. The country garden was well lit, and a paved pathway led to rocky cliffs that fell off sharply. Even from where she stood, Janine could hear the sea roaring below. She could smell its salty tang, mixed with the scent of heath. Thrusting her hands into her blazer pockets, Janine strolled along a narrow path into the garden. The night air was cool and she had no intention of walking far, not more than a few hundred feet. She'd return in the morning when she planned to walk as far as the cliffs with their buffeting winds.

The moon was full and so large it seemed to take up the entire sky, sending streaks of silvery light across the horizon. With her arms wrapped aroung her middle, she gazed up at it, certain she'd never felt more peaceful or serene. She closed her eyes, savoring the luxurious silence of the moment.

Suddenly it was broken. "So we meet again," Zach said from behind her.

"This is getting ridiculous." Janine turned to him and smiled, her heart beating fast. "Meeting on the moors..."

"It isn't exactly a tryst," Zach said.

"Not technically."

They stood side by side, looking into the night sky, both of them silent. During their meal they'd talked nonstop, but now Janine felt tongue-tied and ill at ease. If they'd been worried about having dinner together, they were placing themselves at even greater risk here in the moonlight.

Janine knew it. Zach knew it. But neither suggested leaving.

"It's a beautiful night," Zach said at last, linking his hands behind his back.

"It is, isn't it?" Janine replied brightly, as if he'd introduced the most stimulating topic of her entire vacation.

"I don't think we should put any stock in this," he surprised her by saying next.

"In what?"

"In meeting here, as if we'd arranged a tryst. Of course you're a beautiful woman and it would be only natural if a man...any red-blooded man were to find himself charmed. I'd blame it on the moonlight, wouldn't you?"

"Oh, I agree completely. I mean, we've been thrust together in a very romantic setting and it would be normal to...find ourselves momentarily...attracted to each other. It doesn't mean anything, though."

Zach moved behind her. "You're right, of course." He hesitated, then murmured, "You should've worn a heavier jacket." Before she could assure him that she was perfectly comfortable, he ran his hands slowly down the length of her arms, as though to warm her. Unable to restrain herself, Janine sighed and leaned against him, soaking up his warmth and his strength.

"This presents a problem, doesn't it?" he whispered, his voice husky and close to her ear. "Isn't moonlight supposed to do something strange to people?"

"I…think it only affects werewolves."

He chuckled and his breath shot a series of incredible light-as-air sensations along her neck. Janine felt she was about to crumple at his feet. Then his chin brushed the side of her face and she sighed again.

His hands on her shoulders, Zach urged her around so that she faced him, but not for anything would Janine allow her gaze to meet his.

He didn't say a word.

She didn't, either.

Janine experienced one worry after another, afraid to voice any of them. Zach apparently felt the same way, because he didn't seem any more eager to explain things than she did. Or to stop them…

After a moment, Zach pressed his hands over her cheekbones. Leisurely, his thumbs stroked the line of her jaw, her chin. His eyes were dark, his expression unreadable. Janine's heart was churning over and over, dragging her emotions with it. She swallowed, then moistened her lips.

He seemed to find her mouth mesmerizing. Somewhere deep inside, she discovered the strength to warn him that her grandfather's plan was working. She opened her mouth to speak, but before she could utter a sin-

gle word, Zach's arms came around her and drew her
close against him. She felt his comforting warmth seep
through her, smelled the faint muskiness of his skin.
The sensations were unlike anything she'd ever known.
Then he lowered his mouth to hers.

The immediate shock of pleasure was almost fright-
ening. She couldn't keep from trembling.

He drew back slightly. "You're cold. You should've
said something."

"No, that's not it." Even her voice was quivering.

"Then what is?"

In response she kissed him back. She hadn't meant to,
but before she could stop herself, she slipped her arms
around his neck and slanted her mouth over his.

Zach's shoulders were heaving when at last she pulled
her mouth away and hid her face against his chest.

"What are we doing?" he whispered. He broke hast-
ily away from her.

Janine was too stunned to react. In an effort to hide
his effect on her, she rubbed her face as though struggling to wake up from a deep sleep.

"That shouldn't have happened," Zach said stiffly.

"You're telling me," she returned raggedly. "It certainly wasn't the smartest move we could've made."

Zach jerked his fingers roughly through his hair and
frowned. "I don't know what came over me. Over us.
We both know better."

"It's probably because we're both tired," Janine said
soothingly, offering a convenient excuse. "When you
stop to think about it, the whole thing's perfectly understandable. Gramps arranged for us to meet, hoping
something like this would happen. Clearly the power of
suggestion is stronger than either of us realized."

"Clearly." But he continued to frown.

"Oh, gee," Janine said glancing at her watch, unable to read the numbers in the dark. Her voice was high and wavering. "Will you look at the time? I can't believe it's so late. I really should be getting back inside."

"Janine, listen. I think we should talk about this."

"Sure, but not now." All she wanted was to escape and gather some perspective on what had happened. It had all started so innocently, almost a game, but quickly turned into something far more serious.

"All right, we'll discuss it in the morning." Zach didn't sound pleased. He walked through the garden with her, muttering under his breath. "Damn it!" he said, again shoving his fingers through his hair. "I knew I should never have come here."

"There's no need to be so angry. Blame the moon-light. It obviously disrupts the brain and interferes with wave patterns or something."

"Right," Zach said, his voice still gruff.

"Well, good night," Janine managed cheerfully when they reached the staircase.

"Good night." Zach's tone was equally nonchalant.

Once Janine was in her room, she threw herself on the bed and covered her eyes with one hand. *Oh, no,* she lamented silently. They'd crossed the line. Tempted fate. Spit in the eye of common sense.

They'd kissed.

Several minutes later, still shaking, Janine got up and undressed. She slid under the blankets and tried to find a relaxing position. But she didn't feel like sleeping. Tomorrow she'd have to make polite conversation with Zach and she didn't know if she could bear it. She was sure he'd feel just as uncomfortable with her. She'd seen how he could barely look at her when they entered the inn.

Tossing aside the blankets, Janine decided she had only one option. She'd leave Scotland, the sooner the better. Grabbing the phone, she called the airport, booked a seat on the earliest flight home and immediately set about packing her bags.

Not bothering to even try to sleep, she crept down the stairs a little before midnight and checked out.

"You're leaving sooner than you expected, aren't you, Miss Hartman?" the night manager asked after calling for a cab.

"Yes," she said.

"I hope everything was satisfactory?"

"It was wonderful." She pulled a folded piece of paper from her purse and placed it on the counter. "Would you see to it that Mr. Thomas receives this in the morning?"

"Of course." The young man tucked it in a small cubbyhole behind him.

Satisfied that Zach would know she was leaving and wouldn't be concerned by her hurried return to Seattle, she sat in a chair in the small lobby to wait for her cab.

About fifteen minutes later, Janine watched silently as the cabdriver stowed her luggage in the trunk. She paused before climbing in the backseat of the car and glanced one last time at the muted moonlit landscape, disappointed that she wouldn't have an opportunity to visit the cliffs.

The ride to the airport seemed to take an eternity. She felt a burning sense of regret at leaving Scotland. She'd fallen in love with the country during her short visit and hoped someday to return. Although the memory of her evening stroll through the garden would always bring with it a certain chagrin, she couldn't completely regret that time with Zach. In fact, she'd always remember the fleeting sense of contentment she'd felt in his arms.

Janine arrived at the airport long before her flight was scheduled to leave. She spent an hour drinking coffee and leafing through fashion magazines, several of which she took with her to give to Pam later.

A cup of coffee in one hand, she approached the airline counter with her passport in the other. The bag she had draped over her shoulder accidentally collided with the man standing next to her. An automatic apology formed on her lips, but before she could voice it, that same man turned to face her.

"Zach," she cried, nearly dropping her coffee in shock. "What are you doing here?"

Five

"You think this is intentional, don't you?" Zach demanded. "It's obvious *you're* the one running after me. You found the note I slipped under your door and—"

"I checked out just before midnight so I couldn't possibly have read your note," she said angrily. "And furthermore I left a message for you."

"I didn't get it."

"Then there's been a misunderstanding."

"To say the least," Zach muttered. "A misunderstanding…" His tone was doubtful, as if he suspected she'd purposely arranged to fly home with him. She launched into an indignant protest.

"Excuse me, please."

The interruption was from a uniformed airline employee who was leaning over the counter and waving in an effort to gain their attention.

"May I have your ticket and passport?" she asked Janine. "You're holding up the line."

"Of course. I'm sorry." The best thing to do, she decided, was to ignore Zach completely. Just because they were booked on the same flight didn't mean they had to have anything to do with each other. Evidently they'd both panicked after their encounter in the garden. He was as eager to escape as she was.

Okay, so she'd ignore him and he'd ignore her. She'd return to her life, and he'd return to his. From this point forward, they need never have contact with each other again. Then they'd both be satisfied.

The airline clerk punched something into her computer. "I can give you your seat assignment now," she remarked, concentrating on the screen.

Standing on tiptoe, Janine leaned toward the woman and lowered her voice to a whisper. "Could you make sure I'm as far from Mr. Thomas's seat as possible?"

"This flight is booked solid," the attendant said impaiently. "The only reason you and your…friend were able to get seats was because of a last-minute cancellation. I'll do the best I can, but I can't rearrange everyone's seat assignments just before the flight."

"I understand," Janine said, feeling foolish and petty. But the way her luck had been going, Zach would end up in the seat beside hers, believing she'd purposely arranged that, too.

They boarded the flight separately; in fact, Zach was one of the last passengers to step onto the plane.

By that time, Janine was settled in the second row of the first-class section, flipping through the in-flight magazine. Zach strolled past her, intent on the boarding pass clutched in his hand.

Pretending she hadn't seen him seemed the best tactic, and she turned to gaze out the window.

"It seems I'm sitting here," Zach announced brusquely, loading his carry-on luggage in the compartment above the seats.

Janine had to bite her tongue to keep from insisting she'd had nothing to do with that. She'd even tried to prevent it, but she doubted Zach would believe her.

"Before you claim otherwise, I want you to know I didn't arrange this," he said, sitting down beside her.

"I know that."

"You do?"

"Of course," Janine told him. "The fates are against us. I don't know how my grandfather arranged our meeting at the airport or the adjoining seats, any more than I know why I stumbled on you my first day at the Bonnie Inn. We might never have crossed paths. But somehow, some way, Gramps is responsible." That didn't sound entirely reasonable, but she thought it best not to mention their stroll in the moonlight.

"So you're not ready to unleash the full force of your anger on me?"

"I don't see how I can be upset with you—or the reverse. Neither of us asked for this."

"Exactly."

Janine yawned loudly and covered her mouth. "Excuse me. I didn't sleep last night and now it's catching up with me."

Her yawn was contagious and soon Zach's hand was warding off his own admission of drowsiness. The flight attendant came by with coffee, which both Zach and Janine declined.

"Frankly, I'd be more interested in a pillow," Janine said, yawning again. The attendant handed her one, as well as a blanket, then offered the same to Zach. He refused both, intending to work on some papers he'd withdrawn from his briefcase. The minute the plane was safely in the air, Janine laid her head back and closed her eyes. Almost immediately she felt herself drifting into a peaceful slumber.

She stirred twice in the long hours that followed, but both times a gentle voice soothed her back to sleep. Sighing, she snuggled into the warmth, feeling more comfortable than she had in weeks.

She began to dream and could see herself walking

across the moors, wearing traditional Scottish dress, while bagpipes wailed in the background.

Then, on the crest of a hill, Zach appeared, dressed in a Black Watch kilt and tam-o'-shanter; a set of bagpipes was draped over his shoulder. Their eyes met and the music ceased. Then, out of nowhere, her grandfather appeared, standing halfway between the two of them, looking distinctly pleased. He cupped his hands over his mouth and shouted to Janine. "Is this romance?"

"Yes," she shouted back.

"What else do you need?"

"Love."

"Love," Gramps repeated. He turned to Zach, apparently seeking some kind of assistance.

Zach started fiddling with his bagpipes, avoiding the question. He scowled as he concentrated on his task.

"Look at the pair of you," Gramps called. "You're perfect together. Zach, when are you going to wake up and realize what a wonderful girl my Janine is?"

"If I do get married, you can be sure I'll choose my own bride," Zach hollered.

"And I'd prefer to pick out my own husband!"

"You're falling in love with Zach!" Gramps declared, obviously elated.

"I—I—" Janine was so flustered she couldn't complete her thought, which only served to please her grandfather more.

"Look at her, boy," Gramps directed his attention to Zach again. "See how lovely she is. And think of what beautiful children you'll have."

"Gramps! Enough about babies! I'm not marrying Zach!"

"Janine." Zach's voice echoed in her ear.

"Keep out of this," she cried. He was the last person she wanted to hear from.

"You're having a dream."

Her eyes fluttered open and she saw Zach's face close to her own, her head nestled against his chest. "Oh…" she mumbled, bolting upright. "Oh, dear… I am sorry. I didn't realize I was leaning on you."

"I hated to wake you, but you seemed to be having a nightmare."

She blinked and tried to focus on him, but it was difficult, and to complicate matters her eyes started to water. She wiped her face with one sleeve. Then, straightening, she removed the pillow from behind her back and folded the blanket, trying to disguise how badly her hands were trembling.

"You're worried about what happened after dinner last night, aren't you?"

Janine released a pent-up breath and smiled brightly as she lied. "Nothing really happened."

"In the garden, when we kissed. Listen," Zach said in a low voice, glancing quickly around to ensure that no one could overhear their conversation, "I think it's time we talked about last night."

"I… You're right, of course." She didn't feel up to this, but she supposed it was best dealt with before she had to face her grandfather.

"Egos aside."

"By all means," Janine agreed. She braced herself, not knowing what to expect. Zach had made his views on the idea of an arranged marriage plain from the first; so had she. In fact, even her feelings about a marriage based on love weren't all that positive at the moment. Brian had taught her a valuable lesson, a painful lesson, one she wouldn't easily forget. She'd given him her heart and her trust, and he'd betrayed both. Falling in love had been the most shattering experience of her life, and she had no intention of repeating it anytime soon.

"I'd be a liar if I didn't admit how nice kissing you was," Zach said, "but I wish it had never happened. It created more problems than it solved."

Janine wasn't exactly flattered by his remark. Keeping egos out of this was harder than it sounded, she thought ruefully. Her expression must have revealed her thoughts because Zach elaborated. "Before I arrived in Scotland, we hardly knew each other. We met that first afternoon over lunch—with Anton—and talked a couple of times, but basically we were strangers."

"We had dinner one night," Janine reminded him, annoyed that he could so casually dismiss it.

"Right," he acknowledged. "Then we met at the Bonnie Inn and, bingo, we were having dinner together and walking in the moonlight, and before either of us knew how it happened, we were kissing."

Janine nodded, listening quietly.

"There are several factors we can take into account, but if we're going to place blame for that kiss, I'm the one at fault."

"You?"

"Me," he confirmed with a grimace. "Actually, I'm prepared to accept full responsibility. I doubt you were aware of what was going on. It didn't take me long to see how innocent you are, and—"

"Now just a minute," Janine snapped. Once again he was taking potshots at her dignity. "What do you mean by that?"

"It's obvious you haven't had a lot of sexual experience and—"

"In other words I'm so incredibly naive that I couldn't

possibly be held accountable for a few kisses in the moonlight?"

"Something like that."

"Oh, brother," she muttered.

"There's no need to feel offended."

"I wasn't exactly raised in a convent, you know. And for your information, I've been kissed by more than one man."

"I'm sure you have. But we're getting sidetracked here—"

"I'm sorry you found me so inept. A man of your vast worldly experience must've been sorely disappointed by someone as unsophisticated as me, and—"

"Janine," he said firmly, stopping her. "You're putting words in my mouth. All I was saying is that we—*I*—let matters get out of hand and we can't blame your grandfather for what happened."

"I'm willing to accept my part in this. I can also see where this conversation is leading."

"Good," Zach said. It was clear that his composure was slipping. "Then you tell me."

"You think that because I enjoyed spending time with you and we shared this mildly romantic evening and—"

"*Mildly* romantic?"

"Yes, you did say egos aside, didn't you? I'm just being honest."

"Fine," he said, tight-lipped.

"You seem to think that because you have so much more experience than I do, there's a real danger I'll be *swooning* at your feet." She drew out the word, enjoying her silliness, and batted her eyelashes furiously.

"Janine, you're behaving like a child," he informed her coldly.

"Of course I am. That's exactly what you seem to expect of me."

Zach's fingers tightened on the armrest. "You're purposely misconstruing everything I said."

"Whatever you're trying to say isn't necessary. You figure we had a borderline interest in each other and now we've crossed that border. Right? Well, I'm telling you that you needn't worry." She sucked in a deep breath and glared at him. "I'm right, aren't I? That's what you think, isn't it?"

"Something like that, yes."

Janine nodded grimly. "And *now* you think that since you held me in your arms and you lost your control long enough to kiss me, I'm suddenly going to start entertaining thoughts of the M word."

"The... M word?"

"Marriage."

"That's ridiculous," Zach said, jamming the airline magazine back into the seat pocket in front of him.

"Well?"

"All I mean is that the temptation might be there and we should both beware of it."

"Oh, honestly, Zach," she said sarcastically, "you overestimate yourself."

"Listen, I wasn't the one mumbling about babies."

"I was having a dream! That has absolutely nothing to do with what we're talking about now."

"Could've fooled me." He reached for the same magazine he'd recently rejected and turned the pages hard enough to rip them in two. "I don't think this discussion is getting us anywhere."

Janine sighed. "You were right, though. We did need to clear the air."

Zach made a gruff indistinguishable reply.

"I'll try to keep out of your magnetic force field, but if I occasionally succumb to your overwhelming charm and forget myself, I can only beg your forgiveness."

"Enough, Janine."

He looked so annoyed with her that she couldn't help smiling. Zach Thomas was a man of such colossal ego it would serve him right if she pretended to faint every time he glanced in her direction. The image filled her mind with laughter.

Zach leaned his head back and closed his eyes, effectively concluding their conversation. Janine stared out the window at the first signs of sunrise, thinking about all kinds of things—except her chaotic feelings for the man beside her.

Some time later, the pilot announced that the plane was approaching Seattle-Tacoma International Airport. Home sounded good to Janine, although she fully intended to have a heart-to-heart talk with her grandfather about his matchmaking efforts.

Once they'd landed, she cleared customs quickly. She struggled with her two large pieces of luggage, pulling one by the handle and looping the long strap of her carry-on bag over her shoulder. Zach was still dealing with the customs agent when she maneuvered her way outside into the bright morning sunlight, joining the line of people waiting for cabs.

"Here," Zach said, from behind her, "I'll carry one of those for you." He'd managed to travel with only his briefcase and a garment bag, which was neatly folded and easily handled.

"Thank you," she said breathlessly.

"I thought we'd agreed to limit our expressions of gratitude toward each other," he grumbled, frowning as he lifted the suitcase.

"I apologize. It slipped my mind."

Zach continued to grumble. "What'd you pack in here, anyway? Bricks?"

"If you're going to complain, I'll carry it myself."

He muttered something she couldn't hear and shook his head. "Once we get a cab—"

"We?"

"We're going to confront your grandfather."

"Together? Now?" She was exhausted, mentally and physically. They both were.

"The sooner the better, don't you think?"

The problem was, Janine hadn't given much thought to what she was going to say. Yes, she intended to challenge Gramps but she'd planned to wait for the most opportune time. And she'd hoped to speak to him privately. "He might not even be home," she argued, "and if he is, I'm not sure now would really be best."

"I want this settled once and for all."

"So do I," she said vehemently. "But I think we should choose when and how we do this more carefully, don't you?"

"Perhaps…" His agreement seemed hesitant, even grudging. "All right, we'll do it your way."

"It isn't my way. It just makes sense to organize our thoughts first. Trust me, Zach, I want this cleared up as badly as you do."

His reply was little more than a grunt, but whether it was a comment on the weight of her suitcase or her tactics in dealing with Anton, she didn't know.

"And furthermore," she said, making a sweeping motion with her arm, "we've got to stop doubting each other. Nobody's following anyone and neither of us is in any danger of falling in love just because we were foolish enough to kiss."

"Fine," Zach murmured. He set her suitcase down as a cab arrived and the driver jumped out.

"How is it that we always seem to agree and yet we constantly find ourselves at odds?" she asked.

"I wish I knew," he said, looking weary in body and spirit. The cabdriver opened the trunk, storing her suitcases neatly inside. Zach threw his garment bag on top.

"We might as well still share this taxi," he said, holding the door for her.

"But isn't the Mt. Baker district out of your way?"

"I do need to talk to your grandfather. There're some estimates I need to give him."

"But can't it wait until tomorrow? Honestly, Zach, you're exhausted. One day isn't going to make any difference. And like I said, Gramps might not even be at the house."

Zach rubbed his eyes, then glanced irritably in her direction. "Honestly, Janine," he mocked, "you sound like a wife."

Biting her tongue to keep back her angry retort, Janine crossed her arms and glared out the side window. Indignation seeped through her with every breath she drew. Of its own accord, her foot started an impatient tapping. She could hardly wait to part company with this rude, unreasonable man.

Apparently Zach didn't know when to quit, because he added, "Now you even act like one."

She slowly turned to him and in a saccharine voice inquired, "And what's that supposed to mean?"

"Look at you, for heaven's sake. First you start nagging me and then—"

"Nagging you!" she exploded. "Let's get one thing straight, Zachary Thomas. I do *not* nag."

Zach rolled his eyes, then turned his head to gaze out the window on his side.

"Sir, sir," Janine said, sliding forward in the seat. She politely tapped the driver on the shoulder.

The middle-aged man glanced at her. "What is it, lady?"

"Sir," she said, offering him her warmest, most sincere smile. "Tell me, do I look like the kind of woman who'd nag?"

"Ah… Look, lady, all I do is drive a cab. You can ask me where a street is and I can tell you. If you want to go uptown, I can take you uptown. But when it comes to answering personal-type questions, I prefer to mind my own business."

"Are you satisfied?" Zach asked in a low voice.

"No, I'm not." She crossed her arms again and stared straight ahead.

The cabdriver's eyes met hers in the rearview mirror, and Janine tried to smile, but when she caught a glimpse of herself, she realized her effort looked more like a grimace.

"Me and the missus been married for near twenty years now," the driver said suddenly, stopping at a red light just off the James Street exit. "Me and the missus managed to stay married through the good times and the bad ones. Can't say that about a lot of folks."

"I don't suppose your wife is the type who nags, though, is she?" Zach made the question sound more like a statement, sending Janine a look that rankled.

"Betsy does her fair share. If you ask me, nagging's just part of a woman's nature."

"That's absurd," Janine countered stiffly. She should've known better than to draw a complete stranger into the discussion, especially another male who was sure to take Zach's side.

"I'll tell you the real reason me and the missus stayed together all these years," the cabbie continued in a confiding tone. "We never go to bed mad. I know I look like an easygoing guy, but I've got a temper on me. Over the years, me and Betsy have had our share of fights, but we always kiss and make up."

Janine smiled and nodded, sorry she'd ever gotten involved in this conversation.

"Go on," the cabbie urged.

Janine's puzzled gaze briefly met Zach's.

"Go on and do what?" Zach wanted to know.

"Kiss and make up." The cabbie turned for a moment to smile at them and wink at Janine. "If my wife was as pretty as yours, mister, I wouldn't be hesitating."

Janine nearly swallowed her tongue. "We are *not* married."

"And have no intention whatsoever of marrying," Zach added quickly.

The driver chuckled. "That's what they all say. The harder they deny it, the more in love they are."

He turned off Broadway and a few minutes later pulled into the circular driveway that led to Janine's house. As the talkative cabbie leapt from the car and dashed for the trunk, Janine opened her door and climbed out.

Apparently, Zach had no intention of taking her advice, because he, too, got out of the cab. It was while they were tussling with the luggage that the front door opened and Mrs. McCormick hurried outside.

"Janine," she cried, her blue eyes lighting up with surprise. "What are you doing back so soon? We weren't expecting you for another two days."

"I missed your cooking so much, I couldn't bear to stay away any longer," Janine said, throwing her arms around the older woman in a warm hug. "Has Gramps been giving you any trouble?"

"Not a bit."

Zach paid the driver, who got back in his cab, but not before he'd winked at Janine again. "Remember what I told you," he yelled, speeding off.

"How much was the fare?" Janine asked, automatically opening her purse.

"I took care of it," Zach said, reaching for his garment bag and the heavier of Janine's two suitcases. He said it as though he expected an argument from her, but if that was the case, Janine didn't plan to give him one.

"Is Gramps home?" Janine curved her arm affectionately around the housekeeper's waist as she spoke.

"He went out early this morning, but he should be back soon."

"Good," Zach mumbled, following them into the house.

"I imagine you're both starved," Mrs. McCormick said, heading toward the kitchen. "Let me whip up something for you that'll make you both glad you're home."

Left alone with Zach, Janine wasn't sure what to say to him. They'd spent almost twenty-four hours in each other's company. They'd argued. They'd talked. They'd laughed. They'd kissed.

"Janine—"

"Zach—"

They spoke simultaneously, then exchanged nervous smiles.

"You first," Zach said, gesturing toward her.

"I… I just wanted to say thanks for everything. I'll be in touch," she said. "By phone," she assured him.

"So you don't need to worry about me dropping by the office unannounced."

He grinned sheepishly. "Remember, communication is the key."

"I agree one hundred percent."

They stood facing each other in the foyer. "You wanted to say something?" she prompted after a moment.

"Yes." Zach exhaled sharply, then drew a hand along the side of his jaw. "What that cabbie said is true—even for us. I don't want us to part with any bad feelings. I shouldn't have said what I did back there, about nagging. You don't nag, and I had no right to say you did."

"I overreacted." The last thing she'd expected from Zach was an apology. His eyes, dark and tender, held hers, and without even realizing what she was doing, Janine took a step forward. Zach met her and she was about to slip into his arms when the sound of the front door opening drove them apart.

"Janine," Anton cried, delighted. "Zach. My, my, this is a pleasant surprise." He chuckled softly as he removed his coat. "Tell me, was your tryst on the moors as romantic as I hoped?"

Six

"Our best bet is to present a united front," Janine said to Zach four days later. They'd met at her house early in the afternoon to outline their strategy. Gramps was gone for the day, but by the time he returned, Zach and Janine planned to be ready to talk him out of this marriage idea. The sooner Anton understood that his ploy wasn't working, the better. Then they could both get on with their lives and forget this unfortunate episode.

"It's important that we stand up to him together," Janine said when Zach didn't comment. From the moment he'd arrived, he'd given her the impression that he'd rather not be doing this. Well, she wasn't overjoyed about plotting against her grandfather, either, but in this instance it was necessary. "If we don't, I'm afraid Gramps will continue to play us against each other."

"I'm here, aren't I?" Zach grumbled. He certainly wasn't in one of his more charming moods.

"Listen, if you're going to act like this—"

"Like what?" he demanded, standing up. He walked over to the polished oak sideboard and poured himself a cup of coffee. When he'd finished, he ambled toward the fireplace and leaned against the mantel.

"Like you're doing me a big favor," Janine elaborated.

"You're the one who's left *me* dangling for three days. Do you realize what I've been forced to endure? Anton kept giving me these smug smiles, looking so pleased with himself and the way things worked out in Scotland. Yesterday he went so far as to mention the name of a good jeweler."

Before Janine could stop herself, she was on her feet, arms akimbo, glaring at Zach. "I thought you were going to call me! Weren't you the one who said communication is the key? Then it's as if you'd dropped off the face of the earth! And for your information, it hasn't exactly been a Sunday school picnic around here, either."

"It may surprise you to learn that I have other things on my mind besides dealing with you and your grandfather."

"Implying I don't have anything to do with *my* time?"

"No," he said slowly. "Damn it, Janine, we're arguing again."

She sighed regretfully. "I know. We've got to stop this squabbling. It's counterproductive."

Zach's nod was curt and she saw that he was frowning. "What bothers me most is the way your grandfather found us the other day. We were standing so close and you were staring up at me, practically begging me to kiss you."

"I most certainly was not," she denied, knowing Zach was right. Her cheeks grew pink. She *had* wanted him to kiss her, but she hated having to admit that she would've walked into his arms without a second's hesitation. She decided to blame that unexpected longing on the exhausting flight home.

Zach shook his head and set his coffee cup carefully on the mantel. He thrust both hands into his pockets, still slouching against the fireplace wall. "The problem is, I was ready to do it. If your grandfather hadn't walked in when he did, I would've kissed you."

"You would?" she asked softly, feeling almost lightheaded at his words.

Zach straightened, and a nerve in his jaw pulsed, calling her attention to the strong chiseled lines of his face. "I'm only human," he said drly. "I'm as susceptible to a beautiful woman as the next man, especially when she all but asks me to take her in my arms."

That was too much. Janine pinched her lips together to keep from crying out in anger. Taking a moment to compose herself, she closed her eyes and drew in a deep breath. "Instead of blaming each other for something that *didn't* happen, could we please return to the subject at hand, which is my grandfather?"

"All right," Zach agreed. "I'm sorry. I shouldn't have said anything." He went to the leather wingback chair and sat down. Leaning forward, he rested his elbows on his knees. "What are you going to say to him?"

"Me? I thought… I'd hoped…you'd want to do the talking."

Zach shook his head. "Tact doesn't seem to be my strong point lately."

"Okay, okay, I'll do it, if that's what you really want." She gazed silently down at the richly patterned carpet, collecting her thoughts. "I think we should tell him how much we both love and respect him and that we realize his actions have been motivated by his concern for us both and his desire for our happiness. We might even go so far as to thank him—" She stopped abruptly when Zach gave a snort of laughter. "All right, if you think you can do better, you do the talking."

"If it was up to me, I'd just tell that meddling old fool to stay out of our lives."

"Your sensitivity is really heartwarming," she muttered. "At first, this whole thing was one big joke to you and you really enjoyed tormenting me."

"You're exaggerating."

"As I recall, you played that cow-and-ten-chickens business for all it was worth, but I notice you're singing a different tune now and frankly—"

The library door opened, interrupting her tirade. Her grandfather and his longtime friend, veterinarian Dr. Burt Coleman, walked into the room.

"Zach. Janine," Gramps said, grinning broadly.

"Gramps," Janine burst out, rushing to her feet. They weren't prepared for this, and Zach was being impossible, so she said the first thing that came to mind. Pointing at Zach, she cried, "I don't know how you could possibly expect me to marry that man. He's stubborn and rude and we're completely wrong for each other." She was trembling by the time she finished, and collapsed gracelessly into the nearest chair.

"In case you haven't figured it out yet, you're no angel yourself," Zach said, scowling at Janine.

"Children, please," Gramps implored, advancing into the library, hands held out in supplication. "What seems to be the problem?"

"I want this settled," Zach said forcefully. "I'm not about to be saddled with Janine for a wife."

"As if I want to be *your* wife? In your dreams, Zachary Thomas!"

"We realize you mean well," Zach added, his face looking pinched. He completely ignored Janine. "But neither of us appreciates your matchmaking efforts."

Gramps walked over to the leather chair recently occupied by Zach and sat down. He smiled weakly at each of them, his shoulders sagging. "I thought… I'd hoped you two would grow fond of each other."

"I'm sorry to disappoint you, Gramps, I really am," Janine said, feeling guilty. "But Zach and I don't even like each other. We can barely carry on a civil conversation. He's argumentative and unreasonable—"

"And she's illogical and stubborn."

"I don't think we need to trade insults to get our message across," Janine said. Her face was so hot, she felt as if her cheeks were on fire.

"There's no hope?" Anton asked quietly.

"None whatsoever," Zach said. "Janine will make some man a wonderful wife one day, but unfortunately, he won't be me."

Her grandfather slumped against the back of his chair. "You're sure?"

"Positive," Zach said, loudly enough to convince Mrs. McCormick who was working in the kitchen.

"I love you, Gramps," said Janine, "and I'd do almost anything you wanted, but I can't and won't marry Zach. We know you have our best interests at heart, but neither of us is romantically interested in the other."

Burt Coleman, who stood by the library doors, looked as if he'd rather be anyplace else. His discomfort at witnessing this family scene was obvious. "I think it'd be best if I came back another time," he murmured as he turned to leave.

"No," Anton said, gesturing his friend back. "Come in. You've met Zachary Thomas, haven't you?"

The two men nodded at each other, but Janine noticed how rigidly Zach held himself. This meeting with Gramps hadn't gone the way she'd planned. She'd wanted everything to be calm and rational, a discussion uncluttered by messy emotions. Instead they'd ended up practically attacking each other, and worse, Janine had been the one to throw the first punch.

Without asking, she walked over to the sideboard and

poured Gramps and his friend a cup of coffee. Burt sat across from her grandfather, clearly ill at ease.

"I should be going," Zach said starkly. "Good to see you again, Dr. Coleman."

"You, too," Gramps's friend said, glancing briefly at Zach. His puzzled gaze quickly returned to Anton.

"I'll walk you to the front door," Janine offered, eager to make her own escape. She closed the library door behind her.

Both she and Zach paused in the entryway. Janine tried to smile, but Zach was studying her intently, and her heart clenched like a fist inside her chest. They'd done what they had to do; she should be experiencing relief that the confrontation she'd dreaded for days was finally over. Instead she felt a strange sadness, one she couldn't fully understand or explain.

"Do you think we convinced him?"

"I don't know," Zach answered, keeping his tone low. "Your grandfather's a difficult man to read. Maybe he'll never bring up the subject of our marrying again and we're home free. I'd like to believe that's the case. It's just as likely, though, that he'll give us a few days' peace while he regroups. I don't expect him to back off quite so easily."

"No, I don't suppose he will."

Zach looked at his watch. "I should be going," he said again.

Janine was reluctant to see him leave, but there was no reason to detain him. Her hand was on the door-knob when she suddenly hesitated and turned around. "I didn't mean what I said in there," she blurted in a frenzy of regret.

"You mean you do want us to get married?"

"No," she cried, aghast. "I'm talking about when I

said you were stubborn and rude. That isn't really true, but I had to come up with some reason for finding you objectionable. I don't really believe it, though."

"It was the same with me. I don't think you're so intolerable, either. I was trusting that you knew it was all an act for your grandfather's sake."

"I did," she assured him, but her pride *had* been dented, although that wasn't anything new.

"The last four days have been difficult," Zach went on. "Not only was Anton gloating about Scotland, but like I told you, he's been giving me these amused looks and odd little smiles. A couple of times I heard him saying something in his native tongue—I'm afraid to guess what."

"Well, I know what he was saying, because he's been doing the same thing to me. He's talking about babies."

"Babies?" Zach echoed, his eyes startled.

"Ours in particular."

One corner of Zach's mouth lifted, as if he found the thought of them as parents amusing. Or unlikely.

"That was my reaction, too. Every time I've seen Gramps in the last few days, he's started talking about... well, you know."

Zach nodded. "I do know. The situation hasn't been pleasant for either of us."

"Setting Gramps straight was for the best." But if that was the case, why did she feel this terrible letdown? "If he accepts us at our word—and he just might—then I guess this is goodbye."

"Yes, I suppose it is," Zach responded, but he made no effort to leave.

Janine was glad, because these few moments gave her the opportunity to memorize his features. She stored them for the future, when there'd be no reason for her to have anything but the most infrequent and perfunctory contact with Zach.

"Unless, of course, your grandfather continues to throw us together."

"Of course," Janine added quickly, hating the way her heart soared at the prospect. "Naturally, we'd have to confront him again. We can't allow ourselves to be his pawns."

Zach was about to say something else when the library door flew open and Burt Coleman hurried out, the urgency on his face unmistakable. "Janine, I think we should call a doctor for your grandfather."

"What's wrong?"

"I'm not sure. He's very pale and he seems to be having trouble breathing. It might be his heart."

With Zach following, Janine ran into the library, her own heart in jeopardy. Dr. Coleman was right—she'd never seen her grandfather look worse. His breath came noisily and his eyes were closed as he rested his head against the back of the chair. He looked old, far older than she could ever remember seeing him. She felt a sense of panic as she raced across the room to the desk where there was a phone.

"I'm fine," Gramps said hoarsely, opening his eyes and slowly straightening. He raised his hand in an effort to stop Janine. "There's no need for everyone to go into a tizzy just because an old man wants to rest his eyes for a few minutes." His smile was weak, his complexion still pale. "Now don't go calling any doctor. I was in last week for a checkup and I'm fit as a fiddle."

"You don't look so fit," Zach countered and Janine noticed that his face seemed almost as ashen as her grandfather's. Kneeling beside him, Zach grasped his wrist and began to check his pulse.

"I'm fine," Gramps insisted again.

"Are you in any pain?"

Gramps's gaze moved from Zach to Janine. "None," he answered, dismissing their concern with a shake of his head.

"Dr. Coleman?" Janine turned to her grandfather's longtime friend. "Should I phone his doctor?"

"What does Burt know about an old man and his heart?" Gramps objected. "Burt's expertise is with horses."

"Call the doctor. Having him checked over isn't going to hurt," Burt said after a moment.

"Fiddlesticks," Gramps roared. "I'm in perfect health."

"Good," Janine said brightly. "But I'll just let Dr. Madison reassure me." She punched out the phone number and had to speak loudly in order to be heard over her grandfather's protests. A couple of minutes later, she replaced the receiver and told Zach, "Dr. Madison says we can bring him in now."

"I'm not going to waste valuable time traipsing downtown. Burt and I were going to play a few hands of cribbage."

"We can play tomorrow," Dr. Coleman said gruffly. "You keep forgetting, Anton, we're both retiring."

"I've got things to do at the office."

"No, you don't," Zach said firmly. "You've got a doctor's appointment. Janine and I are going to escort you there and we're not going to listen to a single argument. Do you understand?"

Gramps's eyes narrowed as if he were preparing a loud rebuttal. But he apparently changed his mind, because he relaxed and nodded sluggishly, reluctantly. "All right, if it'll make you feel better. But I'm telling you right now, you're going to look like a fine pair of fools."

The next two hours felt like two years to Janine. While Dr. Madison examined Gramps, she and Zach paced the waiting room. Several patients came and went.

"What could be taking so long?" Janine asked, wringing her hands nervously. "Do you think we did the right thing bringing him here? I mean, should we have gone directly to the hospital emergency room instead?"

"I doubt he would have agreed to that," Zach said.

"Do you honestly believe I would've listened to him?" She sat on the edge of a chair, her hands clenched so tightly together her knuckles whitened. "It's ridiculous, but I've never thought of Gramps as old. He's always been so healthy, so alive. I've never once considered what would happen if he became ill."

"He's going to be fine, Janine."

"You saw him," she cried, struggling against the dread and horror that churned inside her.

Zach's hand clasped hers and the fears that had torn at her composure only seconds earlier seemed to abate with his touch. He lent her confidence and strength, and she was badly in need of both.

When the door leading to the doctor's office opened, they leapt to their feet. Zach's hand tightened around hers before he released it.

"Dr. Madison can talk to you now," the nurse told them briskly. She led them to a compact office and explained that the doctor would be with them in a few minutes. Janine sat in one of the cushioned chairs and studied the framed diplomas on the walls.

Dr. Madison came into the room moments later. He paused to shake hands with Janine and then with Zach. "So far, my tests don't show anything we need to be too concerned about," he said, shuffling through the papers on his desk.

"What happened? Why was he so pale? Why was he gasping like that?" Janine demanded.

Dr. Madison frowned and folded his hands. "I'm really not sure. He claims he hadn't been doing any strenuous exercise."

"No, he was drinking coffee and talking to a friend."

Dr. Madison nodded. "Did he recently receive any negative news regarding his business?"

"No," Janine replied, glancing at Zach. "If anything, the business is doing better than ever. Gramps is getting ready to retire. I hate the thought of anything happening to him now."

"I don't know what to tell you," Dr. Madison said thoughtfully. "He should take it easy for the next couple of days, but there's nothing to worry about that I can find."

Janine sighed and closed her eyes. "Thank God."

"Your grandfather's getting dressed now," Dr. Madison said. He stood, signaling the end of their interview. "He'll join you in a few minutes."

"Thank you, Doctor," Zach said fervently.

Relief washed through Janine like a tidal wave. She got up and smiled at Zach. It was a smile full of gratitude. A smile one might share with a good friend when something has gone unexpectedly right. The kind of smile a woman would share with her husband. The thought hit her full force and she quickly lowered her eyes to cover her reaction.

When Gramps joined them in the waiting room, he looked immeasurably better. His blue eyes were filled with indignation and his skin tone was a healthy pink. "I hope the two of you are satisfied," he said huskily, buttoning his coat. "Most of the afternoon was wasted with this nonsense."

"You were a hundred percent correct, Gramps," Janine said brightly. "You're as fit as a fiddle and we wasted valuable cribbage time dragging you down here."

"I should've been back at the office hours ago," Zach put in, sharing a smile with Janine.

"And whose fault is that?" Anton muttered. He brushed off his sleeves as though he'd been forced to pick himself up off the floor, thanks to them.

Once more Janine and Zach shared an intimate look. They both seemed to realize what they were doing at the same moment and abruptly glanced away.

Zach drove Gramps and Janine back to the house, Gramps protesting loudly all the while that they'd over-reacted and ruined his afternoon. His first concern seemed to be rescheduling his cribbage game.

Afterward Janine walked Zach to his car. "Thanks for everything," she said, folding her arms to repress the sudden urge to hug him.

"If you're worried about anything, give me a call," Zach said as he opened the car door. He hesitated fractionally, then lifted his head and gazed directly into her eyes. "Goodbye, Janine."

She raised her hand in farewell as a sadness settled over her. "Goodbye, Zach," she said forcing a lightness into her voice. "Thanks again."

For the longest moment, he said nothing, although his eyes still held hers. Finally he repeated, "Call me if you need anything, all right?"

"I will."

But they both knew she wouldn't. It was best to end this now. Make a clean break.

Janine stood in the driveway until Zach's car was well out of sight. Only then did she return to the house.

"This is really good of you," Patty St. John whispered, handing the sleeping infant to Janine. "I don't know what I would've done if I'd had to drag Michael to the interview. I need this job so badly."

"I'm happy to help." Janine peered down at the sweet face of the sleeping six-month-old baby. "I apologize if it was inconvenient for you to bring Michael here, but I've been sticking close to the house for the past few days. My grandfather hasn't been feeling well."

"It wasn't any problem," Patty whispered, setting the diaper bag on the floor. She glanced around the house. "This place is really something. I didn't have any idea that you…well, you know, that you were so well off."

"This house belongs to my grandfather," Janine explained, gently rocking Michael in her arms. The warmth and tenderness she felt toward the baby was a revelation. She supposed it was understandable, though. Gramps had spent last week constantly telling her what remarkable babies she and Zach would have, and here she was with one in her arms. All the maternal instincts she didn't know she had came bubbling to the surface.

"I'll be back in about an hour," Patty said. She leaned over and kissed Michael's soft forehead. He didn't so much as stir.

Still carrying the baby, Janine walked to the door with her friend. "Good luck."

Patty gave a strained smile and crossed her fingers. "Thanks. Here's hoping."

No sooner had the door closed than Anton walked into the living room. He paused when he saw Janine rocking in the old chair that had once belonged to his wife. His face relaxed into a broad grin.

"Is that a baby you've got there?"

Janine smiled. "Nothing gets past you, does it, Gramps?"

He chuckled. "Who's he belong to?"

"Patty St. John. She's another volunteer at the Friendship Club. She quit her job when Michael was born, but now she'd like to find some part-time work."

"Are you volunteering to babysit for her?"

"Just for today," Janine explained. "Her regular sitter has the flu."

"I thought you were going out?" Gramps muttered with a slight frown. "You haven't left the house all week. Fact is, you're becoming a recluse."

"I've had other things to do," she returned, not raising her voice for fear of disturbing the baby.

"Right. The other things you had to do were keep an eye on your grandfather," he said. "You think I didn't notice? How long do you plan on being my shadow? You should be gadding about, doing the things you normally do, instead of worrying yourself sick over me. I'm fine, I tell you. When are you going to listen to me?"

"Dr. Madison said to watch you for a few days."

"It's been a week."

Janine was well aware of it. In fact, she was beginning to suffer from cabin fever. She'd hardly spoken to anyone all week. She hadn't heard from Zach, either. Not that she'd expected to. Perhaps Gramps had taken them at their word. Or else he was doing what Zach had suspected and simply regrouping for the next skirmish.

Michael stirred in her arms and she held him against her shoulder, rocking him back to sleep.

"I'm going to the office tomorrow," Gramps announced, eyeing her defiantly as though he anticipated a challenge.

"We'll see," she said, delaying the showdown.

Yawning, baby Michael raised his head and looked around. Gramps's weathered face broke into a tender smile. "All right," he agreed easily. "We'll see." He offered the little boy his finger and Michael gripped it firmly in his hand, then started to chew on it.

Janine laughed, enjoying her grandfather's reaction to the baby. After a couple of minutes, Michael grew tired of the game with Anton's finger and yawned again, arching his back. Janine decided it was time to check his diaper. She got up, reaching for the bag Patty had left.

"I'll be back in a minute," she told her grandfather.

She was halfway across the living room when Anton stopped her. "You look good with a baby in your arms. Natural."

Janine smiled. She didn't dare let him know it felt good, too.

While she was changing the baby, she heard the doorbell. Normally she would've answered it herself, but since she was busy, either Gramps or Mrs. McCormick would see to it.

Michael was happily investigating his toes and making cooing sounds as Janine pulled up his plastic pants. "You're going to have to be patient with me, kiddo," she told him, carefully untwisting the legs of his corduroy overalls and snapping them back in place. When she'd finished, she lifted him high above her head and laughed when Michael squealed delightedly. They were both smiling when she returned to the living room.

Gramps was sitting in the chair closest to the grand piano, and across from him sat Zach.

Janine's heart lurched as her eyes flew instantly to

Zach's. "Hello, Zach," she said, striving to sound as nonchalant as possible, tucking Michael against her hip. She cast a suspicious glare at her grandfather, who smiled back, the picture of innocence.

"Zach brought some papers for me to sign," Gramps explained.

"I didn't mean to interrupt you," she apologized. Her eyes refused to leave Zach's. He smiled that slanted half-smile of his that wasn't really a smile at all. The one she'd always found so appealing. Something seemed to pass between them—a tenderness, a hunger.

"Janine's not interrupting anything, is she?" Gramps asked.

"No," Zach responded gruffly. He seemed to be taking in everything about her, from her worn jeans and oversize pink sweatshirt to the gurgling baby riding so casually on her hip.

Gramps cleared his throat. "If you'll excuse me a moment, I'll go get a pen," he said, leaving them alone together.

"How have you been?" Zach asked, his eyes riveted to her.

"Fine. Just fine."

"I see you haven't had any problems finding another admirer," he murmured, nodding at Michael.

Zach kept his tone light and teasing, and Janine followed his lead. "Michael St. John," she said, turning slightly to give Zach a better view of the baby, "meet Mr. Zachary Thomas."

"Hello," Zach said, holding up his palm. He seemed awkward around children. "I take it you're watching him for a friend."

"Yes, another volunteer. She's looking for a part-time

job, but she's having a problem finding one with the right hours. She's at an interview."

"I see."

Janine sank down on the ottoman in front of Zach's chair and set Michael on her knee. She focused her attention on gently bouncing the baby. "Now that your life's back in order," she said playfully, glancing up at Zach, "have you discovered how much you miss me?"

He chuckled softly. "It's been how long since we last talked? Seven days? I'm telling you, Janine, I haven't had a single disagreement with anyone in all that time."

"That should make you happy."

"You're right. It should." He shook his head. "Unfortunately it doesn't. You know what, Janine? I was bored to death. So the answer is yes, I missed you."

Seven

Before Janine could respond, Gramps wandered back into the living room, pen in hand.

"So where are those papers you wanted me to sign?" he asked Zach.

With obvious reluctance, Zach tore his gaze from Janine's. He opened his briefcase and pulled out several papers. "Go ahead and read over these contracts."

"Do you need me to sign them or not?" her grandfather grumbled.

Once more Zach dragged his gaze away from Janine. "Please."

Muttering under his breath, Gramps took the documents to the small table, scanned them and quickly scrawled his name.

Janine knew she should leave; the two men probably had business to discuss. But she couldn't make herself stand up and walk away. Not when Zach had actually admitted that he'd missed her.

Gramps broke into her thoughts. "Janine, I—"

"I was just going," she said. She clambered to her feet, securing her hold on Michael.

But Gramps surprised her.

"I want you to stay," he declared. "I wanted to talk to you and Zach. Fact is, I owe you both an apology. Burt and I had a good long talk the other day and I told him how I'd tried to arrange a marriage between the two of you. He laughed and called me an old fool, said it was time I stepped out of the Dark Ages."

"Gramps," Janine began anxiously, unwilling to discuss the subject that had brought such contention, "Zach and I have already settled that issue. We understand why you did it and…and we've laid it to rest, so there's no need to apologize."

"I'm afraid there is," Gramps insisted. "Don't worry, Burt pointed out the error of my ways. Haven't got any new tricks up my sleeve." He rose to bring Zach the signed papers, then sat wearily in the chair across from them. He'd never looked so fragile, so old and beaten.

"Janine's a wonderful woman," Zach said unexpectedly. "I want you to know I realize that."

"She's got her faults," Gramps responded, pulling a cigar from his pocket, "but she's pretty enough to compensate."

"Thank you very much," Janine whispered sarcastically and was rewarded with a grin from Zach. Gramps didn't seem to hear her; if he had, he was ignoring her comment.

"I only want the best for my granddaughter, but when I approached her about marrying you, she made a big fuss. Fact is, it would've been easier to pluck a live chicken. She said she needed *romance*." Gramps pronounced the word as if it evoked instant amusement.

"There isn't a woman alive who doesn't need romance," she wailed, defending herself.

"I'm from the old country," Gramps continued. "Romance wasn't something I knew about from personal experience, and when I asked Janine to explain, she had some trouble defining it herself. Said it was a tryst on the moors and a bunch of other hogwash. That's the reason I sent you both to Scotland."

"We figured that out soon enough," Zach said dryly.

"As you'll recall," Janine found herself saying, "that definition was off the top of my head. Romance isn't easy to explain, especially to a man who scoffs at the entire idea."

Anton chuckled, moving the cigar to the side of his mouth. "It's unfortunate the two of you caught on to me so soon. I was looking forward to arranging the desperate passion part."

"Desperate passion?" Zach echoed.

"Yes. Janine said that was part of romance, too. I may be over seventy, but I know about passion. Oh, yes, Anna and I learned about that together." His blue eyes took on a faraway look and his lips curved in the gentlest of smiles. He glanced at Janine and his smile widened.

"I'm glad you find this so funny," Janine snapped.

Gramps dismissed her anger with a flick of his hand and turned to Zach. "I suppose you've discovered she's got something of a temper?"

"From the start!" Zach declared.

"It may come as a surprise to you, Zachary Thomas," Janine said, "but you're not exactly Mr. Perfect."

"No," Zach countered smoothly. "I suspect your grandfather was thinking more along the lines of Mr. Right."

"Oh, brother!"

"Now, children, I don't see that arguing will do any good. I've willingly accepted defeat. Trying to interest you in each other was an old man's way of setting his world right before he passes on."

The doorbell chimed and, grateful for an excuse to leave the room, Janine hurried to answer it. Patty St. John stood there, her face cheerless, her posture forlorn.

"I wasn't expecting you back so soon."

"They'd already hired someone," Patty said, walking into the foyer and automatically taking her son from Janine. She held the infant close, as if his small warm body might absorb her disappointment. "I spent the whole day psyching myself up for this interview and it was all for nothing. Ah, well, who wants to be a receptionist at a dental clinic, anyway?"

"I'm so sorry," Janine murmured.

"Was Michael any problem?"

"None at all," Janine told her, wishing she could think of something encouraging to say. "I'll get his things for you."

It took Janine only a minute to collect Michael's diaper bag, but when she returned to the entryway, she discovered Zach talking to Patty. Janine saw him hand her friend a business card and overheard him suggesting she report to the Human Resources department early the following week.

"Thanks again," Patty said enthusiastically. She lifted Michael's hand. "Say bye-bye," she coaxed the baby, then raised his arm and moved it for him.

Janine let her out, with Zach standing next to her. Gramps had gone into the library, and Zach glanced anxiously in that direction before lowering his voice to a whisper. "Can you meet me later?"

"When?"

"In an hour." He checked his watch, then mentioned the number of a pier along the waterfront. Janine had just managed to clarify the location when Gramps came back.

Zach left the house soon afterward and Janine was able to invent an excuse half an hour later. Gramps was reading and didn't bother to look up from his mystery novel, although Janine thought she saw the hint of a smile, as if he knew full well what she was doing. She didn't linger to investigate. The last time she'd agreed to a clandestine meeting with Zach had been the night they'd met at the Italian restaurant, when she'd all but blurted out the arrangements to her grandfather.

Zach was waiting for her, grim-faced. He stood against the pier railing, the wind whipping his raincoat against his legs.

"I hope there's a good reason for this, because I don't think Gramps was fooled," Janine said when she joined him. "He'll figure out that I'm meeting you if I'm not back soon." She buried her hands in her pockets, turning away from the wind. The afternoon sky was gray, threatening rain.

"Am I interrupting anything important?"

"Not really." Janine wouldn't have minded listing several pressing engagements, but she'd canceled everything for the next two weeks, wanting to stay close to home in case her grandfather needed her.

Zach clasped his hands behind his back and started strolling down the pier, the wind ruffling his neatly trimmed hair. Janine followed. "I'm worried about Anton," he said suddenly, stopping and facing Janine.

"Why?" Perhaps there was something she didn't know about his health, something Dr. Madison hadn't told her.

"He doesn't look good."

"What do you mean?" Although she asked, she already knew the answer. She'd felt the same thing during the past few days. Gramps was aging right before her eyes.

"I think you know."

"I do," she admitted reluctantly.

"Furthermore I'm worried about you."

"Me?" she asked, her voice rising. "Whatever for?"

"If, God forbid, anything should happen to Anton," Zach said, drawing in a ragged breath, "what will happen to you? You don't have any other family, do you?"

"No," she told him, her chest tightening at the thought. "But I'm not worried about it. There are several friends who are very close to the family, Burt Coleman for one, so I wouldn't be cast into the streets like an orphan. I'll have the house and more than enough money to live on. There's no need for you to be concerned. I'm not."

"I see." Zach frowned as he walked to the farthest end of the pier, seeming to fix his gaze on the snow-capped peaks of the Olympic mountains far in the distance.

Janine hurried to catch up with him. "Why do you ask?" she demanded.

"He's always said he was concerned about your not having any other family. But it wasn't until recently that I really understood his motivation in trying to arrange a marriage between us."

"Good, then you can explain it to me, because frankly, I'm at a loss. He admitted he was wrong, but I don't think he's given up on the idea. He'd do just about anything to see the two of us together."

"I *know* he hasn't given up on us."

"What did he do? Up the ante?"

Zach chuckled and his features relaxed into a smile as he met her eyes. "Nothing so explicit. He simply told me that he's getting on in years and hates the thought of you being left so alone when he dies."

"I'll adjust. I'm not a child," she said, although her heart filled with dread at the thought of life without her cantankerous, generous, good-hearted grandfather.

"I don't doubt you would." Zach hesitated, then resumed strolling, apparently taking it for granted that she'd continue to follow him.

"I have plenty of friends."

Zach nodded, although Janine wasn't certain he'd heard her. He stopped abruptly and turned to look at her. "What I'm about to say is going to shock you."

Janine stared up at him, not knowing what to expect.

"When you think about it, our getting married does make an odd kind of sense."

"What?" Janine couldn't believe he was saying this.

"From a practical point of view," he added quickly. "Since the business is in both our names, and we're both alone. I realize I'm not exactly Prince Charming…" Zach paused as if waiting for her to contradict him. When she didn't, he frowned but went on. "The problem has more to do with whether we can get along. I don't even know if we're capable of going an entire day without arguing."

"What are you suggesting?" Janine asked, wondering if she was reading more into this conversation than he intended.

"Nothing yet. I'm trying to be as open and as honest as I can." He gripped the railing with both hands and braced himself, as though expecting a fierce wind to uproot him.

"Are you saying that our getting married wouldn't be such a bad idea after all?" Janine ventured. Initially he'd made a joke of the whole thing. Then he'd seen it as an annoyance. Now he seemed to have changed his mind again.

"I…don't know yet. I'm mulling over my thoughts, which I'm willing to confess are hopelessly tangled at the moment."

"Mine aren't much better."

"Does this mean you'd consider the possibility?"

"I don't know, either." Janine had been so sure she was in love with Brian. She remembered how he'd done everything a romantic hero should do. He'd sent her flowers, said all the things a woman longs to hear—and then he'd casually broken her heart. When she thought about it now, she couldn't really imagine herself married to Brian. But Zach, who'd never made any romantic gestures, somehow seemed to fit almost naturally into her life. And yet…

As she pondered these contradictions, Zach started walking again. "I'm not the kind of husband you want," he was saying, "and not nearly as good as you deserve. I'd like to be the man of your dreams, but I'm not. Nor am I likely to change at this stage of my life." He paused, chancing a look in her direction. "What are you thinking?"

Janine sighed and concentrated as hard as she could, but her mind was filled with so many questions, so many doubts. "Would you mind kissing me?"

Shock widened his dark eyes. He glanced around, then scowled. "Now? Right here?"

"Yes."

"There are people everywhere. Is this really necessary?"

"Would I ask you to do it if it wasn't?"

As he searched her face, she moistened her lips and looked up at him, tilting her head slightly. Zach slipped one arm around her waist and drew her close. Her heart reacted immediately, leaping into a hard fast rhythm that made her feel breathless. He lifted her chin with his free hand and slowly lowered his mouth to hers.

The instant his lips grazed hers, Janine was flooded with a sensual languor. It was as if they'd returned to the moors of Scotland with the full moon overhead, pouring magic onto their small corner of earth. Everything around them faded. No longer did Janine hear the sound of water slapping against the wooden columns of the pier. The blustery day went calm.

She supported her hands on his chest, breathing erratically, when he stopped kissing her. Neither spoke. Janine wanted to, but none of her faculties seemed to be working. She parted her lips and Zach lowered his mouth to hers again. Only this time it was a full-fledged kiss, deep and probing. His hands slid up her back as his mouth abandoned hers to explore the sweep of her neck.

Several glorious moments passed before he shuddered, raised his head and drew back, although he continued to hold her. "Does that answer your question?"

"No," she answered, hating the way her voice trembled. "I'm afraid it only raised more."

"I know what you mean," Zach admitted, briefly closing his eyes. "This last week apart was an eye-opener for me. I thought I'd be glad to put this matter between your grandfather and us to rest. If you want the truth, I thought I'd be glad to be rid of you. I was convinced you felt the same way." He paused, waiting for a response.

"The days seemed so empty," she whispered.

His eyes burned into hers, and he nodded. "You were constantly on my mind, and I found myself wishing you were there to talk to." He groaned. "Heaven knows you deserve a different kind of husband than I could possibly be."

"What about you? I've heard you say a hundred times that when it comes to finding a wife, you'll choose your own."

He blinked, as though he didn't recognize his words. Then he shrugged. "Once I got to know you, I realized you're not so bad."

"Thanks." So much for wine and roses and sweet nothings whispered in her ear. But then again, she'd had those things and they hadn't brought her happiness.

"Like I said—and I hate to admit it—our getting married makes sense. We seem to like each other well enough, and there's a certain…attraction." Zach was frowning a little as he spoke. "It would be a smart move for both of us from a financial viewpoint, as well." He took her by the shoulders and gazed into her eyes. "The question is, Janine, can I make you happy?"

Her heart melted at the way he said it, at the simplicity and sincerity of his words. "What about you?" she asked. "Will you be content being married to me?"

The apprehension in his face eased. "I think so. We'll be good for each other. This isn't any grand passion. But I'm fond of you and you're fond of me."

"Fond?" Janine repeated, breaking away.

"What's wrong with that?"

"I hate that word," Janine said through gritted teeth. "*Fond* sounds so…watered down. So weak. I'm not looking for a grand passion, as you put it, but I want a whole lot more than *fond*." She gestured dramatically with her hands. "A man is fond of his dog or a favorite place to eat, not his wife." She spoke so vehemently that she was starting to attract attention from other walkers. "Would it be too much for you to come up with another word?"

"Stop looking at me as if it were a matter of life and death," he said.

"It's important," she insisted.

Zach looked distinctly uncomfortable. "I run a business. There are more than three hundred outlets in fifty states. I know the office-supply business inside out, but I'm not good with words. If you don't like the word *fond*, you choose another one."

"All right," she said thoughtfully, biting the corner of one lip. Her eyes brightened. "How about *cherish?*"

"Cherish." Zach repeated it as if he'd never heard the word before. "Okay, it's a deal. I'll cherish you."

"And I'll cherish you," she said emphatically, nodding with satisfaction.

They walked along the pier until they came to a seafood stand, where Zach bought them each a cup of steaming clam chowder. They found an unoccupied picnic table and sat down, side by side.

Occasionally they stopped eating to smile at each other. An oddly exciting sensation attacked Janine's stomach whenever that happened. Finally, finishing her soup, she licked the back of her white plastic spoon. She kept her eyes carefully lowered as she said, "I want to make sure I understand. Did we or did we not just agree to get married?"

Zach hesitated, his spoon halfway between his cup and his mouth as an odd look crossed his face. He swallowed once. "We decided to go through with it, both accepting that this isn't the traditional love match, but one based on practical and financial advantages."

Janine dropped her spoon in the plastic cup. "If that's the case, the wedding is off."

Zach threw back his head and stared into the sky. "*Now* what did I say that was so terrible?"

"Financial and practical advantages! You make it sound about as appealing as a dentist appointment. There's got to be more of a reason than that for us to get married."

Shrugging, Zach gestured helplessly with his hands. "I already told you I wasn't any good at this. Perhaps we'd do better if you explained why you're willing to marry me."

Before she could prevent it, a smile tugged at her mouth. "You won't like my reason any better than I like yours." She looked around to ensure that no one could overhear, then leaned toward him. "When we kissed a few minutes ago, the earth moved. I know it's a dreadful cliché—the worst—but that's exactly what I felt."

"The earth moved," Zach repeated deadpan. "Well, we are in an earthquake zone."

Janine rolled her eyes. "It happened when we were in Scotland, too. I don't know what's going on between us or even if we're doing the right thing, but there's definitely…something. Something special."

She wasn't surprised when Zach scowled. "You mean to say you're willing to marry me because I'm good at kissing?"

"It makes more sense to me than that stuff about financial advantages."

"You were absolutely correct," he said evenly. "I don't like your reason. Is there anything else that makes the prospect appealing?"

Janine giggled. "You know," she reflected, "Gramps was right. We're going to be good for each other."

A flash of light warmed his eyes and his hand reached for hers. He entwined their fingers as their eyes met. "Yes, we are."

The wedding was arranged so fast that Janine barely had time to reconsider their decision. They applied for a license that same afternoon. When they returned to the house, Gramps shouted for joy, slapped Zach on the back and repeatedly hugged Janine, whispering that she'd made an old man very happy.

Janine was so busy, the days and nights soon blended together and she lost all track of time. There were so many things to do—fittings and organizing caterers and inviting guests—that for the next five days she didn't talk to Zach even once.

The day before the ceremony, the garden was bustling with activity. Mrs. McCormick was supervising the men who were assembling the wedding canopy and setting up tables and chairs.

Exhausted, Janine wandered outside and glanced up at the bold blue sky, praying the sunshine would hold for at least another day. The lawn was lush and green, and freshly mowed. The roses were in bloom, perfuming the air with their rich fragrance.

"Janine."

She recognized his voice immediately. She turned to discover Zach striding purposefully toward her, and her heart reacted of its own accord. Janine felt as though they'd been apart for a year instead of just a few days. She wore jeans and an old university sweatshirt and wished she'd chosen something less casual. In contrast, Zach was strikingly formal, dressed in a handsome pin-striped suit and dark tie. She was willing to admit she didn't know him as well as she should—as well as a woman who was about to become his wife. His habits, his likes and dislikes, were a mystery to her, yet those details seemed minor. It was the inner Zach she was coming to understand. Everything she'd learned assured her she'd made the right decision.

"Hello," she called, walking toward him. She saw that he looked as tired as she felt. Obviously he'd been busy, too, although the wedding preparations had been left to her.

They met halfway and stopped abruptly, gazing at each other. Zach didn't hug her or make any effort to touch her.

"How are you holding up?" he asked.

"Fine," she answered. "How about you?"

"I'll live." He glanced over at the activity near the rose garden and sighed. "Is there someplace we can talk privately?"

"Sure." Janine's heart leapt to her throat at his sober tone. "Is everything all right?"

He reassured her with a quick nod. "Of course."

"I don't think anyone's in the kitchen."

"Good." Hand at her elbow, he guided her toward the house. She pulled out a chair with trembling fingers and sat down at the oak table. As he lowered himself into a chair opposite her, she gripped the edge of the table. His eyes had never seemed darker. "Tomorrow's the day."

He said this as if he expected it to come as a shock to her. It didn't—but she understood what he was saying. Time was closing in on them, and if they wanted to back out, it would have to be now.

"Believe me, I know," she said, and her fingers tightened on the table. "Have you had a change of heart?"

"Have you?"

"No, but then again, I haven't had much time to think."

"I've done nothing *but* think about this wedding," Zach said, raking his hands through his hair.

"And?"

He shrugged. "We may both have been fools to agree to this."

"It all happened so fast," Janine said in a weak voice. "One minute we agreed on the word *cherish,* and the next thing I remember, we were deciding we'd be good for each other."

"Don't forget the kissing part," he added. "As I recall, that had quite a bit to do with this decision."

"If you're having second thoughts, I'd rather you said so now than after the ceremony."

His eyes narrowed fleetingly before he shook his head. "No."

"You're sure?"

He answered her by leaning forward, slipping his hand behind her neck and kissing her soundly. Tenderly. When they broke apart, they were silent. Not talking, not wanting to.

Janine stared into his dark warm eyes and suddenly she could hardly breathe.

"This is going to be a real marriage," he said forcefully.

She nodded. "I certainly hope so, Mr. Thomas." And her voice was strong and clear.

Less than twenty-four hours later, Janine stood at Zach's side, prepared to pledge her life to his. She'd never felt more uncertain—or, at the same time, more confident—of anything she'd ever done.

Zach seemed to grasp what she was feeling. His eyes held hers as she repeated the words that would bind them.

When she'd finished, Zach slid his arm around her waist and drew her close. The pastor smiled down on them, then looked to the fifty or so family friends who'd gathered on Anton's lawn and said, "I present to you Mr. and Mrs. Zachary Thomas."

A burst of applause followed his words.

Before Janine fully realized what was happening, they were mingling with their guests. One minute she was standing in front of the pastor, trembling but unafraid, and the next she was a wife.

"Janine, Janine!" Pam rushed to her side before anyone else could. "You look so gorgeous," she said softly, and bright tears shone in her eyes.

Janine hugged her young friend. "Thank you, sweetheart."

Pam gazed up at Zach and shook her head. "He sure is handsome."

"I think so, too."

Zach arched his brows, cocked his head toward her and murmured, "You never told me that."

"There's no need for you to be so smug."

"My children," Gramps said, rejoining them. He hugged Janine, and she saw that his eyes were as bright as Pam's. "You've never been more beautiful. I swear you look more like my Anna every year."

It was the highest compliment Gramps could have paid her. From the pictures Gramps kept of his wife, Janine knew her grandmother had been exceptionally beautiful.

"Thank you," she said, kissing his cheek.

"I have something for you." Pam thrust a neatly wrapped box into Janine's hands. "I made them myself," she announced proudly. "I think Zach will like them, too."

"Oh, Pam, you shouldn't have," Janine murmured. Sitting on a cushioned folding chair, she peeled away the paper and lifted the lid. The moment she did, her breath jammed in her throat. Inside were the sheerest white baby-doll pajamas Janine had ever seen. Her smile faltered as she glanced up to see half a dozen people staring at her.

Zach's hand, resting at the nape of Janine's neck, tightened as he spoke, though his voice was warm and amused. "You're right, Pam. I like them very much."

Eight

Janine sat next to Zach in the front seat of his car. Dressed in a pink suit and matching broad-brimmed hat, she clutched her small floral bouquet. Although the wedding had been arranged in seven short days, it had been a lovely affair.

Zach had taken care of planning the short honeymoon. All he could spare was three days, so instead of scheduling anything elaborate, he'd suggested they go to his summer place in Ocean Shores, a coastal town two and a half hours from Seattle by car. Janine had happily agreed.

"So you think I'm handsome?" Zach asked, keeping his eyes on the road. Neither of them had said much since they'd set off.

"I knew if I told you, it'd go straight to your head, and obviously I was right," she answered. Then, unable to hold back a wide yawn, she pressed one hand to her mouth.

"You're exhausted."

"Are you always this astute?"

"Testy, too."

"I don't mean to be," she apologized. She'd been up since before five that morning and in fact, hadn't slept well all week. This wasn't exactly the ideal way to start a marriage. There was an added stress, too, that had to do with the honeymoon. Zach had made it understood that he intended their marriage to be real, but surely he didn't expect them to share a bed so soon. Or did he?

Every now and then as they drove, she glanced in his direction, wondering what, if anything, she should say. Even if she did decide to broach this delicate subject, she wasn't sure how.

"Go ahead and rest," Zach suggested. "I'll wake you when we arrive."

"It should be soon, shouldn't it?"

"Another fifteen minutes or so."

"Then I'll stay awake." Nervously, she twisted the small floral bouquet. Unwrapping Pam's gift had made her all the more apprehensive, but delaying the subject any longer was impossible.

"Zach…are we going to…you know…" she stammered, feeling like a naive schoolgirl.

"If you're referring to what I think you're referring to, the answer is no. So relax."

"No?" He didn't need to sound so casual about it, as if it hardly mattered one way or the other.

"Why do you ask, Janine? Are you having second thoughts about…that?"

"No. Just some reservations."

"Don't worry. When it happens, it happens. The last thing we need is that kind of pressure."

"You're right," she answered, relieved.

"We need some time to feel comfortable. There's no reason to rush into the physical aspect of our marriage, is there?"

"None whatsoever," she agreed quickly, perhaps too quickly, because when she looked at him again, Zach was frowning. Yet he seemed so willing to wait, as though their lovemaking was of minor importance. But as he'd said, this marriage wasn't one of grand passion. Well, *that* was certainly true.

Before another five minutes had passed, Zach left the highway and drove into the resort town of Ocean Shores. He didn't stop in the business district, but headed down a side street toward the beach. The sun was setting as he pulled into a driveway and turned off the engine.

Janine was too enthralled with the house to say a word.

The wind whipped at them ferociously when they climbed out of the car. Janine held on to her hair with one hand, still clutching the flowers, and to Zach with the other. The sun cast a pink and gold reflection over the rolling hills of sand.

"Home, sweet home," Zach said, nudging her toward the house.

The front door opened before they reached it and a trim middle-aged man stepped onto the porch to greet them. He was grinning broadly. "Hello, Zach. I trust you had a safe trip."

"We did."

"Everything's ready. The cupboards are stocked. The firewood's stacked by the side of the house, and dinner's prepared."

"Wonderful, Harry, thanks." Zach placed his hand on Janine's shoulder. "This is my wife, Janine," he said. "We were married this afternoon."

"Your wife?" Harry repeated, looking more than a little surprised. "Why, that's fantastic. Congratulations to you both."

"Thank you," Janine said politely.

"Harry Gleason looks after the place for me when I'm not around."

"Pleased to meet you, Harry."

"So Zach got himself a wife," Harry said, rubbing his jaw in apparent disbelief. "I couldn't be more—"

"Delighted," a frowning Zach supplied for him, ushering Janine toward the front door.

"Right," Harry said. "I couldn't be more delighted."

Janine tilted back her head to survey the sprawling single-story house.

"Go on inside," Zach said. "I'll get the luggage."

Janine started to protest, suddenly wanting him to follow the traditional wedding custom of carrying her over the threshold. She paused, and Zach gave her a puzzled look. "Is something wrong?"

"No." She had no real grounds for complaint. She wasn't even sure why it mattered. Swallowing her disappointment, she made her way into the house. She stopped just inside the front door and gazed with wide-eyed wonder at the immense living room with its three long sofas and several upholstered chairs. A brick fireplace took up an entire wall; another was dominated by a floor-to-ceiling window that looked over the ocean. Drawn to it, Janine watched powerful waves crash against the shore.

Zach followed her inside, carrying their luggage, barely taking time to appreciate the scene before him. "Harry's putting the car away," he said.

"This place is incredible," Janine breathed, gesturing around her. She placed the flowers on the coffee table, then trailed after Zach into a hallway, off which were four bedrooms and an equal number of baths. At the back of the house, she found an exercise room, an office and an ultramodern kitchen where a pot of coq au vin was simmering.

In the formal dining room, the polished mahogany table was set for two. On the deck, designed to take advantage of the ocean view, she discovered a steaming hot tub, along with a bottle of French champagne on ice.

Zach returned as she wandered back into the kitchen and a strained silence fell between them. He was the first to speak. "I put your suitcases in the master bedroom," he said brusquely. "I'm in the one across the hall."

She nodded, not taking time to question her growing sense of disappointment. They'd agreed to delay their wedding night, hadn't they?

"Are you hungry?" he asked, walking to the stove and lifting the pot's lid, as she'd done earlier.

"Only a little. I was thinking about slipping into the hot tub, unless you want to eat first."

"Sure. The hot tub's fine. Whatever you want."

Janine unpacked and located her swimsuit, then changed into it quickly. The warm water sounded appealing. And maybe it would help her relax. Draping a beach towel over her arm, she hurried into the kitchen, but Zach was nowhere to be seen. Not waiting for him, she walked out to the deck and stepped gingerly into the hot tub. The water felt like a soothing liquid blanket and she slid down, letting it lap just under her breasts.

Zach sauntered onto the deck a minute later, still in his suit. He stopped short when he saw her. "I...didn't realize you'd be out so soon," he said, staring at her with undisguised appreciation. He inhaled sharply and occupied himself by uncorking the bottle of champagne, then pouring a liberal glass. When he'd gulped it down, he reached for a second one and filled it for Janine.

"You're coming in, aren't you?" she asked, when he handed her the crystal flute.

"No," he said abruptly. "I won't join you, after all. There were several things I wasn't able to finish at the office this week, and I thought I'd look over some papers. You go ahead and enjoy yourself."

He was going to *work* on their wedding night! But she didn't feel she had any right to comment or complain. She was determined to conceal her bitter disappointment.

"The water's wonderful," she said, as cheerfully as she could manage, hoping her words would convince him to join her.

Zach nodded, but his eyes now avoided Janine. "It looks…great." He strode to the end of the deck, ran his fingers through his hair, then twisted around to face her. He seemed about to say something, but evidently changed his mind.

Baffled by his odd behavior, Janine set aside her glass of champagne and stood up so abruptly that water sloshed over the edge of the tub. "You don't need to say it," she muttered, climbing out and grabbing her towel.

"Say what?"

"You warned me before the wedding, so I walked into this with my eyes wide open. Well, you needn't worry. I got the message the minute we arrived at the house."

"What message is that?"

"Never mind." Vigorously, she rubbed her arms with the towel.

"No," he said. "I want you to tell me."

Against her better judgment, she pointed a quaking finger at the front door. "You went out of your way to tell me how *fond* of me you were and how there wasn't going to be any grand passion. Great. Perfect. I agreed to those terms. That's all fine with me, but—"

"But what?"

Mutely, she shook her head.

He sighed. "Oh, great, we're fighting. I suppose

you're going to ask for a divorce and make this the short-est marriage in Washington state history."

Janine paled. Divorce was such an ugly word, and it struck her as viciously as a slap. Despite her efforts, scalding tears spilled down her cheeks. With as much dignity as she could muster, which admittedly wasn't a lot, Janine went back inside the house, leaving a wet trail in her wake.

"Janine!" Zach shouted, following her into the kitchen. "Listen, Janine, I didn't intend to argue with you."

She turned abruptly. "This marriage doesn't mean anything to you, does it? You won't even interrupt your work long enough to…to act like a man who just got married."

With her head held high, she stared past him to a painting of yellow flowers on the dining room wall. When her tears blurred the flowers beyond recognition, she defiantly rubbed her eyes.

"I'm sorry," he whispered, reaching for her as if he needed to hold her. But then his arms fell to his sides. "I should've realized wedding traditions would be impor-tant to you. Like that carrying-you-over-the-threshold business. I'm sorry," he said again. "I completely forgot."

"It's not just that, it's everything. How many men bring a briefcase with them on their honeymoon? I feel like…like excess baggage in your life—and we haven't even been married for twenty-four hours."

Zach looked perplexed. "What does catching up on my reading have to do with any of this?"

His question only irritated her more. "You don't have the foggiest notion of how impossible you are, do you?"

He didn't answer right away, but seemed to be study-ing her, weighing his answer before he spoke. "I just thought I might have a chance to read over some papers," he said slowly. "Apparently that bothers you."

Janine placed her hands on her hips. "Yes, it bothers me."

Zach frowned. "Since we've agreed to delay the honeymoon part, what would you suggest we do for the next three days?"

"Couldn't we spend the time having fun? Becoming better acquainted?"

"I guess I do seem like a stranger to you," he said. "No wonder you're so nervous."

"I am *not* nervous. Just tired and trying hard not to say or do anything that'll make you think of me as a…a nag."

"A nag?" Zach repeated incredulously. "I don't think of you as anything but lovely. The truth is, I'm having one heck of a time keeping my eyes off you."

"You are?" The towel she was holding slipped unnoticed to the floor. "I thought you said you didn't know how to say anything romantic."

"That was romantic?"

"And very sweet. I was beginning to think you didn't find me…attractive."

Astonished, Zach stared at her. "You've got to be kidding!"

"I'm not."

"I can see that the next few days are going to be difficult," he said. "You'll just need to be patient with me, all right?"

"All right." She nodded, already feeling worlds better.

"How about if I dish up dinner while you're changing?"

"Thanks," she said, smiling.

By the time she got back to the kitchen, wearing gray

slacks and a sweater that was the color of fresh cream, Zach had served their meal and poured the wine. He stood behind her chair, waiting politely.

"Before we sit down, there's something I need to do."

The last thing Janine expected was to be lifted in his strong arms. A gasp of surprise lodged in her throat as her startled gaze met his.

"What are you doing?"

"It's tradition to carry the bride over the threshold, isn't it?"

"Yes, but you're doing it all wrong! You're supposed to carry me from the outside in—not the other way around."

Zach shrugged, unconcerned. "There's nothing traditional about this marriage. Why start now?" He made a show of pretending his knees were buckling under her weight as he staggered through the living room.

"This is supposed to be serious," she chastised him, but no matter how hard she tried, she couldn't keep the laughter out of her voice.

With a great deal of feigned effort, he managed to open the front door and then ceremoniously step onto the porch. Slowly he released her, letting her feet drop first, holding her upper body close against his chest for a long moment. The humor left his eyes. "There," he said tenderly. "Am I forgetting anything?"

It wouldn't hurt to kiss me, Janine told him in her heart, but the words didn't make it to her lips. When Zach kissed her again, she wanted it to be *his* idea.

"Janine?"

"Everything's perfect. Thank you."

"Not quite," he muttered. He turned her to face him, then covered her mouth with his own. Janine trembled, slipping her arms around his neck and giving herself completely to the kiss. She quivered at the heat that began to warm her from the inside out. This kiss was better than any they'd ever shared, something she hadn't thought possible. And what that meant, she had no idea.

Zach pulled his mouth abruptly from hers, but his eyes remained closed. Almost visibly he composed himself, and when he broke away he seemed in control of his emotions once again. Janine sighed inwardly, unsure of what she'd expected.

The next two days flew past. They took long walks on the shore, collecting shells. They rented mopeds and raced along the beach. They launched kites into the sky and delighted in their colorful dipping and soaring. The day before they were scheduled to return to Seattle, Zach declared that he intended to cook dinner. With that announcement, he informed her he had to go into town to buy the necessary groceries. After the first night, he'd given Harry a week off, and Janine had been fixing simple meals for them.

"What are you serving?" she wanted to know when he pulled into the parking lot of the town's only grocery store. "Tell me so I can buy an appropriate wine."

"Wine," he muttered under his breath. "I don't normally serve wine with this dish."

She followed him in, but when he discovered her trailing down the aisle after him, he gripped her by the shoulders and directed her back outside. "I am an artist, and I insist upon working alone."

Janine had a difficult time not laughing outright.

"In order to make this dinner as perfect as possible, I must concentrate completely on the selection of ingredients. You, my dear wife," he said, pressing his index finger to the tip of her nose, "are too much of a distraction. A lovely one, but nevertheless a distraction."

Janine smiled, her heart singing. Zach wasn't free with his compliments, and she found herself prizing each one.

While Zach was busy in the grocery store, Janine wandered around town. She bought a lifelike ceramic sea gull, which she promptly named Chester, and a bag of saltwater taffy. Then on impulse, she purchased a bottle of sun lotion in case they decided to lie outside, tempting a tan.

When she returned to the car, Zach was already there, waiting for her. She was licking a double-decker chocolate ice-cream cone and feeling incredibly happy.

"Did the master chef find everything he needed?" she asked. Two brown paper bags were sitting on the floor and she restrained herself from peeking inside.

"Our meal tonight will be one you'll long remember, I promise you."

"I'm glad to hear it." Holding out her ice-cream cone, she asked. "Do you want a taste?"

"Please." He rejected the offer of the cone itself and instead bent forward and lowered his mouth to hers. As she gazed into his dark heavy-lidded eyes her heartbeat accelerated and she was filled with a sudden intense longing. Janine wasn't sure what was happening between them, but it felt, quite simply, right.

Although the kiss was fleeting, a shiver of awareness twisted its way through her. Neither of them spoke or moved. He'd meant the kiss to be gentle and teasing, but it had quickly assumed another purpose. For a breathless second, the smile faded from his eyes. He continued to hold her, his breathing rapid.

After nearly two full days alone together, Janine

found it amusing that when he finally chose to kiss her, he'd do it in a crowded parking lot.

"I don't remember chocolate being quite that rich," he murmured. He strove for a casual tone, but Janine wasn't fooled. He was as affected by their kiss as she was, and struggling just as hard to disguise it.

They were uncharacteristically quiet on the short drive back to the house. Until the kiss, they'd spent companionable days together, enjoying each other's company. Then, in the space of no more than a few seconds, all that had changed.

"Am I banished from the kitchen?" Janine asked once they were inside the house, forcing an airy note into her voice.

"Not entirely," Zach surprised her by saying. "I'll need you later to wash the dishes."

Janine laughed and pulled her suntan lotion out of her bag. While Zach puttered around inside, she put on her swimsuit, then dragged the lounge chair into the sun to soak up the last of the afternoon's rays.

Zach soon joined her, carrying a tall glass of iced tea. "You look like you could use this."

"Thanks. If I'd known how handy you were in the kitchen, I'd have let you take over long before now."

He set the glass down beside her and headed back to the kitchen. "You'd be amazed by the list of my talents," he threw over his shoulder.

Kissing was certainly one of them, she thought. The sample he'd given her earlier had created a sharp need for more. If she was a sophisticated, experienced kind of woman, she wouldn't have any problem finding her way back into his arms. It would all appear so effortless and casual. He'd kiss her, and she'd kiss him, and then… They'd truly be husband and wife.

Lying on her back with her eyes closed, Janine imagined how wonderful it would be if Zach were to take her in his arms and make love to her....

She awoke from her doze with a start. She hurried inside to change, and as soon as she was ready, Zach announced that dinner was about to be served. He'd set the patio table so they could eat on the deck.

"Do you need any help?" she asked, trying to peek inside the kitchen.

"None. Sit down before everything cools." He pointed to the chair and waited until she was comfortable.

"I only have a spoon," she said, after unfolding the napkin on her lap. He must have made a mistake.

"A spoon is all you need," he shouted to her from the kitchen.

Playfully she asked, "You went to all this trouble for soup?"

"Wait and see. I'll be there in a minute."

He sounded so serious, Janine had to smile. She was running through a list of words to praise his efforts—"deliciously unique," "refreshingly different"—when Zach walked onto the deck, carrying a tin can with a pair of tongs.

"Good grief, what's that?" she asked in dismay.

"Dinner," he said. "The only real cooking I ever did was while I belonged to the Boy Scouts."

As though he was presenting lobster bisque, he set the steaming can in front of her. Janine leaned forward, almost afraid to examine its contents.

"Barbecued beans. With sliced hot dogs," he said proudly.

"And to think I doubted you."

Her reservations vanished, however, the moment she tasted his specialty. The beans were actually quite appetizing. He surprised her, too, by bringing out dessert, a concoction consisting of graham crackers covered with melted chocolate and marshmallows. He'd warmed them in the oven and served them on a cookie sheet.

Janine ate four of what Zach called "s'mores." He explained that once they'd been tasted, everyone asked for "some more."

"I don't know how you've managed to stay single all these years," she teased, forgetting for the moment that they were married. "If the news about your talent in the kitchen got out, women would be knocking at your door."

Zach chuckled, looking extraordinarily pleased with himself.

An unexpected thought entered Janine's mind, filling her with curiosity. She was astonished that she'd never asked Zach about other women in his life. It would be naive to assume there hadn't been any. She'd had her relationship with Brian; surely there were women in Zach's past.

She waited until later that night when they were sipping wine and listening to classical music in front of the fireplace. Zach seemed relaxed, sitting with one knee raised and the other leg stretched out. Janine lay on her stomach, staring into the fire.

"Have you ever been in love?" She was trying for a casual tone.

Zach didn't answer her right away. "Would you be jealous if I said I had?"

"No." She sounded more confident than she felt.

"I didn't think so. What about you?"

She took her time answering, too. She'd thought she was in love with Brian. It wasn't until later, after the pain of Brian's rejection had eased, that she realized she'd been in love with the *idea* of being in love.

"No," she said, completely honest in her response. What she felt for Zach, whom she was only beginning to know, was already a thousand times stronger than what she'd ever felt for any other man. She didn't know how to explain it, so she avoided the issue by reminding him, "I asked you first."

"I'm a married man. Naturally I'm in love."

"You're fond of me, remember?"

"I thought you detested that word."

"I do. Now stop tiptoeing around the subject. Have you ever *really* been in love—I mean head over heels in love? You don't need to go into any details—a simple yes or no will suffice."

"A desperate-passion kind of love?"

"Yes," she told him impatiently. "Don't make fun of me and please don't give me a list of all the women you've been *fond* of."

He grew so quiet and so intense that her smile began to fade. She pulled herself into a sitting position and looped her arms around her bent knees.

Zach stared at her. As she watched the harsh pain move into his eyes, Janine felt her chest tighten.

"Yes," he answered in a hoarse whisper. "I've been in love."

Nine

"Her name was Marie."

"Marie," Janine repeated the name as though she'd never heard it before.

"We met in Europe when I was on assignment with the armed forces. She spoke five languages fluently and helped me learn my way around two of them in the time we worked together."

"She was in the military with you?"

"I was army, she worked for the secret service. We were thrown together for a top-secret project that was only supposed to last a few days and instead dragged on for weeks."

"This was when you fell in love with her?" The ache inside her chest wouldn't go away. Her heart felt weighed down with the pain.

"We both were aware that the assignment was a dangerous one, and our working closely together was essential." He paused, sighing deeply. "To make a long story short, I fell in love with her. But she didn't love me."

"Then what?"

"I wanted her to leave the secret service and marry me. She wasn't interested. If you insist on knowing the details, I'll give them to you."

"No."

Zach took a sip of his wine. "I left the army soon after that. I didn't have the heart for it anymore. Unlike Marie—her work, with all its risks, was her whole life.

She was the bravest and most dedicated woman I've ever known. Although it was painful at the time, she was right to turn down my proposal. Marriage and a family would have bored her within a year. It *was* painful, don't misunderstand me. I loved her more than I thought possible."

They both were silent for a moment, then Janine asked, "What did you do once you left the army?"

"Over the years, I'd managed to put aside some money, make a few investments. Once I was on my own, I decided to go into business for myself. I read everything I could get my hands on about the business-supply field and modeled the way I dealt with my clients and accounts after your grandfather's enterprise. Within five years, I was his major competitor. We met at a conference last year, and decided that instead of competing with each other, we'd join forces. And as they say, the rest is history."

"Was she pretty?" Even as she asked the question, Janine knew it was ridiculous. What difference would it make if his Marie was a former Miss America or had a face like a gorilla? None. Zach had loved Marie. Loved her as he'd probably never love again. Loved her more than he'd thought possible. By comparison, what he felt for her, Janine, was indeed only fondness.

"She was blond and, yes, she was beautiful."

Janine made a feeble attempt at a smile. "Somehow I knew that."

Zach shook himself lightly as if dragging himself back to the present and away from the powerful lure of the past. "You don't need to worry. It was a long time ago."

"I wasn't worried," Janine muttered. She got to her

feet and collected their wineglasses. "I'm a little tired. If you don't mind, I'll go to bed now."

Zach was still staring into the fire and Janine doubted he'd even heard her. She didn't need a crystal ball to know he was thinking of the beautiful Marie.

No more than ten minutes after she'd turned off her bedroom light, Janine heard Zach move down the hallway to his room. For a moment she thought he'd hesitated in front of her door, but Janine convinced herself that was just wishful thinking.

From the second Zach had told her about the one great love of his life, Janine had felt as if a lump were building inside her. A huge lump of disillusionment that seemed to be located somewhere between her heart and her stomach. With every breath she took, it grew larger. But why should she care about Marie? Zach had never confessed to any deep feeling for *her*. He hadn't cheated Janine out of anything that was her right.

An hour later, she lay on her side, wide awake, her hands pressed to her stomach. She didn't mind that Zach had loved another woman so deeply, but what did hurt was that he could never love her with the same intensity. Marrying her, he'd claimed, made practical and financial sense. He was *fond* of her.

Like a romantic idiot, Janine had been frolicking through their short marriage, confident that they'd soon be in love with each other and live happily ever after with their two-point-five children in their perfect little home with the white picket fence.

Zach had loved Marie, who'd dedicated herself to her country.

The most patriotic thing Janine had ever done was cast her vote at election time. She didn't think she should include the two occasions she'd made coffee at Red Cross meetings.

Marie was a linguist. After two years of high-school French, Janine wasn't bad at conjugating verbs, but got hopelessly lost in real conversations.

"I had to ask," she groaned to herself. She was almost certain that Zach would never have mentioned Marie if she hadn't forced the subject. How blissful her ignorance had been. How comfortable.

She could never be the great love of his life and would always remain in the background. Far in the background...

When Janine heard Zach moving around the house a few hours later, she rolled over and glanced at the clock, assuming it was the middle of the night. Then she noticed it was midmorning; they'd planned to be on the road before now. Tossing aside the blankets, she stumbled out of bed and reached blindly for her robe. But she wasn't paying attention. She collided with the wall and gave a shout of pain. She cupped her hand over her nose and closed her eyes. Tears rolled slowly down her cheeks.

"Janine." Zach pounded on the door. "Are you all right?"

"No," she cried, still holding her nose. She looked in the mirror and lowered her hand. Just as she'd suspected, her nose was bleeding.

"Can I come in?" Zach asked next.

"No...go away." She hurried to the adjoining bathroom, tilting back her head and clamping both hands over her nose.

"You sound funny. I'm coming in."

"No," she hollered again. "Go away." She groped for

a washcloth. The tears rained down now, more from humiliation than pain.

"I'm coming in," Zach shouted, his voice distinctly irritated.

Before Janine could protest, the bedroom door flew open and Zach stalked inside. He stopped in the bathroom doorway. "What happened?"

Pressing the cold cloth over the lower half of her face with one hand, Janine gestured violently with the other, demanding that he leave.

"Let me look at that," he said, obviously determined to deal with her bloody nose, as well as her anger. He pushed gently against her shoulders, lowering her onto the edge of the tub, and carefully removed the cloth.

"What did you do? Meet up with a prizefighter?"

"Don't you dare make fun of me!" The tears ran down her cheeks again and plummeted on her silk collar.

It took only a minute or so to control the bleeding. Zach seemed to know exactly what to do. Janine no longer had any desire to fight, and she allowed him to do what he wanted.

Zach wiped the tears from her cheeks. "Do you want me to kiss it and make it better?"

Without waiting for an answer, Zach brought his mouth to hers. Janine felt herself go completely and utterly still. Her heart started to explode and before she realized what she was doing, she'd linked her arms around his neck and was clinging to him helplessly. Zach kissed her forehead and her eyes. His thumbs brushed the remaining tears from her cheeks. Then he nuzzled her neck. Trembling, she immersed herself in his tenderness. No matter what had happened in the past, Zach was hers for this minute, this day.

He lifted Janine to her feet and seemed to be lead-

ing her toward the bed. She might have been tempted
to let him if she hadn't learned about his love for Marie.
Knowing she'd always place a remote second in his af-
fections was a crippling blow to her pride—and her
heart. It would take time and effort to accept that she
could never be the woman who evoked an all-consum-
ing passion in him.

With that thought in mind, she pushed him away,
needing to put some distance between them before it
was too late.

Accepting Janine's decision, Zach dropped his arms
and moved to lean against the doorjamb, as if he needed
its support to remain upright.

Janine couldn't look at him, couldn't speak. She
began fumbling with her clothes.

"I'll give you a few minutes to dress while I begin
loading the car," Zach said a moment later, sounding
oddly unlike himself.

Janine nodded miserably. There was nothing she
could say. Nothing she could do. He'd wanted to make
love to her, and she'd turned him away.

While he packed the car, Janine dressed. She met
him fifteen minutes later, her suitcase in hand. She was
determined to act cool toward him. But not too cool.
Friendly, she decided, but not excessively so.

"I'm ready," she announced, with her most cheerful smile.

Zach locked the house, and they were on their way.
Pretending there was nothing out of the ordinary, Janine chatted amicably during the drive home. If Zach
noticed anything amiss, he didn't comment. For his part,
he seemed as hesitant as she was to talk about what had
happened. They seemed to be of one mind about the
morning's incident. The whole thing was best forgotten.

Only once did Zach refer to it. He asked her if her nose was causing her any pain, but she quickly assured him she was fine. She flashed a smile bright enough to blind him and immediately changed the subject.

The Seattle sky was gray and drizzling rain when they pulled into the parking garage at the downtown condominium owned by Zach. Silently, she helped him unload the car. They were both unusually quiet as they rode the elevator to the tenth floor.

Zach paused outside his door and eyed her skeptically. "Am I obliged to haul you over the threshold again, or is once enough?"

"Once is enough."

"Good." He grinned and unlocked the door, then pushed it open for her to precede him. Curious, she quickened her pace as she walked inside. The living room was a warm mixture of leather and wood, and its wide window offered a breathtaking view of the Seattle skyline.

"It's lovely."

He nodded, seeming pleased at her reaction. "If you prefer, we can move. I suppose now that we're married, we should think about purchasing a house."

"Why?" she inquired innocently.

"I'm hoping we'll have children someday. Whenever you're ready, that is. There's no pressure, Janine."

"I...know that." She looked past him at the panoramic view, and wrapped her arms around herself, her heart speeding up at his words.

Walking to his desk, Zach listened to his voice mail messages; apparently there were a lot.

While he did that, Janine wandered from room to room, eager to see her new home. In the hallway, she noted that Zach had diplomatically left her luggage on the carpet between the two bedrooms. His was in the master. In his own way, he was telling her that where she slept would be her decision. If she wished to become his wife in the fullest sense, all she had to do was place her suitcase in the master bedroom. Nothing more needed to be said.

It didn't take Janine long to decide. She pulled her suitcase toward the guest room. When she looked up, Zach was standing in the hall, studying her, his expression aggrieved.

"Unless you need me for anything, I'm going to the office," he said gruffly.

"See you tonight."

His gaze moved past her and rested briefly on the bed in the guest room. He cocked one eyebrow questioningly, as though to give her the opportunity to reconsider. "Are you sure you'd rather sleep in here?" he asked.

"I'm sure."

Zach raked his fingers through his hair. "I was afraid of that."

A minute later, he was gone.

Zach didn't come home for dinner that night. Janine had been in the bathroom when the phone rang; Zach had left her a message saying he'd be late. So she ate by herself in front of the television, feeling abandoned and unloved. She was just putting the dishes in the dishwasher when he came home.

"Sorry I'm late."

"That's okay," she lied, never having felt more alone.

Zach glanced through the mail on his desk, although Janine was sure he'd looked at it earlier. "You got the message I wouldn't be home for dinner?"

"Yes. Did you want anything to eat? I could fix you something."

"I ate earlier. Thanks, anyway."

They watched an hour's worth of television and then decided to go to bed.

Janine changed into her pajamas—the same no-nonsense type she'd been wearing all week, since she couldn't bring herself to wear the baby-dolls Pam had given her—and had just finished washing her face. She was coming out of the bathroom, her toothbrush between her teeth, when she nearly collided with Zach in the hallway. She'd forgotten her slippers and was going to her bedroom to retrieve them. They'd already said their good-nights, and Janine hadn't expected to see him again until morning. She wasn't prepared for this encounter, and the air between them crackled with tension.

She had to force herself not to throw her toothbrush aside. Not to tell him that she longed for him to love her with the same passion he'd felt for Marie.

His hands reached out to steady her, and when she didn't immediately move away, he ran the tips of his fingers down her thick brown hair, edging her bangs to the side of her face so he could gaze into her eyes.

Janine lowered her head. "Esh-coo me," she managed, but it was difficult to speak with a toothbrush poking out of her mouth.

"Pardon?"

Janine hurried back to the bathroom and rinsed out her mouth. Turning, she braced her hands on the sink. "I said excuse me for bumping into you."

"Will you be comfortable in the guest room?"

"Yes, I'll be fine."

He held a blanket in his arms. "I thought you might need this."

"Thanks," she said as smoothly as possible, coming out of the bathroom to take the blanket from him. She wanted to be swept off her feet. She wanted love. She wanted passion.

He was offering a warm blanket.

"I...phoned Gramps," she said, looking for a way to delay their parting and cursing herself for her weakness.

"I intended to call him myself, but got sidetracked."

"He sounded good. Dr. Coleman and a couple of his other friends were at the house and the four of them were playing pinochle."

"I'm glad to hear he's enjoying his semi-retirement."

"I am, too."

A short silence followed.

"Good night, Janine," Zach said after a moment. He glanced, frowning, into the guest room.

"Good night," she said awkwardly.

Janine was sure neither of them slept a wink that night. They were across the hall from each other, but might as well have been on opposite sides of the state, so great was the emotional distance between them.

In the morning, Zach's alarm rang at seven, but Janine was already awake. She threw back her covers, dressed and had coffee waiting when he entered the kitchen.

Zach seemed surprised to see her. "Thanks," he murmured as she handed him a cup. "That's a very...wifely thing to do."

"What? Make coffee?"

"Get up to see your husband off to work."

"I happened to be awake and figured I should get out of bed and do something useful."

He opened the refrigerator, took out the orange juice and poured himself a glass. "I see." He replaced the carton and leaned against the counter. "You did agree that our marriage would be a real one."

"Yes, I did," she said somewhat defensively. But that agreement had been before she'd learned about the one great love of his life. Zach had warned her their marriage would be advantageous for a variety of reasons, the least of which was love. At the time, Janine had agreed, convinced their relationship would find a storybook ending nonetheless—convinced that one day they'd realize they were in love. Now she understood that would never happen. And she didn't know if she could stand it.

"Janine," Zach said, distracting her, "what's wrong?"

"What could possibly be wrong?"

"Obviously something's bothering you. You look like you've lost your best friend."

"You should've told me," she burst out, running from the kitchen.

"Told you what?" Zach shouted, following her down the hall.

Furious, she hurried into her room and sat on the end of the bed, her hands in tight fists at her sides.

"What are you talking about?" he demanded, blocking the doorway.

"About…this woman you loved."

"Marie? What about her? What's she got to do with you and me?"

"You loved her more than…more than you thought possible. She was brave and wonderful, and I'm none of those things. I don't deal with pain very well and… I'd like to be patriotic but all I do is vote and all I know in French are verbs."

"What's any of that got to do with you and me?" Zach repeated hoarsely, then threw his hands in the air. "What's it got to do with *anything*?"

Knowing she'd never be able to explain, Janine shook her head, sending her bangs fanning out in several directions. "All you are is *fond* of me."

"Correction," Zach said as he stepped into the bedroom. "I *cherish* you."

"It isn't enough," she said, feeling miserable and wretched and unworthy.

"What do you mean, it isn't enough? According to you the only reason you married me was that I was a good kisser, so you can't fault me for *my* reasons."

"I don't, it's just that you…you never told me about loving someone else. Not only that, you *admired* her— she was a hero. All you feel for me is fondness. Well, I don't want your fondness, Zachary Thomas!" She leapt to her feet, trying to collect her scattered thoughts. "If you cared for me, you would've told me about Marie before. Not mentioning her was a form of dishonesty. You were completely…unfair."

"And you weren't?" Zach's expression darkened and he buried his hands in his pockets. "You didn't say one word to me about Brian."

Janine was so shocked she sank back onto the bed. Zach still glared at her, challenging her to contradict him. Slowly gathering her composure, she stood, her eyes narrowing as she studied her husband. "Who told you about Brian?"

"Your grandfather."

"How did he know? I never said a word to him about Brian. Not one solitary word."

"But obviously he knew."

"Obviously." Janine had never felt more like weeping. "I suppose he told you Brian lied to me and claimed to love me when all the while he was seeing someone else." Another, more troubling thought entered her mind. "I…

bet Gramps told you that to make you feel sorry for me, sorry enough to marry me."

"Janine, no."

She hid her face in both hands, humiliation burning her cheeks. It was all so much worse than she'd imagined. "You felt sorry for me, didn't you?"

Zach paced the length of the bedroom. "I'm not going to lie to you, although I suspect it would be better if I did. Your grandfather didn't mention that you'd fallen in love with Brian until after the day we took him to the doctor."

"He waited until we got to know each other a little," Janine whispered, staggered by the realization that her grandfather had known about Brian all along.

"By then I'd discovered I liked you."

"The word *like* is possibly even worse than *fond*," she muttered.

"Just hear me out, would you?"

"All right," she sighed, fearing that nothing he said now mattered, anyway. Her pride had suffered another major blow. The one love of his life had been this marvelous patriot, while Janine had fallen for a weak-willed womanizer.

"It isn't as bad as it seems," Zach tried to assure her.

"I can just imagine what Gramps told you."

"All he said was that he was afraid you'd never learn to trust your own judgment again. For quite a while now, he's watched you avoid any hint of a relationship. It was as though you'd retreated from men and were content just to lick your wounds."

"That's not true! I was seeing Peter Donahue on a regular basis."

"Safe dates with safe men. There was never any likelihood that you'd fall in love with Peter, and you knew it. It was the only reason you went out with him."

"Is…is what happened with Brian why Gramps decided to play matchmaker?"

"I suspect that was part of it. Also his concern for your future. But I don't fully understand his intentions even now. I don't think it matters, though. He wanted you to be happy and secure. Anton knew I'd never purposely hurt you. And in his eyes, the two of us were perfect for each other." Zach sat down next to her and reached for her hand, lacing her fingers with his own. "*Does* it matter? We're married now."

She looked away from him and swallowed hard. "I… may not be blond and gorgeous or brave, but I deserve a husband who'll love me. You and Gramps both failed to take that into account. I don't want your pity, Zach."

"Good, because I don't pity you. You're my wife, and frankly, I'm happy about it. We can have a good life if you'll put this nonsense behind you."

"You'd never have chosen me on your own. I knew what you thought of me from the moment we met. You assumed I was a rich spoiled woman who'd never had anything real to worry about. I bet you thought I'd consider a broken nail a major disaster."

"All right, I'll admit I had the wrong impression, but that was before," Zach insisted.

"Before what?"

"Before I got to know you."

Janine's shoulders heaved with barely suppressed emotion. "As I recall, the reason you were willing to marry me was because I wasn't so bad. And let's not forget the financial benefits," she added sarcastically.

Zach's sigh was filled with frustration. "I told you I wasn't ever going to say the stuff you women like to hear. I don't know a thing about romance. But I care about you, Janine, I honestly care. Isn't that enough?"

"I need more than that," she said miserably. It was the promise of their future, the promise of learning about love together, that had intrigued her.

Zach frowned. "You told me even before we were married that you didn't need romantic words. You were content before I mentioned Marie. Why should my telling you change anything?"

She saw that Zach was losing his patience with her. She stared down at the thick carpet. "I really wish I could explain, but it does make a difference. I'm sorry, Zach, I really am."

A lifetime seemed to pass before he spoke again. "So am I," he whispered before turning away. A moment later the front door opened and almost immediately closed again. Zach had left.

"What did you expect?" she wailed, covering her face with both hands. "Did you think he was going to fall at your knees and declare his undying love?" The picture of the proud and mighty Zach Thomas playing the role of besotted husband was actually comical. If he'd done that for any woman, it would've been the brave and beautiful Marie. Not Janine.

After that disastrous morning, their relationship grew more strained than ever. Zach went to work early every day and returned late, usually past dinnertime. Janine never questioned where he was or who he was with, although she had to bite her tongue to keep from asking.

Zach proved to be a model housemate, if not a husband—cordial, courteous and remote. For her part, she threw herself into her volunteer work at the Friendship Club, spending hours each week with the children. She did her best to hide her unhappiness from her grandfather, although that was difficult.

"You look pale," he told her when she joined him for lunch one afternoon, several days after her return from Ocean Shores. "Are you losing weight?"

"I wish," she said, attempting to make a joke of it. They sat in the dining room, with Mrs. McCormick wandering in and out, casting Janine concerned glances. Janine resisted the urge to leap up and do aerobic exercises to demonstrate that she was in perfect health.

"You can't afford to get much thinner," Gramps said, eyeing her solemnly. He placed a dinner roll on the side of her plate and plunked the butter dish down in front of her.

"I'm not losing weight," she told him, spreading butter on the roll in order to please him.

"I took that sea gull you gave me into the office," Gramps said as he continued to study her. "Zach asked me where I got it. When I told him, he didn't say anything, but I could tell he wasn't pleased. Do you want it back?"

"No, of course not." Janine dropped her gaze. She'd never intended for Gramps to take Chester into the office. On impulse, she'd given him the ceramic bird, reluctant to have it around the condominium to remind her of those first glorious days with Zach.

"I wish I knew what was wrong with you two," Gramps blurted out in an uncharacteristic display of frustration. He tossed his napkin onto his dinner plate. "You should be happy! Instead, the pair of you look like you're recovering from a bad bout of flu. Zach's working so many hours it's a wonder he doesn't fall over from sheer exhaustion."

Janine carefully tore her roll into pieces. She toyed with the idea of bringing up the subject of Brian, but in the end, she didn't.

"So you say you're fine, and there's nothing wrong between you and Zach," Gramps said sarcastically. "Funny, that's exactly what he said when I asked him. Except he also told me to mind my own business—not quite in those words, but I got the message. The thing is, he looks as pathetic as you do. I can't understand it—you're perfect for each other!"

Gramps reached into his pocket for a cigar. "I'll be seeing Zach this afternoon and I intend to give that boy a piece of my mind. By all rights, you should be a happy bride." He tapped one end of the cigar against the table.

"We'll be fine, Gramps. Please stay out of it."

For a long moment, he said nothing; he only stared at the cigar between his fingers. "You're sure you don't want me to talk some sense into the boy?" he finally asked.

The mental picture of him trying to do so brought a quivering smile to her lips. "I'm sure," she said, then glanced at her watch. Pam would be waiting for her. "But since you're seeing Zach, would you please let him know I'll probably be late for dinner? He…should go ahead and eat without me."

"Do you do this often?" His question was an accusation.

"No," she replied, shaking her head. "This is the first time. Pam needs my help with a school project and I don't know when we'll be finished."

Gramps glowered as he lit his cigar, puffing mightily before he spoke. "I'll tell him."

As it turned out, Janine spent longer with Pam than she'd expected. The homework assignment wasn't difficult, but Pam begged Janine to stay with her. Pam's father was working late and the girl seemed to need Janine more than ever. They made dinner together, then ate in the kitchen while Pam chatted about her friends and life in general.

It was almost nine by the time Janine pulled into the parking garage. The first thing she noticed was Zach's car. The atmosphere had been so falsely courteous between them that she dreaded each encounter, however brief. Since that first morning, Zach hadn't made any effort to talk about her role in his life. Janine wasn't looking for a long flowery declaration of love. Just a word or two more profound than *fond* or *like* to let her know she was important to him.

Drawing a deep breath, she headed for the condominium.

She'd just unlocked the door when Zach stormed into the room like a Minnesota blizzard. "Where the hell have you been?" he demanded.

Janine was so shocked by his fierce anger that she said nothing.

"I demand to know exactly where you were!"

She removed her sweater, hanging it carefully in the entry closet, along with her purse. Zach scowled at her silence, fists clenched at his sides. "Do you have any idea of the time? Did it even cross your mind that I might've been concerned about you? Your cell phone was off and you didn't return any calls."

"I'm sorry." Janine turned to face him. "But you knew where I was," she said calmly.

"All Anton said was that you'd be late. Not where you were going or who you were with. So naturally I was worried."

"I'm sorry. Next time I'll tell you myself." Janine yawned; the day had been exhausting. "If you don't mind, I think I'll go to bed now. Unless there's anything else you'd like to know?"

He glared at her, then shook his head. Wheeling around abruptly, he walked away.

Hours later, Janine was awakened by a gruff sobbing sound coming from the other room. It took her a moment to realize it was Zach. Was he having a nightmare?

Folding back the covers, she got out of bed and hurried into his room. The cries of anguish grew louder. In the light from the hallway, she could see him thrashing about, the bedding in disarray.

"Zach," she cried, rushing to his side. She sat on the edge of the bed and placed her hands gently on his shoulders. "Wake up. You're having a dream. Just a dream. It's okay...."

Zach's eyes slowly opened. "Janine." He ground out her name as though in torment and reached for her, hauling her into his arms with such force that he left her breathless. "Janine," he said, his voice so husky she could barely understand him. "I thought I'd lost you."

Ten

"Zach, I'm fine," Janine whispered. Emotion clogged her throat at the hungry way his eyes roamed her face. He seemed to have difficulty believing, even now, that she was unhurt.

"It was so real," he continued, his chest heaving. He hid his face as if to block out the vivid images the dream had induced. Making room in the large bed, he pulled her down beside him. His hands stroked her hair as he released several jagged breaths. "We were at the ocean," he told her, "and although I'd warned you against it, you decided to swim. A huge wave knocked you off your feet and you were drowning. Heaven help me, I tried, but I couldn't get to you fast enough." He shut his eyes briefly. "You kept calling out to me and I couldn't find you. I just couldn't get to you fast enough."

"Zach," she whispered, her mouth so close to his that their breath mingled, "I'm right here. It was only a dream. It wasn't real."

He nodded, but his eyes still seemed troubled, refusing to leave her face. Then ever so slowly, as though he expected her to object, he moved his mouth even closer to hers. "I couldn't bear to lose you. I'd rather die myself."

Helpless to deny him anything, Janine turned her face to receive his kiss.

His hands tangled in her thick dark hair, effectively holding her captive, while his mouth seized hers in a kiss that sent her senses swirling. Nothing mattered except his touch. Overcome for a moment by the fierce tenderness she felt in him, Janine eagerly fed his need.

"Janine, oh, my dear sweet Janine. I couldn't bear to lose you."

"I'm here… I'm here." Melting against him, she molded her body to the unyielding contours of his, offering her lips and her heart to his loving possession. Again and again, he kissed her. Janine slid her hands up his chest and twined them around his neck. This was what she'd longed for from the first, the knowledge that he needed her, and she gloried in the sensation.

With a groan, he reluctantly pulled his mouth from hers. He held her firmly to his chest, his breathing harsh and rapid. Peace combined with a delirious sense of happiness, and Janine released a deep sigh. Pressing her ear to his chest, she listened, content, to the heavy pounding of his heart.

"Did I frighten you?" he asked after a minute.

"No," she whispered.

He resumed stroking her hair as she nestled more securely in his arms. Zach had made her feel wondrous, exciting things every time he kissed her, but the way he held and touched her now went far beyond those kisses. She'd experienced a bonding with Zach, a true joining of spirits that had been missing until now. He had told her he'd cherish her, but she hadn't believed it until this moment. Tears clouded her eyes and she struggled to restrain them.

For a long while neither of them spoke. But Janine didn't need words. Her eyes were closed as she savored this precious time.

When Zach did speak, his voice was little more than a hoarse whisper. "I had a sister who drowned. Her name was Beth Ann. I'd promised I'd always be there for her—but I failed her. I couldn't bear to lose you, too."

Janine tightened her hold, knowing how difficult it must be for him to speak of his sister.

"I never forgave myself." His body tensed and his fingers dug roughly into her shoulder. "Losing Beth Ann still haunts me. She wouldn't have drowned if I'd been with her. She—"

Lifting her head slightly, Janine's misty gaze met his. "It wasn't your fault. How could it have been?"

"But I was responsible for her," he returned harshly.

Janine suspected that Zach had rarely, if ever, shared his sorrow or his guilt over his sister's death with anyone. A low groan worked its way through him and he squeezed his eyes tightly shut. "For years, I've drummed out the memories of Beth Ann's death. The nightmare was so real, only this time it wasn't her—it was you."

"But I'm safe and sound. See?" She pressed her hands to both sides of his face, smiling down on him.

He sighed and smiled back, a little uncertainly. "I'm all right now. I shouldn't have burdened you with this."

"It wasn't a burden."

His arms tightened around her, and he inhaled deeply as if absorbing her scent. "Stay with me?"

She nodded, grateful that he needed her.

Within minutes, Janine felt herself drifting into drowsiness. From Zach's relaxed, even breathing, she knew he was already asleep.

When Janine next stirred, she was lying on her side, and Zach was cuddling her spoon fashion, his arm about her waist. At some point during the night, she'd slipped under the covers, but she had no recollection of doing so. A small satisfied smile touched the edges of her mouth. She rolled carefully onto her back so as not to disturb

Zach, and wondered what she should do. When Zach woke and found her in bed with him, she was afraid he might regret what had happened, regret asking her to stay. He might feel embarrassed that he'd told her about his sister's death and the guilt he still felt.

Closing her eyes, Janine debated with herself. If she left his bed and returned to her own room, he might think she was rejecting him, shocked by his heart-wrenching account of Beth Ann's death.

"Janine?" He whispered her name, his voice husky with sleep.

Her eyes flew open. "I...we fell asleep. What time is it?"

"Early. The alarm won't go off for another couple of hours."

She nodded, hoping to disguise any hint of disappointment in her voice. He didn't want her with him, she was sure of it. He was embarrassed to find her still in his bed. "I'll leave now if you want."

"No."

The single word was filled with such longing that Janine thought she'd misunderstood him. She tipped her head back to meet his gaze. The light from the hall allowed her to see the passion smoldering in his dark eyes. Turning onto her side, Janine lovingly traced the lines of his face.

"I'm sorry about the way I behaved over... Marie," she whispered. "I was jealous and I knew I was being ridiculous, but I couldn't help myself."

The corners of his eyes crinkled with his smile. "I'll forgive you if you're willing to overlook the way I behaved when you got home last night."

She answered him with a light kiss, and he hugged her to him. Janine surrendered to the sheer pleasure of being in Zach's arms, savoring the rush of warm sensations that sprang to life inside her.

"I don't know how to say all the words you deserve to hear, but I know one thing, Janine. I love you. It happened without my even being aware of it. One day I woke up and realized how important you'd become to me. It wasn't the grand passion you wanted, and I'm sorry for that. The love I feel for you is the quiet steady kind. It's buried deep in my heart, but trust me, it's there. You're the most important person in my life."

"Oh, Zach, I love you so much."

"You love me?"

"I have for weeks, even before we were married. That's what bothered me so much when I learned about Marie. I wanted you to love *me* with the same intensity that you felt for her...that I feel for you."

"It isn't like that. It never was. Marie was as brave as she was beautiful, but what we shared was never meant to last. And she was smart enough to understand that. I fell in love with her, but she was too much of a professional to involve her heart. She was the kind of person who thrives on excitement and danger. It wasn't until you and I met that I realized if I were ever to marry, it would be to someone like you."

"Someone like me?"

He kissed her briefly. "A woman who's warm and gentle and caring. Someone unselfish and—" he hesitated "—desirable."

Her throat tightened with emotion, and it was all she could do to meet his gaze. Zach found her desirable. He wanted to make love to her. He didn't need to say it; the message was there for her to read in his eyes. It wasn't the desperate passion she'd once craved, but his love, his need to have her in his life, was far more potent than any action he could have taken, any words he could have said.

"Love me, Zach," she whispered simply.

Zach's mouth touched hers with a sweet desperate ardor. If she had any lingering doubts they vanished like mist in the sun as his lips took hers, twisting her into tight knots of desire.

His arms locked around her and he rolled onto his back, pulling her with him. His hands outlined her face as though he half expected her to stop him.

"Make me your wife," she said, bending forward to brush her moist mouth over his.

Zach groaned, and then he did the strangest, most wonderful thing. He laughed. The robust sound echoed across the room and was so infectious that it made Janine laugh, too.

"My sweet Janine," he said. "You've changed my life." And then he kissed her again, leaving her with no doubts at all.

For a long time afterward, their happiness could be heard in their sighs and gasps and whispered words of love....

The buzzing sound refused to go away. Janine moaned softly and flung out her hand, hoping to find the source of the distraction. But before she could locate it, the noise ceased abruptly.

"Good morning, wife," Zach whispered.

Her eyes remained closed as she smiled leisurely. "Good morning, husband." Rolling onto her back, she held her arms open to him. "I had the most marvelous dream last night."

Zach chuckled softly. "That wasn't any dream."

"But it must've been," she said, slipping her arms

around his neck and smiling lazily. "Nothing could be that incredible in real life."

"I didn't think so, either, but you proved me wrong." He kissed her tenderly, and then so thoroughly that by the time he lifted his head, Janine was breathless.

Slowly, almost against her will, her eyes drifted open. His were dark with desire. "You'll be late for work," she warned him.

His smile was sensuous. "Who cares?"

"Not me," she murmured. And with a small cry of pleasure, she willingly gave herself to her husband.

Zach was already an hour late for the office when he dragged himself out of bed and headed for the shower. Wearing her husband's pajama top, Janine wandered into the kitchen and prepared a pot of coffee. She leaned against the counter and smiled into space, hardly aware of the passage of time.

A few minutes later—or perhaps it was longer—Zach stepped behind her and slid his arms around her waist, nuzzling her neck.

"Zach," she protested, but not too strenuously. She closed her eyes and cradled her arms over his, leaning back against his solid strength. "You're already late."

"I know," he murmured. "If I didn't have an important meeting this morning, I'd skip work altogether."

Turning in his arms, Janine tilted back her head to gaze into his eyes. "You'll be home for dinner?"

"Keep looking at me like that and I'll be home for lunch."

Janine smiled. "It's almost that time now."

"I know," he growled, reluctantly pulling away from her. "We'll go out to dinner tonight," he said, kissing her again. His mouth was hot on her own, feverish with demand and passion and need. He raised his head, but his eyes remained shut. "Then we'll come home and celebrate."

Janine sighed. Married life was beginning to agree with her.

At precisely five, Zach was back. He stood by the door, loosening his tie, when Janine appeared. A smile traveled to his mouth as their eyes met. Neither moved. They stared at each other as if they'd spent years apart instead of a few short hours.

Janine was feeling distinctly light-headed. "Hi," she managed to say, shocked that her voice sounded more like a hoarse whisper than the cheery greeting she'd intended. "How'd the meeting go?"

"Bad."

"Bad?"

He nodded slowly and stepped forward, placing his briefcase on the desk. "I was supposed to be listening to an important financial report, but unfortunately all I could do was wonder how much longer the thing would take so I could get home to my wife."

"Oh." That wasn't the most intelligent bit of conversation she'd ever delivered, but just looking at Zach was enough to wipe out all her normal thought processes.

"It got to be almost embarrassing." His look was intimate and loving as he advanced two more steps toward her. "In the middle of it, I started smiling, and then I embarrassed myself further by laughing outright."

"Laughing? Something was funny?"

"I was thinking about your definition of romance. The tryst on the moors was supplied by your grandfather. The walk along the beach, hand in hand, was supplied by me after the wedding. But the desperate passion, my dear sweet wife, was something we found together."

Her eyes filled with tears.

"I love you."

They moved toward each other then, but stopped abruptly when the doorbell chimed. Zach's questioning eyes met hers. Janine shrugged, not knowing who it could possibly be.

The second Zach answered the door, Anton flew into the room, looking more determined than Janine had ever seen him.

"All right, you two, sit down," he ordered, waving them in the direction of the sofa.

"Gramps?"

"Anton?"

Janine glanced at Zach, but he looked as mystified as she did. So she just shrugged and complied with her grandfather's demand. Zach sat down next to her.

Gramps paced the carpet directly in front of them. "Janine and I had lunch the other day," he said, speaking to Zach. "Two things became clear to me then. First and foremost, she's crazy in love with you, but I doubt she's told you that."

"Gramps—" Janine began, but her grandfather silenced her with a single look.

"The next thing I realized is that she's unhappy. Terribly unhappy. Being in love is difficult enough but—"

"Anton," Zach broke in, "if you'd—"

Gramps cut him off with the same laser-eyed look he'd sent Janine.

"Don't interrupt me, boy. I'm on a roll and I'm not about to stop now. If I noticed Janine was a little melancholy at lunch, it was nothing compared to what I've been noticing about you." Suddenly he ceased his pacing and planted himself squarely in front of Zach. "All week I've been hearing complaints and rumors about you. Folks in the office claim you're there all hours of

the day and night, working until you're ready to drop."
He paused. "I know you, Zach, probably better than anyone else does. You're in love with my granddaughter,
and it's got you all tangled up inside."

"Gramps—"

"Shh." He dismissed Janine with a shake of his head.
"Now, I may be an old man, but I'm not stupid. Maybe
the way I went about bringing the two of you together
wasn't the smartest, or the most conventional, but by
golly it worked." He hesitated long enough to smile
proudly. "In the beginning I had my doubts. Janine put
up a bit of a fuss."

"I believe you said something about how it's easier
to pluck a live chicken," Zach inserted, slanting a secret
smile at Janine.

"True enough. I never knew that girl had so much
spunk. But the fact is, Zachary, as you'll recall, you
weren't all that keen on the idea yourself. You both think
because I'm an old man, I don't see things. But I do. You
were two lonely people, filling up your lives with unimportant relationships, avoiding love, avoiding life. I
care about you. Too much to sit back and do nothing."

"It worked out," Janine said, wanting to reassure him.

"At first I thought it had. I arranged the trip to Scotland and it looked like everything was falling neatly into
place, like in one of those old movies. I couldn't have
been more pleased when you announced that you were
going to get married. It was sooner than I'd expected,
but I assumed that meant things were progressing nicely.
Apparently I was wrong. Now I'm worried."

"You don't need to be."

"That's not the way I see it," Gramps said with a
fierce glare. "Tell him you love him, Janine. Look Zach
in the eye and put aside that silly pride of yours. He

needs to know it. He needs to hear it. I told you from the first that he wasn't going to be an easy man to know, and that you'd have to be patient with him. What I didn't count on was that damnable pride of yours."

"You want me to tell Zach I love him? Here? Now?"

"Yes!"

Janine turned to her husband and, feeling a little self-conscious, lowered her eyes.

"Tell him," Gramps barked.

"I love you, Zach," she said softly. "I really do."

Gramps gave a loud satisfied sigh. "Good, good. Okay, Zach, it's your turn."

"My turn?"

"Tell Janine what you feel and don't go all arrogant on me."

Zach reached for Janine's hand. He lifted her palm to his mouth and brushed his lips against it. "I love you," he whispered.

"Add something else," Gramps instructed, gesturing toward him. "Something like…you'd be a lost and lonely soul without her. Women are impressed by that sort of thing. Damn foolishness, I know, but necessary."

"I'd be a lost and lonely soul without you," Zach repeated, then looked back at Janine's grandfather. "How'd I do?"

"Better than most. Is there anything else you'd like him to say, Janine?"

She gave an expressive sigh. "I don't think so."

"Good. Now I want the two of you to kiss."

"Here? In front of you?"

"Yes," Gramps insisted.

Janine slipped into Zach's arms. The smile he shared with her was so devastating that she felt her heart race with anticipation. Her eyes fluttered closed as his mouth settled on hers, thrilling her with promises for all the years to come.

Gently, provocatively, Zach moved his mouth over hers, ending his kiss far too soon to suit Janine. From the shudder that coursed through him, Janine knew it was too soon for him, too. Reluctantly they drew apart. Zach gazed into her eyes, and Janine responded with a soft smile.

"Excellent, excellent."

Janine had all but forgotten her grandfather's presence. When she turned away from Zach, she discovered Gramps sitting across from them, his hands on the arms of the leather chair. He looked exceedingly proud of himself. "Are you two going to be all right now?"

"Yes, sir," Zach answered for them both, his eyes hazy with desire as he smiled at Janine. She could feel herself blushing, and knew her eyes were foggy with the same longing.

"Good!" Gramps declared, nodding once for emphasis. A slow grin overtook his mouth. "I knew all the two of you needed was a little assistance from me." He inhaled deeply. "Since you're getting along so well, maybe now would be the time to bring up the subject of children."

"Anton," Zach said, rising to his feet. He strode across the room and opened the door. "If you don't mind, I'll take care of that myself."

"Soon?" Gramps wanted to know.

Zach's eyes met Janine's. "Soon," he promised.

* * * * *

SWEET DREAMS
ON CENTER STREET

Sheila Roberts

For Lilly-Anne, Pat and the gang at
A Book for All Seasons in Leavenworth, Washington

Acknowledgments

Sometimes when we think of an author writing a novel
we envision the poor thing hunched over a keyboard
for hours on end, starting at a computer screen, all
by herself, consuming vast quantities of chocolate,
growing fat on her hips. Oh, my gosh, that's me!

Except writing isn't always a solitary pursuit.
After all, a girl has to do research. And this is the part of
the book where I get to thank the people who helped me
with that research. I owe a big thank-you to my long-
suffering husband for sharing his banking expertise and
doing copious research to help me try to get my business
details correct. Also, a huge thank-you to Laura at
Bainbridge Island City Hall for explaining all the work
that goes into putting on a community event. When it
comes to community events, Bainbridge knows how to
do it. Big thanks to Brett at Theo Chocolate in Seattle for
being so willing to answer all my questions about what
goes into running a chocolate company. They do it right
over there. Thanks to my Facebook friends and fans
who sent me recipes—wish there was room in this book
for every one of them. To the brain trust—Susan Wiggs,
Anjali Banerjee, Kate Breslin and Elsa Watson—you
girls rock. And finally, huge thanks to the gang at the
Chamber of Commerce in Leavenworth, Washington,
for making their resources available to me—
the history of how your town built itself into
a charming alpine village and successful
tourist destination is truly inspiring.
Icicle Falls is the closest I can come to a tribute.

One

Manage your relationships well and your business will go well. Because what, after all, is business but a relationship with some dollar signs attached?
—Muriel Sterling, *Mixing Business with Pleasure: How to Successfully Balance Business and Love*

Samantha Sterling sat next to her mother in the first pew of Icicle Falls Community Church and fought back the urge to jump up, run to the front of the sanctuary, grab her stepfather, Waldo, by the neck and throttle him. She didn't, for two reasons. One, a girl didn't do things like that in church. Still, she could have overcome her reservations if not for the second reason—God had already taken Waldo out. Waldo was as dead as roadkill on Highway 2. In addition to a daughter from his first marriage, he'd left behind his grieving wife, Muriel, his three stepdaughters, Samantha, Cecily and Bailey, and the family business, which was nearly as dead as Waldo.

Sweet Dreams Chocolates had been healthy when Samantha's father was alive. The company had been started by her great-grandmother Rose and had slowly but steadily grown under his leadership—one big, happy family to mirror the happy family who were living off its profits. All three sisters had spent their summers working at Sweet Dreams. All three had it drummed into them from an early age that this business was the source of both the family's income and honor (not to mention chocolate). But it was Samantha who had fallen in love with it. Of the three girls, she was the one who'd stayed and she was the heir apparent.

But then her father had died and everything came to a halt. Samantha lost the man she and her sisters idolized, and her mother lost her way. Muriel left it to Samantha and the bookkeeper, Lizzy, to keep the company running on autopilot while first she mourned and then later searched for a new husband.

Enter Waldo Wittman, a tall, gray-haired widower recently retired, encouraged to do so by his company, which was downsizing. (Now, looking back, Samantha suspected there were other reasons Waldo had been turned loose.) He'd wanted to get away from the rat race, or so he'd said. With its mountain views, its proximity to eastern Washington wine country, its small-town friendliness and its attractive widow, Waldo decided Icicle Falls would fit the bill. And Muriel decided the same about Waldo. So, after a year and a half of widowhood, she got a new man.

And now there he was, at the front of the church, stretched out in his favorite—expensive!—gray suit. Sweet, beloved Waldo…the money-eater. *Oh, Waldo, how could everything have gone so wrong so fast?*

It was early January, the beginning of a new year. And what a nightmare year it was promising to be, all because Mom had made her new husband president of their family-owned business. She'd left Samantha as VP in charge of marketing; much good that had done. Now Samantha was VP in charge of disaster and she could hardly sit still thinking of the mess waiting for her back at the office.

"You're fidgeting," whispered her sister Cecily, who was sitting next to her.

Fidgeting at a funeral probably wasn't polite but it was an improvement over standing up, pulling out her hair and shrieking like a madwoman.

Why, oh, why hadn't Mom and Dad done what needed to be done to make sure that if something happened to Dad the business passed into competent hands? Then Mom could have skipped happily off into newlywed bliss, no harm no foul.

None of them had expected her to remain alone forever. She was only in her fifties when Dad died and she didn't function well alone.

When Waldo arrived on the scene she came back to life, and Samantha had been happy for her. He was fun and charming, and she and her sisters gave him a hearty thumbs-up. Why not? He'd brought back Mom's smile. At first everyone got along well. Like Samantha, he'd been a shutterbug and they'd enjoyed talking photography. Her favorite joke when she'd stop by the house to talk business with Mom (or try, anyway) was to ask, "Where's Waldo?"

But once Mom dropped him on the company like a bomb, Samantha didn't have to ask. She knew where Waldo was. He was at the office, in over his head and making her crazy.

She ground her teeth as she mentally tallied how much money he'd squandered: new business cards with his name on them, new stationery, new equipment they hadn't needed, a fancy phone system they couldn't afford that a slick-tongued sales rep had talked him into buying. How could a businessman be so bad at business? Of course he'd convinced both himself and Mom that every purchase was necessary, and Samantha hadn't had the veto power to stop him.

That had been just the beginning. Six months ago

their profits sank and they started having trouble paying their suppliers. Waldo cut back on production, which then affected their ability to fill orders, and Lizzy, their bookkeeper, began looking as if she'd been invited to dinner with the grim reaper. "We're behind on our IRS quarterlies," she'd informed Samantha. "And that's not all." She showed Samantha expenditures on the company credit card that made no sense. A gun. Ammunition. Cases and cases of bottled water, enough to keep the whole town hydrated. Waldo was a financial locust, devouring the company.

Where's Waldo? Busy dumping their lives in the toilet. *Flush, flush, flush!* She could have happily stuffed his head in a toilet and—

"And I believe that if Waldo could speak to us now he'd say, 'Thank God for a life well-lived,'" Pastor Jim said.

Her mother let out a sob and Samantha felt a pang of guilt. She should be crying, too. She'd liked Waldo. He'd been a man with a big heart and a big appetite for life.

"We know he'll be missed," Pastor Jim was saying, and Cecily laid a comforting hand on Mom's arm. That, of course, gave Mom permission to start crying in earnest.

"Poor Mom," whispered Bailey, who was sitting on the other side of Samantha. "First Dad and now Waldo."

Losing two husbands—talk about a double whammy. Mom had not only loved both her husbands, she'd loved being married. She had no head for business (which probably explained why Grandpa had been perfectly happy to let Dad run Sweet Dreams), but she had a gift for relationships. She'd even had a couple of relationship books published with a small publisher and before

Waldo died she'd been about to start on a new book, *Secrets of a Happy Remarriage*.

Samantha hoped that now Mom would turn her attention to learning how to have a happy life—with *no* marriage. At least, no marriage until they could get the business off the critical-care list and Samantha was put officially in charge.

The sooner, the better. Her first order of business would be to rehire Lizzy, who Waldo had fired in a misbegotten attempt to economize. She only hoped Lizzy would come back and help her sort through this mess.

She heaved a sigh. Here her mother was grieving and all she could think about was saving the family business. What was wrong with her? Did she have a calculator for a heart?

"Now I'd like to give the rest of you a chance to say something about Waldo," Pastor Jim said.

He made me nuts probably wouldn't cut it. Samantha stayed seated.

Lots of other people were happy to oblige, though.

"He was the most generous man I ever met," said Maria Gomez, his regular waitress at Zelda's. "He gave me two hundred dollars to get my car fixed. Just like that. Said not to worry about paying him back."

Samantha pressed her lips firmly together and envisioned hundred-dollar bills with wings flying away, circling ever upward and off toward Sleeping Lady Mountain.

You do have a calculator for a heart. People were talking about how nice Waldo had been, and all she could think about was money. She was a terrible person, a terrible, terrible person. She hadn't always been like that, had she? A tear slipped from a corner of her eye.

Ed York, owner of D'Vine Wines, stood. "I can still

remember sitting with Waldo out on his deck, looking at the mountains, sharing a bottle of wine, and him saying, 'You know, Ed, it doesn't get any better than this.' That Waldo, he sure knew how to enjoy life."

While everyone around him was pulling out their hair.

"He was a dear soul," old Mrs. Nilsen said. "Last month he stopped in the freezing cold to change my tire when I had a flat on Highway 2."

On and on went the praise. Good, old, wonderful Waldo. Everyone here would miss him—except his rotten, ungrateful, Scrooge-in-drag, calculator-for-a-heart stepdaughter. She was pathetic. Another tear sneaked out of her eye and trickled down her cheek.

Pastor Jim finally called a halt to the festivities and the party made its way under cloudy skies to Festival Hall, where everyone could mingle, sing Waldo's praises further and devour cold cuts and potato salad. Inside, the three sisters smiled and commiserated.

Waldo's brother and his daughter, Wanda, had flown in from the East Coast. Taking in the woman's red eyes as she approached, Samantha managed to find empathy in the swirl of guilt and resentment and frustration she was experiencing

"I'm sorry we're having to see each other again in such sad circumstances," Wanda said.

"So are we," Cecily told her.

"I'm sorry for your loss," Samantha added. And she was. She knew how horrible it was to lose a father and she wouldn't wish that on her worst enemy.

Wanda dabbed at her eyes with a soggy tissue. "I can't believe he's gone. He was the best father. And he was always so positive, so upbeat."

So clueless. "I wish we could turn back the clock," Samantha said.

Wanda sniffed and nodded. "You were all so good to him."

Samantha couldn't think of anything to say to that. She hardly wanted to confess that during the past few months she'd been anything but good.

Cecily stepped into the gap. "He was a nice man."

True. He was just a bad businessman.

"He sure loved Muriel," Wanda said. "He was so lonely after Mother died. Muriel gave him a new lease on life."

"And I don't know what her life would've been like without him," Samantha said.

"I think Muriel would like to hear that, Wanda," murmured Waldo's brother, Walter, as he led their long-distance stepsister away.

"I need a drink," Samantha said.

"Great idea," Bailey agreed, and they all drifted over to the punch bowl.

Samantha really wasn't much of a drinker, but a good stiff belt sure seemed to help a lot of movie characters through stressful moments and right about now she was willing to give it a try. "I wish this was spiked," she muttered.

Bailey looked across the room at their mother. "I feel so bad for Mom."

Muriel Sterling-Wittman sat on a folding chair framed by the weak winter light coming through the window behind her, a beautiful tragic figure starting the new year alone. Her basic black dress discreetly draped her Betty Boop curves and her hair was still the same shiny chestnut it had been when Samantha was a girl, courtesy of the geniuses at Sleeping Lady Salon. The green eyes

Waldo once raved about were bloodshot from crying but still looked lovely thanks to lashes thick with waterproof mascara. Half the men in the room were hovering around with tissues in case she found herself in need.

"Well, at least we won't have to worry about her being lonely," Bailey said. She was the spitting image of their mother and the most like her, as well—sweet, positive and naive.

Cecily gave a cynical snort. "Much good any of those men will do her. They're all married."

"Not Ed," Bailey pointed out.

"He's got the hots for Pat over at the bookstore," Samantha said, and mentally added, *Thank God.*

"Arnie's not married," Bailey said. "Neither is Mayor Stone. Or Waldo's brother. Wouldn't it be sweet if—"

Samantha cut her off. "Let's not even put that thought out in the universe." All they needed was another man coming along and convincing Mom that the third time would be the charm.

"Look at them. Waldo's barely gone and they're already circling around her like some old-guy version of *The Bachelor.*" Cecily shook her head. "Men."

"You know, for a matchmaker you sure have a sucky attitude," Bailey observed.

"Where do you think I got it?" Cecily retorted.

"How do you manage to stay in business?" Bailey asked in disgust.

"By staying superficial." Cecily gave them a wicked grin.

Cecily was the only blonde in the family and she was the prettiest of them all with perfect features and the longest legs. Samantha had been cute with her red hair and freckles, but it was Cecily the boys drooled over. Still, in spite of her good looks, Cupid had never been kind to her. So far she'd gone through two fiancés. Samantha didn't understand how Cecily could make money matching up beautiful people in L.A. but couldn't seem to get it right when it came to her own love life.

Like you're doing so well?

Touché, she told her snarky self.

"You're enough to make a woman give up on love," Bailey muttered as she nodded and smiled politely at old Mr. Nilsen, who was ogling her from the other side of the hall.

"That would be the smart thing to do," Cecily said.

"Well, I don't think Mom's ready to give up on love. Maybe you could match her up with someone," Bailey suggested.

"No!" Several people turned to stare and Samantha downed a slug of punch in an effort to put out the fire in her cheeks. What was wrong with her? Could a woman suddenly get Tourette's at thirty?

The wicked in Cecily's grin kicked up a notch. "I know what you mean. No one will ever be able to replace Waldo."

"I liked Waldo, I really did," Samantha said. "But no more men. I've got enough to deal with already."

"Gosh, Sammy." Bailey frowned at her.

Samantha frowned back. "Hey, baby sister, you two get to go back to sunny California and match up lonely millionaires and cater events for starlets. I'm the one stuck with the fallout here."

Cecily sobered. "I'm sorry. You're right. We're leaving you with a mess. You've got the business to sort out, plus Mom's affairs."

"Except if anyone can do it, you can, Sammy," Bailey said, linking arms with her.

Samantha sighed. As the oldest it was her job to be

the rock everyone leaned on—although right now she didn't feel like a rock. She felt like a pebble on a beach about to be swept away by a tsunami.

And her own mother had been the one to unwittingly drop her there. She and Muriel loved each other dearly, but they often disagreed. And before Waldo died they'd disagreed a lot, especially when Samantha tried to get her mother to talk sense into him.

"He's not feeling well," Mom kept saying, but when pressed for details she'd remained vague.

Maybe the poor guy's heart had been acting up all along. Maybe he'd been so worried about his bad health he hadn't been able to concentrate and that was why he'd made such poor decisions. Except that didn't explain his odd purchases. Or the answers he'd given her when she asked about them.

"A man needs to be able to protect what's his," he'd said when she'd questioned him about the gun.

"In Icicle Falls?" she'd countered. The biggest crime they'd had all year was when Amanda Stevens keyed Jimmy Rodriguez's Jeep after he'd cheated on her with another girl. And Jimmy hadn't pressed charges.

"You never know," Waldo had hedged. "I saw someone. In the parking lot."

"Doing what?" she'd asked.

"He was following me. And don't tell your mother," he'd said. "I don't want to worry her."

Like he'd just worried his stepdaughter? Then there'd been the water.

"We could have an avalanche and be trapped here for days," he'd said.

She'd let that slide, too. Until things started getting really bad. And then, just when she'd decided she and her mother would need to have a very unpleasant conversation, Waldo had walked from their house on Alpine Drive into town and keeled over dead right in front of Lupine Floral. Poor Kevin had dropped the roses he'd been storing in the cooler and run out to give him CPR while his partner, Heinrich, called 9-1-1, but Waldo was dead within minutes.

And now she was stuck dealing with the mess he'd left behind. Her sisters were leaving on Monday and she was the one who'd be dealing with their mother and figuring out how to pay the people who depended on Sweet Dreams for their livelihood. Great-grandma Rose, who'd started this business on a dream, was probably turning in her grave at what her descendants had done to it.

Samantha frowned at her half-empty punch cup. *The glass is half empty...the glass is half full.* Either way, "This stuff needs booze."

Two

Your biggest asset is your family.
—Muriel Sterling, *Mixing Business with Pleasure:*
How to Successfully Balance Work and Love

Two hours later, friends and extended relatives had exhausted themselves on the topic of Waldo and consumed all the potato salad and cold cuts. The party was over. Sent on their way with one final hug from Olivia Wallace and a paper plate containing half a dozen lemon bars, the three sisters and their mother stepped outside to a cold, cloudless night.

Mom looked as drained as Samantha felt. Only Mom's exhaustion was from pure grief. Samantha's was contaminated by a less pure mixture of feelings.

"I'll follow you guys back to the house," she said, and went in search of her car.

It was now five-thirty on a Friday afternoon and the old-fashioned lampposts along Center Street stood sentinel over a downtown shopping area about to go to sleep for the night. Nearby restaurants like Zelda's and Schwangau would open for business, but here, on what the locals dubbed Tourist Street, the shops were closed and only a smattering of cars remained.

Samantha loved their little downtown, its park with the gazebo and multitude of flower beds, its cobbled streets edged with quaint shops, the mountains standing guard over it. Normally this time of year the mountains would have worn a thick blanket of snow, and both cross-country and downhill skiers, as well as snowboarders, would be in town for the weekend, shopping, eating in the restaurants, enjoying the little outdoor skating rink and admiring the Bavarian architecture. But these days there were few visitors. It had been a lean year for snow. Heck, it had been a lean year, period, and several once-thriving shops were now shuttered.

Businesses going under—don't even think about that.

Too late. That was all it took to make her angry once more about her own company's troubles and she had to remind herself that her world, unlike her mother's, had not come to an end. Somehow she'd manage to pull the business from the brink but Mom would never have her husband back. This was the second one she'd lost in five years. What was that like, to be in love and happy and lose it all not once but twice? Samantha thought back to her own romantic troubles and realized she had no point of reference. She could only imagine.

She needed to be a supportive daughter, lock any negative thoughts inside her head and keep her big mouth shut. *Mouth shut, mouth shut, mouth shut.* She chanted it for the last several steps to her car. Then she got in, closed the door and said it one more time. "Mouth shut." Okay. She was ready.

She got to the house to find Cecily starting a fire in the big stone fireplace, the sound of crackling cedar already filling the great room. Bailey was arranging cards along the mantelpiece where Waldo's ashes reposed in a brass urn, while in the kitchen Mom made tea. The plate of lemon bars sat on the granite countertop. It was a regular postwake party.

Bailey turned at the sound of the door and knocked

the urn, making it wobble and their mother gasp. Fortunately, Cecily grabbed it before it could tip.

"Sorry," Bailey said.

Mom shot a look heavenward. "Put him on the hearth, honey."

Cecily nodded solemnly and moved Waldo to safety.

Samantha shed her coat and hung it in the closet, then forced herself to walk to the kitchen and ask her mother if she needed help.

Mom shook her head, her gaze riveted on the mugs lined up in front of her on the counter. "Would you like some tea?"

The offer came out stiffly. No surprise. The way they'd been not getting along lately, she could almost envision her mother lacing hers with arsenic. "No. Thanks."

She suddenly longed for the comfort of her little one-bedroom condo at the edge of town, where she'd find no emotional undercurrents and the new man in her life would be waiting to welcome her—Nibs, her cat. Everyone would be fine here without her. Mom had Cecily and Bailey to keep her company and listen to her Waldo stories. And they could do it guilt-free.

"I think I'll take off."

"Stay for a little while," Mom said.

Or not. Samantha nodded and went to slump on the couch.

"Tea is ready," Mom announced. Cecily and Bailey both picked up their mugs and returned to join their sister, Cecily taking up a position on the couch next to Samantha and Bailey settling on the hearth beside Waldo.

Mom followed and sat on the yellow leather chair she always read in. She took a sip of her tea, then set the mug on the coffee table, laid back her head and sighed

deeply. "I just want you girls to know how much I've appreciated the moral support. I still can't wrap my mind
around the fact that Waldo is gone."

"He'll be missed," Bailey said.

"Yes, he will," Mom agreed, giving Samantha a look
that dared her to say any different.

No way was she taking that dare. "I need a lemon
bar," she muttered.

"Never mind that. Let's get the hard stuff," Cecily
said. "Break out the chocolate."

But there wasn't so much as a shaving of chocolate in
the house. Mom had gone on a binge. So Bailey stayed
with her while Samantha and Cecily made a run to the
shop.

Sweet Dreams Chocolate Company occupied prime
real estate a few streets back from Center Street on a
block the locals nicknamed Foodie Paradise. Across
from them was Gingerbread Haus, Cassandra Wilkes's
fantasy bakery, specializing in fanciful baked goods. At
Christmas she was swamped with orders for her gingerbread houses and shipped them all over the world. Next
to that was the Spice Rack, which carried every exotic
spice known to man. Every time the door opened, the
scent of lavender or sage drifted out to tickle noses and
tempt shoppers inside, and whenever she was in town
Bailey practically lived there. On the other side of Gingerbread Haus sat Bavarian Brews, where everyone went
to chitchat and indulge in great coffee—very convenient
when Samantha needed a quick pick-me-up. Down the
street they could see Schwangan's, a five-star restaurant and another popular destination. Its owner and head
chef, Franz Reinholdt, made a mean schnitzel.

The Sterlings had the biggest piece of land, though—
so far, anyway—and an inspiring view, with their

second-story offices looking down on the town from one side and out over the Wenatchee River from the other. The factory and retail store occupied a full block. The warehouse, part of the company's pre-Waldo expansion, occupied another. It should have been full of a lot more supplies and inventory than it currently was. Sigh.

Samantha unlocked the store, flipped on the light and turned off the alarm as Cecily strolled in.

"Sometimes I miss this place," Cecily said, taking in the gift shop with its various shelves and display tables of treats. There was plenty to drool over—goodie bags of enrobed fruit, chocolate-dipped apples, potato chips and cookies, boxes of mixed chocolates, gift boxes of salted caramels, cognac truffles made from Great-grandma Rose's secret recipe, fudge and hot fudge sauces (Mom's contribution to the line) that ranged from spicy Mexican to chocolate mint. Over in the corner under the TV that played a video feed of the gang in the factory hard at work, shoppers could find all manner of nonedible goodies, including candy dishes, chocolate scented candles, little kitchen signs with chick-centric statements like "The Best Kisses Are Chocolate" and "I'd Give Up Chocolate but I'm No Quitter."

"You can take the girl out of the chocolate company but you can't take the chocolate out of the girl," Samantha teased, snagging a box of truffles and walking over to the cash register. "Have you got any money? All I have on me is a five." And she was lucky to have that.

Her sister looked at her in shock. "Since when do we have to pay?"

"Since we went broke." Samantha held out a hand, palm up.

Cecily frowned and dug out her wallet. "I have to pay for chocolate from my own company? This sucks."

"Welcome to my world."

"Keep the change," Cecily said, and handed over a twenty.

"Thanks. I will."

"It really is bad, isn't it?"

"No," Samantha said firmly. Maybe if she said it enough she'd believe it.

As a little girl she'd loved hearing the stories of how Great-grandma Rose started the company in her kitchen, of the recipes that literally came to her in her dreams, how she and her husband, Dusty, used their life's savings to buy this piece of land and build a modest shop back when Icicle Falls was nothing but a rough-and-tumble collection of mismatched buildings. Sweet Dreams wasn't just a company. It was a family legend. It was also a source of income for thirty families and she was going to pull them out of this tailspin no matter what it took.

Cecily leaned on the counter and gave her an assessing stare. "Are you lying to me?"

"Yes, but things could be worse. We still have inventory." Samantha stowed away the money, then opened the box, pulled out a truffle and popped it in her mouth. It hit her taste buds like a drug and she let the sweetness travel over her tongue. She could almost feel a troupe of endorphins doing a happy dance through her body. A girl could bite off even the biggest challenge if it was coated in chocolate.

"So what are we going to do besides eat the inventory?" Cecily asked.

Cecily had been the one dissenting voice way back when they'd talked about taking out a loan and expanding the company, ignoring both Samantha's charts and

Dad's confidence. At the time Samantha had accused her of a lack of vision.

That was both ironic and stupid, she now had to admit, since Cecily had uncanny instincts. In high school she could always sense a surprise quiz lurking around the corner, and she knew when her sisters were going to break up with their boyfriends long before they ever had a clue. After Dad died, she'd predicted Mom would be remarried within the year. She'd only been off by a few months.

But when it came to business Samantha had prided herself on her expertise and bulldozed over all objections, dreaming big and ready to gamble big, and Dad had backed her. Now, between her ambition and the disaster that was Waldo, she was in danger of losing big. Her father's confidence had been sadly misplaced. Suddenly the box of truffles was looking all wavy, like they were underwater. She blinked and a tear dropped on the counter.

She felt a hand on her shoulder. "Hey, it's okay," Cecily said. "You'll sort things out. I know you will."

Samantha rolled her eyes. "Do you really believe that or are you trying to make me feel good?"

"A little of both. Meanwhile, though, maybe you could talk to Arnie over at the bank, see what he can do?"

"Arnie's on his way out."

Cecily blinked. "What?"

"I heard Cascade Mutual is bringing in a new manager. I have no idea what that person will be like." Maybe he'd turn out to be as nice as Arnie. She could hope. But realistically, she suspected that the good old days of having a community bank that cared were gone. Arnie had cared a little *too* much, which had a lot to do with why the bank was under new management.

Cecily twirled a lock of blond hair. "Maybe I could get a loan."

"No," Samantha said. "We could be on the *Titanic* here and if we are, I don't want you going down with us."

"We're family and this is a family business. We stick together. Remember?"

"Thanks." Her sister's words were comforting, but when it came right down to it, Samantha was both captain and crew of this ship and steering clear of disaster was going to be her responsibility.

"I'm sure I could come up with something," Cecily insisted.

L.A. was not a cheap place to live and do business, and Samantha had no intention of saddling her sister with a big chunk of debt. Anyway, Cecily would never be able to come up with the kind of money they needed. "I'll manage."

"You always do, but I just want you to know that you don't have to do this alone. After all, I still owe you for stealing your diary," Cecily said with a smile.

Samantha couldn't help smiling, too, at the memory of finding her sister reading her deepest twelve-year-old thoughts to her friends. Pretty darned funny now. Not so much at the time. "You were lucky you lived to see middle school."

Cecily sobered. "I want to do something to earn my share of the profits when they start coming in again."

"If I think of something, I'll let you know," Samantha told her, but they both knew she didn't really mean it. She'd already had one person—Waldo—"helping" and that was enough for a lifetime.

Cecily reopened the box and bit into a truffle, then

offered another to Samantha. "I know things will turn around."

"I hope you know as much as you think you know," Samantha said. Otherwise… Oh, no. She wasn't going down that rocky road. Not yet, anyway.

Three

Always stop and think before you act. This is the
first rule of good relationships and good business.
—Muriel Sterling, *Mixing Business with Pleasure:
How to Successfully Balance Business and Love*

It was Monday, and all was quiet now that the girls
were gone. In a way Muriel relished the solitude. It gave
her a chance to grieve freely. But the house seemed so
empty and she felt so alone. Her daughters had lives of
their own to return to, though, and she couldn't blame
them for running off. It certainly wasn't any fun being
with her. She hadn't even made them breakfast before
Samantha took them to the airport.

Muriel poured herself a mug of tea and padded bare-
foot over to her picture window to gaze at the winter
scene outside. Fir and pine trees shook off a thin blanket of snow too wet to stick. The houses on her block sat
empty and unlit, waiting for their owners, who all had
lives, to return. A truck sloshed down the street, making only a momentary dent in the smothering silence.

Okay, she'd seen enough. She got her tea and went
back to bed, placing the mug on the nightstand for easy
access. Even though she was wearing a sweater over her
favorite silk pajamas the bed still felt cold. Both her husbands had been bed hogs, especially Waldo. He not only
slept diagonally, every time he rolled over he pulled the

covers with him like a giant ebb tide. It used to irritate her no end. No ebb tide now.

Hot tears pricked her eyes. Hard to believe she had any left after the past week. She wiped them away and took a determined sip of tea. "You can't just stay in bed all day," she told herself.

And then argued back. "Why not?" Who cared whether she stayed in bed or got up?

She was alone again.

Oh, stop, she scolded herself. *Waldo's sudden death was a blessing. Would you have wanted him to suffer?*

The answer, of course, was no.

With that settled in her mind (for today, anyway), she drank some more tea and surveyed the room like a pioneer checking out new territory. What to do in this new territory? Where to start?

Normally by ten o'clock in the morning she'd already be hard at work on her next book for Mountain Crest Publications, a small Pacific Northwest publisher. She hadn't made much money as a writer but she'd enjoyed the experience. It held no appeal for her now, though, not when she was back in this dark place.

Those months after Stephen died had been a nightmare, even worse than losing either of her parents—and she'd thought nothing could top that. Widowhood went beyond loneliness. It cut off half your soul.

Now, going through it again so soon was more than she could handle. All she could do was drift through the house like a wraith. With no one to cook for she had no interest in food, not even chocolate, the family's lifeblood. Planning Waldo's funeral had been torture. Walking past his desk and seeing all those bills had been terrifying. She had no head for money and math was a mystery, one she'd never needed to solve. After all, she'd had Stephen. When he died the only thing that kept her from throwing herself (or at least her checkbook) off Sleeping Lady Mountain had been the patient helpfulness of Arnie at Cascade Mutual.

She'd breathed a sigh of relief when Waldo rode into her life like a knight on a white horse, but he'd gone out like Don Quixote and here she was again, lost and adrift. Why Waldo, of all people? He'd been so sweet, and his laugh—everyone, including her, had loved to hear him laugh. Without him the house was a tomb and she felt numb. And the book she'd been working on was as dead as her husband.

Her editor had wanted Muriel to capitalize on her chocolate connection more than she had in her previous books and had urged her to do a cookbook featuring chocolate recipes. She'd resisted. She'd been so happy with Waldo she'd wanted to write about how to start over again. She couldn't write about that now. She couldn't write. Period.

She set the mug on the nightstand and slipped under the covers. Cocooned beneath her down comforter, she eventually drifted off to sleep and found Waldo.

But he wasn't the only one keeping her company in her dreams. Stephen showed up, too, and there they were, all at a dance at Festival Hall, dressed in German attire.

She had just danced with Stephen, who looked dashing in lederhosen, and now Waldo was sweeping her away in a polka. "Come on, Muriel, old girl, let's have fun. Life is short."

Suddenly the doors to the hall blew open and a swirling black tornado entered the room, whisking Muriel off her feet and separating her from him. Salted caramels swirled all around her and she kept grabbing for them, but she couldn't catch even one. And now the wind was whooshing her out the door. "No, I'm not ready to leave!"

Muriel's eyes popped open. It took her a second to realize she was home in bed with late-afternoon shadows sprawled across the bedspread. She couldn't have slept the day away. She looked at the clock. It was going on four. She had.

And what had that strange dream been about? What was her subconscious trying to tell her? Maybe that she was going insane.

Bailey gave Samantha one more hug and then followed Cecily into Sea-Tac Airport to catch their late-afternoon flight to L.A.

Once through the sliding glass doors both sisters turned and waved a final goodbye. She waved back and swallowed a lump in her throat. Not for the first time she wished they lived closer, but a girl had to follow her dreams. It was too bad their dreams had led them all in different directions.

She heaved a sigh, then got in her trusty Toyota and began the two-hour drive back to the other side of the mountains. She'd barely get home in time to bake cookies before going to hang out with her other sisters, sisters of the heart. Monday wasn't normally a party night but tonight was an exception.

Back home, Samantha baked up the cookie dough Bailey had left in her freezer. Then she pulled on her down coat and her winter boots and walked the short distance from her condo to her friend Charley's snug little house, which overlooked Icicle Creek. A moonlit sky speckled with stars lit her way, but she could have found the house just as easily by following the noise. A soundtrack of Gloria Gaynor singing "I Will Survive" was blasting an accompaniment to raucous laughter. Obviously the party was in full swing.

She walked around to the back of the house. The deck was lit with several strings of pink flamingo party lights. Patio chairs sprawled every which way and a picnic table was laden with salads and desserts. But the action was taking place around the fire pit on the lawn, and in the center of it all stood Charlene Albach. Charley, a slender woman in her mid-thirties with dark hair cut in a messy bob, looked fashionable in jeans, ankle boots and a faux-fur-trimmed jacket. She was holding what had to be the world's largest wineglass and dumping a handful of photos onto a roaring bonfire.

"Samantha, get yourself down here," she called. "We're burning weenies."

The symbolism wasn't lost on Samantha and she smiled as she put her cookies on the table. She plucked one off the plate and then walked down to join the group of women gathered around the fire. One she recognized as Charley's older sister, Amy, who had come up from Portland for the occasion. And there was Elena, Samantha's loyal secretary; Lauren, her teller from the bank; her pal Cassandra Wilkes from Gingerbread Haus; Heidi Schwartz, who worked part-time in the Sweet Dreams gift shop; and Rita Reyes and Maria Gomez, who worked for Charley at her restaurant, Zelda's—all present to help Charley celebrate her first official day of freedom. Earlier that morning Charley's divorce had become final.

She set aside her glass and handed Samantha a hot dog skewered on a stainless-steel toasting fork. "Welcome to the celebration. Have a dick-on-a-stick."

From their side of the fire Rita and Maria laughed

uproariously. "I need more wine," Rita said. "Can I get you some?" she asked Samantha.

Samantha didn't have much of a palate for wine. She shook her head. "Nah, I'm good."

"You have to drink something. We're going to be toasting my future, you know," Charley said. "Get her some of that ChocoVine. It tastes just like Baileys. You'll like it," she informed Samantha. "Trust me."

"'Trust me'—isn't that what worthless old Richard said to you?" quipped her sister.

Charley scowled. "Yes, he did." She picked up more pictures of her ex and sprinkled them over the fire. "Here, baby, make yourself useful."

All the women sent up a cheer, including Samantha. Even as she did, she thought of her mother, probably sitting home in that yellow leather chair of hers, wishing Waldo was still alive. But there was leaving and there was leaving. Waldo hadn't left voluntarily. Richard had opted for a dishonorable discharge from marriage, taking off with the hostess from Zelda's.

Either way, though, both women had wound up on their own. When it came right down to it, Samantha concluded, the one person a girl could count on was herself.

"So," Cass said, raising her glass after Rita had returned to the fire. "To a new and better future for our girl here."

"To a new and better future," they all echoed and drank.

"And to never having to watch another football game," Cass added.

"I'll drink to that," said Maria. "My boyfriend." She rolled her eyes. "One of these days he's going to turn into a football."

"Better than turning into a cheater." Charley threw

another pile of photos on the fire. "I am so glad I found out what kind of man Richard really was before I wasted another twelve years on him."

"Twelve years is a long time," Amy said.

For a moment Charley's eyes glistened with tears but she lifted her chin and said, "Too long, and I'm not wasting so much as a minute missing that man. He can have his new woman and his new restaurant in the city. Seattle's loss is my gain. *And* I have the bed all to myself now."

"I'm jealous," her sister murmured.

"I can watch as many episodes of *What Not to Wear* as I want," Charlie continued, "leave the dishes in the sink and spend my money however I decide. And I bet I've lost more weight than anyone here."

"You do look great," Samantha agreed.

"You would, too, if you'd lost a hundred and fifty-five pounds of dead weight," Charley cracked, "and good riddance."

"You know, I never liked him," Cass said.

"Me, neither," Charley's sister threw in.

"Why didn't you guys say something?" Charley demanded. "No, never mind, don't answer that. I probably wouldn't have listened."

"Love is blind," Cass said. "And dumb."

As the night went on the women shared memories, collecting evidence that Richard the defector was indeed nothing but a rat. The wine flowed and the party got increasingly loud, especially when Charley cranked up the CD and the women started singing at the top of their lungs to "Before He Cheats," "Over It" and "I Can Do Better."

Finally a neighbor a couple of houses away hollered, "Shut up over there," and everyone giggled.

The food and drink was consumed and the fire had flickered down to embers and the women remembered they had to work the following day. Charley smiled around the circle at all of them. "Thanks for coming, you guys, and for helping me feel positive about the future."

"You're always positive about the future," Heidi said. "I'm not sure I could be if I was in your shoes."

Samantha doubted Heidi—with a husband who adored her and an adorable baby—would ever have to worry about that.

Charley managed a shrug. "There were a few times this past year when I didn't feel very positive at all. But you know what? I'm taking back my life. I've got a lot of years ahead of me and I intend to enjoy every one of them."

"You think you'll ever get married again?" Heidi asked.

Charley made a cross with her fingers as if warding off a vampire. "Bite your tongue."

"You might want somebody around to bite yours once in a while." Rita laughed. "Or other parts of you."

"Men are still good for some things," Elena put in. "In fact, they're good for a lot of things. You shouldn't give up on all of them just because you got a bad one."

"Yes," said Lauren, who was dating Joe Coyote, the nicest man in town.

"Well, when you find a good one, let me know and I'll take him—to the cleaner's." Charley's comment made everyone laugh. "Seriously," she added, "love's a gamble, and I'm done gambling."

"Heck, all of life's a gamble," Samantha said.

Charley gave her a one-armed hug. "You're right. But I'm going to make sure the deck's stacked in my favor, so from now on I'll just keep men as friends."

"Friends with benefits?" Rita teased as they tossed the last of the paper plates on the embers.

"Maybe." Charley shrugged. "Who knows what the future holds. I'm open to anything but marriage."

"But don't you want kids?" Heidi asked.

Samantha thought of Elena's handicapped daughter and the baby Rita had lost last year. Parenthood could be as risky as marriage.

"I don't need a man to have children," Charley said. "That's why there's adoption. Meanwhile, you'll share James, right? I'll be his Aunt Charley and spoil him rotten."

Baby-sharing. It saved a girl from those pesky little complications, like men. And childbirth. Still, it wasn't the same as having a child of your own.

As Samantha walked home she had plenty to think about. Did she ever want to try and have a serious relationship? Her parents had had a great marriage. It could be done. Every man out there wasn't a Waldo or a Richard. And just because she'd picked one Mr. Wrong didn't mean she couldn't find Mr. Right. Although she was beginning to wonder what the odds of that were. She hadn't dated anyone since college who even qualified as Mr. Maybe. Sheesh.

Look at it this way, she told herself. *Your life has nowhere to go but up.*

Or not. At the office the next morning Samantha ground her teeth as she sat at Waldo's old desk, which was now going to be hers, and sorted through a mountain of papers in preparation for meeting with Lizzy, who had, thank God, consented to return. There was the mock-up for their spring catalog that he'd insisted on looking at three weeks ago and then ignored. And what did he need with a week's worth of old newspapers? In another pile she found several threatening letters from suppliers who hadn't been paid. She'd have to start calling them this afternoon, explain about Waldo's death and beg for mercy. Oh, and here was a week-old invitation from Cascade Mutual to come to their open house and meet the new manager, Blake Preston, who, according to the invite, was anxious to assist her in any way he could.

Blake Preston? The former football hero of Icicle Falls High? He'd been four years ahead of her in school and she'd been too young for his crowd, but it was a small school and everyone knew everyone. He'd winked at her a few times when they'd passed in the hall, like that was supposed to make her day. It had.

Yes, good old Blake had been a player both on and off the field. But how the heck had he wound up as a bank manager? Banking and football didn't exactly go hand in hand.

She frowned, remembering the jocks she'd shared classes with as a college business major, not to mention the one she almost married. Guys like that spent more time studying their playbooks than listening to what the professor had to say in lecture hall. Some of those doofs should never have been given a business degree, but they'd gotten one, anyway. Her doof not only got a degree, he'd dumped her and gotten the richest girl in their graduating class. (And a cushy job with Daddy, too.) Thank God she'd gone out of state for her college education. At least she'd never have to see him and Mrs. Doof again. Wherever he'd ended up, he was probably busy ignoring his company to play golf and lunch with his old frat buddies.

So what old frat buddy had given Blake Preston entrée into the world of banking? Whoever it was, he hadn't done Icicle Falls any favor. She tossed the invite in the wastebasket and kept digging.

One more layer of paper down she found a ticking time bomb—another piece of correspondence from the bank, this one not so nice. Her heart shifted into overdrive and she fell back against Waldo's big leather chair, sure she was going to have a heart attack. There, under the Cascade Mutual letterhead, was a cold but polite missive informing her stepfather that Sweet Dreams was behind on its loan payment. "As you are aware"—were they?—"Cascade Mutual Bank has a strict ninety-day grace period regarding overdue installment payments. This grace period has expired on your note in the amount of…"

Ooooh. The numbers danced in front of her eyes like tiny demons. No, this couldn't be happening! She read on.

"Because Sweet Dreams Chocolates and Cascade Mutual Bank have a long-standing relationship, we are extending the grace period until February 28, at which time the aforementioned amount is due in full. It is hoped this matter can be resolved as soon as possible."

Only if she started printing money in the basement. What in the name of Godiva was she going to do?

Hyperventilate! A bag, where was a bag? She couldn't breathe. She was going to be sick. She needed chocolate! Her cell phone rang. The ring tone—Gwen Stefani's "Sweet Escape"—told her it was Cecily and she grabbed it like a lifeline. "Cec, we… Oh, I'm going to pass out. Where's a bag?" She rifled through desk drawers, but came up all she came up with was an old cigar, paper clips, rubber bands and—what was this? A stress ball. She scooped it up and strangled it.

"What's wrong?"

"We— The bank. Oh, my God, I can't believe this!" Samantha wailed, and burst into tears.

Now she'd made so much noise that Elena had rushed into the office. "What's going on?" One look at Samantha and the blood drained from her face. *"Madre de Dios."*

"Get me chocolate," Samantha panted, and squeezed the stress ball again. These things were useless. She threw it across the room and grabbed a fistful of hair as Elena rushed off to find a dose of restorative chocolate.

"Sam, tell me what's going on," Cecily demanded.

"The bank is calling in their note. As if everything wasn't already enough of a mess. As if we didn't already owe the whole friggin' world! My God, what did I ever do to deserve this? Is it because I bossed you guys around when we were little? I'm sorry. And I shouldn't have stood up Tony Barrone for homecoming. No, that's not it. It's because I yelled at Waldo."

"Sam, please," Cecily pleaded. "You're scaring me."

Be afraid. Be very afraid. What old movie was that from? Probably one where everybody died.

Samantha laid her head on the desk and pulled a newspaper over her. Now she understood why the groundhog went back underground when it saw its shadow. She wished she could dig a hole and pull it in after herself and never come out.

From a distance her sister called, "Sam? Sam!"

"I give up," she moaned, pulling the phone under her paper tent and back to her ear. "I surrender. Match me up with a millionaire. I just want to lie around on a yacht somewhere in the Mediterranean and drink ChocoVine."

"No, you don't," Cecily said firmly. "You're not wired that way and you'd be bored out of your mind in a week."

"I'm not wired for *this*," Samantha whimpered.

"It's going to be okay."

Elena was back now, slipping an open box of truffles under the newspaper.

"Thank you," Samantha said. She shoved a handful in her mouth.

Elena lifted a corner of the paper and peered under it. "What else do you need?"

"A new life." Samantha pulled the newspaper off her head and forced herself to sit up and push her hair out of her eyes. "I'm fine," she told both Elena and herself. "Just a temporary meltdown."

Her secretary hovered, looking doubtful.

"Really. It's okay." What a big, fat liar she was.

Elena still looked dubious, but she got the hint and left, shutting the door behind her.

Samantha picked up her phone. "Okay. I'm okay now." No, she wasn't. Who was she kidding? Where were they going to get that kind of money?

"Maybe you could go over to the bank and charm the new guy in charge into giving you a little more time," Cecily suggested.

They'd given her a little more time. Very little. "This is business. Charm doesn't enter into it." *Damn.*

"Charm enters into business more than you realize," Cecily said.

Samantha sighed. "You're right. I'll have to go over there and talk to the new manager. Sweet Dreams is a vital part of the town's economy. It's in everyone's interest for the bank to work with us and help us get through this rough patch." That was exactly what she'd say to him. Rules could be bent if everyone benefited in the long run.

She took a deep cleansing breath and told herself she felt better already. *Big, fat liar.*

"There you go," Cecily said encouragingly.

"And I'll take him some of our wares," Samantha decided. "Who doesn't like chocolate?"

"Charm and bribery, a businesswoman's best friends."

Samantha sure hoped so. She thanked her sister for the shrink session, then buzzed Elena on the office phone.

"You okay now?" Elena asked.

"Yes," Samantha lied. "Call down to Luke and tell him to put together the mother of all gift baskets."

At 10:00 a.m. Samantha walked into the bank bearing a cellophane-wrapped basket filled to the brim with goodies from Sweet Dreams Chocolates. If this didn't melt Blake Preston's heart—well, then, he had no heart to melt.

Speaking of, there he sat at the manager's desk in the far corner, a sandy-haired tackling dummy in a suit. Blake Preston looked more suited to a WWE Friday night smack down than to sitting behind a bank manager's desk, deciding the fate of local businesses.

Lauren sent Samantha a welcoming smile from her teller's counter, but the one she got from Blake Preston when he saw her approach his desk wasn't quite so friendly. *Wary* would've been a better word for it. Even wary, it qualified for a toothpaste commercial. Whoa, that was some wattage, and she felt the electricity clear across the room. She couldn't help checking his left hand for signs of a ring as he stood to greet her. None.

Never mind his ring finger or any other part of him. You're here to do business.

She could almost hear her sister whispering in her ear, "Charm enters into business more than you realize."

She donned her most charming smile and said, "Hi," injecting her voice with goodwill. *You like me. You want to give me a longer extension on my loan.* "I'm Samantha Sterling from Sweet Dreams Chocolates. We went to high school together," she added, hoping that would earn her some brownie points.

He held out his hand for her to shake. She took it and felt an even bigger jolt than she'd gotten from his smile. Maybe that was a good sign. Maybe they were going to hit it off. Maybe he'd be happy to grab a mop and help her clean up the mess she was in.

"I remember," he said.

Right. You were older and too busy partying and cutting classes to pay attention to a nerdy underclassman. "I was just a lowly freshman, but you made quite an impression." There, that was pretty darned charming if she did say so herself. "I thought you might enjoy some samples from the best chocolate company in Washington," she said, handing over the gift basket.

He took it and stood there as if uncertain what to do with it. His computer and several piles of papers were taking up all the surface space on his desk. "Well, thanks. That was…nice. Have a seat."

She sat and he sat, still holding the goodies.

"You'll really like the chocolate-covered potato chips," she said, pointing to her basketful of bribes. "Those are our newest product."

"Interesting." He shifted the fortune in chocolate sitting on his lap as awkwardly as though he were an old bachelor who'd just been handed a baby.

Okay, that took care of the charm. Next, she decided to play the sympathy card. "I'm not sure if you're aware of it, but we've had a few challenges in our business. We just lost my stepfather."

"I heard. I'm sorry," he said, and looked properly sympathetic.

"Things have been a little chaotic and then this morning I discovered a letter from you."

He cleared his throat. "I'm afraid we have something of a problem. You're behind on your loan."

As if she wasn't aware of that? As if she hadn't read the friggin' letter? She could feel her blood pressure rising and it took every last ounce of willpower she had to remain professional. "This business has been in my family for a long time. I'm the fourth generation."

"Ms. Sterling. Samantha. I understand what this business must mean to you."

No, you don't. You have no idea. She was probably radiating anger. She tried her best to look charming. "Not just to me. We employ a lot of people, all who have families and live in this town."

"I know that. I grew up here. But—"

Oh, no. Here came the *but.*

"But the kind of leniency the bank indulged in under the previous management is what got them in so much trouble."

"I'm not asking for any more money," she said, keeping her voice low so everyone in this fishbowl wouldn't hear her. "I just need a few months to sort things out. If you could give us a little extra time, extend the loan…"

Now he was shaking his head sadly. "I'm afraid I can't. I'd like to, but I can't. As I said in the letter, Cascade Mutual has a strict ninety-day policy on past-due loans. We've already extended yours until the end of next month."

"I recognize that," she said, and trotted out her most

charming smile, "but surely you can make an exception for extreme circumstances. All we need is another six months while we restructure the company."

"I'm sorry," he said earnestly. "I really am. I wish I could extend the deadline but my hands are tied. You're going to have to come up with that money before the end of February."

"That would take a miracle," she protested.

He heaved those big boulders that passed for shoulders in a helpless shrug. "We've got several churches in town. I think if I were you I'd have them start praying."

She narrowed her eyes at him. "You know, you have a sick sense of humor."

"I wasn't kidding," he said. "I'm sorry. I wish I could help you further but I've got my orders."

What was this, the military? "You're a bank manager," she said between gritted teeth. "You could do some managing and find a way to work with me."

He shook his head. "Don't think I haven't been trying. I'm aware of what your company means to the community and I appreciate your situation."

"I'll just bet," she growled. *Oh, very charming, Samantha.*

Well, who cared? Her ship had already gone down and she was now bobbing in the icy waters of despair. And she'd given him treats to eat while he watched her turn blue. All her business training, all her sister's advice to be charming, fled before her rage. She stood and plucked the basket from his lap.

He blinked in shock. "What—"

"There's no use wasting fine chocolate on those who don't value it enough to want to save it from extinction." And with her peace offering clutched to her chest, she turned and marched out of the bank.

* * *

The gaze of every bank employee was on Blake Preston, making him feel like a cockroach under a magnifying glass. Arnie Amundsen had left him here, an invader in a hostile land.

Of course, no one was overtly hostile. They were all too glad to have jobs for that. But he could sense his unpopularity from the polite yet lukewarm reception he'd been given, from the looks, sometimes thoughtful *(What the hell are you doing here?)*, sometimes resentful *(Who asked you to come back and meddle in our business?)*. He was there to get them out of the disaster their beloved Arnie had created. And if he hadn't come to meddle in their business, they wouldn't have a business, damn it! He knew it and they knew it. They just resented it.

And *he* resented the quickly snuffed snicker he'd heard in one corner of the room, the way Lauren Belgado over at her teller's counter swallowed her serves-him-right smirk and went back to serving Heinrich Blum, who was making a deposit for Lupine Floral. The way heads lowered to hide smiles.

He pressed his lips firmly together in the hope that it would, somehow, stop the sizzle on his cheeks and neck. This would be all over town by five o'clock. Of course, no one would know the details. All anyone would be able to pass on was what they saw—him being an obvious jerk and upsetting their reigning queen of chocolate. *Great, just great. Welcome back, Preston.* He'd barely returned to his hometown, and he was already campaigning for Public Enemy Number One.

What was he supposed to do, anyway? He wasn't king of the world. He was a bank manager and if he didn't manage this bank well, it would go under. And all those old high school buddies and friends of a friend who wanted special treatment were going to have to get that through their thick heads.

Maybe that old saying was true and you couldn't go back. Icicle Falls had been a great place to grow up. Church picnics, Boy Scout camping trips, fishing the river with Gramps. But now Blake found himself thinking he should have left small-town life in the idyllic past where it belonged. Taking this position hadn't been a step up. It had been a step into a big pile of shit.

He adjusted his shirt collar that had gone suddenly tight and then went back to work on the loan application papers in front of him. But all he could see was Samantha Sterling's full lips frowning at him. What had he been smoking when he decided to go into banking after he graduated from college? Heck, he could have followed his folks when they moved to Seattle and helped his dad run that Honda dealership. Or gone into computer sales and made a fortune. Or become a construction worker. Truck driver. Prison warden.

Right now he felt like a prison warden with everyone around him planning to stick him with a shiv, and all because of one angry woman. Correction, angry and unbalanced.

Of course, he could see how his predecessor had gotten sucked into making poor decisions. That long red hair, those big hazel eyes, that cute little tush—Samantha Sterling was hotter than the Wenatchee Valley in August. So were her sisters and her mother. He'd seen them around. They were a tag team of damsels in distress. He could imagine Muriel flashing a bit of cleavage and batting those thick-lashed eyes of hers at old Arnie and putting him in a trance where he'd happily give her everything, including the keys to the vault. Watching her and her daughter struggle so valiantly to keep the family business going, watching those big eyes fill with tears—the poor slob hadn't stood a chance.

But Blake was made of sterner stuff. Of course he'd do all he could to support Samantha. He'd buy chocolates even though he was allergic to chocolate. Gram had a birthday coming up soon and he'd get her the biggest box of candy they had, and when his mother and sister were in town he'd send them to the Sweet Dreams gift shop to go crazy with his debit card. He'd even be willing to help Samantha brainstorm ways to raise funds—private investors or a loan from some of her cronies at the Chamber of Commerce. He'd have told her all that if she hadn't had a meltdown and stomped off. But he couldn't change bank policy just for her. He'd already gone out on a limb by extending her loan to the end of February.

It's not your business to fix other people's mistakes, he reminded himself. *You can't save every failing business in the state.* Still, it seemed a shame to let this one die. He was well aware of the company's history and it was the stuff of movies. Except right now the Sterlings' story wasn't looking like it was headed for a happy ending.

He forced himself to focus on the papers in front of him. It was impossible. All he could think about was what a villain he felt like. Sweet Dreams was Samantha Sterling's baby and she was trying desperately to save it. If he had to lock the company's doors and sell off its assets he'd be a baby-stealer and everyone in town would hate him. Almost as much as he'd hate himself.

Elena took one look at Samantha storming into the office and muttered, *"Mierda."*

Samantha set the basket on Elena's desk. "Take it home to your family and enjoy."

Elena's eyebrows drew together. "That is a lot of money there."

"Consider it a bonus," Samantha said. "God knows it's probably the last one I'll be able to give you."

"You mustn't talk like that," Elena scolded. Sixteen years older and forty pounds heavier than Samantha, she sometimes forgot she was an employee and morphed into an office mother. "And why are you back with this?"

"Long story," Samantha said, "and one I don't want to tell." Having shut the door on a fresh lecture, she then shut her office door on the world, plopped down at her desk and stared bitterly at the array of pictures on the wall.

Generations of successful family smiled at her. Great-grandma Rose and her husband, Dusty, wearing their best clothes, stood in front of the newly purchased building that would house Sweet Dreams Chocolates. Then there was Great Aunt Fiona and Grandma Eleanor posing in their aprons behind the counter of the retail gift shop in the fifties, and Grandpa Joe, smiling over his shoulder for the camera while he worked the line in the factory with a young José Castillo and George Loomis. There was a shot of Mom before she married Dad, sitting at the receptionist's desk. And one of her and Grandpa, displaying the logo Mom had created for the seal on the candy boxes. There was Dad in front of the store, posing with his three daughters, the whole Sweet Dreams team gathered around and beaming. A caption beneath it read Success, How Sweet It Is!

She felt sick. She laid her head on the desk and closed her eyes.

A moment later Gwen Stefani started singing on her

cell phone. Cecily again. Head still on the desk, she fumbled the phone to her ear. "Tell me you're calling because you had a vision of money falling from heaven."

"Sorry, no pennies from heaven. I had a feeling you might need to talk."

What she needed was a rewind button. "I blew it at the bank."

"What, did you walk in and shoot the new manager?"

"Worse. I gave him chocolate."

"Bribes are good."

"And then took it away." What the heck was wrong with her, anyway? Was she having a psychotic break? Maybe she had multiple personalities and didn't know it.

"Oh," her sister said weakly. She could imagine Cecily falling into a chair in her little pink office at Perfect Matches.

"I started out charming, I really did," Samantha defended herself. "But then he just sat there looking all smug, repeating that he couldn't help me—like a big dumb parrot in a three-piece suit—and… I blew it, pure and simple."

A sigh drifted over the phone line. "What would Dad say if he was here?"

He'd say, "What were you thinking, princess?" Or maybe he'd say, "You should have punched the guy's face in." Okay, probably not that.

"I don't know," Samantha said miserably.

"He'd say temper…"

Oh, yeah, that. "…and good business don't mix," Samantha finished with her. He'd told her that often enough, especially when she was young and impetuous.

And now she was so mature. Ha!

There was a long moment of silence before Cecily asked, "Maybe you should apologize to him?"

"Apologize! As in, 'Gee, Mr. Dragon, I'm so sorry I got mad at you for breathing fire and devouring my village'?"

"He's trying to save the bank like you're trying to save Sweet Dreams."

Ever the mediator, Samantha thought sourly. "He's just trying to save his butt."

Her sister heaved another sigh. "Well, you're the business major. You know best."

"Oh, that was cute."

"Sorry. It's just that, well, when it comes to business, you're usually more in control than this."

Samantha scowled. She hated it when her sister was right. Samantha was the oldest. She was supposed to be the most mature, the one who always knew what to do. Except when it came to Sweet Dreams, she seemed to lose all perspective.

"I wish I was up there to help you."

"I'll be okay," Samantha said with a sigh. "No more meltdowns, I promise."

"Call me if you need to."

"Thanks I will. Meanwhile, go make some money."

"Yeah, I should go. I've got a match-up cocktail party to plan and a client coming in ten minutes."

Finding rich men for beautiful women, throwing parties at swanky restaurants—no wonder Cecily had opted for L.A. over Icicle Falls, Samantha thought as she hung up. Who would want to live in a small town when she could have the big city and beautiful people?

Samantha, that was who. She loved her mountain town with its picturesque setting and its friendly people, and she was proud that her family and their company were part of the town's history.

She wanted them to continue to be part of its present,

too. She drummed her fingers on her desk. What options did she have other than robbing the bank? *Think, Samantha.*

After an hour of thinking she had a headache and one last option—Waldo's life insurance money. She wanted to go hit her mother up for a chunk of that about as much as she wanted to stick a knife in her eye. But it was for the good of the business and all their employees, she reminded herself, and she'd pay the money back. *So get up and get over there.*

She laid her head down on the desk again. Tomorrow. Like Scarlett O'Hara, she'd think about it tomorrow.

Except the clock was ticking and she couldn't afford the luxury of waiting until tomorrow. She took a deep breath, stood and strode out of the office.

Four

No one is perfect. It's important to remember this
when working with family.

—Muriel Sterling, *Mixing Business with Pleasure:
How to Successfully Balance Business and Love*

Muriel was in a swimming pool full of melted chocolate, competing in a swim meet, doing the butterfly
stroke and trying desperately to catch up with her competition in the other lanes. Waldo stood at one end of
the pool holding up a giant silver trophy cup brimming
with fudge, and Cecily and Bailey were at the front of
the throng, cheering wildly. "Go, Mom! You can do it!"
But the chocolate was so thick that no matter how hard
she pulled against it, she couldn't make any progress.

She was halfway across the pool and heavily winded
when in swept the Wicked Witch of the West on her
broom. The witch wasn't wearing her usual black garb.
Instead, she was in an old-fashioned bathing suit from
the early 1900s and she looked suspiciously like Samantha with hazel eyes and long red hair flying out from
under her pointy black hat.

"Tsunami! Quick, everybody out of the pool," cried
the witch. She flew out over the water, reached down
and yanked Muriel out by her hair. "Mom, you can't stay
here. Mom. Mom!"

"Mom?"

Muriel opened her eyes to see Samantha leaning over

her, a hand on her shoulder, her expression anxious. "Are you okay?"

Of course she wasn't okay. Muriel shoved her hair out of her eyes and sat up. "What time is it?"

"Eleven forty-five."

Almost noon. Here she was, sleeping away another day.

"Have you eaten?" Samantha asked.

"I'm not hungry, sweetie."

"When was the last time you ate?"

What did it matter? Muriel waved away the question. She slipped out of bed and went into the bathroom and shut the door on her daughter.

Samantha's voice followed her. "I'll make coffee."

Coffee, ugh. Muriel had always loved a good cup of coffee but her taste buds, like the rest of her, seemed to have given up on life.

She stood at the bathroom counter and stared at her reflection. Beneath those artificially brown curls the face of an old woman looked mournfully back at her. The dark circles under her eyes showed how poorly she was sleeping in spite of all the mattress time she was logging in.

She flipped off the light and left the bathroom. The bed called to her, but the smell of brewing coffee reminded her that Samantha was expecting her in the kitchen. She put on her bathrobe and sat on the edge of the bed, willing herself to get out there. Her body refused to obey.

Finally Samantha entered the room bearing a steaming mug. At the sight of her mother she managed a tentative smile. "How about I draw you a bubble bath and make us an omelet?"

Muriel took the mug. "Is that a hint?" That sounded snippy. Well, she felt snippy.

Samantha's fair skin glowed like an ember. "No, I just…"

"Go ahead and make yourself something. I'll be out in a few minutes." Muriel returned to the bathroom with as much dignity as she could muster. She was too young for her daughter to be telling her what to do.

Although Samantha was right. She needed a bath.

Twenty minutes later she emerged to find her daughter huddled on a stool at the kitchen counter, nursing her own mug of coffee. Muriel joined her and they sat side by side, looking at the empty kitchen.

"I can't seem to get my feet under me," Muriel murmured.

"You will," Samantha said.

And, if her daughter had anything to say about it, the sooner, the better, but all that busyness seemed like a waste of time. Her head suddenly hurt.

"So, how about an omelet?" Samantha coaxed.

Waldo loved a big, hearty breakfast. "It starts the day out right," he used to say.

There was no right way to start this day. "No, I don't want anything," Muriel said. *Except to have my husband back.*

"Let me at least get you some toast."

Fine, if it would make her happy. Muriel nodded.

It wasn't until Samantha had toasted and buttered a piece of rye bread, put it on a plate and set it on the counter that Muriel's foggy brain made an observation. "You're not at the office."

Samantha nudged the plate closer. "Have some toast."

Muriel took a bite and chewed. She might as well

have been chewing sawdust. She pushed the plate aside. "I thought you'd be at the office."

Once again Samantha inched the plate closer. "Have another bite."

Again Muriel pushed it away. She narrowed her eyes at her daughter. "Samantha Rose. Why are you here?"

Samantha dropped her gaze to the counter and gnawed her lip. Behind that pretty face lived a will of steel that showed itself in a strong chin always set in determination. Today, though, her daughter looked like she'd collapsed in on herself.

Maternal mode overpowering grief, Muriel reached across the counter and laid a hand on Samantha's arm. "Tell me," she commanded even though she didn't want to hear. Between her daughter and the doctors, she'd been hearing enough miserable news the past few months to last her a lifetime. She shuddered inwardly and braced herself.

Samantha looked up at her, eyes filled with desperation. "I don't even know how to say this."

Of the three girls this daughter had never been afraid to tell her mother exactly what she thought. "Just tell me. It can't top any of the bad news I've had in the past month."

"The bank is calling in its note. If I don't come up with the money by the end of next month they'll seize our assets and we'll lose the business."

She'd known the company was having trouble, but hearing this, Muriel felt like she'd been knocked over by an avalanche. First that horrible diagnosis, followed by Waldo's sudden death, now the business. What next?

If she'd stayed in the modest paid-for house where she and Stephen had raised the girls, she and Samantha could have gone to the bank and gotten a home equity loan and solved this problem. But instead, she'd traded up and bought a big, new house to go with her new husband and her new life. Real estate values in the region had fallen and even she knew what that meant—her house wasn't worth what it once was. And that meant the amount of equity she had to trade on amounted to zilch.

It seemed wrong to ask your daughter, "What are we going to do?" She should've had an answer. But she didn't. So she sat there and stared at Samantha, feeling like the world's worst mother, willing her brain to become math-friendly.

"I've been to the bank," Samantha said. "They won't help us. Right now there's only one thing I can think to do."

She'd thought of something. Good. Whatever it was, Muriel would support her.

Samantha hesitated, chewing her lip. She obviously wasn't happy with the solution she'd come up with.

"I'm listening," Muriel said encouragingly even though she felt an overwhelming urge to run away.

"I hate to ask this, but did Waldo have life insurance?"

Life insurance. Just hearing the words made Muriel's stomach churn. Waldo was not only dead, his life was reduced to a check. But it was a check they needed. She could use it to help her daughter save the company and maybe pay down this ridiculous mortgage.

Oh, how crass that sounded! *Waldo, I'm sorry.*

"Mom, I wouldn't ask if I could think of anything else but I'm out of options," Samantha was saying. "If you could just lend me enough to catch us up with the bank, I'll make sure you get repaid as soon as possible."

She patted her daughter's arm. "This is our business, honey. I'll give you the money."

Samantha's lower lip trembled and she took a deep breath. "Thanks," she said with tears in her eyes.

"We're a family. Family sticks together." Muriel hugged her.

Samantha wrapped her arms around Muriel like a drowning person would grab a life preserver.

Independent as her daughter was, she still needed her mother, and no matter how much Muriel wanted to sit life out for a good long while, maybe forever, she wasn't about to abandon her child to fight this battle on her own. "I won't let us lose this business," she promised. "Grandma Rose would turn in her grave."

"So would Daddy." Samantha pulled away and Muriel saw both relief and guilt on her face. "Thanks, Mom. I'm sorry we're having to go about things this way."

She pushed a lock of red hair behind Samantha's ear. "I'm not. And Waldo would be happy to know he was helping."

That remark tugged her daughter's lips down at the corners, and even though Samantha didn't say it, Muriel could hear her thinking, *It's the least he could do, considering the circumstances.*

But she didn't say it, and for that Muriel was grateful. She held in a thought of her own, too. *Yes, Waldo made some mistakes but he wasn't the one who took out that expansion loan in the first place.* Sometimes her daughter forgot that.

"I'll find the policy and call the insurance company this afternoon," she promised.

Samantha nodded, still looking uncomfortable. "Thanks." And then she was all business, ready to recommence fighting the world. "I'd better get back to the office. Call me after you talk to them."

"I will," Muriel assured her.

She sent Samantha on her way with a kiss, then stood at the window and watched her run down the walk to her car. For a moment she saw her daughter at eighteen, climbing into the passenger seat next to her father, driving to her summer job in the Sweet Dreams office. "Someday I'm going to run this company," she'd announced when she was sixteen, "and we'll be big."

Such dreams and ambition. "She's a natural," Stephen had said.

Muriel sighed. She should have remembered that and left her daughter in charge instead of bringing in Waldo and complicating things. She hadn't trusted her own judgment or her daughter's business smarts, and now she realized that had been a mistake. But Samantha had been so young.

As if age had anything to do with business smarts. Muriel herself was living proof that wasn't true.

Well, it was a new day. Samantha was in charge now and it seemed fitting that Waldo's life insurance money would allow her to resuscitate Sweet Dreams and take the company to the next level.

Muriel went up to the loft they'd turned into an office and opened the filing cabinet. The files were all jumbled, with manila folders stuck in haphazardly rather than in alphabetical order. She finally found the one marked Life Insurance and pulled it out, only to discover it contained papers on the house.

Panic began to simmer inside her. She set the file on the cabinet and checked the house file, thinking maybe Waldo had mixed things up. No life insurance policy. She moved to the desk, pawing through the scattered papers piled on top. A past-due notice for Waldo's Beemer payment made her swallow hard but didn't distract her from her search. It had to be here somewhere.

Three hours and two more cups of coffee later, she found a letter from the insurance company. She picked it up and began to read.

Words jumped out and slapped her. *Due to nonpayment...policy...canceled.*

There had to be some mistake. She'd call the insurance company first thing in the morning and straighten this all out.

Oh, Lord, please let there be some mistake.

But there wasn't. No matter how many superiors Muriel spoke to the following morning, no matter how much she pleaded, the answer was always the same: "We're sorry, but we can't help you."

And now she had to call the office and say the same words to her daughter. She stared at the phone and wished she could just go back to bed.

Five

If you can't depend on your family in your time
of need, who can you depend on?
—Muriel Sterling, *When Family Matters*

Samantha sat at her desk, gnawing her fingernails while
staring out the office window at the Wenatchee River.
The sun was out today and the river was a sparkling
sapphire-blue, but she could barely see it. Her view was
eclipsed by the vision of the end of life as she knew it.
Sweet Dreams was going to be history. The possibility of using Waldo's life insurance money had been her
last hope. What was going to happen to her employees?
What was going to happen to Mom without that extra
income? How could she fix this mess?

Maybe another bank would lend her money. Then she
could use that to pay off Cascade Mutual. She made a
couple of calls to test the water. The water was frigid.
Another fingernail went bye-bye.

Her cell phone started playing "Girls Just Want to
Have Fun." Bailey.

She forced herself to answer even though she didn't
want to. She'd already talked to Cecily, who'd at least
had the decency to let her be depressed. Bailey, the family cheerleader, would be calling to pump her up. And
she didn't want to be pumped up, damn it all, she wanted
to be pissed. Pissed, pissed, pissed!

"I'm here," she snarled.

"Well, of course. Where else would you be?" Bailey replied reasonably. "You wouldn't be you if you weren't in the office busy saving the company."

"I'm not busy saving the company. I'm busy…" What *was* she busy doing? Oh, yeah, feeling sorry for herself and doing a darned good job of it, too.

"Cecily told me about the bank. Are you okay?"

"No."

There was silence on the other end and she could just see her baby sister biting her lip, considering what to say next. "I'm sorry, Sammy," she finally said. "I feel like we're leaving you holding a big, stinky mess up there."

Samantha rubbed her aching forehead. "At the rate we're going I won't be holding it much longer." And then what would she do? Worse, what would Mom do? She wasn't exactly making a fortune as a writer. Cecily would have to find millionaires for both of them.

"But you can't let Sweet Dreams go out of the family," Bailey said. "That would just be wrong, Sammy."

Sometimes Samantha felt it was wrong that she was the only one of the sisters who'd stayed in Icicle Falls to keep Willy Wonka Land going. Here she was, like Davy Crockett at the Alamo. Or the Last of the Mohicans. Or…something.

"Do you have any ideas for how to save the company?"

Offer to sleep with Blake Preston in exchange for making an exception to bank policy. Oh, cute. Where had that come from? No place good. "No," Samantha said. But there had to be something they could do. Why couldn't she think of anything? She'd never lacked for ideas in the past, so where was all that brilliant inspiration now? Obviously, her idea factory had been shut down.

"We need a family brainstorming session," Bailey said firmly.

If she couldn't think of anything, what did Bailey suppose the rest of them were going to come up with? "Listen," she began.

Bailey cut her off. "I know you think nobody can run the company like you, but we're all pretty creative."

There was no denying that. Samantha looked at the shredded nails on her left hand and decided manicures were overrated.

"I'm calling Cec," Bailey said decisively. "I'll go over to her place tonight and we'll Skype you at Mom's at seven."

By seven all Samantha wanted was to be in her condo, escaping into a computer game or a movie on TV with Nibs curled up in her lap. "I don't think—" she began.

"Come on now, don't balk. Let's at least give it a try."

Her baby sister would stay on the phone and harass her until she caved. Might as well cave now and be done with it, she told herself. "All right. Seven tonight."

"Good," Bailey said in a tone of voice that sounded as though they'd already accomplished something.

Cecily stared in surprise at the buxom blonde in the low-cut top and overdone jewelry sitting on the other side of her desk, hardly able to believe what she was hearing. Liza and Brad should have been a perfect match. He wanted a woman with boobs the size of life rafts and she wanted a man with a deep well of money to support her Rodeo Drive spending habit. Brad not only had money, he was good-looking to boot, another requirement of Liza's, and now Liza was saying she didn't want to see him again? Seriously?

"So you didn't hit it off?" Cecily asked.

"We should have. He took me to Melisse, and the food was to die for. We both love great food."

"Common interests are important," Cecily said. They could have happily eaten their way through life while Liza ate her way through Brad's bank account.

"Then he said he liked my hair."

"Compliments, that's good."

Liza made a face. "Oh, yeah? Not when he says it's the same color as his mother's hair and then he starts talking about *her*."

"Maybe he thought you'd like his mother?"

"Not by the time he was done. I swear it was like there were three of us on that date. And she lives with him. He's forty and he lives with his mother? Sheesh. I can't believe you don't screen your guys better."

"Well…" Cecily stumbled to a halt. She wasn't even sure what to say to that. She didn't have a place on her forms to check off *mama's boy*. "I'm sorry, Liza. I thought he'd be perfect."

"Well, he wasn't. You've *got* to do better."

That might not be so easy, considering the fact that Liza had tried to sucker the last two guys she'd gone out with into taking her shopping on the second date. "I'll try," Cecily said. "But you have to remember not to ask these guys to buy clothes for you when you've barely started dating them. It makes them think that's all you want out of the relationship."

Liza scowled at her. "Of course that's not all I want. What do I look like, a hooker?"

Actually, yes, and not a very high-class one. "No, no," Cecily said quickly. "Don't worry. We'll find your perfect match."

"I hope so. I mean, I *could* go to someone else, you know."

The Millionaire Matchmaker on TV? Cecily smiled the diplomatic smile that had always stood her in good stead. "Of course, I want you to be happy." The rest of that sentence should have gone something like, "And I'm going to do everything in my power to find the perfect guy for you." But the rest of the sentence never got out of her mouth. Instead, she discovered she had an evil twin, and the evil twin said, "So if that's how you feel, then you should trot those Jimmy Choos somewhere else and see if they can find you a man who's into gold diggers." Oh, dear God, had she just said that?

Liza obviously couldn't believe she had. Her jaw dropped. "Excuse me?"

Oh, boy. "I don't think I can help you," Cecily said simply. And then the evil twin added, "And I don't think I want to."

Liza's eyes flashed. "I want my money back!"

Good luck with that, thought Cecily. That money was long gone, just like her patience. "You got your money's worth. I've matched you up with six eligible men. It's not my fault you blew it."

Liza glared at her. "Fine. I'm telling all my friends never to come to you. Ever!" And with that, she grabbed her Kate Spade bag and teetered out of the office on her three-inch heels.

Cecily ran a hand through her hair. This was abysmal. Not losing Liza as a client—she'd had a feeling all along that she wouldn't be able to help the woman. No, it was the way she'd reacted to Liza's threat—so tacky, so unprofessional. What was wrong with her? She was burned out, plain and simple.

She told Willow, her secretary, to hold her calls and locked herself in her office with a cup of chamomile tea, but the tea didn't make her feel any better. She tossed out the remains and went back to her emails. And with each new one she opened, she kept asking herself, *What are you doing here?*

Good question.

Samantha was about to leave the office when her mother called to ask how she was doing.

"I haven't slit my wrists yet," Samantha reassured her.

"Don't even joke about things like that," Mom scolded. "I just talked to Cecily. It sounds like we're set for a brainstorming session tonight and I was wondering if I should make dinner."

While Samantha always preferred other people's cooking, especially her mother's, the idea of sitting across the table from Mom after everything that had happened, and now this latest development—she couldn't face it. "I've got a million things to do before we Skype." *Please don't ask what.* "Can I take a rain check?"

"Of course," Mom said. "But let me send some food home with you after. I'm up to my nose in casseroles."

Free food. That would work. And stuffing herself with Mrs. Nilsen's triple-threat mac and cheese was a step above medicating her pain with goodies from their gift shop or chewing off what few fingernails she had left.

She pulled up in the driveway at 6:55, turned off the ignition and sighed. It was wrong not to want to spend one-on-one time with her mother. She loved her mother. But right now she felt a big, lumpy wall between them, a misshapen, awkward pile of resentment, guilt and who knew what else, that she wasn't sure how to scale. Mom was trying, though, God bless her. Which, of course, made Samantha feel all the more guilty.

Learning that Waldo had no life insurance hadn't helped. Mom had felt awful when she called with the bad news and Samantha had felt numb. But not so numb that she couldn't exclaim, "How could he have been so irresponsible? My God! First the business and now this."

"Let's not panic," Mom had advised.

"Mom," Samantha had said sternly, "we're in a burning building and the fire department is on strike. What do you expect me to do?"

"We'll think of something," Mom had assured her.

Easy for her mother, the queen of clueless, to say. She knew nothing about business or finance. "You're right," Samantha had lied, trying to make up for her gaffe. "I'd better go." *Before I explode.*

After she hung up she'd felt awful. If there was an award for the most insensitive daughter, she'd win it hands down.

Now she made her way up the walk, slo-o-owly, and then let herself in, hoping to hear Mom's voice drifting down from the loft as she talked to Cecily and Bailey on the computer. Instead, she found her mother rooted in her favorite yellow leather chair, nursing a cup of chocolate-mint tea. The aroma drifted across the room to greet her.

"I have a pot of tea on the counter," Mom said as Samantha bent to kiss her cheek, "and Pat brought over white-chocolate raspberry brownies. Vitamin C," she added, referring to the family joke that chocolate was the equivalent of vitamins.

At the rate Samantha was going, she'd wind up overdosing on chocolate. She moved to the counter, poured herself some tea and took a brownie. Just one. She'd make this the last fattening thing she ate for the rest of her life. Okay, for the rest of the month. The week. The night, anyway.

"How are you feeling?" Mom asked.

Like French royalty about to face the guillotine. Samantha shrugged. "I've been better."

Her mother's face was a picture of sympathy and regret. "I'm so sorry, sweetie."

That made two of them. "Mom, about this morning. I'm sorry I snapped at you." Daughters were supposed to be a comfort to their mother. She was about as comforting as a kick in the shins.

Mom waved away the apology. "Don't give it another thought. I know you're under a lot of stress."

Stress, the all-American excuse for bad behavior. Could she go back to the bank and try that one out on Blake Preston?

Mom gave her a motherly pat on the shoulder. "Somehow this will all work out, sweetie."

Samantha had to find a way to make that prediction come true. The weight of responsibility on her shoulders felt like twin elephants. How was she going to get them out of this mess? *Panic!*

No, no. No panicking. Stay calm and think.

"So they haven't called yet?" she asked, stating the obvious. Suddenly she was eager to talk to her sisters. Even though there was nothing they could do to help, a big dose of moral support would be good.

"Not yet," Mom said. "I was just about to go up to the loft. We can start talking to Cecily. You know how to do this Skype thing, right? Waldo always…" Mom's sentence trailed off.

Samantha simply nodded and led the way upstairs. At first it looked like Mom had done some serious cleaning in the office, but on closer examination Samantha realized her mother had only stacked all of Waldo's paperwork in neat piles.

"I'm working through your stepfather's papers," Mom said as she sat down and booted up the computer.

"I can help you with that," Samantha offered, pulling up a chair next to her and clicking on the Skype icon.

"It can wait," Mom said. "You've got enough on your plate."

Not as much as Mom had. Yes, Samantha was feeling responsible for keeping the company going, but Mom was coping with the loss of a husband and probably her house, on top of all this trouble with Sweet Dreams. All the sparkle had drained out of her and she looked like a zombie with her eyes bloodshot from crying. Samantha, with her ill-considered outbursts, wasn't helping.

Their call went through and Cecily appeared on the screen. She was perched on a brown microfiber love seat in her living room, looking comfy in sweatpants and an old sweater, her blond hair pulled back in a ponytail. On the wall behind her Samantha could see Mom's 1979 Moskowitz print that Cecily had taken with her when she'd moved to L.A. It depicted three pastel-colored ostriches, one with its head in the sand, two staring out at the world with perplexed expressions. Rather symbolic of most of the women in her family if you asked Samantha. Not that anyone had.

"Bailey isn't here yet," Cecily told them. "She called to say she's running late."

"What a surprise," Samantha murmured.

"Baby of the family. What can we say?" Cecily said. She widened her eyes. "Is that a brownie you're eating?"

Samantha stuffed the last of her brownie in her mouth. "Mmm."

Cecily made a face. "Unfair."

Kind of like her being up here all by herself, worrying about Mom and the business. Then she reminded herself that she'd been the stupid martyr who insisted her sisters return to their lives in L.A.

"But better your waist than mine," Cecily taunted.

"By the time everyone in Icicle Falls is done bringing food we'll have no waists. We'll be tree trunks," Mom predicted. "Still, it's very thoughtful."

And it's free, Samantha thought. Right now free was good, as her savings account was on the verge of flatlining.

"So, have you come up with any ideas for how to get the money we need?" asked Cecily.

The elephants sitting on Samantha's shoulders settled in for a nice, long stay. "Other than robbing the bank, no."

"I still think I should take out a loan," Cecily said. "Maybe I could get a home equity loan on my condo."

"Nice try, but I told you, no loans," Samantha insisted. "This family isn't going any deeper into debt." Mom being upside down on her house was bad enough. They didn't need to put her sister in the same position.

Cecily gave a fatalistic shrug. "You know, I always thought I was pretty good at thinking outside the box, but I've got to admit that so far I'm at a loss. Other than matching you up with a rich man," she teased Samantha.

"Meeting a nice man, there's an idea," Mom said, perfectly happy to take her seriously. "Maybe someone who'd be willing to make you a personal loan."

"No problem," Samantha said irritably. "Let's run down to the rich-guy mart and pick up a sucker."

"We wouldn't have any luck, anyway," Cecily said. "Your boobs aren't big enough."

Now Mom was looking thoughtful. "What's the new bank manager like?"

"He's no Arnie," Samantha said bitterly. An image of

Blake Preston with his broad shoulders and superhero chin came running into her mind, all dressed up in his football regalia. Samantha benched it.

"Still, surely he could be of some help," Mom said.

Samantha shook her head. "I've met him. He's useless."

"Maybe you didn't get off on the right foot," Mom persisted.

If snatching back the bribe she'd brought him counted, no, they hadn't. Samantha shot her sister a look that warned bodily harm if Cecily ratted her out to Mom and said, "Trust me, he won't be any help. A man can't always fix things," she couldn't keep from adding.

Her mother heaved a sigh. "I wish your father was alive. He'd know what to do."

"If Dad was alive we wouldn't be in this mess in the first place," Samantha said, and then wanted to bite off her tongue. *Just shoot me now,* she thought, watching her mother's shoulders stiffen. "Sorry. I didn't mean that the way it sounded," she muttered. Except she had and they both knew it.

"It's okay," her mother said even though they both knew it wasn't.

Now Samantha could hear Bailey's voice in the background. A moment later her youngest sister appeared on the screen, plopping onto the love seat next to Cecily and pulling off a red leather jacket, probably a consignment store find. Ever since the company's profits had evaporated they'd all been shopping secondhand. Or, in Samantha's case, not shopping at all.

"So what have you guys come up with?" she asked.

"Nothing," Samantha said. This was going to be a big waste of time.

"Well, I was thinking about something on the way

over," Bailey told them. "What about some kind of fundraiser? You know, with a big thermometer so people could see how much money we've raised."

"No," Samantha said. "Perception is important in business and the last thing we want is to announce to the whole world that we're going under."

"But we are going under," Bailey pointed out.

"No thermometers," Samantha said sternly.

Bailey frowned and fell back against the couch cushions, deflated.

"Speaking of perception," Cecily said, "does anybody know how to contact Mimi LeGrande? If she featured Sweet Dreams on a show, we'd be golden."

Why hadn't *she* thought of that? Mimi LeGrande hosted the Food Network's brand-new hit show *All Things Chocolate.* There wasn't a bakery or chocolatier in the country who didn't dream of getting included in one of her shows. If she were to give them a nod, orders would pour in from foodies and chocoholics, and their future would be secure.

"I heard she lives here. I could ask around," Bailey offered. "There's got to be someone who knows her."

"That would be great," Samantha said. Heck, it would be more than great. It would be a miracle. "But it's a long shot. I think we need a more immediate plan." There had to be one. Why wasn't she seeing it?

Silence reigned for a full five minutes until Cecily said, "You know, our baby sis could be on to something."

"Oh, not you, too," Samantha groaned.

"What if we did come up with some sort of event to bring in money for the business?"

"A chocolate dinner?" Bailey suggested, coming back to life. "Every course could use chocolate. And we could do it at Zelda's."

"Guys, I appreciate the thought," Samantha said, "but a dinner wouldn't even come close to raising the kind of money we need." Maybe they were on the right track, though. "Let's think on a grander scale."

"I did a chocolate tour in Seattle once," Bailey said.

"A chocolate tour, a chocolate weekend," Samantha mused. Maybe they could pull that off. They could have a dinner and a chocolate high tea at Olivia's B and B. But anything they got from that would only be a drop in the bucket. "A chocolate festival." Too bad they didn't have more time. Festivals brought in a lot of people and a lot of money.

"Now, that's brilliant!" Cecily exclaimed.

"Brilliant but not practical," Samantha said. "We need that money in six and a half weeks. It would take six months to plan something on such a grand scale."

"Then let's plan on a baby grand scale," Bailey said. "We can have it the weekend before Valentine's Day when people are feeling romantic and buying candy."

Samantha shook her head regretfully. "There isn't time. It's a lot to plan, and you have to promote it."

"If you had people helping, you could do it," Bailey insisted. "And with the internet and social media you can promote things fast now."

"It's a great idea," Cecily said.

Was her entire family certifiably insane?

Suddenly she could envision Icicle Falls buzzing with throngs of visitors all on a chocolate high. Something like this wouldn't just help their company, it would help the whole town.

Was she insane, too?

"Let's do it," Bailey said eagerly.

What was with this *let's do it* stuff? They were down there and she was up here. On her own.

"We can sponser a bunch of events, maybe have some sort of contest," Bailey continued. "I couldn't come up till just before, but I could help with planning over the phone and on email in between catering jobs."

"Actually, I can come up right away," Cecily said.

"You've got a business to run," Samantha protested.

"Things are quiet right now. I've got the time."

Quiet? What did that mean? Wasn't her dating service doing well?

Cecily tended to keep things to herself. When she had a crisis they never heard about it until it was long over.

Still, this worried Samantha. "Not that I don't want you," she said, "but you can't just up and leave your business for several weeks."

Cecily put on what Samantha thought of as her poker face; her expression gave nothing away. "I'm closing the business. It's a long story," she added before Samantha could press her for details. "Anyway, I've had all the sun I can take. I need seasons. I can rent out my condo, and I bet Charley would let me have a job waiting tables at Zelda's a couple of nights a week. That would leave me free during the day to work on the festival with you guys. Mom, can I stay with you?"

"Of course," Mom said. "But I think you girls need to figure out a few more things first, like where we'd hold this festival."

"All over town." Bailey almost whacked Cecily in the nose with her sweeping hand gesture.

"I bet we could get all the B and Bs to participate and offer some special rates," Samantha said thoughtfully. "No one has full occupancy these days, so maybe some of them would offer a special discount for that weekend."

"Oh, and the restaurants can feature special chocolate desserts," Bailey said.

"We could award a plaque to the one that comes up with the most creative dessert, using our candy, of course," Cecily suggested. "Bragging rights for them, profit for us."

"I love it," Samantha said. This scheme was looking better by the minute.

Bailey nodded eagerly. "Our local artists can set up booths in the park along Center Street. Heck, we can all have food booths over on Alpine like we do on the Fourth of July."

"Girls, this all sounds lovely, but you have to have time to get people on board," Mom said.

"Since when isn't the Icicle Falls Chamber of Commerce on board with anything that brings in tourist business?" Samantha argued. "I could work that angle."

"Me, too," said Bailey. "I can phone people from here. Oh, this could be really big. We can hand out samples, give tours of the factory, all kinds of cool stuff."

"But there's the matter of permits," Samantha said, coming down to earth with a thud. "We can't just decide to have a festival without getting permits for the sale of food and alcohol. And we need a special-event permit that all the departments sign off on. It takes time for all that to make the rounds in city hall."

"But if it's good for Icicle Falls I bet you can find someone to move the process along," Cecily said.

Hmm. Her sister had a point there.

"Let's try it, anyway," Bailey urged. "Think of all the chocolate-lovers we can lure up here. Oooh, and we could have a chocolate ball," she added dreamily. "I can see it now, an old-fashioned masked ball where everyone dresses up."

"And have that chocolate dinner before," Cecily put in.

"We can sponsor the dinner and the ball and sell hot

chocolate and truffles in a booth." Bailey was beaming now, on fire with a million ideas.

If they could manage to pull off even some of them... Samantha felt the fire catching in her, too. "We'd need to advertise in the Seattle papers, set up a website." She grabbed a piece of paper from Waldo's desk and began scribbling notes to herself.

"That will cost money," Mom pointed out. "Girls, I just don't think we can raise what we need by sponsoring something like this. Sponsoring, by its very nature, involves cost."

Now that they were going down the tubes she was deciding to grow a head for business? "Everything involves cost," Samantha argued.

But Mom had a point. This whole thing was a huge gamble and it could bomb big-time.

What did it matter, though, if the bank was going to take the business, anyway? Chances were slim that they'd even come close to making enough money to get the bank off their backs—but if they did nothing their chances went from slim to none. And maybe they could at least raise enough to allow her to renegotiate with the bank. If she came in with a check...

"I've got a good feeling about this," Cecily said.

Samantha put a lot of stock in her sister's instincts. "Then let's do it. What have we got to lose?"

Their business, of course. And maybe their sanity.

Oh, wait, trying to pull off something this big in such a short time—they'd already lost their sanity. So what the heck. Sweet Dreams Chocolates was about to sponsor a chocolate festival.

Six

The man of your dreams is the one who shares
your dreams.
—Muriel Sterling, *Mixing Business with Pleasure:
How to Successfully Balance Business and Love*

After their family conference call, Samantha's mother
loaded her up with chicken casserole, tuna surprise and
brownies, gave her an encouraging hug and then sent
her home feeling slightly ill. She hoped the queasiness
was due to all the sugar she'd been consuming lately
and not fear of failure.

She went to bed half hoping she could save the day
by dreaming up a fabulous chocolate candy recipe just
like Great-grandma Rose had done all those years ago.

Could she, though? No-o-o. Instead of dreaming up
a new recipe that would put them on the map, she spent
her REM sleep hours running from King Kong–size
candy-bar monsters that chased her all over town, trying to squash her with their big, flat feet. Finally three
of them cornered her right in front of the bank.

"Get her," growled one, and raised a giant foot.

"No," she cried. "I'll do anything. Anything!"

So far in her dream she'd appeared to be the last
living soul in Icicle Falls but suddenly the bank door
opened and Blake Preston stood in the doorway dressed
in leopard-print boxers. "Did you say you'd do *anything?*" he asked.

"Anything," she panted. He took her by the arm and pulled her inside the bank.

There she saw that all the desks had been replaced with round beds draped in pink satin bedspreads and the ceiling was one gigantic mirror. In another corner sat a hot tub, bubbling with chocolate.

Blake slipped an arm around her waist. "I've been waiting for you," he whispered. He tucked a lock of hair behind her ear and nibbled her earlobe, turning her insides gooey. "Why don't you lose that dress and join me in the hot tub?"

"Will you save me from the monsters?" she asked him.

"Of course. That's what men are for, isn't it? Look how Waldo saved your mother."

"Aack." She covered her face with her hands.

Blake started chuckling and she glanced up to see that he'd put on some sort of Dracula cape and sprouted fangs. And they were dripping chocolate.

She let out a shriek and ran for the door. But then she caught sight of a big, brown monster eye peering in at her and dashed blindly in the other direction with Blake in hot pursuit, his cape flying out behind him.

"Bwa-ha-ha. You know you want me," he cackled.

"I want to save my company!" she yelled over her shoulder. "Sign something that guarantees you'll save my company."

"First let's seal the deal," he called as he chased her around a bed. "Come on, Samantha, you know you want to."

"I shouldn't do this," she said, and hesitated, which gave him time to get around the bed and catch her. "It's all right," he murmured as he kissed her neck. "Trust me."

Next thing she knew he was helping her strip off her little black dress. And lo and behold, she was wearing leopard-print panties and a matching bra.

"Now, sign this," he said, and produced some sort of contract and a pen shaped like a licorice stick. Samantha took it and scrawled her name across the bottom of the document. "What did I just sign?"

Blake scooped her up in his arms and smiled at her. "You signed your life away, baby. You sold your company to Madame C."

The cheap chocolate company in Seattle? "No!" she protested, and struggled to get free.

"And now nobody needs you anymore." With her still squirming in his arms, he flew over to the hot tub and dropped her in. "*Sayonara,* sweet cheeks," he said, and began pushing her head down.

She wakened just before she drowned, sitting up with a jerk and panting, covered in sweat. What kind of sick subconscious did she have, anyway? She pushed her hair out of her eyes and lay back down with a whimper. Nibs slowly made his way across the bed to investigate and she drew him close.

"Okay, it was only a dream," she told herself. And one that had convinced her that no matter how bad things got, she didn't want to end it all by drowning herself in chocolate.

Blake was picking up his midmorning Americano at Bavarian Brews when he spotted Samantha Sterling coming through the door. She wore a short, faux-fur-trimmed jacket over jeans that hugged her thighs and tall black boots—typical Icicle Falls business casual. Except this woman made business casual look erotic and he had to beat down a surge of red-hot lust. The memory of her losing her temper at him doused any remaining embers—until an unbidden thought fueled a fresh fire, suggesting that with so much passion she'd be a real firecracker in bed.

She saw him and her cheeks, already rosy from the cold, deepened to red. She shot a sidelong glance at the door but then seemed to think the better of turning tail and running, instead donned a polite mask and moved toward the order counter. He smiled at her, determined to meet her halfway. They lived in the same town. Might as well manage a difficult situation civilly.

"Good morning," she said, her voice as stiff as her smile.

He held up his cup. "It is—now that I've got my coffee."

She nodded. "I'm running on empty myself."

"Can I buy you something?"

She blushed again and dropped her gaze to his chest. "No, thanks. That is—" she cleared her throat "—about the other day."

This was awkward. He held up a hand. "Consider it forgotten."

Now she did look at him. She had great eyes. And then there was her mouth. And other parts of her.

"It was very unprofessional of me," she said, "and I'm not normally like that."

"I'm sure you're not," he agreed. "And believe me, this isn't any more fun for the bank than it is for you."

A delicate eyebrow cocked, turning her earnest expression into something a little more cynical. "It hurts you more than it does me?"

"Well, sort of." That had sounded stupid and made him look like a real jerk. This wasn't going well. "I don't like having to be the bad guy," he said. Boy, there was an understatement. Why, of all the business choices in the world, had he chosen banking?

Oh, yeah, he'd wanted to help people fix their money problems, make their dreams come true, blah, blah. Talk about naive. Banks didn't cure financial stupidity. They profited from it. He was no hero. He was a profiteer.

"Then don't be a bad guy," she urged. "Work with us."

She looked so helpless, so desperate. He wanted to wrap his arms around her and tell her he'd come up with some way to save her.

Wait a minute. What was he thinking? He wasn't, of course. Women like this one, they made a man's brain melt. He gave himself a stern reminder that Samantha Sterling wasn't the only person in town with financial needs. He had employees and other bank customers depending on him.

None of his other customers looked like this one.

Oh, no. He wasn't about to follow old Arnie right over the cliff and take the bank with him. Yes, legions of men did dumb things for women. They spent money they didn't have on women, stole for them, even committed murder for them. He didn't have to join the legions.

"We're making plans for something that could benefit not only Sweet Dreams but the whole town," Samantha said earnestly.

There. She'd be fine. He'd known it all along.

This was a town full of fighters. It had been ever since the shutdown of the lumber mill and the relocation of the railroad left Icicle Falls in bad straits during the Depression. It'd been almost a ghost town by the fifties, but the people of Icicle Falls had self-administered CPR and spent the early sixties transforming their town into an Alpine village and haven for skiers. Sweet Dreams Chocolate Company was one of their success stories, weathering the hard times and giving the town a source of pride, and how it was founded had become a local legend. Like the other residents of Icicle Falls, Samantha Sterling was a fighter. She'd pull out of this.

"If we could have a little more time," she added.

That again. So much for the false rosy picture he'd been painting. His morning coffee began churning up acid in his gut. "I wish I could," he said. And he did. No lie.

There went the eyebrow once more. "Do you?"

Yes, damn it. But what was he supposed to do, rob the bank for her? Did he look like a money tree with hundred-dollar bills sprouting out of his ears? "Like I said before—"

"I don't think I want to hear what you said before," she snapped. "It was depressing the first time around."

In under a minute she'd reduced him from six feet two to twelve inches, the world's smallest man with the world's smallest heart. "If there's any other way I can help," he began.

"You're helping enough," she said coldly, and marched off to the order counter, her back stiff.

But not her tush. How did women manage to walk like that? *Honky-tonk badonkadonk, mmm-mmm.*

Nice, Preston, he scolded himself. *You're about to take her business and you're thinking about her butt.* What kind of bastard did that make him? He supposed his ex-girlfriend would be glad to tell him.

There had been a superficial relationship that was doomed from the start. After they broke up he'd vowed to be more cautious and not let his common sense get anesthetized by a pretty face. Or a nice tush.

Talk about doomed relationships… *Samantha Sterling is not for you.* Still…that didn't mean he couldn't step back and analyze her situation once again and maybe come to a new conclusion. Really, was the bank wise to be so hard-nosed to a business that played a vital part in the local economy?

He tossed his coffee and stepped out into the cold. Instead of returning to the bank he went down to Riverfront Park. With the exception of a couple of brave walkers the footpath was deserted. He took out his cell and dialed Darren Short, his district manager, all the while telling himself that he was not following Arnie over the cliff.

"Blake, how's it going?" Darren greeted him. "Are you settling in?"

"Well enough," Blake said. "But now that I'm here I'm getting a bigger picture than we had on paper."

"Oh?" Now Darren sounded cautious.

"Look, I think we need to reevaluate a few of these loans, especially the one to Sweet Dreams Chocolates."

"Don't go soft on me now," Darren said. "You're up there to stop the hemorrhaging."

"I know."

"Then don't let me down. You're our wunderkind and we're depending on you to turn that branch around and make it an asset for Cascade Mutual. Hell, the people who work up there are depending on you, too."

"I have every intention of doing that, but—"

Darren cut him off. "Good. I stuck my neck out for you. Don't make me regret it."

"Don't worry, I'm doing my job," Blake said. "But part of that job involves evaluating the situation and—"

Darren cut him off again with a brusque, "It's *been* evaluated and I'm sure I don't have to remind you of bank policy—to which you've already made an exception."

"I haven't forgotten," Blake said through gritted teeth.

"I'm glad to hear it. You can give me a full report when we meet on Friday."

"I will." In fact, Darren was going to get a much fuller report than he expected. One way or another Blake was now determined to make his boss see reason. He had to. He couldn't take living the rest of his life as the world's smallest man.

Samantha had been looking forward to a caramel latte all morning, but once she had it she took no more than two sips before throwing it out. She started back to the office but changed direction at the last minute, instead walking over to Gingerbread Haus, owned by her business buddy Cassandra Wilkes.

Between her visits to the bakery, and Cass's visits to Sweet Dreams it was inevitable that the women would become friends. In addition to a love of food and a passion for business, they also seemed to share a common snark bone.

Cass was a single mom, now in her early forties, with three children. She'd come to town a bitter thirty-four-year-old divorcée with barely a penny to her name and went to work for Dot Morrison, who owned the Breakfast Haus restaurant. Dot had lent her the money to start her fantasyland bakery seven years ago and Cass had taken the money and run as fast as she could for success. She'd never looked back.

Samantha opened the door and was greeted with a rush of warm air carrying the scent of cinnamon and nutmeg. From behind the glass counter gingerbread cookies in every imaginable shape beckoned. Cream puff swans swam inside a refrigerator display case, along with German-style kuchen loaded with whipped cream.

A huge gingerbread castle perched atop the counter and the shelves behind it displayed other examples of Cass's creativity.

Today she was in the kitchen, covered in flour and rolling out cookie dough for sugar cookie pizzas, but when she saw Samantha standing at the counter talking to her oldest daughter, twenty-year-old Danielle, she washed her hands, slipped off her apron and decided to take a coffee break.

Cass wasn't a bad-looking woman in spite of the fact that she tried her best to look bad. She never bothered with makeup and when her dark hair wasn't in a net it was pulled into a sloppy bun. She was thirty pounds overweight and proud of it, and she rarely dressed up beyond jeans and a sweatshirt or T-shirt. But it was probably more her attitude than her looks that kept her single. Where something about Muriel said, "Call me," Cass sent out signals that said, "Don't even think about it."

Now she regarded Samantha with that penetrating gaze of hers and said, "Okay, who do you want to kill today?"

Samantha couldn't help smiling at her perceptiveness. "Not my mother and not myself."

"That's a step in the right direction," Cass said as they settled at a corner table with some cake pops.

"But maybe the new bank manager."

"I didn't get to the open house but I was in making a deposit this morning and saw our hometown boy." Cass shook her head and smiled. "I've gotta say, even though my ideal man is made of gingerbread, this one brought my hormones back to life for a minute there."

"I always knew you were a cougar," Samantha teased.

"So have you been in to talk to him about helping you sort out your Waldo mess?"

Cass and Charley were the only ones who knew Samantha had been struggling with the business but she hadn't told either of them just how desperate the struggle was. "He won't be any help," she said, and left it at that.

Cass shook her head. "The man must have a heart of stone and gonads of dough."

"That about covers it. We're going to try and find some other ways to fix the business. My mom and sisters and I were kicking around something last night and I want to get your impression." Cass was an astute businesswoman. If she was in their corner, that would help sell other members of the Chamber of Commerce on the idea.

She sat back and slung an elbow over the back of her chair. "Okay," she said, her voice noncommittal.

"We're thinking of sponsoring a chocolate festival."

Cass nodded thoughtfully. "Sounds interesting. Tell me more."

And so Samantha did, and as she talked, Cass's skeptical body language changed. She leaned forward, arms on the table, listening intently. "You know, this could be good," she said at last.

"Do you think it could work?"

"Why not? We're always trying to find new ways to bring visitors to town. When were you hoping to do it? You have to make sure you don't eclipse anything that's already in place."

"Next month."

Cass blinked and fell back against her chair. "Next month?"

"I realize it's kind of a rush job." That was the understatement of the century.

"Kind of?" Cass raised both eyebrows. "You know how long it takes to plan something like this?"

Samantha slumped in her seat. "It's hopeless, isn't it? I knew it." She'd been deluding herself—which was exactly what crazy people did.

"I didn't say that, but damn."

"We could start small," Samantha ventured.

"Why February?"

"I need a ton of money by the end of next month. I'm out of options, Cass." It was painful to have to say it out loud and Samantha found herself blinking back tears.

"Not necessarily. You have friends in this town."

Samantha shook her head. "I don't have enough friends for what I owe. Anyway, I wouldn't do that to my friends. If the bank could have worked with me…" There was no sense completing that sentence.

"Okay, so when next month?"

"We'd like to have it the weekend before Valentine's Day."

Cass nodded slowly. "A chocolate festival the weekend before Valentine's Day. Perfect timing. You should be able to lure lots of couples up here for that. Good for the B and Bs, restaurants, wineries. Bakeries," she added with a grin.

"So, if we didn't go too wild, could we pull it off?"

Cass shrugged. "I say give it a shot. You've got nothing to lose."

Except her business, and she wasn't letting go of that without a fight.

Cass returned to work and Samantha hurried back to the office, a woman ready to wage war.

Elena looked at her uneasily. "I was getting worried. Where've you been?"

"Out getting inspired. I need you to look up festivals on the internet and print out everything you can find."

"Okay," Elena said. "But—"

"And call Luke and tell him to plan to triple production on our mint chocolate hearts."

"What in the world is going on?"

"We are about to sponsor Icicle Falls first annual chocolate festival," Samantha said, and then marched into her office, a general about to form her battle plan and conquer the world. Or at least the bank.

Seven

A positive attitude in you inspires a positive attitude in others.
—Muriel Sterling, *When Family Matters*

Wednesday morning found the members of the Icicle Falls Chamber of Commerce assembled in the banquet room of Dot Morrison's Breakfast Haus.

"Do you want me to bring up the idea of the festival?" Cass asked Samantha.

"I appreciate the offer, but no." It would be nice if someone would just take the reins and gallop them off into the sunset (or over the cliff) but Samantha knew she had to do this herself. Her glance sneaked to the far end of the table, where Blake Preston sat talking with Ed York, who owned D'Vine Wines. Would he weigh in and advise everyone present not to listen to a woman whose business was in ruins?

Don't be ridiculous, she scolded herself. It was in the bank's best interest for her to succeed. Otherwise, they'd have a chocolate company on their hands, and what would the bank do with a chocolate company?

"Just remember to stress that we'll all benefit from this," said Charley, whom she'd filled in on their way to the meeting. "We need to figure out how to make Icicle Falls a tourist destination all year long, snow or no snow."

Samantha nodded and pushed her plate away. What

little she'd eaten of her Belgian waffle was lying in her stomach like a brick.

Another fifteen minutes of small talk and Ed brought the meeting to order. There was much to discuss, like how to encourage everyone to put out hanging baskets and window boxes full of flowers come spring so they could keep their Alpine village theme consistent throughout town.

During this discussion several of the women present cast scornful frowns in the direction of Todd Black, whose sports bar, the Man Cave, camped at the edge of town—rather like the embarrassing relative everyone at the family picnic wishes would just go away. His concession to the requisite Bavarian look they were going for had been to add the carved wooden overhang to his roofline and commission one of his buddies to paint a Neanderthal in lederhosen holding a club on the front of the building. Many thought it in poor taste. Rather like the brawls that often took place there on a Saturday night.

Another hot topic of discussion was whether or not to foot the bill for a new town sign welcoming visitors to Icicle Falls with a quaint German phrase.

"Really," said Annemarie Huber, who had recently purchased the Bavarian Inn, "if we're an Alpine-style village we should have an Alpine-style welcome sign."

"You have a point there, Annemarie," Ed told her. "We should check with Bill Jacobs to see how much it would cost."

"Too much," Todd muttered.

"It will add to our town's charm," Annemarie insisted. She got as far as having everyone agree that the matter should be looked into.

The brick in Samantha's stomach grew heavier. If

nobody wanted to fork out for something as small as a sign, they sure weren't going to be excited about coughing up cash for putting on a festival.

"We have one more piece of new business from Samantha." Ed smiled at her encouragingly.

She'd just had to open her big mouth and tell him she had a proposition to discuss that could benefit the whole town. Now her feet weren't simply cold, they were frozen solid. Would everyone think she was being completely self-serving? They'd probably shoot her down. Heck, if she didn't need this so badly she'd shoot herself down.

People were studying her with speculative interest. *Sell this idea. It's the only one you've got and it needs to fly.* She steeled herself and put on her game face. "Yes, I've kicked this around with several people." Charley and Cass, her family—that was several. "And I've been getting some positive response." Especially from her family.

"Let's hear it," Ed said. "I don't know about the rest of you, but I'm open to ideas. Business hasn't been the best this winter."

"You can say that again," agreed Olivia Wallace, who owned Icicle Creek Lodge.

"We need to do some things to bring in business and make Icicle Falls more of a tourist destination throughout the year," Samantha said. "After all, it's lovely here all year-round. We have great hiking in the summer, and in the fall when the leaves turn, it's gorgeous. Plus we're near some of the best wineries this side of Napa."

Ed nodded. "Amen to that. So what did you have in mind?"

"Well, it's an idea my family's been toying with for some time." *Some* being the operative word. She continued, the big lie tumbling out of her mouth before she could bite her tongue. "And it's a dream my stepfather, Waldo, had hoped to make happen." If he'd known about it he'd have been all over it, she rationalized, willing the guilty burn off her cheeks. Waldo loved a good party, and this would be the party to end all parties. Anyway, he'd been useless to the business in life. He could darn well contribute something in death.

"God rest his soul," someone murmured.

If they pulled this off, he could rest in peace with Samantha's blessing.

"So what is it?" prompted Ed, who was practically salivating now.

She could feel Blake Preston's gaze on her as she stood there all dolled up in the business equivalent of the emperor's new clothes and felt her cheeks go warmer. "Well, what's the third-biggest spending holiday of the year?"

"Mother's Day," Annemarie guessed.

"Close," Samantha said. "Actually, it's Valentine's Day, coming in right after Christmas and Thanksgiving, and I'm thinking we could celebrate it here in Icicle Falls, which is why Sweet Dreams would like to sponsor a chocolate festival in honor of Cupid's big day. I'm sure, as you all know, a festival can bring loads of business into a town." Okay, there it was. Had she baited the hook enough?

Some people had caught the excitement; she could tell by the glint in their eyes. Others, like Dot and Todd Black, Mr. Alpine Neanderthal, were looking dubious.

"What exactly did you want to do?" Dot asked.

Samantha launched into her spiel, making the sales pitch of her life, all the while hoping no one would suggest there wasn't enough time to plan something like this.

"But that's only a month away," Hildy Johnson protested. Hildy was a stocky woman whose smile was as thin as the rest of her was fat. Her husband, Nils, was a pharmacist and he took care of filling prescriptions over at Johnson's Drugs but Hildy ran everything else, including him.

And now she'd just found the proverbial fly in the ointment. "I know it's less than six weeks," Samantha admitted, "but my family has already done a lot of the groundwork." Some anyway. They'd logged in a ton of phone calls over the weekend talking about it and Cecily and Bailey were working on schedules and venues for possible events. "We'd have to start small this year, but if we all pulled together to offer something fun and visitors enjoyed themselves, well, word of mouth would bring us twice as many people next year. And, let's face it, this is a day that lends itself well to merchandising—lovers' packages at our B and Bs and motels, wine-tastings, romantic dinners, special floral arrangements."

Now more eyes were lighting up. She still didn't dare look at Blake. She pressed on, throwing out enticing details like so many Hershey's Kisses.

"What about advertising? How are you going to promote this?" Hildy wanted to know. "You can't get the word out overnight."

"But you can get it out fast, thanks to the internet and social media," Samantha argued, parroting Bailey's words.

"How many friends have you all got on Facebook who don't live here? How many hits are you getting on your websites?" Todd asked cynically, making Samantha want to kick him.

"Obviously, we'd need to promote other places, too," she said. "Radio, newspaper—"

"They all cost money," Hildy interrupted.

Now Samantha couldn't help looking in Blake's direction. The pity in his eyes made her want to cry. Instead, she pinned on her best saleslady face. "I realize we're racing against the clock, but if we all worked together, pooled our resources, we could bring some good business into town."

"And God knows we could use it," muttered Heinrich, owner of Lupine Floral.

"So, would we like to be involved in this?" Ed asked. "What do you think, people?"

"What the hell," Dot said with a shrug. "I can hang up some foil hearts and offer a breakfast special."

"We have limited funds in our lodging tax fund," Hildy said. "And this." She shook her head. "It'll get costly. We'd have to pay overtime to the police for security and we'd have to pay for maintenance and cleanup."

"That's what the fund is there for, isn't it?" Samantha asked reasonably.

Hildy frowned at her. "Of course, but it's not there for every cockamamie idea that gets thrown out at Chamber meetings. Money doesn't grow on trees and we need to be wise with ours. I think we need a committee to look into this," she concluded.

"With only a little over a month until V Day, I think we have to decide today to either pass or jump in," Dot said.

"Then I say let's jump," Charley said. "I agree with Samantha—we can start small."

God bless you, Samantha thought, shooting her a grateful smile.

Hildy shook her head again. "I think we should pass."

"You can't pull this off," Todd said.

"I think we can," Samantha insisted. "If the whole

town supported it, we *could* pull it off and we'd all benefit."

"What do you think, Blake?" Hildy asked, obviously looking for someone to side with her.

He tugged at his necktie. "It's a big undertaking," he said. "You'll probably spend more money than you take in this first year."

"There you go," Hildy said as if that settled it.

Go ahead, stab me in the heart, thought Samantha bitterly, narrowing her eyes at him.

He refused to look in her direction. "But if you're asking me whether I think it's an idea that, with a little more time to plan and execute, could increase tourism, I'd have to say yes," he added. Now he did look at Samantha, who still hadn't removed the scowl from her face, and regarded her with those blue eyes of his in a way that dared her to accuse him of being biased.

She'd take that dare. He was.

"I dunno," Todd said with a shrug. "It doesn't do much for me. I don't sell chocolate at my place."

"But I sell wine," Ed reminded him, "and it goes pretty damn good with chocolate. We should put our heads together and see what we can come up with," he said to Samantha.

"I think it's a smart idea," Heinrich put in. "And if it brings people here, it's good for all of us. Why not capitalize on the fact that our town has a chocolate factory?"

"I like the idea, too," Annemarie said.

"God knows we need to do something after the dead winter we've had," Olivia added. "And I'd rather offer some special packages and have my place full than sit around and do nothing until the bank takes it." Her cheeks turned red and she cast an apologetic glance at Blake. "No offense."

"None taken," he assured her. "Cascade Mutual wants to be part of this community, and working together is in all our best interests."

What a hypocrite, thought Samantha.

Discussion continued for another ten minutes, with Hildy raising every kind of imaginable objection. Finally Todd shrugged and said, "Do what you want. It won't affect my business either way."

"That's for sure," Charley muttered in disgust. "As long as there are losers and beer in the world, he'll be fine."

"We'll take a vote," Ed announced. "Do I have a motion?"

The vote was almost unanimous, with Todd abstaining and Hildy casting a resounding *no.*

"This is a waste of money," she informed Ed as she left, but several people lingered to congratulate Samantha on her great idea.

"I'll be happy to help with the planning," Olivia volunteered.

"Me, too," Cass said.

"I'm already thinking about the menu for your chocolate dinner," said Charley. "How does chocolate pasta with French cheese and artichokes sound for one of the courses?"

"Heavenly," Samantha murmured. And expensive. "Remember, we need to turn a profit."

"Trust me, we will."

"I think this will be *wonderful,*" Heinrich gushed. "We could become the perfect Northwest destination for lovers. Annemarie," he called, hurrying after her. "We should work together on a romantic package."

"Don't forget to include chocolates in it," Samantha called after him, and he grinned and gave her a thumbs-up.

They were on their way. She beamed as people walked past, promising to help.

"I think you'd better set up an email loop," Jonathan Templar suggested. He was her computer tech expert and owner of Geek Gods Computer Services. "So you can all keep one another up-to-date."

"Gee, I wonder who we can get to do that," she teased. "Hopefully, someone who works cheap."

"Since it's for the town, I'll offer my services for free," he said, pushing his glasses up his nose. "And I'll build you a special website. I can have it up and running in a couple of days."

"You're my hero," she said, and kissed him on the cheek, making his whole face turn russet.

From the corner of her eye she caught sight of Blake, old Mr. Community Spirit, talking with Ed while watching her. He gave her what he must have considered an encouraging smile, which made her seethe. Oh, yeah, the bank wanted to do what it could to help the community, all right. Unless a business was really in trouble. Then they could forget it.

She turned her back on him and said to Charley, "Let's go. I've got a lot of work to do." Like saving a company.

Eight

If you can't manage your family, what hope do you
have of managing a business?
———Muriel Sterling, *When Family Matters*

It was going on two in the afternoon and Muriel had
done about all she wanted to for one day. She'd gotten
dressed. Now she was on the couch, looking through
one of her photo albums.

The cordless phone rang and she picked it up from the
coffee table where it was slowly losing juice. Caller ID
told her that her eldest was on the other end of the line.

Not now, she decided, and set the phone back down.
She loved her daughter, but sometimes Samantha simply exhausted her.

This was nothing new. She'd begun by keeping her
pregnant mother awake half the night with her in-the-
womb acrobatics, and she hadn't been any easier to cor-
ral once she'd left for the big wide world. Samantha had
never been fond of the word *no,* which had made her a
top seller in school fund-raisers. It also made her a challenge to raise. She'd always pushed the boundaries on everything from allowances to clothing styles to curfews.
By the time the other two girls came along, Muriel had
given up on her idea of holding the reins of parenthood
tightly and had gone lenient.

"*I* never got to stay out that late," Samantha would

complain when Bailey came dragging home at midnight. "And you're going to let her stay out all night for prom?"

Frustration with her mother's choices hadn't stopped with such minor issues. "Mom, you can't put Waldo in charge of this company. He's a sweet man and I know he wants to be involved, but he doesn't understand how we do things."

"He's a businessman," Muriel had insisted. "And he'll bring new ideas to the table."

The fallout from that decision had taken her relationship with her firstborn to new lows, and so far she hadn't been able to atone for her bad judgment. So she'd vowed that whatever her daughter needed to do, she'd be supportive. But putting on this festival just seemed so impossible. Merely thinking about it exhausted her. The last thing she wanted to do today was talk about it.

With a frown, Muriel refocused her attention on the pictures from her honeymoon cruise with Waldo. There they stood at the ship's railing, the turquoise waters of the Caribbean serving as a backdrop, smiling like a couple who had many good years ahead of them. She sighed and turned the page and fingered the picture of them seated at the captain's table, her in her evening gown and Waldo in his tux. They should've just kept cruising and left Samantha to run the business.

She flipped through the pages, blinking back tears at the snapshots of their short life together: picnicking at Lost Bride Falls, enjoying dinner at the Space Needle in Seattle, posing in front of the tree last Christmas. She looked at the brave face he was putting on and felt tears forming. They'd known about his condition for a month by then but hadn't told the girls. The holidays hadn't seemed like the right time. Now there was no point in saying anything, especially to Samantha. She'd only feel bad about how angry she'd been with him.

Samantha. With a sigh, Muriel picked up the phone to check the message.

Her daughter's voice was filled with energy. "Good news, Mom. The Chamber is behind us. Our chocolate festival is a go. Looks like you're going to be busy for the next several weeks."

Busy for the next several weeks, and all with a daughter living at home again.

Not that she didn't want Cecily back—she would be a comfort. But she would also be…here. And even though Muriel loved her daughter, she'd rather not expend valuable energy pretending she was doing well. She just wanted to sleep or sit in the office and stare into space or look at pictures. She'd been down this road before and it didn't get any easier the second time around. In fact, she was sure it was harder.

And how to explain that to her daughters, to anyone? How could you explain the ache of loss, the deep well of sorrow, to people who hadn't experienced it yet?

The moment that thought emerged, she knew she wasn't being fair. Her daughters had experienced the loss of a father they adored.

Still, they were young. They had their whole lives before them. They'd find men who loved them and build lives with those men. Muriel wouldn't. She'd been blessed to find two wonderful men in one lifetime. There would be no third time for her. And, that being the case, what would she do with the rest of her life? She'd spent so many years as a wife and companion. What was she now?

Still a mother, she reminded herself, and that was a role a woman never stepped out of. Life goes on.

What a depressing saying! On days like this it seemed wrong that life kept going when someone you loved died. Now hers wasn't going to simply keep going it was about to turn into a whirlwind, and she wasn't ready. But she would be. For everyone's sake she had to be. She'd call Samantha…tomorrow.

"That's great," Cecily said after Samantha told her the news.

"And it will be really good for Mom," Samantha said. "She can't keep sitting in the house doing nothing."

"Well." Cecily was thoughtful. "I don't know. We're not giving her any time to grieve."

"There isn't time, not if we want to keep our business."

"Whoa, Scrooge lives."

"Scrooge has to. Did she tell you Waldo let his life insurance lapse?"

"What? You mean—"

"She gets nothing. Nada. Zip."

"The new house isn't paid off, is it?" Now Cecily sounded worried.

And so she should. Someone besides Samantha needed to be. "Nope, and she's upside down on it."

Cecily let out her breath. "This is not good."

Samantha agreed. "The sooner you get here, the better, because Mom's not answering her phone."

"Well, maybe she's out running errands."

"No, she's in the house moping."

"How do you know?"

"Because that's what she was doing last time I went over." There was silence, and suddenly Samantha felt guilty. "What?" she demanded, ignoring the little voice jeering, *Rotten daughter, rotten daughter, rotten,* rotten *daughter.*

"You're not cutting her much slack."

Her sister was right and that made Samantha testy. "There's no time to cut anybody any slack."

"You've got a point there," Cecily said diplomatically.

Darn right she did. Oh, who was she kidding? She was the world's biggest bitch. Her sisters should get her a dog collar for her next birthday.

She heaved a sigh. "You're right. Mom needs a chance to grieve and I need to see a shrink."

"Don't worry. We'll get you whipped into shape," Cecily teased.

"I think it's hopeless," Samantha said. "I should go. I've got to get over to city hall and start things moving on the permits."

"Okay. I'll be there by the end of the week."

Samantha only hoped her sister wasn't closing shop on her account. "Are you positive you want to do this?"

"Absolutely. You probably don't really need me, though. Knowing you, everything's under control."

Even though she'd felt put-upon when her sisters left her holding the bag at Sweet Dreams, she had to admit she liked being in control. Except this was still a family business. Had she really made Cecily think she didn't need her?

That last thought came as a bit of a revelation. "I need you to help me keep all these balls in the air," she said. "And to keep me sane."

"Well, I'm not sure about that last one, but I can help with the juggling."

"Thanks," Samantha said. "Have I told you recently what a great sister you are?"

"No. But you're right. I am."

She could hear the smile in Cecily's voice, and when she hung up she was smiling, too. She wasn't going to have to hold down the chocolate fort alone. Reinforcements were coming. She shot an email to Ed to let him know she was getting the permit process started, then grabbed her purse and coat and left her office.

"I'm off to city hall to apply for permits," she told Elena, who had stopped a rapid-fire conversation in Spanish to ask where she was going. "I shouldn't be long."

Elena nodded and returned to her conversation, frowning and gesticulating madly. The waving arm and Spanish could only mean one thing—she was talking to her mother. Samantha was glad she'd be out of the office for a while. It always took Elena at least half an hour to calm down after one of her mother-daughter chats.

What was it about moms? They could be a girl's best friend one minute and her worst enemy the next. *Your mother was never your enemy,* she reminded herself. Mom wasn't psychic; she couldn't have known how things were going to turn out. She'd been nothing but supportive all of Samantha's life. Well, until Waldo.

Samantha frowned. And there was the rub. She'd resented Mom's decision to put him in charge then and she still resented it, even now that he was gone.

I do need a shrink, she thought as she made her way toward the end of Center Street, where Icicle Falls City Hall and the police department were located. But she didn't have time for one now.

Priscilla Castro was on the front desk and she greeted Samantha with a superior smirk, her usual greeting for her former rival. In high school Samantha and Priscilla had battled each other over everything from grade point supremacy to boys. Priscilla's friends had called her

Cilla. The other girls called her Prissy, which quickly got changed to Pissy. Samantha had beaten her out as class valedictorian and—worse—taken the Miss Icicle Falls crown and the college scholarship money that went with it, leaving Pissy in the dust as third runner-up. Pissy got even by stealing Samantha's boyfriend, Neil Castro, right before senior prom. She wound up marrying Neil, who went to work in a fruit-packing warehouse in Wenatchee. Not exactly the catch of the century as far as Samantha was concerned. Or Pissy, either. They got divorced after a couple of years, something Pissy probably blamed Samantha for, too. If Sweet Dreams went under, Pissy would probably climb on the roof of city hall and crow. Long live high school.

"Hi, Piss… Priscilla," Samantha said.

"Samantha, what brings you here?" Pissy's tone of voice added, *Not that anyone wants to see you.*

"I need permits for a special event and I figure you're the go-to gal," Samantha said with forced pleasantness.

"Special event?" Pissy cocked her head like the inquisitive crow she was. "Who's doing a special event?"

"The Chamber."

"This is the first I've heard of it," Pissy said.

"Well, that's because it was just decided." Samantha strove to keep her smile in place.

"Does Mayor Stone know?"

Del Stone, like Pissy, didn't like anything happening in town that he didn't know about. "Not yet, but I'm sure Ed York will give him all the details. So, what do I need to fill out?"

Pissy handed over the appropriate form. It was a mile long. "You can bring it back tomorrow."

"You know, I think I'll take care of it now," Samantha said sweetly. The sooner she got the process going, the better.

Pissy shrugged. "Suit yourself. We close in ten minutes." She sauntered off in the direction of the mayor's office to tattle, leaving Samantha at the counter.

Samantha had barely begun when Del Stone emerged from his office, a short stocky man who loved to pair crazy neckties with his conservative suits. Today he was sporting a black necktie featuring a leaping salmon and the caption Born to Fish.

"Samantha," he greeted her, taking her hand and giving it a fatherly pat. "How is your mother doing?"

She has no money and she's sleeping all day. "She's fine," Samantha lied.

"Well, if there's anything I can do…"

Just don't ask her to marry you. "Thank you," Samantha said.

"I hear the Chamber is talking about a festival," the mayor said. "This is news to me."

He was smiling but Samantha knew a scolding when she heard one. She looked over to where Pissy now sat at her desk, still in smirk mode. "Well, we just voted on it today."

He shook his head. "I wish I could've been there. I'm afraid I had business in Wenatchee. Is it something for summer perhaps?"

Once more it hit Samantha how crazy it was to try and slap this together in such a short time. "Um, no, a little sooner than that."

"Oh?" he probed.

She could feel her cheeks warming. "More like Valentine's Day."

The good mayor's smile did a Cheshire Cat fade. "Valentine's Day," he repeated.

"Actually, Sweet Dreams is going to sponsor it."

"Figures," Pissy muttered over at her desk.

"Samantha, this really isn't very practical," the mayor said.

"We're going to start small," Samantha assured him.

"With so little time you'll have to start microscopic."

"I think we can do it," she said.

Now the mayor was frowning. "If this comes off half-baked, it won't look good for our town."

"It won't, I guarantee it," Samantha insisted. He was standing there like a two-legged rain cloud ready to dump on her festival, so she hurried on. "Why don't you let Ed and me take you out to dinner at Zelda's tonight and tell you more about it? You'll find that this is something we can all get behind." Great. There went more money flying off over Sleeping Lady Mountain. The mayor loved to eat. And drink. Dinner would cost a fortune.

Del nodded thoughtfully. "All right. And why don't you bring your mother? It would do her good to get out."

Just what her mother always wanted, dinner with Del Stone, swinging bachelor. Del had been divorced for years. With no wife on the scene he'd done his best to turn himself into an urbane ladies' man, and it was looking like Mom was the new lady of choice.

"I'll see if she's feeling up to it," Samantha said.

Mayor Stone nodded again. "I'll see you tonight. Shall we say around seven?"

Samantha nodded, too. She hoped Ed would be free. Del rarely got excited about any idea that hadn't come out of his own balding head. It would take some convincing to get him in their corner—but getting him there was bound to move the permit process along.

He checked his watch. "Well, then, see you tonight. And don't forget to bring your mother."

As she watched him return to his office, she wondered if that was a condition for receiving Del's blessing. Probably.

Now the clock on the wall said one minute until closing time. Samantha frowned at the half-finished form on the counter in front of her. Between them, Pissy and Del had managed to prevent her from getting her form turned in. And Pissy's smirk had grown.

Samantha folded the form, put it in her purse and smirked right back. "I guess I'll see you tomorrow." And for the rest of today she'd be seeing red. Why did people have to keep complicating her life?

She marched out of city hall, her pace fueled by frustration. This called for a large dose of…coffee.

She had just gotten a double-shot mocha latte at Bavarian Brews and was envisioning herself back at city hall first thing in the morning, stapling her completed form to Pissy's forehead, when at the end of the order line she spotted—did he live here?—Blake Preston, business gobbler and festival saboteur. The steam coming from her to-go cup was nothing compared to what she could feel coming out of her ears.

At the sight of her, his jaw set in determination. "Samantha."

Oh, no. I do not want to talk to you. She averted her gaze and skirted the edge of the tables, occupied by retail clerks taking an afternoon coffee break and high school students fresh out of school for the day.

"Samantha, wait," he called.

She pretended deafness and scooted past a table where two older women were enjoying coffee and scones. He cut her off.

"I really don't have time to talk to you," she snapped, and headed the other way around the table.

"I just want five minutes," he said.

"I'd give you five minutes," one of the women said, patting hair that had been dyed a color found nowhere in nature.

Samantha picked up her pace. Or tried to. Unfortunately, she tripped over a large purse lying by the woman's chair. Instead of making a rushed but dignified exit from the coffee shop, she did a clown-style lurch, sloshing her latte from the cup onto her gloves, her coat and the floor. She landed with a squeak in the lap of a burly high school boy.

"Whoa," he said in pleased surprise, and his friends snickered.

This was like being in a movie where everyone froze so all eyes could be on her.

There was no "like" about it. All eyes *were* on her. Her face flamed. "Sorry," she muttered, and scrambled to her feet.

"Anytime," the kid said.

Abandoning all attempts at dignity, she made a dash for the door.

Blake followed her out and caught her by the arm. It was hard to ignore the jolt she felt at the contact.

"Samantha, wait," he said.

She waited. And removed his hand from her arm. Irritation with both herself and him filled her with a strong desire to kick him. Grown-up that she was trying to be, she resisted it. "If I didn't know better, I'd swear you were stalking me."

He frowned. "Very funny."

"These days I have to find humor where I can."

"Look, I know you think I should have said more at the meeting today."

"You could have," she said coldly.

"I was honest," he said. "You're not going to make much money this first time around with so little time to plan."

"Well, I'd love to have a year to pull this together, but, as you know, the bomb is ticking and I don't have that luxury."

"Samantha, it may not look like it, but I'm in your corner."

Watching her get pummeled to death. "Oh, please," she said, and rolled her eyes.

He let out an angry hiss. "You can't believe I want to call in that note."

Okay, she'd had about all the hypocrisy she could stomach for one day. "It's a free country. I can believe whatever I want," she informed him. "And once I pull my company out of this mess, I will be taking our business to a bank that puts its money where its mouth is and really helps its customers." He started to speak and she held up a hand. "Don't. Say. Anything. If you do, I just might trip again and spill the rest of my latte all over you."

"Go ahead, if it'll make you feel better." He threw out his arms and puffed out his chest, turning himself into a target.

But all she could see was how big his chest was.

She raised her chin. "No, I think not. There's no point wasting a perfectly good latte." Having delivered her parting shot, she turned her back on him and crossed the street to return to her one true love—her business.

Nine

There is a difference between selling your ideas
and selling yourself.
> —Muriel Sterling, *Knowing Who You Are:*
> *One Woman's Journey*

With its art deco decor and a menu that featured Northwest-style specialties, Zelda's restaurant was a hopping place when winter sports enthusiasts were in town, and locals couldn't get in without a reservation. No reservations needed for tonight, though. It was a weekday and the tourists had been few and far between, thanks to the sparse snowfall. That, combined with a cold sleet falling outside, left the restaurant less than half-full with a couple of families and some couples taking advantage of the twofer coupon Charley had run in the *Mountain Sun* on Sunday.

The aroma of spices and seared beef greeted Samantha as she and her mother walked in the door. The sizzle of cooking meat from the open kitchen, where Charley's new chef was hard at work creating culinary masterpieces, provided background music for the spurts of laughter coming from a table of three women, who had obviously gotten a head start on their drinking. Later they'd drift into the bar to meet up with local guys, but for now they were indulging in Zelda's huckleberry martinis and shrimp tarts. Over by the window Samantha caught sight of Luke, their production manager, out on a date with his four-year-old daughter, Serena, who was finishing up a hot fudge sundae. He gave Samantha a smile and a wave.

Luke was a single dad, not by choice. His wife had been tragically killed two years earlier, hit by a car when she was out jogging. He was a nice man and a hard worker, one of many employees who depended on her company for his livelihood. She waved back, trying to ignore the weight of responsibility that was suddenly crushing her appetite.

A group whoop from the party girls made Mom frown. "I shouldn't have let you talk me into this."

"They'll be gone soon," Samantha said.

"It's not them, it's me. I'm not ready for socializing, sweetie. You entertain the men. I can walk home."

She turned to leave, but Samantha laid a pleading hand on her arm. "Mom, please. It's only for an hour. I really need your support."

And she needed Mom to bat her eyes at Del so he'd want to get behind the festival. Pimping out her own mother. She was pathetic.

Ed was waving at her from a corner table. Next to him sat Del, looking downright eager. "Anyway, they've seen us," she added. "It would be rude to leave." Playing the courtesy card always worked with her mother.

Sure enough, Mom resigned herself to her fate with a sigh. "All right. But I don't want to be here all night."

Charley, taking the place of the hostess who'd been overly hospitable to Charley's now-ex-husband, greeted them with menus in hand. "Ed and Del are already here. I've got you at a nice corner table where you can talk." To Mom she said, "Good to see you, Mrs. Wittman."

Mom managed a smile and murmured her thanks, and Charley led them to their table.

Both men stood politely as they approached. Next to Ed, who was tall and lean and still had his hair, Del, with his paunch and bald head, didn't exactly show well in spite of his black suit and crisp white shirt and impress-the-ladies lavender tie he'd exchanged for his earlier fish number.

Ed took both of Mom's hands in his and said, "I'm glad you came."

Del did him one better, raising a hand to his lips and kissing it. "You look lovely tonight, Muriel."

No lie there. Mom wore a simple black dress and hadn't bothered with any makeup other than mascara and eyeliner (which she wouldn't be without, even on her deathbed), but her pale face made her appear vulnerable. Which was exactly what she was.

Mom's polite smile slid south. "Thank you," she murmured, and extricated her hand.

They all sat and Del gave Mom a genial smile. "How about something to ward off the cold?" he asked. Judging from the near-empty glass in front of him, Del had already driven away the cold.

"A cup of tea would be nice," she said.

"I was thinking something a little stronger," Del said. "Some white wine, perhaps?"

Mom shook her head, and Del looked disappointed.

Maria came to the table, ready to take their orders. "May as well get a bottle, don't you think?" he said to Ed.

"Sure," Ed agreed.

Samantha hoped he was going to pick up the tab for it.

Once the wine had arrived and they'd chosen their dinners—steak for the men, chicken with raspberry sauce and baby potatoes for Samantha and a small salad for Mom—Samantha introduced the subject of the festival.

Del took a sip of his wine and shook his head. "Plenty of time to talk about that," he said. "But first let me just say, Muriel, that if there's anything you need, I hope you know you only have to ask."

"Thank you, Del. I appreciate that," Mom said.

And here would have been the perfect opportunity for her mother to say, "I need you to support this festival we're planning." Instead, she took the little pot Maria had brought and poured tea into her cup.

Samantha forced herself not to drum her fingers on the table. She glanced at Ed. He was busy enjoying his wine and seemed in no hurry to get down to business. *And that* is *how you do business,* she had to remind herself. *Don't rush right into talking about what you want. Get the other person relaxed and receptive first.* Actually, Del was already relaxed. So was Ed. She was the one who was tense.

Del was pouring a third glass of wine when dinner arrived. Now would be the time to bring up the subject of the festival. Samantha took a sip from her water glass, then plunged in. "I'm glad you could join us tonight," she began.

"I'm happy to spend an evening with my old pal Ed, here, and two of my favorite women in town," Del said, and beamed at Mom.

"We're really excited to share what the Chamber's come up with to bring more visitors to town," Samantha plunged on.

Del took another swallow of wine. "Let's enjoy our dinner, shall we? We can talk business a little later."

After how many more glasses of wine? Samantha looked to Ed, who just shrugged and cut into his steak.

Samantha sighed inwardly and told herself that buttering people up required a lot of time. And there was a lot of Del to butter.

As the evening wore on and the wine flowed, Del's fish stories got harder to swallow and his laugh got as big as the one that got away. "Ah, but there's nothing like being in the great outdoors," he concluded. "When you're out on the river, you can let the whole world go by. And if a man's out there with a beautiful woman, it's like being in Eden."

Del's hand disappeared under the table and Mom suddenly shifted in her seat. Uh-oh.

"Well, it is a little piece of paradise up here," Samantha said in an effort to distract him, "which makes it the perfect place to hold a festival."

Del was obviously more interested in holding other things, like her mother's leg. Now he was pouting.

And Mom had become the ice queen. She turned to Samantha. "I'm not feeling well. If you don't mind, I'll take the car and head home."

"I'll be glad to drive you," Del offered, probably hoping for more grope time.

"I don't think you should drive anywhere," Mom told him. "Ed, would you mind giving Samantha a lift? Del, too."

"Not at all."

"Mom, I'll take you," Samantha said. That was the least she could do. Oh, man, what a dumb idea this had been.

Mom's Miss Manners mask was firmly in place, but Samantha could feel the waves of irritation radiating off her. "No, dear, you stay and enjoy yourself."

Like that was going to happen. There had been nothing enjoyable about this little dinner party, and Samantha suspected it was going to be downhill from here on.

Sure enough. Mom left and Del lost interest in everything but the second bottle of wine Ed had ordered. And when Samantha tried to redeem the situation by bringing up the subject of the festival, his only response was, "I wish you'd talked to me about this. I don't see how you can pull it off."

Maria came to the table, to ask if they wanted dessert.

They'd blown enough money on Del. "We'll take the check now," Samantha said.

Fortunately, Ed insisted on picking up the tab.

"I'm afraid we wasted your money," Samantha said after they'd loaded a tipsy Del into Ed's car.

"Nothing is ever wasted, Samantha," he said. "Sure I can't give you a lift?"

She shook her head. "I'd rather walk. Anyway, I think I've spent enough time with our good mayor."

Ed grinned. "Del's a decent sort. Just can't hold his liquor. Never could. Don't worry. I'll have another go at him when he's sober. He'll come around."

She hoped so. It was important to have Del's support. She might not have her mother's anymore. She hunched inside her coat and made her way back to Mom's house, bracing herself for a well-deserved lecture.

Mom was in her yellow leather chair, nursing a mug of tea and frowning at the TV when Samantha let herself in. Her mother looked up as she entered but didn't smile. Not a good sign.

"How are you feeling?" Samantha ventured.

Mom cocked an eyebrow.

Samantha knew that gesture. She'd learned it at her mother's knee. It didn't bode well for their conversation. She bit her lip and perched on the edge of the couch.

"I'm sorry about tonight. I had no idea Del was going to behave like that."

"He always behaves like that when he's had too much to drink, and he always drinks too much."

"Mom, I'm really sorry. I thought—"

Her mother cut her off. "I know perfectly well what you thought. Samantha, I understand we need to save our company."

"Not only the company. This benefits the whole town," Samantha insisted.

Her mother held up a hand. "I don't care if it benefits the whole world. I will not have my own daughter pimping me out."

"Mom!" Samantha protested. Bad enough she'd thought it, but to hear it voiced by her mother... Her cheeks flamed.

Mom set down her mug and gave Samantha a look that made her feel eight years old. "Samantha Rose, I will do all I can to help you behind the scenes, but I am not putting up with this sort of nonsense. Is that clear?"

Samantha bit her lip again and nodded.

Mom nodded, too. "Good. Now, give me a kiss and go home."

Thoroughly chastised Samantha kissed her mother's cheek, took her car keys and fled. She cried all the way back to her condo, then burned off her misery by playing games on her laptop until two in the morning. But no matter how many zombies she killed, it didn't really help.

She was still killing zombies in her sleep (they all looked like Del) when her alarm went off at seven the next morning. She shut it off with a groan and forced herself to get out of bed. Winners never quit and quitters never win. She was no quitter.

She fed Nibs, who was, as usual, starving. Then she put on her favorite dance workout DVD and got busy. Exercise always made her feel better and she was really getting into it when an angry thump on her living room floor from Lila Ward, her cranky neighbor downstairs, told her she needed to curb her enthusiasm. She stomped on the floor a couple of times to show Lila she'd gotten the message, then switched from dancing to doing crunches. After that it was a quick shower, some scrambled eggs and out the door.

She had a full day ahead of her. In addition to dropping off that form at city hall, she had to email the members of her newly minted festival committee, check out the website Jonathan was designing and meet with Lizzy, her bookkeeper.

"So how much can we spend on advertising?" she asked later that day after Lizzy had assured her that she and her employees could survive another month.

Lizzy looked at Samantha over her pink bifocals. "Seriously?"

Samantha leaned back in her chair and sighed. "Yeah. Dumb question."

Blake Preston had had a hard time getting Samantha Sterling out of his mind. Here was a woman who'd inherited a business that had been left in chaos, who could have taken one look at the odds and thrown in the towel. But she was still swinging, fighting for all she was worth. How could anyone not admire that? In addition to being a fighter, she was a walking idea factory. She could turn her company around, given half a chance.

He knew all the reasons he couldn't make an exception and give her that chance, but it would go a long way toward good community relations if he did. And what was Cascade Mutual going to do with a chocolate factory, anyway?

He pressed his point to his regional manager, Darren Short, as they ate schnitzel at Schwangau, Blake's favorite restaurant.

Darren cut off a gigantic chunk of meat and stuffed it in his mouth. "Don't worry. We won't end up stuck with anything."

Blake frowned at Darren. Fifteen years Blake's senior, Darren had been both his mentor and his champion. Right now Blake took in Darren's scrawny build and weak chin and thought him a wimp. "And why is that?"

Darren washed his schnitzel down with a hearty swig of beer. "Because we have someone who's interested in taking over their assets."

"Who? Who the heck would want those assets?"

"Madame C in Seattle."

Blake pushed away his plate, his appetite gone. "Their competitor."

"Big fish eat little fish," Darren said with a shrug.

"And we serve up little fish on a platter."

Now Darren set down his knife and fork. "Was it a mistake sending you back to your hometown?"

Maybe. "You've seen my report. You tell me."

Darren took another swig of beer, then leaned back in his chair and studied Blake. They sat there for a moment, locked in a stare-down, while in the background other diners talked over an old German drinking song.

Darren was the first to break eye contact. He picked up his knife and fork and resumed attacking his meat. "You're doing a fine job. I'd hate to see you follow in Arnie's footsteps."

"I have no intention of doing that," Blake said. "But I *am* trying to do what's best for the bank. Maintaining good community relations by helping a business that's been part of this community for generations is a sensible way to bring in more business."

"We don't want the kind of business that costs us large amounts of money. Come on, Blake, you've been in banking long enough to know the bottom line."

"Yeah, and it sure isn't people, even though we say it is," Blake muttered.

"Trevor Brown is people, too, and if Sweet Dreams goes under, his company will benefit from their loss."

Blake's eyes narrowed suspiciously. "So you know Brown."

Darren calmly cut off another piece of meat. "I know a lot of businessmen in Seattle. Look, Darren. I'm not saying I want this company to fail. I hope they succeed. But in case they don't, either way, the bank will be fine and someone will be happy. Someone goes down, someone else goes up. And that, my boy, is business," he said, and popped the meat in his mouth.

"Like you said, either way the bank comes out fine," Blake said in disgust.

"That about sums it up. And all the people who work in the Icicle Falls branch will still have jobs come March 1 because you're doing what has to be done." He picked up his glass and saluted Blake. "Cheers."

Yeah, cheers.

Ten

Luck is what you make it.
—Muriel Sterling, *Knowing Who You Are:*
One Woman's Journey

The day before had been ugly, with unsympathetic creditors to deal with and an unexpected computer crash. Miraculously, Jonathan Templar had been able to fix it, but that minor miracle had taken several hours, and he'd warned Samantha it was only a temporary fix. She'd finally left the office at seven, a drained dishrag in heels, thoroughly depressed by what felt like a never-ending run of bad luck.

But now their luck was going to turn, she was convinced of it. Her sister being able to come and help was surely the first of many lucky breaks, she told herself as she drove to Sea-Tac Airport on Friday to pick up Cecily. Reinforcements had arrived and things were already humming right along for the festival.

Shop owners as well as the restaurants and B and Bs were on board and promising to offer special sales. Jonathan had their website up and, with the exception of one thing, it looked good. For the home page he'd used a landscape shot of the town and surrounding mountain peaks for background and then superimposed a glorious box of bonbons in the foreground. Looking at Center Street with its Bavarian shops and window boxes and hanging baskets full of spring flowers (not to mention that box of goodies), who wouldn't want to come to Icicle Falls and enjoy a weekend dedicated to shopping, fun and chocolate?

Cecily's flight was on time, more good luck.

"How are you doing?" Cecily asked as soon as they had her bags loaded in the car.

"Great," Samantha said. "Did you check out the website?"

Cecily nodded. "It's fabulous. I can't believe how much progress we're making."

"It's amazing how much you can accomplish with so many people pitching in," Samantha said. "But…that schedule of events you had Jonathan put up— I'm not so sure about this Mr. Dreamy contest." She had a sneaking suspicion their baby sister was behind it. "Was this Bailey's idea?" Whoever came up with it should have run it by her first before posting the event. Was it too late to remove the contest? Even though the website had already gotten a lot of hits, no one had entered yet, and she'd know if they had, since, according to the website, contestants could download the form and drop it off at the Sweet Dreams gift shop. Another little detail no one had run past her.

"Yes, it was Bailey's brainchild," Cecily said, "but it's a clever idea."

Translation: *I didn't stop her because I didn't want to hurt her feelings.* Samantha frowned.

"It'll stir up lots of local interest," Cecily said, "and you can bet Festival Hall will be packed with women the night we have the competition. We're charging for the event, so we'll make a ton of money."

"And you know that because?"

"Because I've been to events where the firefighters who do those fund-raiser calendars make an appearance.

The women go crazy. We'll give everyone a small box of chocolates and a chance to watch their favorite man walk the catwalk shirtless, and they'll think they scored big."

"It all seems a little tacky."

"I suppose it is," Cecily admitted, "but with the ball, the dinner and the chocolate high tea at Olivia's we already have enough classy events. This gives people a chance to cut loose and get silly. And Bailey's rounded up some really cool prizes, so I suspect we'll have a lot of men wanting to enter, not to mention women volunteering their boyfriends."

"I don't know," Samantha said dubiously.

"Sam, you're not going to micromanage us, are you?"

"I don't micromanage." She shot a glance in her sister's direction to see Cecily giving her a look that said, *Oh, yeah?* "I don't," she insisted.

"Okay, then, since you don't, don't. You've delegated the events and publicity to us. Let us handle them. You've got your hands full overseeing the festival and running the business. That means you just have to make sure we're doing our jobs. You don't get to tell us how to do them."

"I would never do that. I mean, I might offer some suggestions once in a while." That was part of overseeing, after all.

"Suggestions are always welcome, but don't worry. Everything's under control," Cecily said.

"Okay, so tell me where we are with promotion."

"I found the name of the producer of that Seattle talk show, *Northwest Now.* I'm going to email her and see if they'll do a story on the festival. I know the *Mountain Sun* will do one."

"Free publicity, the best kind," Samantha said approvingly.

They spent the rest of the drive home talking about Cecily's ideas and brainstorming other ways to promote the festival. By the time they entered town both sisters were excited.

"This really is going to be great," Cecily predicted.

Samantha nodded. "I think our luck is about to change."

And to prove it, her car started *ka-thwumpity-thwumping* down the road.

"What the heck?" Cecily asked as Samantha gripped her jiggly steering wheel.

"We've got a flat. That's a real pain." Samantha pulled off into the parking lot of the Man Cave.

She got out to inspect her car and discovered that her left rear tire was flat. "My lucky day," she grumbled as she got back in the car to fish out her cell phone and call a tow truck.

"What is this place?" Cecily asked, although the Bud Light neon sign in the window was a pretty big clue.

Still, she couldn't help asking. It was such an eyesore with its tacky mural, the potholed parking lot and the smattering of beat-up trucks and motorcycles parked in front.

This business was a new addition to town since she had moved to L.A. She remembered the building itself. It had been a mom-and-pop grocery store before Safeway came to town and cornered the grocery market. Then it had enjoyed a short life as an office supply store. After that it sat empty and became party central for kids bent on fun their parents wouldn't approve of. She'd been one of those kids for a short time until she decided getting high wasn't going to get her the kind of attention she wanted in life or the kind of boys.

Not that she'd gotten the type of men she wanted after high school. Pathetic to be able to tell who was right for whom when people came to her dating service (not that they listened), but never able to figure it out for herself. She eyed the gigantic mural of the Neanderthal in lederhosen on the side of this old building, which was being given a dubious new life. That was the type of man she'd always seemed to gravitate toward. Why? Had her life been so boring that she had to spice it up with cavemen?

"It's been here about a year," Samantha said. "A guy named Todd Black bought it and turned it into a sports bar. He's one of the few people who's not on board with the festival," she added with a frown.

"Interesting taste in decorating," Cecily observed.

"The Neanderthal says it all. Oh, and speak of the devil."

Handsome devil. Cecily took in the lean man with the broad shoulders walking across the parking lot toward them. He had the dark hair and swarthy pirate complexion she typically fell for. He dressed like the kind of man she always fell for, too, in jeans and leather jacket hanging open over a gray T-shirt that showed off a fine set of pecs.

Oh, no, she told herself, *those pecs are attached to the wrong man.*

But a girl could look.

You look, you'll want. Don't look.

As he got closer she saw he had light blue eyes. Blue like ice. Mysterious. *Stop. Don't go there.* She swallowed hard and looked away. *Out of sight, out of mind.*

She could hear the car window on her sister's side sliding down. Then she heard his voice. "Planning on coming in for a beer?" Oh, she was a sucker for a low, sexy voice. Its magnetic pull turned her head toward him.

"How'd you guess?" Samantha retorted. "We had a flat. I was just about to call Swede."

"Swede'll gouge you good. I assume you've got a spare."

Her sister was always prepared. If there was no spare in the back, then Samantha had been kidnapped by aliens and this cranky woman sitting behind the driver's seat was a fake. "Of course," she said, insulted.

"Pop your trunk and I'll change it for you."

"Thanks, but you don't need to do that," Samantha said. "We'll be fine."

"I know. Pop the trunk."

She popped it and got out. Cecily decided to stay inside. It didn't take two women to supervise changing a tire. And besides, she didn't need to see any more of Todd Black than she already had.

Their voices drifted toward her through the open window.

"So, you pissed because I'm not into chocolate?"

"Should I be?"

"Actually, no. What's the point of getting pissed just because someone disagrees with you?"

"None, of course, but there's a difference between disagreeing and trying to discourage people," Samantha said.

"Hey, I happen to think you're biting off too much and it's going to blow up in your face. I don't want to be part of that."

"You're about the only one in town who doesn't," Samantha countered.

Cecily couldn't help smiling. *Don't waste your time arguing with my sister.*

"It only took one kid to see the emperor was buck naked," Todd said. "Anyway, it's a free country. Knock yourself out."

This man was quick with a comeback, but it wasn't a very nice comeback. Cecily knew her men. They all fell into categories and now she had this one pegged. He was a mule man—stubborn, intractable, always positive he was right. Ugh.

A tap on her window made her jump. She turned to see the blue-eyed mule man. "You mind getting out? I'm about to jack up the car. If you move around in there, you might move it off the jack."

She nodded and got out.

"I'm Todd Black," he said. "You new here?"

"I've lived here all my life," Cecily informed him.

That smile on his face… Was he mocking her? "Ah, part of the old-timers' club," he said with a knowing nod. "I've been here a year and I haven't seen you. Where've you been hiding?"

"L.A." And she hadn't been hiding. "I'm Cecily, Samantha's sister."

"That explains it," he said. Now his smile was definitely mocking.

"Explains what?" she demanded.

"The warm reception I'm getting." He walked back around to the other side of the car and started cranking the jack.

"Todd, we do appreciate you bailing us out," Samantha said. "I just wish I could get you to see how good this festival can be for the whole town."

"I don't need a festival to boost my business."

"Oh? You don't need paying customers?"

"I already have paying customers," he said as the car levitated.

"This will bring in more," Cecily put in.

He grinned at her over his shoulder. "So, you drank the poisoned Kool-Aid, too, huh?"

"I think my sister's right," she said. "That's why I'm up here, to help her."

He shrugged. "Well, blood is thicker than water. And what do you do when you're not planning festivals?"

Cecily could feel her cheeks burn, a sure sign that she was blushing. But she had no reason to be embarrassed. She offered a vital service. "I have a business." Well, she *had* a business.

"Me, too," he said, jerking his head to indicate the dump at the far end of the parking lot. "What's yours?"

"It's a dating service." *And a very good one at that.*

At least it was, until the final straw had glowered his way into her office—Clyde Dangler-Dunn. Mr. Double D, she'd called him, and he'd been a typical stud man— the kind of man who thought he was God's gift to women and was more interested in exercising his favorite muscle doing the horizontal bop than in finding a life companion. She had tried to do the impossible and find someone for Clyde but had failed—not for lack of trying but because there was no perfect woman for a man like him. Except for a hooker, and since she wasn't a madam she couldn't help him with that.

"None of the women your service introduced me to have met my standards," he'd informed her, his double chin raised to its haughtiest level. (Clyde was a little on the hefty side, but since he also had a hefty bank account he expected women to overlook that.)

Which probably meant they'd refused to sleep with him on the first date. "Now, Clyde," she'd said sweetly, "I've found you six beautiful, talented women half the men in America would die to date." And coming up with that many women had been a miracle.

"I'm not half the men in America. I told you I want women with big breasts. Real ones."

Like she could find those easily in L.A.?

"Cancel my contract immediately and refund my money or you'll be hearing from my lawyer."

Cancel his contract? She'd gladly have canceled *him*. But not wanting to repeat the disaster she'd had with Liza, she'd restrained herself. Instead, she'd said all that was diplomatically required and written him a check right then and there. And that had drained her business account.

And her patience. Burnout had destroyed both her dreams and her business. Men like Stud Man and this mule man here made it hard for Cupid and his helpers. She'd decided that Cupid was on his own. Cecily was too disgusted to care anymore. Let those losers go online and lie through their teeth, let them do their own screening and set up their own meet-and-greet parties to their hearts' content. She was done, done, done. She'd tied up loose ends, made a few final matches, then closed her doors.

"A dating service, huh?" said this latest poor specimen of the male species.

"I can guess what you're thinking," she hurried to say. "But not all dating services exist to match gold diggers up with millionaires." Although that had been the case with most of her customers.

"Good. You set my mind at ease."

Sarcasm, always a nice trait in a man. Cecily managed a polite smile, then turned her back and contemplated the thin icing of snow on the mountains. When she'd been up here for Waldo's funeral she'd thought it was nice to see the town growing. This kind of growth, however, they didn't need.

"There you go, ladies," he said at last. "This will hold you until you can get over to Swede's and pick up a new tire. He charges an arm and a leg for towing but his tire prices are reasonable."

As if they didn't know that? Swede Lind had been in business in Icicle Falls for the past twenty years. In fact, he was the grandfather of the new bank manager who was giving Samantha grief.

"Thanks," Samantha said. "I'd offer you some chocolate to show our appreciation but since you don't like it—"

"Who said I don't like it?" he asked. "I just think the festival is a dumb idea."

Samantha shook her head, but she promised him a box. Then they got into the car and left the Neanderthal to go back to his drooling Neanderthal customers.

"Well, he's something else," Cecily said contemptuously.

Samantha sneaked a look in Cecily's direction. "But he's hot."

"A great cover doesn't make a great book."

"Is that something you told all your customers?"

"There wouldn't have been any point," Cecily said. "They never listened."

"Well, make sure you listen to yourself. When it comes to guys—"

Cecily cut her off. "I know. You don't have to remind me."

"Okay. Just sayin'."

Thankfully, Samantha let it go at that. There was no need for a sisterly lecture. Cecily had learned her lesson. No more bad boys who insisted they wanted to get mar-

ried but cheated on you with your best friend. No more
men who pretended to have money and then asked you
for loans and then forget to pay you back. No more losers! Heck, no more men. Period. Look at all the grief a
girl got from them.

And, speaking of grief. Mom was still in her jammies when they arrived at the house, even though it
was midafternoon. "Welcome home," she said, and gave
Cecily a hug.

Their mother normally smelled like Calvin Klein's
Obsession. Today she smelled like…well, it wasn't Calvin Klein.

Cecily remembered after their father died waking up
in the middle of the night to hear her mother crying, but
during the day Mom used to put up a good front. This
time around, she wasn't trying to hold up that false front.
Maybe she figured this time around she didn't need to.
Who knew? Regardless of the reason, it was unnerving.

"You're earlier than I expected," Mom said. "I haven't
had a chance to get dressed."

What had she been doing? Cecily looked around the
house. A fine layer of dust coated the furniture. A couple of photo albums lay open on the couch and a half-
finished mug of chocolate mint tea sat on the coffee
table. Well, she was allowed, no matter what Samantha thought.

"Would you like some tea?" Mom asked.

"We can make it if you want to get dressed," Samantha said in an attempt to be diplomatic.

"I'll be right back."

"No rush," Cecily told her.

As soon as their mother was out of earshot Samantha
said in a low voice, "This is how she's been."

Cecily gave a helpless shrug. What did Samantha

expect her to do about it, slap Mom and tell her to snap out of it? "We've got to give her time."

Samantha frowned and Cecily decided to drop the subject and search the kitchen for tea and distraction.

Samantha followed her. "She'll be better now that you're here. I think she needs someone to need her. Once we get her involved with the festival she'll be fine."

Cecily wasn't so sure about that. Busyness wasn't a miracle cure for a broken heart. She knew from personal experience.

Half an hour later Mom joined them, looking more like herself with her hair freshly washed and wearing gray wool slacks and a black sweater—a V-neck, which had become her trademark ever since she learned that turtlenecks weren't flattering to older women.

"How are you doing?" Cecily asked, handing her a cup of Earl Grey.

"I'm fine," Mom said. "It's good to have you home, sweetie."

"It's good to be home," Cecily said. Here she'd gone off to follow her heart, prove herself and fill the world with love only to realize that her heart had misled her. Filling the world with love was a Herculean task when the world was overflowing with selfish, shallow people.

And then there were the people who were simply too busy for love, like her sister. Samantha managed to sit still long enough to drink a mug of tea, but then she got fidgety.

"I know you need to get back to the office," Mom said, giving her permission to escape to work.

"I should." To Cecily she said, "Maybe you can tell Mom about some of the things we were discussing in the car."

Cecily agreed, and after Samantha left she started to

talk about the festival. But somehow, they drifted from the subject of Mr. Dreamy to Mom's own dream man, Waldo, and out came the photo albums. Cecily didn't mind looking at them, though and, unlike Samantha, she didn't have a problem reconciling the man they'd all liked with the man who'd brought so much chaos into their lives.

"He didn't have the best head for business," Mom admitted, touching a picture of Waldo sitting on the deck, raising a glass of wine in toast to her, "but he had the best heart. And I was so happy to find love again. I never thought I would."

Lucky Mom. She'd found true love not once but twice.

"I keep hoping you girls will find the right man soon." She smiled at Cecily. "They say there's someone for everyone. But I guess you know that."

"I used to believe that," Cecily said. "I'm not sure I do anymore. People expect too much. And give too little," she added, thinking of her two ex-fiancés.

"Not always. You'll find someone," Mom said, patting her arm.

She'd found two someones in the exotic soil of sunny California but neither had turned out to be good. Obviously she was about as qualified to find her own Mr. Right as a surgeon was to operate on himself. "And how do you know that?"

"Because you're too wonderful to be wasted."

Her mother had said the same words to her when she was going through her rebellious phase, only much more sternly. "Seems to me I've heard those words before," she teased.

"They're still true." Mom leaned back against the couch and regarded her. "I think God has been waiting for you to come home. I think He's got the perfect man for you somewhere right here in Icicle Falls."

Cecily envisioned the Neanderthal who had been her welcome-home committee. *Or not.*

Samantha had a quick conference with Jim, their sales rep, promised the moon to a supplier and then put in a call to city hall to see how the permits were moving along.

This time she was spared having to deal with Pissy. Emily Brookes, one of the office workers, answered the phone. "Just calling to see how the permits for our chocolate festival are coming along," Samantha said cheerily.

"Gosh, I guess okay," Emily said. "I haven't heard anything one way or another. Do you want to talk to Priscilla?"

Not any more than Pissy wanted to talk to her. "No, that's okay," Samantha said. "I'll check later." These things took time and her form was probably making the rounds of different departments—unless Pissy had shredded it.

Think positive, she told herself, and went back to work. She answered a slew of emails and then shot one to Ed York, running the Mr. Dreamy contest idea past him (not that she was micromanaging—she simply wanted another opinion). Ed gave the idea a resounding thumbs-up and Samantha resigned herself to going along with what she still considered a very tacky event.

Well, good news for Cecily, she supposed, and put in a call home.

"Bailey just phoned," Cecily told her. "Now she's not only got the two-day winery tour package, she also talked Adventure Outfitters into donating a kayak to give our Mr. Dreamy, as well."

"That's some prize package," Samantha said, impressed.

"That's not all. It looks like we've also got a twenty-five-dollar gift certificate for both Italian Alps and Big Brats—free Italian and German food. And I think Cass is going to give us a certificate for her place, too. So, we'll have a nice prize package for our Mr. Dreamy."

"Sounds like it. Ed York thinks it's a great idea." Samantha regretted the words the minute they were out of her mouth.

"You were running this by Ed?"

"Just keeping him up-to-date," Samantha said, improvising quickly. She heard a big sigh on the other end of the line. "No micromanaging. Really."

"I hope not," Cecily said. "By the way, we're about to make dinner. Want to come by?"

"With my malnourished bank account my new motto is never turn down a free meal."

It would be good to get in some sister time and, much as she hated to admit it, she'd appreciate having Cecily present as a cheerful third party for what could be a slightly strained meal with Mom.

The casserole supply had finally dwindled but Cecily had found some chicken soup Bailey had made and left in the freezer and she'd coaxed Mom into making biscuits. The aroma of baking biscuits and simmering soup reminded Samantha that it had been a long time since she'd eaten and her stomach rumbled in anticipation.

"This is the perfect meal for our drizzly mountain weather," she said as she kissed her mother's cheek.

"Too bad that drizzle isn't snow." Cecily placed bowls around the dining table.

"We could have used it. It's been a tough season," Samantha said. "But things are bound to improve," she added. "I think we're on the right track with this festival. We need events to attract tourists. Once they come here and see how beautiful it is, hike the trails, hit the shops and the restaurants, we'll have them hooked. We're every bit as pretty as those high-priced ski resort towns and a better bargain."

"We should put that somewhere in our advertising," Cecily said thoughtfully. "Resort living at affordable prices. What do you think, Mom?"

"That sounds like a good idea," their mother said as she filled a serving bowl with biscuits.

"Do you like that better than 'Icicle Falls, Your Mountain Destination'?" Cecily asked.

"Either one would be lovely," Mom said noncommittally.

Their mother used to love to brainstorm clever slogans and advertising ideas for the company. No storm tonight, just a calm *Stepford Wives* smile. She didn't have much to contribute to the conversation, either, other than agreeing with Cecily that Bailey's soup was excellent.

"So, should we watch a movie?" Cecily asked after they'd finished eating.

"Why don't you girls go out and enjoy yourselves?" Mom suggested instead.

Because we're broke, thought Samantha.

"We'd rather stay here with you," Cecily said. "Let's watch a movie."

Mom shook her head. "If you don't mind, I'm going to go to bed and read."

"Oh. Sure, if you'd rather." Cecily sneaked a look at the cuckoo clock in the kitchen.

"Mom, it's only seven," Samantha protested. Mom never went to bed before eleven. But then she never used to sleep in till noon, either.

"I know. I'm tired," Mom said. "You two go have fun."

Like they could have fun with disaster hanging over their heads, held off by mere threads of hope and determination?

Their mother kissed them both on the cheek, then scooped up a photo album and disappeared into her bedroom.

"She's really struggling," Cecily said as soon as Mom was out of earshot. "I kept trying to interest her in coming up with ideas for ads but I couldn't hold her attention. Hardly surprising, but still."

"I know," Samantha agreed. "She seems like a ghost of her former self. I thought having you here would help her perk up."

"You can't rush grieving. It's going to take time."

The one thing they didn't have. Samantha raised a finger to her mouth to gnaw on a nail and then remembered she didn't have any left. She frowned at her mangled fingertips.

"I see your old habits have returned," her sister observed.

"Yeah, well, it beats eating the inventory," Samantha retorted, then sighed. "I need a new vice."

"You wanted to take up drinking. Why don't we go over to Zelda's?"

"I'm too broke to take up drinking."

"Don't worry. I'll buy. I still have money in savings." Cecily walked to the coat closet and got her jacket. "Let's go cheer you up."

"The only thing that could cheer me up would be winning the lottery," Samantha muttered, and followed her out into the cold.

Zelda's wasn't packed, but Friday night had brought

out a few more warm bodies. A retired couple finished up their meals with coffee and pie. Several younger families were still eating, the parents digging into their smoked salmon chowder while their kids devoured gourmet burgers and sweet-potato fries.

Samantha saw Pissy and one of her underlings from city hall at a table by the window and feigned blindness. Instead, she went to say hello to Heidi Schwartz, who sat toward the front with her new husband. Baby James was in a high chair, slapping the tray in excitement at the sight of a spoon loaded with mashed potatoes.

Cecily came over, too, and Heidi greeted them both enthusiastically. "Sit down. Join us."

"No, you guys go ahead and enjoy your meal. We're heading to the bar, anyway," Samantha said. "Girls' night."

"Sounds like fun," Heidi said agreeably, but from the way she'd been smiling at her husband, Samantha could tell she wouldn't trade her former single life for the one she had now.

A little ping of jealousy hit Samantha—but she brushed it off. Yes, it would be nice to settle down someday, if she could have the kind of happy ending Heidi had found. But there were no guarantees. She could as easily end up with a loser like Charley had.

Blake Preston, with his big shoulders and his small heart, came to mind, giving her a ping of a very different kind. Oh, no. Men like Blake Preston were why she was single. She was happy with her life just as it was. Well, just as it was going to be once she got everything back on an even keel.

"Are you here for the festival?" Heidi asked Cecily.

"I am."

"That's so cool that you can take time off to come up."

Cecily nodded, offering no other information. Samantha couldn't say that she blamed her sister. She wouldn't be announcing it all over town if she'd closed up shop. That thought led to more sobering ones, which she quickly shoved aside.

"Well, enjoy your meal, guys," she said again, and turned to leave. That was when she discovered that while they'd been visiting, Charley had seated some new customers at a table they'd have to pass en route to the bar. Crud. There had to be a way to skirt around that table. More fake blindness required. They should've stayed at Mom's and watched a movie.

"Samantha," Ed York called, smiling and waving at her.

She could have pretended blindness, maybe even deafness, too, but with her sister standing right next to her, smiling in Ed's direction, that would have been pushing it. She swore under her breath, pasted on a smile and waved back at Ed, who was seated a few tables over with her nemesis, Blake Preston.

"Charm," Cecily said under her breath, and led the way to their table.

"Samantha, this is becoming our second home, isn't it?" Ed greeted her. "And, Cecily. What brings you back to town so soon?"

"I'm here to help with the festival," she said.

"We'll take all the help we can get, won't we?" Ed stood and pulled out a chair. "Join us for a drink ladies. We can talk."

That was what Samantha wanted to do, all right, sit down for a chummy little drink with Blake Preston, business killer.

"Maybe they have dates," Blake said. He probably

didn't want to get cozy any more than she did. Or was he insinuating she couldn't get a date?

"If not, you could join us for dinner," Ed offered.

"Oh, no. We've already eaten," Samantha said.

"Well, a glass of wine, then."

"A glass of wine sounds wonderful," Cecily said, making the decision for them and instilling in her sister a desire to throttle her. Blake stood to pull out another chair and she held out her hand for him to shake. "I'm Cecily Sterling. I was a few years behind you in school but—"

"I know who you are. Everyone knows the beautiful Sterling sisters," Blake said gallantly.

Blech. This man was wasted in banking. He should've been a salesman. On a used-car lot. Or at a fair, selling overpriced kitchen gadgets.

"So I think we're making real progress, don't you?" Ed said heartily.

"Absolutely," Samantha agreed. "Everyone's on board with this," she added, practically daring Blake to even hint otherwise.

At that moment, Charley walked by with Samantha's downstairs neighbor, Lila Ward, and another older woman in tow. Lila was a retired teacher, skinny as a pencil, with short gray hair and thin lips. She told everyone she was widowed. Samantha didn't believe it. She suspected the former Mr. Ward had run away.

Tonight Lila wore gray slacks and a heavy fisherman knit sweater—a scarecrow bundled up for winter. At the sight of them seated all together, her lips pursed and Samantha braced herself for an unpleasant encounter.

Sure enough. Lila stopped at the table, leaving her friend and Charley to move on without her. "I hear you're planning some kind of festival, Ed," she said, ignoring his tablemates. Lila obviously hadn't taught manners.

"As a matter of fact, we are," he said jovially. "If all goes according to plan we should have a town full of people next month."

"And there goes our peace and quiet," Lila snapped. "I didn't retire up here to see the place overrun with yuppies and hoodlums. I don't know what you're thinking."

"We're thinking it'll give our town's economy a boost," Samantha put in, unable to resist entering the fray.

"You're a smart woman, Lila." Ed spoke in a soothing voice. "You understand economics. No business, no town. And then where will you buy your groceries?"

"We don't need crowds and crowds of people to stay in business," Lila said.

Ed sobered. "You didn't notice? We haven't *had* any crowds this winter."

"Of course I noticed. And we're all still here, aren't we?"

"Not all of us," Ed said, his smile completely gone.

"This won't help. It's foolish and silly." Lila shot a disapproving look at Samantha. "Chocolate festival, indeed." And with that parting shot she took her skinny self off.

"Well, almost everyone's on board," Ed murmured.

Just then Maria arrived to take their orders, ending the conversation.

"I'd love a glass of pinot grigio," Cecily told her.

While Samantha had been busy being a stellar overachiever, her sister had been learning the art of sophisticated social drinking.

"How about you, Samantha?" Maria asked.

"ChocoVine."

"You'll have to go to a party at Charley's for that, *amiga*," Maria said. "Why don't you try the huckleberry martini? It's a little sweet. You'll like it."

"Okay, I'll try it."

"We should get Hank to make up a signature chocolate drink for the festival," Cecily said, giving a lock of hair a thoughtful twirl as Maria left to fill their drink orders. "A chocolate kiss. Doesn't that sound good?" she asked the table in general.

"A kiss sounds good to me," agreed Blake.

Samantha ignored him.

She continued to ignore him as they sipped their drinks, and Ed and Cecily tossed plans back and forth. The men ordered dinner and Ed insisted the sisters have another drink on him. He didn't have to force Samantha. She decided she liked huckleberry martinis.

But she still didn't like Blake Preston. He was a snake.

"Lila Ward is definitely in the minority when it comes to the festival," Ed was saying.

"Few ideas get one hundred percent support," Blake said. "I hope this flies for you, though."

Samantha cocked an eyebrow. "Do you?"

"Of course I do," he said earnestly.

She took a giant-sized sip from her martini. "Well, of course. Silly of me to doubt you. The bank has already been *so* supportive."

"We should probably get going," her sister said.

Excellent idea.

There was no enjoying herself after that. (Not that Samantha had planned on enjoying herself, anyway. Stress and fun didn't mix.) Running into Blake the Snake had been enough to curdle her entire weekend.

She tried putting him out of her mind by going for an early-morning run on Saturday, but with every slushy footfall she could hear his voice. *Hope this flies, hope this flies.* Did he? Really?

Attending Cass's weekly chick-flick night on Sunday evening didn't improve Samantha's mood. It had been Charley's turn to pick and she brought *You've Got Mail.* Samantha found herself squirming as she watched Meg Ryan's character fall for the man who'd ruined her business.

Well, unlike Meg, she wasn't going to give in to temptation.

Eleven

Every day brings something new. But if you don't
open your arms to receive it, it will pass you by.
—Muriel Sterling, *Knowing Who You Are:*
One Woman's Journey

Samantha had work to do before the festival committee
meeting. She didn't have time to hand-deliver the chocolates she'd promised to Todd Black. So Cecily, being a
good sister, volunteered for gofer duty.

"That's the only reason, right?" Samantha asked, regarding her suspiciously. "I mean, I'll admit he's a hunk
and a half, but I'd be willing to bet that man has a trail
of broken hearts stretching from here to Tahiti."

"Don't worry, Mother," Cecily said, tucking the pink
box tied with gold ribbon under her arm. "I've been
vaccinated."

"I'm not sure the vaccine for that one has been in-
vented."

"I'm just going to drop it and run," Cecily assured her.

"Okay. If you're not back here in twenty minutes I'm
sending out a search party."

Cecily smiled and shook her head. Really, sometimes
Samantha could be so overprotective. But there was no
need. Cecily had weathered two crappy relationships.
She wasn't about to strike out a third time. And she was
only running this errand to be helpful. That was why
she was here, to help.

Anyway, he probably wouldn't even be there. It was morning. Taverns never closed until the wee hours and he was probably home, wherever that was, in bed.

Bed. Todd Black in bed. What did he wear to bed?

What did she care? She was so going to drop this candy and run.

She got to the tavern to find the neon beer sign in the window turned off and the potholed parking lot deserted except for one lone car—a mud-spattered Jeep. One caveman left in the Man Cave. It wasn't hard to guess who it belonged to.

She didn't see any lights on inside, though. Maybe Todd Black had been too drunk to drive home after work. Maybe he was passed out on the floor somewhere.

Cecily got out of her car and picked her way across the parking lot. As she got closer she could see through the window into Todd Black's kingdom. Chairs were up-ended on top of tables, waiting for someone to sweep the floor. In the dingy light she spied a dartboard hanging on a wall and a vintage pinball machine in a far corner. The requisite TV hung over the bar, which held upended bar stools that looked like they'd been imported from some old movie set. Places like this always seemed so seedy and forlorn in the daytime.

She'd heard this one really hopped at night, attracting a rowdy crowd, mostly men. No surprise there. What woman in her right mind would come in here when she could be drinking wine or huckleberry martinis at Zelda's? Maybe a woman who liked to play pinball, she thought with a smile, and then added, *But not you.*

She knocked tentatively on the door. No one came.

Just as well, she told herself. She didn't want to see Todd Black.

She knocked again, a little louder. She was here, after

all, and she hated to leave the candy outside to get ruined by the weather or eaten by a passing dog. Chocolate was poisonous to dogs. She owed it to the canine population to make sure this candy got to Todd. She knocked one last time—and was rewarded by the sight of a shadow moving across the room toward the door. A moment later it opened and there stood Todd Black in jeans and a black sweater, unshaved and scruffy and tempting.

He leaned one hand on the door frame and treated himself to a lazy perusal of her from head to toe. "Well, if it isn't the California girl."

When a hot guy was single after a certain age there was usually a reason. Now she knew why this one was on his own. He had a real gift for irritating a woman.

She decided not to respond in kind. Instead, she simply smiled and handed over the box of candy. "I'm dropping off a thank-you from my sister for changing her tire."

He grinned. "Pink, just my color."

"I thought so."

He swung the door open wider. In the distance the vintage pinball machine beckoned. "Want to come in and help me eat these?"

Step into my parlor, said the spider to the fly. "I'm sure you can handle that all by yourself."

"Yeah, but it won't be as much fun. Anyway, I could use a break. Couldn't you?"

She'd come up here to get a break. From men. "I really need to go," she said, and took a step back.

"I bet girls like you don't go in places like this," he taunted.

"What kind of girl am I?"

"Stuck-up?"

All because she'd turned down his invitation to enter

his seedy domain—talk about conceit. "Nope, just busy," she said, and turned to go back to her car. "Lucky for you because I'm a wizard with a pinball machine." And that was something stuck-up girls didn't play. So there.

"Anytime you want to come by and show me what you've got…" he called after her.

She picked up her pace. The sooner she was in her car and away from here, the better. Todd Black was obviously an expert at getting women to show him what they had.

"We're almost at full occupancy for the weekend of the festival," Olivia announced to the rest of the committee as they met over breakfast at Dot's Breakfast Haus.

"I'm a little over half full now," Annemarie said. She smiled at Samantha. "This was a great idea."

"And the Mr. Dreamy contest was positively inspired," Olivia said. "I'm going to enter both my sons."

Samantha could feel Cecily's superior smirk without even looking at her. The elbow in the ribs was quite unnecessary.

"We don't have permits yet," Samantha told them.

"Maybe you should see what the holdup is," Olivia suggested.

As if she hadn't been trying. On the issue of those permits, Samantha felt like a salmon trying to spawn in quicksand. No one at city hall seemed to know anything and they kept referring her to Pissy, which was a joke since every time Samantha called, Pissy always managed to be out of the office or on the phone or just plain unavailable.

When she'd finally cornered her archrival, Pissy had gotten, well, pissy about the whole thing. "Do you think we're incompetent around here?" she'd demanded.

"No, of course not," Samantha had said, getting in touch with her inner Cecily. *Just spiteful.*

But even Pissy wouldn't be so small as to sabotage this merely to one-up Samantha. At least, Samantha hoped not. Unless she didn't get that it was good for the whole town.

"Especially when this is going to benefit so many businesses," Samantha had added, just to make sure Pissy was seeing the whole picture.

"Yours especially," Pissy had said. "Now, if that's all you need I've got to go. I have an important meeting."

"With your shrink?" Samantha had snapped.

But Pissy was long gone and the only reply she'd gotten was a dial tone.

Obviously, it would help if someone besides Samantha bugged the gang at city hall. "Maybe someone with a little more pull should try to get things moving. Ed, would you mind giving Del a call?"

"I'm sure he's on top of it," Ed replied, "but I'll talk to him. It would be good to know where we are." He rubbed his forehead.

"Are you feeling okay?" Olivia asked him, sounding like a concerned wife. Samantha suspected she'd like to step into that role, but Ed only had eyes for Pat Wilder, the statuesque widow who owned Mountain Escape Books.

"Just got a touch of headache," said Ed. "I'll be fine. But I think I'll go home and take a rest. I'm feeling kind of tired."

"I hope you're not coming down with something," Olivia said.

Me, too, thought Samantha. *If you are, don't get sick until you talk to Del.*

Selfish, she scolded herself. "Feel better soon," she

told Ed. "And let me know what Del says," she added, a subtle hint to call the mayor before he collapsed. Okay, so she wasn't the most noble girl in Icicle Falls, but damn it, she had a business to save and a town depending on her.

Ed's departure, along with the fact that the pancakes had been consumed, signaled the end of the committee meeting, but Samantha decided she needed a private meeting with her sister. "Walk with me to the office," she said as they left the restaurant.

"Is that an invitation or a command?"

"Uh, yes?"

Cecily frowned but obliged.

It was a lovely day for a walk, anyway, Samantha reasoned. The sun was out, the sky was blue, the rugged beauty of the mountains was breathtaking and the crisp mountain air invigorating. Talk about a jewel of a setting for a town. This festival was bound to attract new visitors, and once they saw how lovely Icicle Falls was, they'd return and bring family and friends.

"Is there a problem?" Cecily asked, bringing her back to the present.

These days it seemed like there was always a problem. Samantha didn't say that, though. Instead, she said, "I wish you'd held off a few more days before running that piece about the contest in this morning's *Sun*."

"You can't wait until the last minute with this sort of thing."

"I know."

"You're worried about the permits, aren't you?"

Samantha nodded. "We're doing things backward. That makes me nervous."

"If you wait until you have the permits in hand you won't have time to set up all your events," Cecily said.

Of course her sister was right. They were racing against the clock and that meant they couldn't follow standard operating procedure. Still. She liked to get her ducks in a row and these ducks were swimming in all directions. Now she rubbed her forehead. Ed's headache was catching.

"I know I'm obsessing," she admitted, "but without the arts and crafts and food booths the festival won't really feel like a festival. People will feel cheated."

"We'll have to manage the best we can," Cecily said with a shrug.

Her sister was right. Worrying wasn't helping anything. At the rate she was going she'd be prematurely gray by Valentine's. Samantha forced herself to stay on track. "So, what's this I hear about a kickoff for the Mr. Dreamy contest at Zelda's bar?" She could only imagine how tacky that would turn out to be. "Is it really necessary?"

"Yes, it is. It'll be a fun evening and get people excited. And it's another way to remind everyone that they want to buy tickets for the pageant, not to mention chocolate."

"I suppose," Samantha said grudgingly. "Who have you suckered into judging that, by the way?"

"You, for one."

"Me?" Oh, that was what she wanted more than anything in the world, to be a judge in a male beauty contest.

"Do I detect a sneer in your voice, Miss Icicle Falls?"

Samantha pointed a warning finger at her sister. "That was for college scholarship money. And we at least had a talent competition."

"Well, this is for valuable prizes," Cecily said. "And we'll have interview questions."

"Like if they want world peace?" Samantha scoffed.

"Nothing so boring," Cecily said with a grin.

"I don't know about this," Samantha muttered. Although it didn't make any difference. Her sisters had turned into event bulldozers, plowing over her objections and concerns. Not that she had many when it came to the classier events. It was only this stupid Mr. Dreamy contest she wasn't wild about.

"It'll be great," Cecily assured her. "Guys will have to tell us their favorite Sweet Dreams candy, so of course they'll buy lots to do research, and that's good for sales. Anyway, everyone's on board and this train is already down the track."

"Well, you can let it go down the track without me," Samantha said.

"I'm afraid we can't. Sweet Dreams is sponsoring this and you're the face of Sweet Dreams. By the way, Nia Walters wants to interview you for the paper. So you're not only getting sales out of the contest, you're getting free publicity."

It was hard to argue with free publicity. Still, Samantha would rather have jumped naked into the icy Wenatchee River than judge this stupid contest. "Who else is judging?" she asked grumpily.

"Mom and me."

"Sounds like you have plenty of faces. You don't need mine. And what's Bailey doing?"

"Mistress of Ceremony, since she loves the spotlight. And yes, we do need you."

"So is that it? I mean, shouldn't we have someone else?"

"I thought maybe Cass. She'd be unbiased."

"Have you asked her?" Somehow, Samantha couldn't picture Cass going along with such silliness.

"I hoped you would," Cecily said, careful not to meet Samantha's gaze.

"You little chicken."

"Cluck, cluck," replied her sister. "Look at it this way. I've given you a chance to micromanage."

They were at Sweet Dreams now, and before Samantha could come up with a comeback her sister had breezed into the gift shop to see if any men had stopped by for an entry form.

"We've already had six guys," Heidi said.

"I knew this was going to be popular," Cecily crowed.

Samantha decided to say nothing other than, "I've got to get to work," and escaped to her office.

"Don't forget to talk to Cass," her sister called after her.

"Why me?" she grumbled.

The answer to that was easy. She was the oldest. She got to do the dirty work.

Later she found Cass and her daughter, Danielle, busy draping a necklace holder with necklaces and bracelets made of chocolate cookie hearts with pink icing.

"They're for the festival," Cass said. "What do you think?"

"I think they're adorable," Samantha gushed. "Who's the designer?" She didn't really need to ask. Danielle was beaming and Cass was looking like a proud mama.

"It was Dani's idea," Cass said. "Is she good or what?"

"Or what. You're an artiste," Samantha told the girl.

"Try one," Danielle urged.

They were almost too pretty to eat. Almost. Samantha bit into one and got sent straight to taste-bud heaven. "These will sell like crazy," she predicted.

"Especially with middle-grade girls," Danielle said.

"If they go over well, then maybe Mom will sell them on the website," she added, looking to her mother.

Cass nodded slowly. "It's a possibility."

"Could Luke help me figure out how to box them so they don't break?" Danielle asked Samantha.

"I'll send him over later today," Samantha promised, happy to support a budding entrepreneur.

Two teenage girls entered the store in search of after-school sustenance and Danielle went to serve them.

"You have such a great daughter," Samantha said.

"Yes, I do," Cass agreed, looking at Dani with pride. "I just wish her sister would stop driving me crazy," she said, brows furrowing.

Amber, Cass's youngest child, was fourteen going on trouble. "Willie's doing okay, though," Samantha said in an attempt to help her look on the bright side. Between wrestling and football and Boy Scouts, her son had plenty of activities to keep himself out of mischief.

Cass gave a snort. "Two out of three's not bad. Is that what you're saying?"

It had been. Lame. "She'll come around. Cecily went through a phase where she drove our parents nuts and she came out of it."

"I'm sure Amber will, too," Cass said. "It's either that or I'm going to kill her. I know, maybe I'll adopt her out. Would you like a fourteen-year-old?"

"In about twenty years," Samantha quipped.

Cass shook her head. "I love her dearly but sometimes… If only she didn't take after her father. She can be so surly. And stubborn."

As far as Samantha could tell, that described most fourteen-year-old girls.

"And, of course, I'm the bad guy these days, getting on her about her grades, ruining her social life," Cass continued, "while he gets to look like a cross between Santa and Saint Christopher. Men," she added in disgust.

Cass was obviously not feeling generous toward the opposite sex right now. Maybe this wasn't the moment to ask if she wanted to help choose Icicle Falls' first Mr. Dreamy.

But Cass was always unhappy with her ex, so there'd probably be no good moment. "Speaking of men, we need an impartial judge for our Mr. Dreamy contest. Cecily was hoping we could recruit you."

"As long as none of them look like Mason I can be unbiased," Cass said with a grin.

"We'll work on that." Samantha sobered. "You know, I've got to admit I'm surprised you're willing to do this."

"Oh? Why?"

"Well, for one thing, it's silly."

"It's also fun and I'll enjoy watching those men jump through whatever hoops Cecily dreams up. And I assume there'll be chocolate in it for me, right?"

"Absolutely."

"Then call me Your Honor."

Well, that was easy, Samantha mused as she left. In fact, other than the frustration of not knowing where those permits were in the tangle of city hall red tape, plans for the festival were coming along nicely. What should have required months was falling into place in record time, thanks to an entire town full of enthusiastic volunteers. And things like that just didn't happen except in books and movies.

So, when was the other shoe going to drop?

Cecily started a buzz in the grocery store when she stopped by to put up a poster for the Mr. Dreamy contest on the community bulletin board.

"How fun!" exclaimed Lauren Belgado, who had ducked in on her coffee break. "And, oh, my gosh, look at the stuff the winner gets. I'm so nominating Joe."

Her boyfriend, Joe Coyote, had a nice face and a nice build. Due to a scar on his face and a limp (a souvenir from a construction accident) Cecily wasn't sure he could compete against some of the better-looking men in town. Still, if a man could win on heart alone, the prize was Joe's.

Now another woman had come over. "Oh, wow, I read about this in the paper. I'm going to pick up an entry form. If my boyfriend wins, we can take that wine tour."

"What all do the guys have to do?" asked Lauren. "Is there, like, a talent competition? Joe's kind of shy."

"No talent."

"Then what do they have to do?" the other woman asked.

"Oh, we'll have some questions for them to answer, like what their favorite Sweet Dreams candy is."

"Research," Lauren said happily, making Cecily wish her sister was present to hear this conversation. "What else?"

"Nothing too hard," Cecily assured her. "Probably walk out on stage without their shirts."

The women giggled.

"Dumb," a deep voice said behind Cecily.

She turned to see that Todd Black had emerged from his man cave to purchase sustenance for the Neanderthals. If you could call a grocery cart filled with soft drinks and pretzels sustenance. The first thought that came to mind was *There's our first Mr. Dreamy.*

She quickly squelched it. She didn't know Todd

Black's educational background, but wherever he went to school he must have majored in obnoxious behavior. "No dumber than the Miss America Pageant," she said.

"True," he agreed in a tone of voice that told her what he thought of that competition.

"Or the Victoria's Secret special," she said sweetly, determined to strip off his P.C. camouflage and reveal that he was just as superficial as any other man.

He didn't disappoint her. "That's worth watching," he said with a grin.

Now two more women were eavesdropping and she felt the need to put him in his place. Diplomatically, of course. "Not to us," she told him. "And that's why we're having a Mr. Dreamy contest. Since women are the ones who like chocolate—"

"Guys like chocolate, too. Remember?" he said.

"Just not chocolate festivals."

"Have a Miss Chocolate Kiss competition. I'll come," he said. "I'll even vote for you," he added with a wink, and wheeled his cart out the door.

"My God, he's gorgeous," one woman breathed.

"Better than chocolate," another said.

"*Nothing* is better than chocolate," Cecily informed them even as her traitorous hormones muttered that she'd sell off all the stock in the Sweet Dreams warehouse for a night with him.

Fortunately, her brain was in charge now. Her hormones had proved they couldn't be trusted.

Oh, but she was willing to bet he was an exceptional kisser.

Lots of practice, said her brain. *Leave him in his man cave where he belongs.*

Good idea.

* * *

Muriel had meant to get dressed, she really had. But somehow the day had gotten away from her. Now the doorbell was ringing and she was in the living room in her pajamas.

She wouldn't answer. The drapes were drawn. She could just hide in here until whoever was pestering her went away.

But then she heard voices and a key in the front door lock and she had to find a new hiding place. She scurried down the hall to her bedroom and shut the door.

A moment later Cecily's voice drifted down the hall to her. "She's home and I'm sure she'll want to see you."

No, she wouldn't, whoever it was. She slipped into the bathroom and shut that door, too, putting another barrier between herself and the world.

She heard a knock on the bedroom door, then, "Mom?" followed by tentative tapping on the bathroom door. "Mom, Pat's here."

"Tell her I'll call her later," Muriel said. "I'm not feeling well." That was certainly no lie.

"Okay."

She sounded disappointed, like Muriel had failed some sort of test. This was hardly surprising. She seemed to be failing all kinds of tests lately.

Pat was a good friend. It would be rude not to see her. Reluctantly, Muriel opened the door and said, "Never mind."

Cecily looked at her in surprise. "I thought you didn't feel good."

She wasn't sure she'd ever feel good again. She wasn't sure she'd ever *feel* again. But she was still here and she had to interact with people. That was how life worked, or at least how it was supposed to work.

"I'll be fine," she told both her daughter and herself, and went to the living room to greet her friend.

Also a widow, Pat Wilder was a tall, attractive woman who, like Muriel, kept her youthful hair color with the aid of regular visits to Sleeping Lady Salon. Unlike Muriel, her roots weren't starting to show. Pat was a sharp dresser and today she wore jeans and boots and a black leather jacket over a cream-colored cashmere sweater and a wealth of silver jewelry. A knit scarf in hunter-green—probably a gift from Olivia, who loved to knit—completed her ensemble. The faintest hint of her favorite floral perfume wafted toward Muriel as Pat reached out to hug her.

Muriel hated to think what was wafting off her. Suddenly she felt self-indulgent and embarrassed.

"I'm not going to ask how you're doing," Pat said, "because I know. I'm so sorry you're having to go through this again."

Muriel could feel the tears collecting but she tried to be brave and murmured her thanks.

Cecily hovered at the corner of the room as if uncertain whether to go or stay. "Would you like some tea?" she asked Pat.

"I'd love some," Pat said, and settled on the couch. She patted the cushion next to her and Muriel seated herself, acutely conscious of the contrast in their appearances.

"It's going to take time before you can string two thoughts together," Pat said comfortingly, and Muriel couldn't help wishing her daughters understood that. "And you've got all this craziness with the festival going on."

Craziness they could have avoided if she'd been a

more astute businesswoman and hadn't landed their company in this mess.

"But I'm hoping I can talk you into going out for dinner."

Muriel stared at her friend. Of all the people in the world, Pat should have understood how little taste she had for socializing these days. And after the fiasco with Del the other night she had even less. "Oh, I don't think—"

Pat cut her off. "This isn't exactly a social dinner."

Now Cecily was there with two steaming mugs, eavesdropping shamelessly.

Muriel felt cornered. "I'm not interested in some multilayered business plan," she said flatly.

Pat chuckled. "You mean multilevel and that's not what this is. Olivia and I formed a little group about a year and a half ago, after she lost George."

"A book club." Of course. Pat owned a bookstore. But Muriel didn't have time to join a book club. The girls needed help and she was busy…sitting around in her pajamas looking through photo albums.

"No, no. Nothing like that," Pat said. "This is a support group."

Muriel didn't want support. She opened her mouth to refuse but Pat was too quick. "A widows' club," she added bluntly. "Dot is in it, too."

Dot, with her chain-smoking and sharp tongue, was no one Muriel wanted to get chummy with. "Thanks, but I'm not interested."

"I just want you to try us out. Come to dinner with us tomorrow."

"Pat, I'm not ready," Muriel said firmly.

"You weren't ready for Waldo to die, either," Pat said, her gentle tone taking the sting from her words. "We're not ready for much of life. It happens, anyway. Come on, what do you say? Dinner is on me."

"Why don't you go, Mom?" Cecily urged.

It was all Muriel could do not to reply, *Why don't you mind your own business?*

"Come this once," Pat coaxed. "If nothing else it will be a chance to share your memories of Waldo."

That would be nice. Her daughters were too involved with the festival to ramble down memory lane with her. Maybe talking with women who'd gone through what she had would help her feel better equipped to cope with staking out new real estate in the land of the living.

"All right."

Her daughters loved her dearly but they couldn't take her where she needed to go emotionally. As an only child she'd missed out on having sisters. Could girlfriends fill the gap? Maybe she should find out.

Twelve

The best way to handle anything unpleasant is
with a sense of humor.
— Muriel Sterling, *Mixing Business with Pleasure:
How to Successfully Balance Business and Love*

Tuesday evening found Muriel back at Zelda's. Olivia,
gray-haired and plump, dolled up in a sequin-studded
black sweater and her favorite elastic-waist slacks,
greeted her with a hug. "I'm so glad you decided to
join us, lovie."

Actually, now that she was here, so was Muriel. Instead of feeling pressured and on edge, she hoped she
could exhale and let herself fall into the deep comfort
that could only come from the camaraderie born of a
shared profound experience. No one would push her to
plan events. No one would ask if she'd called Lupine
Floral yet to see about getting floral arrangements do-
nated for the ball or if she'd thought of any clever questions for the Mr. Dreamy competition. Here she could
say how much she missed Waldo and how lost she felt
and no one would merely pretend to be sorry for her
loss. They would feel it.

Charley had just seated them at a corner table when
Dot Morrison arrived. She was skinny with short gray
hair over a long face with a sharp nose. She had nice
eyes, Muriel would give her that, but they seemed to be
stuck in a perpetual squint, most likely in an effort to

hide from all the smoke. In short, Dot looked like a real-life version of Maxine, the greeting-card cartoon character. Muriel had never bought Maxine greeting cards.

Dot slid into her seat, bringing the scent of cigarette smoke with her. "What a night," she said in a voice deep enough to sing bass in a barbershop quartet. "If we get much more of this damned freezing rain we're all going to rust." Now she seemed to notice Muriel for the first time. "I see we have a new LAM. Although I'm laying odds you won't be with us for long," she said to Muriel.

Lamb, as in lamb to the slaughter? And what did she mean Muriel wouldn't be with them for long? Were they going to blackball her?

She smiled stiffly. "Lamb?"

"Not lamb," Olivia corrected her. "*L.A.M.* LAM."

"It's an acronym," Pat explained. "It stands for 'life after men.'"

Life after men; that sounded depressing.

"It's meant to be positive," Olivia said, as if reading Muriel's thoughts, "to remind us that just because our marriages are over it doesn't mean our lives are." She smiled gratefully at Pat. "If Dottie and Pat hadn't taken me under their wing after George died, I don't know how I would have coped. Helping the boys, running the inn alone, it was all so overwhelming. Sometimes I felt like the entire Cascade Mountain Range had fallen on me. And some days I still feel alone, but the truth is, I'm not."

Until you go to bed at night, Muriel thought.

"Still, it's hard to make that adjustment," Pat said.

"But don't worry," Dot said to Muriel. "I bet you'll find another man and be off within six months."

She'd been wrong. There was no comfort to be found here. Disappointed and irritated, Muriel bristled. "Excuse me?"

"You're still young and pretty," Dot said, as if age had anything to do with finding love, and as if a woman just skipped over to the park and began poking around under the bushes for a new soul mate like a child hunting Easter eggs.

Or maybe Dot was insinuating that she wasn't very picky. Whatever she was implying, Muriel didn't appreciate her condescending attitude. In spite of that smoke-aged skin and gray hair Dot wasn't much older than she was, so she hardly qualified for the role of wise old woman.

"I've been lucky enough to be married to two wonderful men," Muriel said, emotion giving her voice a sharp edge. "I'm certainly not going to run out and settle for someone simply because I'm lonely."

Dot raised both eyebrows. Translation: *Really?*

Of all the nerve. If this was support, she could do without it. Muriel was about to remember a pressing need at home and excuse herself when Maria came to take their drink orders.

"Hi, ladies. Time for another LAM meeting?"

"Yes," Pat said. "So bring on the champagne."

Maria nodded and hustled off and Pat smiled at Muriel. "We need to toast our newest member."

Newest member? Muriel had made no commitment. She'd just said she'd come to dinner. "Well, we'll see," she murmured. It would be impolite to leave now. She'd stay for one drink, wish them all well and *then* leave.

As they waited for the champagne, talk fell to mundane things like the exploits of Pat's grade-school-age grandsons, the new diet Olivia was on—something about seven days of vegetables followed by seven days of protein. Then the women began to discuss their businesses and Muriel felt like a fish out of water. These

women were all competent businesswomen. She was…
clueless. Another reason not to stay.

Maria brought the champagne and filled their glasses.

Pat lifted hers and said, "To Muriel. May lovely memories cradle you and new beginnings lead you."

"To strong women," Dot said, raising her glass to Muriel. "Harsh winds may bend us but we don't break."

"And though you're now on your own, may you always remember you're not alone," Olivia finished. "To the LAMs."

"To the LAMs," the other two echoed.

As they sipped their champagne Muriel drank in the words of their toasts. Maybe she would stay for dinner, after all. It would be rude to rush off.

Cecily was surprised to awake to the aroma of bacon frying. Mom couldn't be up already. And making breakfast? Really? She went to the kitchen and found her mother not only making breakfast but dressed. Mom's red eyes betrayed a secret morning crying jag but it was encouraging to see her up and functioning.

Cecily gave her a kiss. "That smells wonderful."

Her mother patted her cheek. "I'm sure you've got a million things to do today. I figured you could use a good breakfast."

"You thought right," Cecily said, and poured herself a cup of coffee.

Mom put bread in the toaster. "What's on your agenda for today?" she asked for the first time since Cecily had arrived.

"I'm going to print out pictures of all the men who've entered our Mr. Dreamy contest and hang them in the shop. And sometime before Bailey and I Skype this afternoon, I'd like to nail down a theme for the ball and start pulling together details on that."

Mom nodded and cracked eggs into a pan.

"I could use some creative help," Cecily ventured.

She'd already asked Mom to come up with some questions they could ask their Mr. Dreamy contestants, hoping to take advantage of her mother's writing skills and take her mind off her troubles, but had gotten a polite yet firm refusal so she wasn't sure why she was asking.

"Maybe I can come up with something," Mom said.

Other than the family brainstorming session, which she'd pretty much been forced into, it was the first time since Waldo's death that their mother had taken any interest in the life that was still going on around her. Cecily didn't know if her dinner out the night before with Pat's support group had anything to do with this—Mom hadn't shared details when she got home—but if it had, they all owed Pat chocolate for life.

"That would be great," she said. And Samantha would be really pleased to see Mom involved.

"I don't want you girls to think you're pulling this load alone," Mom said. She slid an egg onto a plate, added toast and handed it to Cecily.

"You're dealing with a lot," Cecily said, feeling suddenly guilty that she'd asked for help.

"We're all dealing with a lot," her mother said, "but together we're strong enough to knock down any obstacle. We'll get through this."

Mom was still the word queen. She could lay out a phrase like a comforting blanket. Cecily set down the plate and hugged her. "You're always there for us."

"Thank you, dear," her mother said in a choked voice, and hugged her back.

It was a perfect way to start the day and Cecily left

for the shop wearing a smile along with her jeans, turtleneck and winter jacket.

Samantha wasn't at the office when she poked her head in to say hi. "She went over to Bavarian Brews," Elena said. "She's meeting Nia Walters."

Of course, the interview for the *Mountain Sun* that Cecily had set up for her. "Great. I'm going to put up a display of our Mr. Dreamy contestants down in the shop. Maybe I'll have her bring Nia over to see it when they're done."

"That's going to be some contest," Elena predicted. "Heidi said another couple of guys dropped off entries this morning. Not surprising, considering the prizes."

Bailey had outdone herself. "It feels like every woman in town is entering her man." Cecily smiled.

"Not me," Elena said with a snort. "Even if we could enter, I wouldn't. Mine wouldn't stand a chance with that big belly of his. He wanted to, though."

"What did you tell him?"

"That he was *loco.*"

"Do you think we were *loco* to have this contest?"

"*Loco* like a fox. We'll sell lots of chocolates at this, eh? I'm going to be there and I'm bringing my sisters."

Samantha could squawk all she wanted, Cecily thought as she went downstairs to the shop, but this was going to pack Festival Hall. Hopefully, the ball and the other events would be equally successful.

"I never realized we had so many good-looking men in Icicle Falls," Heidi said, handing over pictures and entry forms from the latest entrants.

One photo was of Olivia's younger son, Brandon, posing in full ski regalia. He was a ski bum and a bad boy, and he'd left a trail of broken hearts, including Bailey's, scattered from Icicle Falls clear to Ellensburg. Bailey had hoped to see him when she came up for Waldo's funeral but, thankfully, he'd been out of town. It looked like he was planning to be around for the festival, though, which could mean trouble for little sister.

Cecily studied the picture, trying to decide what movie star he resembled. That square chin and brown wavy hair made her think of Orlando Bloom but he definitely had Jake Gyllenhaal eyes, and a lean Jude Law–style body. She finally concluded that he was simply a composite of gorgeous.

And here was... She blinked. Blake Preston? Seriously? The man had his nerve.

"What's he doing in here?" she asked Heidi.

Heidi replied, "Why shouldn't he be?" reminding Cecily that their company troubles weren't common knowledge. Thank God.

"It doesn't seem very dignified for a bank manager," she said, improvising fast.

"Tell that to his grandma," Heidi said. "She thinks he's gorgeous. And he is."

It was sad that such a handsome man had such an ugly heart. But not unusual. Most of the men Cecily had met were Shallow Sams who didn't consider their heart their most important organ.

She took the picture to the side of the shop where she was setting up her display and called her sister. "You'll never guess who's entered our contest."

"Who?"

"Blake Preston."

There was a charged silence on the other end of the phone. Then Samantha exploded. "Oh, for the love of chocolate. Of all the rotten, two-faced, low-class—"

"That about sums it up," Cecily agreed. "Should I lose his picture?"

"No, save it. I might want to throw darts at it."

"At least you can tell Nia we've got the blessing of the local movers and shakers."

"I'd like to shake him, right off the top of Sleeping Lady Mountain," Samantha grumbled. "Oh, here comes Nia now. Gotta go."

Cecily ended the call and got to work, still mulling over this latest development.

She'd barely started when the shop bell tinkled and in walked Billy Williams, who worked at the River Bend guest ranch. One of their first entrants, Bill Will, as everyone called him, was another local bad boy and Cecily had run with his crowd for a brief time in high school. She'd grown up but it appeared Billy hadn't. Heidi had caught Cecily up on his exploits in one succinct sentence: *He loves to hang out at the Man Cave.* That said it all, considering who owned the place.

"Hi, Bill Will," Heidi greeted him. "Did you come in for some chocolate?"

"I came in to give Samantha a treat." He pulled off his cowboy hat to reveal tousled chestnut curls. "Hey, Cec," he said to Cecily. "Heard you were back in town."

"I am and I'm really busy with the festival," she said before he could offer to show her a hot time.

He shrugged good-naturedly. "So where's your sis?"

"She's over at Bavarian Brews."

He nodded. "Okay. Guess I'll go find her there."

"What do you need?" Cecily asked. And what was this mysterious treat? She'd never stopped to consider that anyone would try to bribe the judges.

"Oh, nothing. Just thought I'd show her why I'm the best Mr. Dreamy in town. See you girls around." Then he was out the door.

The two women exchanged looks. Bill Will was a bit of an exhibitionist.

"Should we warn Samantha?" Heidi asked.

Bill Will putting on a show would be good publicity. Whatever he planned to do was bound to spice up that article Nia was writing for the *Sun*. "Let's keep it a surprise."

Samantha and Nia had settled at a corner table with their lattes when in walked Billy Williams, a beefcake poster come to life in tight-fitting jeans and a shirt that was about to burst from straining to hold in well-developed pecs. His cowboy hat was pushed back on his head and he was carrying a rope.

"Samantha Sterling. I got something to show you, girl," he called across the coffee shop, pulling all eyes to himself.

And there were plenty of eyes to pull. Shop owners and retail clerks in search of a morning caffeine hit stood in the order and pickup lines. Three middle-aged women occupied one table, while at another four young moms with babies in their laps or parked next to them in strollers were looking at Billy like he was a tray of truffles marked down fifty percent. And at another table sat—oh, no—Hildy Johnson and Lila Ward, both wearing disapproving frowns. Oh, boy, this couldn't be good.

Sure enough. Now Bill Will had his rope out and was swinging a lasso over his head. And—oh, please, God, no—breaking into song, belting out "Save a Horse, Ride a Cowboy." He began to do a hippity-hop bump and grind in her direction, and the table of young moms clapped and let out whoops of encouragement. Even the baristas stopped production and the hiss of the espresso machines paused, leaving the floor to Bill Will.

He was making the most of it, too. Now he was at Samantha's table. She slid down her seat, wishing she could make herself invisible. That turned out to be a mistake because it only got her up close and personal in a truly embarrassing way as Bill Will bumped and pumped. And—oh, no—Nia Walters, girl reporter, now had her trusty camera out and was snapping blackmail pictures while Bill Will went at it as if he expected Samantha to put a five-dollar bill down his jeans. Nia wasn't the only one. Everyone with a cell phone was recording this moment for posterity.

She tried to look anywhere but at Billy and that proved to be another mistake, because her embarrassed gaze drifted to the door.

Why, of all the coffee joints in all the world, do you keep walking into mine?

Thirteen

It's not so hard to find where you belong in this world. You belong where you're needed.
——Muriel Sterling, *Knowing Who You Are: One Woman's Journey*

Bill Will ended his routine by throwing his hat in the air and letting out a big "Yeehaw!" Hildy sat watching in shock while Lila scowled like an angry schoolmarm, but the rest of the crowd gave him a round of applause.

There was also plenty of laughter and Samantha felt as if her whole face was on fire. She managed a cool, "That was quite a show, Bill."

He grinned. "Just wanted you to see your future Mr. Dreamy in action." He turned his full-watt smile on Nia. "Am I gonna be in the paper?"

"Definitely," Nia said, and it was all Samantha could do not to swear.

One of the moms called him over to their table and Bill Will swaggered off. Samantha couldn't help sneaking a look in Blake's direction. He'd moved to the order counter and was keeping his distance.

He should. Coming over to comment on his competition would make him even more hypocritical than he already was.

She turned to Nia. "You're not really going to run that picture, are you?"

"Of course. People will love it."

"But the festival is about so much more than the Mr. Dreamy contest," Samantha protested.

"Don't worry. I know that," Nia assured her. "Now, tell me how you got the idea and what we can expect."

Samantha launched into her spiel and Nia typed away on her laptop. By the time they were done, Samantha had infected herself with a dose of excitement even greater than what she'd pumped into Nia.

Then she saw Bill Will making his way toward them, probably for a repeat performance. "I've got so much to do," she said. "I'd better get back to the office."

Nia had seen him coming, too. "Yeah, you'd better," she agreed. "And lock the door."

Samantha beat it out of there. In her hurry to escape Bill Will, she failed to see that she'd run right into Blake. Or nearly. He moved his cup away just in time to prevent their near-collision from spilling coffee on his suit.

"Sorry," she said, reaching for the door.

He pushed it open and followed her out. "I didn't know you produced musicals on the side. I guess auditions are over for the day?"

She could feel her cheeks sizzling. "You're very amusing. Maybe you should give up banking and be a stand-up comic."

"Would you come watch me?"

"Could I throw rotten tomatoes?"

He smiled. "I prefer money."

Didn't she know it?

Aware that he'd stuck his foot in his mouth, he cleared his throat. "So, is that one of your Mr. Dreamy contestants?"

She snorted. "Why are you asking? Worried about the competition?"

He just shook his head.

She looked at him in disgust, then said a brisk, "Well, I'd like to stand here all day while you try to butter me up, but I have a company to save." Then, before he could say anything, she dashed across the street. Cecily was right. Men!

Blake watched Samantha run across the street to her business. When God handed out perfect bodies, she must have been at the head of the line. And those full lips. Did women have any idea what it did to a man when they wore that lip gloss stuff?

He frowned and tossed his coffee in a nearby garbage can. He admired Samantha's determination to save her company and the clever ways she was coming up with to do it. He'd love to tell her that, but if he did she'd tell him where to stick his admiration. He was the villain in her story and nothing he could say or do was going to change that. What a sick twist of fate. He wasn't sure what he'd done to deserve it, but obviously Somebody Up There had it in for him.

Cecily had just finished putting up her Mr. Dreamy photo gallery when her sister returned. "Did Bill Will find you?" Dumb question considering the expression on Samantha's face.

Samantha scowled. "Was that fiasco your idea?"

"What did he do?" Heidi asked, replacing stock on the shelves.

"He practically gave me a lap dance in the middle of Bavarian Brews," Samantha muttered. "And, naturally, Nia got a picture."

Cecily snickered. It was rude but she couldn't help it. The image of her perfect older sister getting the Bill Will treatment in public was just too funny.

"I'm glad you find it amusing. Are you sure you and Bailey didn't set that up?"

"No, honestly," she said.

"It's true," Heidi seconded. "He came here looking for you and we told him you were over there. We had no idea what he was going to do."

Except knowing Billy Williams, Cecily had suspected it would be something over-the-top. And he hadn't disappointed. His little stunt had been worth a thousand ads.

"If anyone else comes looking for me, I'm not here. I moved to Tahiti," Samantha said, and stomped upstairs to her office.

"Your poor sister." Heidi tried unsuccessfully to hide a smile.

"It's not easy being the queen of chocolate," Cecily said. "Royalty has its price."

Being a queen with no king had its price, too, Cecily thought. Poor Sam carried a heavy burden of responsibility on her shoulders. Her life would be easier if she had a king.

And Cecily had been getting these funny impressions about who that king should be. She couldn't seem to figure out a thing for herself, but when it came to other people she had a gift for seeing who should be with whom. It was crazy, but she kept seeing her sister with Blake Preston.

That was, of course, preposterous. She was obviously losing her edge. Another reason to get out of the matchmaking business.

What she was going to wind up doing, though, she had no idea. Short-term, she'd help her sister with the festival and work for Charley. She'd gone by Zelda's and offered her services, and Charley had been more than happy to hire her as a hostess on weekends. With the stipulation that she could have the festival weekend off, of course. That money, plus the little she had in savings, would carry her through until spring. Then…who knew? Samantha would have everything up and running at Sweet Dreams again and wouldn't need her. Mom was slowly pulling out of her tailspin and would be fine and no one would really care if she moved on.

She'd often felt invisible as a child. Mom had not only filled out Samantha's baby book, she'd added extra notes and pictures. Cecily's got half-completed. Not that Mom didn't love her. Her mother hadn't been stingy with kind words or kisses. But time was a commodity she'd had difficulty distributing evenly, especially once Bailey arrived on the scene.

It was hard to feel special when you were the middle child, sandwiched between Miss Perfect and Miss Adorable. Samantha was the stellar firstborn and Bailey was the baby of the family who kept everyone entertained with her antics. Cecily was…the quiet one, the little supporting actress for the two stars.

So what did she do when she grew up? She became a matchmaker and took on another supporting role, working to give other people the love story they wanted while managing her own love life on the side and doing a poor job of it. Pathetic.

Well, after the festival she'd make a new beginning, maybe move over the mountains to Seattle and… Do what? Her future was a thick fog.

Hopefully, she'd be able to turn on her fog lights and find her way. Meanwhile, she'd go back to the house and have some lunch. "I guess that's it for today," she told Heidi. "I'll get out from underfoot before your lunch-hour rush starts."

Oh, that there would be a lunch-hour rush. Their midweek traffic so far had been spotty, yet another thing to worry Samantha.

"Too late," Heidi said as the door burst open.

In rushed a little girl with blond curls and cornflower-blue eyes, followed by a short, slender, middle-aged woman Cecily immediately recognized as Bernadette Goodman, the mother of Luke, their production manager.

Luke had about ten years on Samantha and had been at Sweet Dreams ever since he was a teenager, when he first started working on the production line. When their production manager was lured away a few years ago by a bigger company, Luke's strong work ethic and good people skills had made him the perfect man to step in and take over. His wife had died two years earlier. Bernadette was helping him raise his daughter.

Cecily hadn't seen the child since she was a toddler. Serena had lost that baby look. She was a gorgeous little girl. How sad that her mother wasn't alive to see her daughter grow up.

"We're here to visit my daddy," the child announced gleefully. "My daddy is going to take us for hangabuggers."

"Hangabuggers," Heidi repeated seriously. "That sounds yummy."

"Grammy said we can come back and have a chocolate after," Serena continued.

"An excellent idea," Cecily said, and greeted the older woman.

"Cecily, I heard you were back in town. Are you working on the festival?" Bernadette asked.

"I am." She'd never been around the company as much as Samantha and she certainly wasn't as high-profile as Bailey, so it pleased her that Bernadette remembered her.

"I'm sure Samantha appreciates the help," Bernadette said.

Cecily remembered her sister's aggravation only a short while ago and smiled. "I'm sure she does." She bent over and said to Serena, "You're a big girl now, aren't you?"

Serena nodded, making her blond curls bounce. "I'm four." She held up four fingers to prove it.

"That's definitely old enough for a chocolate." Cecily smiled. "What's your favorite?"

"Milk chocolate!"

Cute. The girl already knew her chocolate. "You know, we just happen to have some here with your name on it," Cecily told her. "Would a piece spoil her appetite?" she asked Bernadette.

"Not at all," Bernadette said, and opened her purse.

"No charge for any of the Sweet Dreams family." She donned a plastic glove and fished a good-size piece from the jar of seconds they sold by the pound, while Serena jumped up and down with anticipation. She handed it to the child, who took it eagerly.

"What do you say?" Bernadette prompted.

"Thank you," Serena sang. She studied the candy and her brow furrowed.

"What's wrong?" Cecily asked.

"I don't see my name on it." Serena held it out for inspection.

The three women smiled. "That's an expression, honey," Bernadette said. "It means Miss Cecily was saving that piece just for you."

Serena beamed and popped the whole thing in her mouth, fearlessly going where no grown-up would dare to go. "Good," she said, and a little trail of chocolate dribbled down her chin.

"Oh, Serena Hope," Bernadette said, taking a tissue to her granddaughter's chin. "What will your daddy say if he sees you all covered in chocolate?"

"He'll say, 'Another satisfied customer,'" a male voice said.

Cecily turned to see Luke entering the shop from the hallway that led to the factory. He was a large man with fair skin and hair, blue eyes and a round face—not good-looking enough to win a Mr. Dreamy contest, but nice. In fact, *nice* seemed to sum up Luke Goodman. He was the boy next door, the perfect big brother, the friend who sat beside you in homeroom.

And that was about all the chemistry Cecily felt looking at him. A hard-working, loyal family man was every woman's ideal. Why, oh, why didn't her stupid hormones wake up at the sight of him the way they did every time she saw Todd Black?

"Daddy!" Serena squealed, and ran to him.

He scooped her up in his arms and kissed her cheek. "You smell like chocolate," he informed her. "I'm going to eat you all up." He gobbled on her neck, making her giggle and squirm.

"Don't, Daddy," she protested halfheartedly.

He gave her one more kiss, then set her down and turned his attention to Cecily. The look in his eyes told her that his hormones weren't snoozing. "Hi, Cecily. It's been a while since we've seen you."

Who wouldn't want a man like this? Wake up in there!

Her hormones dozed on.

He's big. You like big men.

Zzzz.

Give up, she told herself, *you were obviously meant to be single.*

Todd Black's swarthy face came to mind. *Or stupid.*

No. No more stupidity. She was done with men like Todd Black. She was done with men, period. After two years of running a dating service she'd had too much opportunity to study them up close. *She has to be a D cup.... What? I never said I was interested in marriage, just a relationship.* (Translation: sex.) Oh, yes, she'd had enough of the male of the species to last her a lifetime.

Not every man who came to her service was like that, she reminded herself. This one surely wasn't. She smiled back at him. "How's it going?"

"Can't complain," he said. "I heard you were back."

Apparently everyone in town had. "And busy," she said, pointing to the Mr. Dreamy pictures.

He shook his head. "Whatever brings in business, I guess."

Okay, so it was a little cheesy. And maybe just a little hypocritical, considering how judgmental she'd been of some of her clients. She quickly shied away from that last thought.

"Daddy, I'm hungry," Serena said.

"Right. We're off to Herman's," he told Cecily. "Would you like to join us?"

Herman's Hamburgers was one of the most popular spots in town, famous for its Herman the German hamburgers, which were almost more than any human mouth could get around.

It would be interesting to see little Serena try, but Cecily didn't want to give Luke the wrong idea. "Actually, I've got to get back to the house," she said.

His smile looked a little less jovial now.

"But thanks for the offer," she added, trying to soften the blow to his ego.

"Sure, no problem."

"Let's go, Daddy," Serena urged.

He shook off his disappointment like a big dog shedding water. "Right. Come on, girls. We're gonna go take on Herman the German and some garlic fries."

"Lovely to see you again," Bernadette said as they left the shop. "Come by for coffee sometime."

"I'll do that," Cecily lied.

"What a nice guy," Heidi said as the door closed after Luke and his family.

"He is," Cecily agreed. There had to be some perfect woman out there for him.

You're out of the matchmaking business, she reminded herself. Luke would just have to get along without her.

Fourteen

No business is immune to a certain amount of un-
pleasantness.
   —Muriel Sterling, *Mixing Business with Pleasure:*
   How to Successfully Balance Business and Love

Nothing tops off a day of public humiliation like a little
family insanity, thought Samantha as she tried to rein
in an overly enthusiastic Bailey via Skype.

Once more the Sterling women were gathered for a
brainstorming session, and much of it had been productive. They'd gone with Mom's suggestion of "Moonlight and Magic" as the theme for the masked ball and
the problem of music had been settled economically. It
would've been nice to have an orchestra or local band,
but a DJ from a radio station in Wenatchee was going
to spin tunes for them for half the price. To play on the
theme, he'd be tucked away behind a decorative screen
and the speakers would be concealed by floral arrangements from Lupine Floral so the source of the music
would be hidden. The owners of the Mad Hatter had
agreed to stock some exotic masks, so attendees could
pretend to be mysterious until the unmasking at midnight. Bailey had reported that plans were well under
way both for the high tea and the chocolate dinner. And
that was all well and good and should have been enough
to keep her busy, but now she had a new idea, one she'd
gotten from reading a historical romance.

"I think a kissing booth would be great," she insisted. "People used to do stuff like that all the time."

"That was before people got so sexually active," Samantha said. "Nobody's going to be interested in a kissing booth." At least nobody she'd want her baby sister kissing.

"People probably said that about bikini baristas," Bailey countered, "and now you see them all over the place."

"But nobody's kissing anybody in those. Anyway, I don't even think that would be legal. It's like soliciting for sex."

"We'd only be selling kisses," Bailey objected.

"It does seem a little tacky," Mom said.

Just like the Mr. Dreamy contest. "We're already pushing the envelope with some of the other things we're doing," Samantha said, making Cecily frown.

"You could make a fortune," Bailey began. "You—"

"You could also get cold sores," Samantha broke in.

Bailey made a face. "Eew."

"Yeah, eew," Samantha said. "No kissing booth."

At the rate they were going, maybe there wouldn't be any booths at all, she worried later as she let herself into her condo. She'd called Ed's wine shop to see if he'd any luck at city hall and learned that he was home with the flu. That meant the chances he'd been able to do any lobbying for moving those permits forward were slim to none.

From down the hall she heard the soft thump of sneaky cat paws hitting the floor, which told her that Nibs had been up on the kitchen counter again where he knew he wasn't supposed to be. Not that such unimportant details ever stopped a cat.

Now he came trotting up to her, all innocence. "You are a naughty boy," she said, and picked him up.

Naughty boy. Her mind did a word-association free fall to Bill Will's racy serenade in the coffee shop. Maybe the pictures Nia took wouldn't turn out. Maybe there wouldn't be room to put any of them in the paper. That was a strong possibility…in a parallel universe.

Samantha set down the cat and went in search of aspirin.

She found herself reaching for more aspirin the next day when she got to the office and Elena gave her a copy of the morning paper. There was the picture Nia had taken right on page one, capturing all the action from the day before. She'd caught Samantha trying not to look at Bill Will's crotch, except that the camera angle gave the illusion that Jockstrap Land was exactly where her gaze was directed. The caption read Competition for Mr. Dreamy Heats Up.

Just shoot me now and kill me dead. Wasn't it enough that she had to deal with saving her company? How was she supposed to go out in public after this?

"I know what you're thinking but it's not that bad," Elena said.

"According to whom?"

"It will be fine, *amiga.* You'll see. *A veces, todo el mundo tiene un dia de pelo revuelto.*"

Samantha crumpled the paper and tossed it in the garbage. "Okay, what does that mean?"

Elena shrugged. "It means that sometimes everyone has a bad hair day."

"I would welcome a bad hair day. I'd trade a lifetime of bad hair days for this."

Elena shrugged. "It will blow over. And meanwhile, you will get lots of free publicity."

"I don't need this kind of publicity," Samantha grumbled.

Elena fished the paper out of the garbage and handed it to her. "Read the whole article," she advised.

Samantha shut herself in her office and read. Nia had done a first-rate job of promoting the festival, naming the various events and even going so far as to suggest contestants get over to Sweet Dreams and buy some of their chocolates. "For surely any man representing our favorite hometown chocolate company had better know what his favorite chocolate is."

Okay. She had to hand it to Nia. She'd managed to convey the excitement that Samantha and the other Chamber of Commerce members were feeling in such a way that readers couldn't help but get excited, too, and want to participate. And that was a good thing.

"This is great free publicity," Cecily said when she called twenty minutes later.

"It is," Samantha agreed. "Except that picture, ugh. I'm going to have to put a bag over my head when I go out."

Cecily chuckled. Then sneezed.

"You're not getting sick, are you?" Samantha asked.

"Me? You know I never get sick."

"Well, take it easy today," Samantha said. None of them could afford to be sick until after the festival.

"Don't worry about me," Cecily said. "And don't take any bribes from Mr. Dreamy wannabes. We don't want to be accused of rigging the contest."

"Ha, ha." Samantha hung up.

Cecily wasn't the only one she heard from. Emails poured in from other members of the committee commending her on the exposure she'd gotten them, and in each reply she made sure her sister got the credit. As the morning wore on, some of her embarrassment wore off.

It helped that she'd stuffed the newspaper in a drawer where she didn't have to look at it.

By midmorning she'd put the whole embarrassing incident behind her. At least that was what she told herself.

Ed was still down for the count, so she called city hall and got put through to Pissy. Of course.

"Nice picture in the paper," Pissy said snidely.

"You sound jealous," Samantha retorted. Oh, way to win friends and influence people. Not that Pissy would ever be her friend and even offering the woman a lifetime supply of chocolate probably wouldn't influence her.

"I'm not going to dignify that with a response," Pissy said in her snootiest voice. "What do you want, Samantha?"

A million dollars. "Just calling to see how things are coming with the permits."

"I'll have to get back to you on that," Pissy said.

Great. "And when do you think you might be able to do that?" Samantha asked, keeping a tight rein on her patience.

"As soon as I know something. Now, quit hounding me," Pissy snapped, and hung up.

Samantha slammed the phone down and growled, "Bee-atch." If only she had a magic lamp. She'd use it to strand Pissy on a desert island with no chocolate.

She sat drumming her fingers on her desktop. Something or someone was holding up those permits. Samantha didn't believe Pissy had that kind of power, even though she liked to think she did. So why was this taking so long?

Obviously, she wasn't going to get to the bottom of the problem over the phone. She'd have to go over there.

She'd catch Del before lunch and talk to him, see if he'd pull some strings to get things moving.

She almost had Center Street to herself as she walked down it. She did encounter one couple who were strolling along and window-shopping and couldn't help overhearing their conversation as she approached.

"It's a cute town," the woman commented.

"I guess," the man said. "But there's no snow."

That wasn't true. There was some, enough to ski on… if you were a rabbit.

"This was a waste of vacation days," Mr. Good Sport said.

It took every ounce of willpower for Samantha to press her lips firmly together, but she was sure she had enough steam coming out of her ears to melt what little snow there was right off the highest peak. A waste of vacation days? Ha! She'd show him.

She was still steaming when she got to city hall, and encountering Pissy on her way out didn't improve matters, especially when Samantha saw that she was on her way out with Blake. "We're going to lunch so I can't help you." Pissy smirked.

Blake was taking Pissy out to lunch? Well, how perfect, two stone-cold hearts beating as one over bratwurst. "I wouldn't dream of keeping you from your lunch."

"Good, because I know Blake is a busy man," Pissy said, linking her arm through his.

Gack. Even though these two deserved each other, even though Samantha couldn't care less whom he took to lunch, she couldn't resist stealing a glance to see if Blake had swallowed this wad of flattery. His cheeks had taken on a ruddy tinge and he didn't look Samantha in the eye.

He cleared his throat. "Well, we'd better get going."

"We have reservations at Schwangau," Pissy said.

La-di-da. The two of them were probably off to conspire on how to keep those permits tied up. She hoped they choked on their schnitzel.

"Oh, and if you want Mayor Stone, you're too late. He's gone to lunch," Pissy called over her shoulder.

Samantha glared at Pissy's departing back. Wouldn't it be nice if looks could kill?

Blake was not having a good day. In fact, the day before hadn't been so good, either. First Samantha Sterling had left him smarting from that disgusted look she'd given him on the steps of city hall, as if it was a crime to take someone to lunch. Of course, he'd like to have told her he was taking Priscilla Castro to lunch in order to sweet-talk her into making sure those permits made the rounds and got signed in a timely manner, but that wasn't something he could explain with Priscilla standing right there. And when he'd finished buttering up Priscilla like she was corn on the cob, he'd tracked down Del Stone and given him a friendly nudge, too.

After accomplishing his mission, he'd thought of stopping by Samantha's office to let her know what he'd been up to. He'd envisioned her hugging him gratefully and saying, "I had no idea. That was so sweet of you." That happy vision had put a smile on his face and he'd still been smiling when he answered his phone.

Darren Short had quickly wiped it off. "I'm coming your way tomorrow and I'll have Trevor Brown from Madame C with me. I want to show him the Sweet Dreams facility."

"You—you what?" Blake had stammered.

"I want to show him the facility."

"We don't own that business yet," Blake reminded him.

"We hold the note. We're within our rights to inspect our investment."

"You're not coming up to inspect it."

"I am in a sense. This is all totally legal," Darren assured him.

But not even remotely ethical. "There's no need to rush. Let's hold off until March."

"Trevor wants to scope out the place, see what kind of condition it's in. There's no harm in looking."

Yeah, tell that to the Sterlings, Blake thought. "I'm not going along with this."

A moment of deathly quiet hung between them. "Am I suddenly working for you?" Darren finally asked.

"No," Blake said, "but why have you got me up here if you don't trust me to do the bank's business?"

"Come on now, Blake, there's no need to get stiff-necked about this. I'm looking out for the bank's interests—just like you are."

The implication was plain. Blake's loyalty was suspect and if he didn't cooperate he'd show his true turncoat colors. He *didn't* want to go along with it. But he didn't want to get fired, either. Then he'd be in no position at all to help any of his customers, especially the Sterlings.

Like you're being such a big help to them now?

That question had nibbled away at his peace of mind the night before and all morning long. Now, as he saw Darren walk into the bank beside a thin gray-haired man with jowls, dressed in slacks and a sweater, it went from nibbling to gobbling.

"Blake, meet Trevor Brown," Darren said jovially.

"Nice to meet you," Brown said, and held out a greedy paw.

Shake hands with the devil. Blake clasped the man's hand and nodded curtly. "Trevor."

"I'm anxious to see this place," Brown said, not wasting any time.

"I think you'll find it well worth the trip," Darren told him. "Don't you, Blake?"

"You do understand, of course, that this is a family business and the family is doing everything in its power to keep it," Blake said, making Darren scowl.

"Of course." Brown nodded genially. "But frankly, they don't stand a snowball's chance. We all know that."

Sadly, they did.

"So," said Darren, giving Blake a look that threatened not only termination but dismemberment, "shall we go?" Blake was about to claim a heavy workload and stay behind when Darren said, "Lead on, Blake."

Blake clenched his jaw and walked with them out of the bank, feeling like a Judas goat about to lead the sheep to slaughter.

Fifteen

Sooner or later, trouble is bound to knock on your door. Welcome it. Then poison it.
> —Muriel Sterling, *Knowing Who You Are:*
> *One Woman's Journey*

Del wasn't in his office. Again. "When will he be back?" Samantha asked Pissy.

"By noon, but he has a lunch date so he's not going to be able to talk to you."

"I'm sure he can spare a minute," Samantha said, and plunked herself down on a chair to wait. This time she was not leaving until somebody told her something about those permits.

Pissy shrugged. "Suit yourself." Then she went back to her desk and got busy looking busy.

Really, if people could get a degree in immaturity, Pissy would have a doctorate. Samantha took out her phone and began checking email.

She'd barely gotten started when Elena called. "You'd better get back here."

The urgency in her voice made Samantha's heart stop. "What's going on?"

"Something fishy. The manager from the bank is here with two other men and they want to inspect the factory."

"What?" Samantha bolted from her seat and hurried out the door. "Where are they now?"

"I sent them to the gift shop for some free samples. I didn't know what else to do."

"You did the right thing," Samantha said.

"Why are they here? Does this have anything to do with your meltdown a couple weeks ago?"

"Yes, but it's under control. Don't worry."

"Don't worry? *¿Estás demente?* I know a shark when I see one. What's going on, *chica?*"

"Nothing I can't handle," Samantha assured them both. Oh, Lord, she hoped she was right. She ended the call and broke into a run.

But when she reached her street she realized she needed to face these buzzards from a position of strength, not weakness. Entering her business establishment breathless, sweaty and panicked was no way to put up a strong front. She slowed down, finger-combed her hair and found a tissue in her purse to blot her damp forehead. Then she took a deep breath and marched into battle.

She'd expected to see Blake the Snake and maybe another bank manager, but not the third man, and her heart seized at the sight of him. She knew this man, just like she knew all her competitors. She'd made it her business to check out the competition. Trevor Brown was a busy boy. Every year he lobbied for Madame C to become the official candy of Washington State, as the Liberty Orchards people who made Aplets and Cotlets did, and Brown & Haley, producers of Almond Roca—as if he was even in their league—and Sweet Dreams, the chocolate contender. He had big suppliers and a big appetite. He'd already gobbled up two small companies, and now he was looking to swallow hers. Well, he wasn't going to get it.

She donned her business smile and forced herself to move forward, hand out. "I heard we had visitors."

Blake shook her hand. She felt a jolt at the contact and told herself it was rage, pure rage.

He looked embarrassed. He should. He should be mortified by his behavior. Entering the Mr. Dreamy contest and now bringing the vultures for a little deathbed visit. She ended the handshake as quickly as possible. Shaking hands with the other two men as he made introductions wasn't any more pleasant. No jolt there, just panic. *Don't panic!*

"Nice to meet you," she said to Trevor Brown even though they both knew it was a lie. "Your reputation precedes you." *As a maker of inferior chocolates.*

"Does it?" He smiled and took another bite of the pecan butter crunch fudge Heidi had given him.

Meanwhile, Heidi was standing behind the counter, a question mark in her big blue eyes.

Samantha smiled reassuringly at her, then returned her attention to the trio of vipers in front of her. "So, gentlemen, what can I do for you?"

"Actually, we're here to tour your facility," said the man Blake had introduced as Darren Short.

"I'm afraid we don't give tours." Samantha smiled with faux regret.

"To the bank that's calling in your note you do," Darren said pleasantly.

Samantha's veins turned to ice. Heidi's shock came at her like a wave; before the day was over, all her employees would be in a panic. She suddenly felt like the proverbial little Dutch boy trying to plug a multitude of holes in the dike. "The bank doesn't own Sweet Dreams." Not yet, anyway.

"No," Darren said, "but as holder of the note we do

have the right to inspect the facility at any time and make sure it's in good working order."

"Then I suggest you send in someone who's qualified to do so."

"We have," Darren said. "That's why Trevor is with us."

This had to be how a cat felt when it was cornered by a pack of dogs. Both Darren Short and Trevor Brown were slobbering to devour her, and Blake the Snake stood there, his jaw clenched like he wished she'd just shut up and die and be done with it.

Well, she'd be damned if she would. She raised her chin. "I'm sorry, gentlemen, but I'm afraid Mr. Brown doesn't qualify as an inspector." The only title he qualified for was king of mediocrity. "If you're concerned about the condition of our building or equipment you can, of course, send someone appropriately qualified, although I can assure you everything is in perfect working order." Now she smiled, the charming businesswoman offering hospitality. "Mr. Brown, I know you've got a long drive back to Seattle, but I'm sure you'll want to check out one of our fine restaurants. Zelda's is popular, and if you like Mexican there's Der Spaniard. And Schwangau can give you some wonderful authentic German fare." She moved to the door and opened it.

"Now, wait a minute," Darren sputtered.

"Gentlemen, I think it's time for lunch," Blake said, moving to the door.

Trevor shrugged. "I've seen enough. Great chocolate, by the way," he said to Samantha as he sauntered past.

Darren wasn't such a good sport. He punched a finger at her. "I want reports on all your equipment and the condition of your building on Blake's desk by the end of business today. Got it?"

In his dreams. Samantha glared at him. "Get. Out."

He stormed off, but Blake lingered. "Samantha, this was not my idea."

She glared at him, too. "But here you are, anyway."

"Not by choice."

"Said the hangman to the prisoner," she retorted.

"Believe it or not, I'm trying to help you."

"Yes, I can tell," she said through gritted teeth. She nodded at his departing partners in crime. "You'd better hurry and catch up. I'd hate to see the vultures start lunch without you."

For a moment he stood there, his jaw working.

"I guess that was too polite. Let me translate. Leave."

He nodded curtly and strode off down the street and she closed the door behind him, then collapsed against it.

"What's going on?" Heidi asked in a small voice.

"A temporary glitch with the bank," Samantha said. "Don't worry. We'll be fine."

She said the same thing to Elena a minute later.

"*No me digas mentiras, chica.* We have troubles, don't we?"

"We have troubles, yes, but we're going to pull out of them," Samantha insisted. "Hang in there with me, okay?" It was asking a lot. Elena needed both the money and the health insurance.

She nodded. "You know I will."

Samantha's throat tightened and her eyes stung with tears. "Thanks," she managed to say, and shut herself in her office.

The rest of the day was torture. More than one employee came to her wearing a worried expression.

That night she tossed and turned and stared at the ceiling. When she finally slept, her dreams took her to the factory, where she stood alone on the assembly line, trying to gather a million chocolates off the conveyor belt as they scooted by and put them in boxes. Above her a giant grandfather clock began striking the midnight hour. With the final bong the factory door shot open and the flying monkeys from *The Wizard of Oz* swooped in. One snatched her up and out the door they flew. Over a frozen Wenatchee River, it let go and she began to fall.

She woke up right before she hit the ice, her heart pounding. And she'd wanted to go to sleep? What had she been thinking?

She called a meeting with her employees the next day and assured them that Sweet Dreams was not closing its doors, all the while hoping she didn't end up a liar. "With Waldo's death we've had a few challenges to work through." *Yeah, and the great flood of Genesis was just a rainstorm.*

"But what were those men doing here?" Heidi asked.

"Snooping," Samantha said.

"I heard one of them was from the bank," said Chita Arness, a single mom who worked the production line. "Are they trying to close us down?"

None of Samantha's business classes had prepared her for this. She took a deep breath. "No one is closing us down. My family owes them money and they were checking on their investment. It's that simple." And that ugly. She didn't have the heart to tell everyone that if they didn't pay up, Cascade Mutual would be selling Sweet Dreams to the highest bidder.

But Chita obviously wasn't fooled.

"What if you can't pay the bank?" she asked. "What about our jobs?"

"If we were to get bought out, I'm sure you'd still have them." Trevor Brown would keep everyone employed, wouldn't he? Samantha's stomach churned. "Don't worry," she said as much to herself as her employees. "We're restructuring and, as you all know, we're gearing up for a lot of business the weekend of the chocolate festival. We have no plans to shut our doors, no matter what you may hear to the contrary." That was her story and she was stickin' to it.

She went back to her apartment drained and ready to do nothing but stare at her TV like a two-legged squash. But vegging out wasn't an option. It was Friday and she had to go to Mr. Dreamy Night—the brainchild of her sister and Charley—which was taking place in the bar at Zelda's. And, according to Cecily, the face of Sweet Dreams needed to be there for the big contest kickoff.

"Well, you'll have to find another face," she'd said when Cecily had first asked her to attend. "I'm not going."

Then Cecily had caught a bad cold. She was still in bed, slurping Mom's homemade chicken soup and watching old movies on her computer and guess who was going to Mr. Dreamy Night.

Samantha pulled her hair into a sloppy ponytail, put on a black skirt, her favorite V-neck gray sweater and a pair of boots and left it at that. No way was she freshening up her makeup or getting all dolled up for what could very well prove to be a repeat of the Bill Will incident. Cecily and Charley had promised her things wouldn't get out of hand, but she knew better. Her whole life was out of hand. Why would tonight be any different?

There wasn't much to eat in the fridge but that was okay. Since her confrontation with the vultures earlier in the week she'd had no appetite, anyway.

She got to the restaurant at quarter to eight. The dining area was almost empty with only a few older people and one or two couples. From the noise drifting out from the bar, it wasn't hard to figure out where all the customers had gone.

"Everyone's raring to go," Charley told her. "Go on in and order a drink. I'll be there as soon as I can get away."

Samantha entered the bar. It was so packed with people both standing and sitting, she could hardly see the vintage pictures of twenties gangsters and flappers that hung on the wall. Laughter and loud talk rolled over her like a tidal wave. This was going to be a zoo. No one under the age of forty had stayed home tonight; they were all here, slurping huckleberry martinis and chowing down on hot wings and pretzels. Samantha looked around and saw that most of the tables were occupied by couples, but there were also plenty of singles. Four women sat at one table, clearly out hunting for their own Mr. Dreamy. They were dressed to the max in outfits designed to show both cleavage and leg and wore full makeup. At another table she spotted a couple of grocery checkers from Safeway, probably new Mr. Dreamy contestants.

Rita Reyes, looking hot in her simple black shorts and shirt and requisite flapper headband, came over to Samantha, bearing a sheaf of papers. It was impressively thick. "New entries," she said.

"Just from tonight?"

"Yeah. Oh, Charley said to ply you with booze. What would you like?"

The way her week had been going? Arsenic. "I don't know."

"Your sister had Hank invent a drink for the night—a chocolate kiss. They're pretty popular. Want to try one?"

What she really wanted was to go home and feel sorry for herself but that wouldn't help, so she said, "Sure."

"Charley will be here soon. We're about done out in the restaurant."

Samantha was about done in here and they hadn't even started.

"The shirtless-man parade's in twenty minutes. She'll be MCing it."

Shirtless-man parade. Oh, Lord. Cecily had conveniently neglected to tell her about that. "Hurry up with my drink," Samantha said weakly.

She tried her best to shrink into the shadows, but failed. Several women dragged their boyfriends over to schmooze and a couple of guys offered to buy her drinks. And then—oh, no—here came Bill Will.

"Samantha!"

She held up a hand. "No singing."

He grabbed a chair from the other side of her little table and set it next to her, then slid onto it and slipped an arm around her shoulders. "Oh, come on," he teased.

Rita arrived with her drink and she grabbed the glass and took a swallow. "Wow, this is good," she said in surprise.

"What it needs is a Sweet Dreams chocolate in it," Bill Will said, going for shameless flattery.

Actually, though, that was a good idea.

Red Ralston, who worked on the guest ranch with Bill Will, came over and seated himself in a chair on her other side. "Hey, is Bill Will trying to bribe you?"

"I can't be bribed," she said. "Anyway, the competition isn't tonight. You both know that. This is just the kickoff."

"We know," Red said amiably.

"And I'm not the only judge."

"You're the most important one," Bill Will said, giving her a playful bump with his shoulder.

She had to smile; Bill Will was so full of it. "How much have you had to drink?" she asked him. Like he needed alcohol to be outrageous?

He raised both hands. "Just one beer. Honest."

"Well, go get yourself another," Samantha said. "You, too," she told Red. "This table is reserved."

"Okay, fine," Bill Will said with a shrug.

"Bill Will, over here!" called one of the Mr. Dreamy hunters.

That was all it took. He sauntered off, his buddy following him. Samantha watched them go and took another slug of her drink. This was *re-e-eallly* good. A couple of these could go a long way toward helping a girl forget her problems.

Now Rita was back with a bowl of pretzels. "This is good stuff," Samantha told her.

Rita smiled. "We thought you'd like it."

"Can I have another?"

"Sure. But go easy. It's sweet but it packs a wallop."

As hard as she'd already been walloped this week, Samantha wasn't afraid of a little old drink. "I can handle it," she said.

Rita seemed dubious, but went to put in the order.

"I can handle my liquor," Samantha muttered, then smiled. She'd heard that expression before. Never thought she'd use it, though.

Now Charley was at the table. "I guess you got the entries," she said, pointing to the pile of papers on the table in front of Samantha.

"Oh, yeah. Looks like we're going to have quite the pageant."

"I'd say so," Charley said. "Make yourself at home with the pretzels. I've got to announce our shirtless-man parade."

Samantha frowned. "That is so disgusting."

"Don't blame me. It was your sister's idea."

"Which one?"

"The one who conveniently isn't here," Charley said, and made her way to the tiny stage at one corner of the bar, where a mike had been set up.

Blake had been in a corner booth when Samantha Sterling entered the restaurant. Brave man that he was, he hid behind his menu at the sight of her. Ever since she'd disappeared into the bar he'd tried to consume the medium-rare steak and baked potato he'd ordered, but with little success. Thinking about the mess she was in had taken away his appetite. Samantha Sterling had been in his thoughts since the first day she'd walked into the bank. Even worse, she'd quickly migrated from his thoughts to his dreams, and they weren't the kind of dreams a guy shared with his mom.

Those dreams would never come true. He was the unwilling villain in her life. He recalled the very unpleasant scene with Darren after the factory fiasco. Brown had merely shrugged off their encounter with Samantha. He had the patience of a croc. He'd wait. Darren, on the other hand, had seethed with a barely controlled rage all through lunch. And before he and Brown took off for Seattle, he made sure he got a minute alone with Blake to rake him over the coals for his lack of team spirit.

"If Trevor wants this," Blake had retorted, "he'll wait. Meanwhile, Sweet Dreams is still a bank customer."

"Not for long, just like your run as bank manager," Darren had snarled, and stormed off.

Wounded pride, Blake had reasoned. He'd calm down. And in another couple of months Trevor Brown would happily swallow a new chocolate company. The only one who'd come out of this badly was Samantha Sterling.

"Shouldn't you be in the bar?" Maria asked as she gave him his check.

"What's going on in there?" he asked.

"It's the kickoff for the Mr. Dreamy pageant," she said. "You're one of the contestants. Why aren't you in there?"

"I'm what?" Was she making some kind of sick joke?

"Nobody told you?"

He shook his head.

Maria made a face. "Well, you're on the list."

"What list?" Was he in the *Twilight Zone?*

Now she shook *her* head and put a hand on her hip. "The one with all the contestants. You have some serious competition."

"I didn't enter," he protested.

"Somebody nominated you, because your picture's hanging up with all the other contestants in the Sweet Dreams shop."

He grabbed his wallet and pulled out his credit card. "Well, it's news to me."

She shrugged and went to ring up his bill, and he sat and drummed his fingers on the table, trying to figure out who'd done this to him. Someone had a sick sense of humor.

Or thought he was fabulous. He frowned. *Gram.* Oh, man, this was sick.

Maria returned with his receipt. He added a generous tip and scrawled his name, then headed for the bar to make sure he was removed from the infamous list. After what happened this week, he had no doubt Samantha Sterling would be happy to remove him, right off the face of the earth.

He arrived just in time for roll call. Charlene Albach, the owner of the restaurant, was bringing the contestants to the little stage at the end of the bar, one by one. Judging by the hoots and applause as each man took his place, it appeared that the contestants had all brought their cheering sections.

"Joe Coyote," she called, and Blake's old football buddy limped self-consciously up to the stage while Lauren Belgado and a girlfriend cheered him on. He knew Joe and Lauren had been seeing each other. Things had to be pretty serious for her to be able to talk quiet old Joe into something like this.

"Bill Williams."

The bar erupted with screams and clapping as the cocky cowboy in a Western shirt and jeans tight enough to show off his package swaggered up to the stage. Bill was obviously a crowd favorite and Blake couldn't help glancing in Samantha Sterling's direction to see if the guy was a favorite of hers. Apparently not. She was frowning.

"Blake Preston."

Now Samantha looked as if she'd just drunk vinegar and Blake felt his face catching fire as all eyes turned to him. Lauren seemed surprised but she and her girlfriend dutifully clapped and cheered along with a couple of other women.

"Sorry, I'm not competing," he called.

"Oh, come on. No chickening out," Charlene teased, clearly enjoying his discomfort. She started the crowd chanting, "Blake, Blake, Blake."

He shook his head and moved to Samantha's table, seating himself next to her. She bristled at his arrival.

The crowd gave up and moved on to fresh meat and,

under cover of the loud talk and laughter, Samantha hissed, "This table is taken."

"I can see that," he said. "That's why I chose it. I wanted to talk to you."

She downed what was left of her cocktail in one gulp and then hiccupped. "Well, I don't want to talk to you."

"You didn't give me a chance to explain yesterday."

"Like your actions needed an explanation?"

"Yes, as a matter of fact, they did."

She cocked her head and stared at him as if trying to bring him into focus. How many of those drinks had she gulped down?

The cocktail waitress was at their table now, asking him what he'd like to drink.

"Jack Daniel's straight up," he said.

"And I'll have another of these." Samantha held up her near-empty martini glass.

"How many of those have you had?" he asked.

"None of your business," she informed him.

The waitress seemed hesitant. "You're not much of a drinker, Samantha. Two might be your limit."

"Three is a nice even number," Samantha said. "Bring me one more."

The waitress frowned. "Okay, but after that Hank's gonna cut you off. I can tell you that right now."

"Fine," Samantha said with an airy flick of her hand. Now she turned her attention back to Blake. "Are you still here?"

"I'm afraid so," he said agreeably.

"You know, you really are a snake. And a hypocrite. Entering our Mr. Dreamy contest while you're trying to steal our company."

"I didn't enter your contest and I am not trying to steal your company," he said.

"Yes, you are. You want to give it to Trevor Brown. I'm not stupid."

"I never said you were." Actually, he thought she was one smart cookie.

"You're probably the reason our permits are lost somewhere in city hall," she said, pointing a finger at him.

"What?" Oh, that smarted. After enduring a lunch with Priscilla Castro drooling over him, he deserved a medal, not a cold shoulder.

"We need permits to have all those festival booths downtown. You can't just plant 'em like flowers. We need permission to sell food and alcohol and have musical performances. We need an event permit. And so far we have nothing. Nothing!" She waved a hand, almost taking off his nose. "Do you know what a bust the whole thing will be if we can't put up booths downtown?" He opened his mouth to speak, but she talked right over him. "Not that it matters," she said, contradicting herself. "We'll still have our dinner and our ball and our Mr. Dreamy contest and we'll sell lots and lots of chocolate. And I'll pay you and your bank buzzards everything I owe you." She grabbed her martini glass and tossed back the last of her drink.

"Hey, you're supposed to sip that stuff," Blake cautioned.

"I am," Samantha said. "I like big, long sips."

"And now, before we start our shirtless-man parade, let's have a few words from Samantha Sterling, one of our judges," Charlene said from the mike.

Amid much clapping and hooting, Samantha stood—a little unsteadily but she made it to her feet and then to the mike. "Thank you all for turning out," she told the crowd. "Ladies, if you haven't gotten your tickets for the Mr. Dreamy pageant yet you can purchase them at the Sweet Dreams gift shop, along with our fabulous chocolates. Nothing is better than chocolate, especially if it comes from Sweet Dreams." With that, she gave the mike back to Charlene, who started down the line of men, having them peel off their shirts one at a time. Fired by alcohol and hormones, the women went wild.

Samantha returned to the table and fell into her seat. "Oh, good. My drink is here." She frowned at Blake. "And so are you. Don't you have somewhere to go?"

"Huh-uh," he said.

She continued to frown and took a sip from her glass. "You always did think you were hot fries, didn't you? Big man on campus, giving all the girls a thrill. Did you play football in college?" she demanded as if that was, somehow, a crime.

"No, I blew out my knee my freshman year."

Down went more of that cocktail. She was drinking it like it was soda pop. "Too bad," she sneered. "I guess you had to work for your degree, then."

"Actually I did. Same as you." Now she was beginning to bug him. Samantha Sterling had a mouth on her.

She grunted and took another swig. "What did you major in?"

"Business."

"Monkey business, I'll bet," she muttered. "Why are you at the bank, anyway?"

"That's not what you're really asking, is it?" he countered.

"Oh? What am I really asking?"

"You're asking, 'Why aren't you Arnie?'"

Her face fell and she stared into her glass. "Well, why aren't you?" she said, her voice tremulous. "He wouldn't stand by and let my family lose our company. He understood the importance of community."

"That may be, but he didn't understand the importance of being wise with money. Sadly, a lot of people don't."

She reared back her head and looked at him through bleary eyes. "Are you accusing me of not being wise?"

He knew she'd inherited the mess she was in. "Not at all. I'm just saying—"

"I don't want to hear what you're saying. I don't want to talk to you. I want to have fun. Girls just want to have fun, you know. Why does everyone get to have fun but me? Why do I have to worry about the company and Mom keeping a roof over her head and not letting everyone down? I should be partying. I think I will," she decided, and began to climb up on her chair, showing enough leg to bring every shirtless man running from the other end of the bar. It was a wobbly assent, sure to summon disaster.

Blake grabbed for her and she shied away, ricocheting off another table and upending a drink in a woman's lap. "Oops, sorry," she said to the sputtering woman, and giggled. "Girls just want to have fun, you know. And I'm gonna have fun." She started dancing, waving her arms back and forth over her head. "I want to dance in the sun or the moonlight or whatever it was." Once more she tried to scale the chair, but wound up draped over the table. "Who's spinning this thing?"

"Those drinks you inhaled," he told her.

She managed to crawl up on the table but was now stuck on all fours, glaring at him through a curtain of red hair. This was hardly the moment to be turned on, but Blake was.

She tried to blow her hair out of her face, then scowled

at him. "You keep pretending you want to help me. Well, help me up on this table."

"I don't think that would be a good idea," he said. Bad enough that he couldn't stop her from making a fool of herself. He didn't want her falling and knocking herself unconscious on top of that.

"Fine, if you won't help I'll do it myself. I don't need anyone to help me, anyway." She struggled to get up, leaving him no choice but to assist her.

Oh, boy, this would be one more thing she'd blame him for once she was sober.

"Oh, it's high up here. I can see everyone. Go, Mr. Dreamy!" She pumped the air with one hand and immediately lost her balance, toppling from the table. He caught her before she could bang her head.

"I think it's time to go home," he said, setting her on her feet.

Now Charlene was at the table. "Samantha, how many of those have you had?"

Samantha's brow furrowed. "How many what?"

"Never mind." Charlene thrust out one hand, palm up. "Give me your car keys."

"Don't worry. I'm taking her home," Blake said.

"To *her* home," Charlene said.

What did she think he was? He didn't bother to dignify that remark with a response. Instead, he got out a bill and laid it on the table. "Come on, party girl," he said to Samantha. "You've had enough fun for one night."

He put an arm around her and started moving her out of the bar. No one noticed. They were all too busy cheering on the Mr. Dreamy wannabes as the men paraded through the maze of tables accompanied by the Weather Girls singing "It's Raining Men."

They passed the now-empty restaurant. Patrons had either fled the noise or gone to the bar to add to it.

"Is my head still connected to my neck?" Samantha asked as he opened the door for her. "It feels like a balloon."

"Yes, it's still connected but not enough for you to be driving."

"I don't want to go home with you," she said petulantly. "And I'm not going to run around the bank in my underwear or let you drown me in a vat of chocolate, either."

He blinked. "What?"

She blinked. "Uh, never mind."

They were at his car now, a classic red Camaro in which he took great pride. He opened the door and she fell onto the black leather seat, giving him a view of leg and beyond that sent the blood rushing from his head to an area slightly farther south.

Alcohol and a gorgeous female he was attracted to— that was all it took to make him want to do what men were designed to do. There were only a couple of drawbacks. Three actually. One, she was drunk. Two, she despised him. Three, he pretty much despised himself.

His parents had raised him to be a gentleman and that was exactly what he was going to be. But his fingers itched to touch her.

He got behind the wheel and started the engine, and the car roared to life like a giant beast. That made two beasts on the road. She leaned her head back against the cushions and closed her eyes, unaware of how sexy she looked with that long neck exposed, just waiting for someone to nibble on it.

"I'm tired," she sighed.

That comment had nothing to do with the time. He

slanted a look her way. Now she was staring at him with those big hazel eyes.

A tear slipped from one and rolled down her cheek. "I'm trying so hard."

Oh, no. Don't cry. Please don't cry. "Samantha," he began.

She held back a sob and turned her face to the window. "I've drained my savings, I've had to beg all our suppliers to keep—" She pressed her lips firmly together to stop any more secrets from leaking out and wiped at a corner of her eye.

He pulled off the street. Now they were by the park. The giant fir tree that the town made great ceremony of lighting every Christmas loomed, creating the illusion of privacy. "Come here," Blake said, and drew her close to him, not an easy task considering the fact that this damned car had bucket seats.

She looked up at him, her head on his shoulder. Her hair brushed his cheek like a caress. "So many families in this town depend on us. What would Icicle Falls be without Sweet Dreams? Without chocolate? What would the world be without chocolate?"

This probably wasn't the time to tell her he was allergic to the stuff.

"Nothing in this world is better than chocolate," she murmured.

"Oh, there are some things," he said, staring at her lips. *Don't do it.*

"Ha! Like what?" He knew the second she recognized the glint in his eye. Her eyes widened, then her gaze dropped, showing him a flutter of long lashes. She looked at his lips and wet hers.

Okay, gentleman or no, he knew an invitation when he saw one. He leaned over and kissed her. She whimpered and he deepened the kiss, threading his fingers through her hair. He could feel her melting, all that female softness surrendering to him. Oh, yeah, there was something in this world a *lot* better than chocolate.

He had just gotten her into his lap and had a hand sliding along her thigh when her fingers froze in the middle of taking a trip up his neck. She pulled back and gaped at him in horror. "You...you..."

Beast. She was right. He was taking unfair advantage and they needed to stop. But not this way, not with her wearing that look of betrayal. "Samantha," he protested. "I'm not your enemy."

"Yes, you are and I almost slept with you!" she cried.

A few hot kisses on a cold night did not equal sleeping with the enemy.

She didn't give him a chance to tell her that, though. She was already scrambling off his lap. Now she had her hand on the door handle. "Samantha, wait," he begged.

She didn't. She got out of the car, pulling her purse after her, and slammed the door. Then she was off, marching a crooked path down the street.

He fumbled the keys in the ignition and started the car, then rolled down the window. "Where are you going?" he called.

"Home!"

He cruised alongside her. "I'll take you."

"You've taken me far enough for one night," she snapped. "I'll walk."

"You can't walk," he protested. But of course she could. It was perfectly safe in Icicle Falls. Really, the only danger to her had been the wolf behind the wheel, he thought glumly as he watched her lurch away.

He swore and smacked the steering wheel. This whole situation sucked.

He needed to reconsider his career choice.

Sixteen

Helping your family is the equivalent of helping your family's business.
—Muriel Sterling, *Mixing Business with Pleasure: How to Successfully Balance Business and Love*

After two days in bed feeling like Death had put out the welcome mat, Cecily awoke on Saturday morning to the realization that she was going to live, after all. She called Charley to let her know she'd be able to work that night. Then she enjoyed a long, hot shower followed by a breakfast of fruit and her mother's homemade white-chocolate-lavender scones. That, along with two cups of tea, left her feeling ready to get back to work. It was now almost ten in the morning. Samantha should be awake. She'd check to see how the kickoff for the Mr. Dreamy competition had gone.

It took several rings for Samantha to answer with a weak hello.

"Were you still asleep?" Cecily asked. Samantha probably got in late. She should have waited to call.

"No."

Then why did she sound so funny? "Are you okay?"

"I have the mother of all headaches," Samantha said. "I think I had one too many chocolate kisses."

There had been an inspired idea. Not that Cecily was fishing for compliments or anything, but... "How did those turn out?" Okay, so she was fishing for compliments.

"Fabulous. They're also death in a glass. My head feels like somebody stomped on it."

"How many did you have?" Her sister had never been a big drinker. It wouldn't take much to put her under the table.

"I can't remember."

"You know, most of us get this drinking thing sorted out by the end of college."

"Well, I'm a late bloomer."

"Can you remember anything about last night?"

The only answer Cecily got was silence.

"Oh, no," she groaned. "What happened?"

"Nothing," Samantha said irritably. "The kickoff was a smashing success with shirtless men and girls going wild. We'll probably have a population explosion nine months from now. And yes, I made sure to put in a plug for Sweet Dreams."

"That's all good."

"Yes, it's all good. Everything's good."

"Okay," Cecily said dubiously. "Do you still want to work this afternoon?"

"Not particularly," Samantha said, "but we need to. Let's meet at the office around one. Maybe by then these rhinos stomping around in my head will have settled down for a nap."

They ended the call and Cecily sat at the kitchen table, idly twirling a lock of hair and wondering what had happened the night before that her sister hadn't told her.

Mom came into the kitchen and poured herself a cup of tea. "Did everything go well last night?"

"It sounds like it." Why didn't it feel like it?

Mom sat down at the table and studied Cecily. "Is something wrong?"

"No, I guess not." Mom looked worried, so Cecily added, "I'm sure everything's fine."

Mom didn't say anything to that. She just kissed the top of Cecily's head and disappeared into her bedroom.

Cecily remained alone in the kitchen. When she'd first offered to come home and help with the festival, she'd had a vague feeling that her family needed her, that destiny was waiting for her in Icicle Falls.

So far her destiny seemed to consist of irritating her sister and running unimportant errands. As for Mom, well, all she really needed was time and that obviously wasn't something Cecily was in a position to give.

"Why am I here?" she muttered.

The cuckoo clock on the kitchen wall struck the hour and the little cuckoo popped out the door to tell her just what he thought of her. She left before he could finish.

Blake had several errands to run this morning, but a visit to his grandmother topped the list. Janice Lind was one of the town's old-timers. She'd been a young woman when Icicle Falls pulled itself from the brink of extinction by transforming a collection of boarded-up storefronts and empty streets into an alpine village. Blake's maternal grandfather, Tom, whom everybody called Swede, had been the town's only mechanic for years. He'd owned the gas station where Blake's dad worked as a teenager before he married Blake's mother and went into car sales. Even Blake had worked at the station a summer or two. Since he was the only boy in the family, both his dad and his granddad had plans for him. Gramps had wanted him to run the garage after he graduated. Dad had wanted Blake to come and work with him selling cars in Seattle. If he'd done either, he could've connected with Samantha under different circumstances. Maybe they'd have been an item by now. He frowned as he made his way up the front walk to his grandparents' cozy log home.

She must have seen him coming because he was halfway up the walk when she opened the door, a slim modern granny with a flour-dusted apron over her slacks and tiger-print bifocals dangling from a chain around her neck. "This is a nice surprise," she greeted him.

A surprise? Rather like learning he'd been entered in the Mr. Dreamy contest.

"I'm making oatmeal cookies."

"My favorite. You must've known I was coming."

"Well, they're almost your favorite. I'm trying out a new recipe," she said, leading him into the kitchen. "This one uses Sweet Dreams chocolates. I figure it can't hurt to try and impress the judges."

He wished all Samantha Sterling needed to be impressed with him was home-baked cookies. He took a seat at the old red Formica table. Gram's kitchen always smelled great. This morning the aroma of the day was spices mixed with coffee. Not only did the place smell good, it looked like a stage for some cooking show. Everything was state-of-the-art, from the stainless-steel fridge to the ceramic-top stove. Copper pans polished to a high sheen hung from a rack over her counter, and two baking racks were stacked with man-size cookies.

She poured him a mug of coffee and set it in front of him, along with a plate of cookies. "If they've got chocolate, I'll pass."

"Silly," she said, tapping his shoulder playfully. "I made a special batch just for you. No chocolate, only raisins and nuts."

"In that case." He took one and stuffed half in his mouth.

"How is it?"

"Good," he said around a mouthful of fabulous. "Where's Gramps?"

"At the garage, doing some paperwork. And making sure the new mechanic really knows what he's doing." She shook her head. "Your grandpa just can't stay away from there. So much for semiretirement."

Blake had known all along that his grandfather wouldn't ease up, no matter how many mechanics he hired. Running that garage and filling station was his passion. Lucky guy. He'd found something he loved to do and been able to do it his whole life.

Once Blake had believed that banking was what he wanted, but life in the real world hadn't matched his vision, especially lately.

"Did the people from Sweet Dreams contact you?" his grandmother asked, bringing up the very reason he'd come. She was smiling like she'd done a wonderful thing.

"That's why I came by."

The smiling stopped. "Oh. I can see you're not pleased."

"I don't want to be in a male beauty pageant."

"Oh," she said again, sounding downright disappointed. "I saw all those wonderful prizes and...well, you truly are the handsomest young man in Icicle Falls."

He had to smile at that. "I think you might be prejudiced."

"I most certainly am not," she said stoutly.

"I appreciate the thought." Not really, but she'd meant well and he didn't want to hurt her feelings. "But it wouldn't look right. Not fitting the position of a bank manager."

"Yes, I suppose so. Your mother and I just felt it would be fun for you."

So his mother had been in on this, too. Why was he not surprised? He supposed he could be thankful that only one of the women in his life was currently living in town. He shuddered to imagine the mischief his mother and grandmother would dream up if they were both here. Factor in his sister, and he'd have had a triple threat.

"We hoped maybe it would loosen you up a little," Gram continued.

"Loosen me up?"

She reached across the table and laid a hand on his arm. "You used to be such a happy young man. You seem so serious these days."

"I'm happy," he insisted. But as he did, he realized that he hadn't laughed once since he'd moved back. Taking over the management of a troubled bank and feeling like some sort of cartoon villain whenever he saw Samantha Sterling was sucking his soul dry.

"Are you?" Gram said, and observed him over the rim of her coffee mug.

"For the most part. I have a lot of responsibility at the bank."

"Your grandfather has a lot of responsibility at the station and your father has a lot of responsibility at the dealership. They still enjoy themselves."

"That's different. They don't have people's lives depending on them."

She raised an eyebrow. "Oh? No families to support? No families working for them?"

She had a point there.

"Everyone has responsibilities, dear."

"I guess you're right," he conceded. "But I still don't want to be Icicle Falls' first Mr. Dreamy."

Not that he would have been. These days he was anything but Samantha Sterling's idea of a dream man. Somehow, someway, he had to do something to change that.

Grief was a heavy burden to carry but guilt was even worse and Muriel didn't think she could bear the load any longer. Her poor daughters were working so hard to clean up the mess she'd created. She had to do her part.

But how? She knew nothing about business. Yes, she'd worked at Sweet Dreams off and on over the years but she'd never been involved in any aspect of running the company. Her most important business had been her family. It still was and now she needed to help them put Sweet Dreams back in the red. Or the black. Or whatever it was. She might not know business, she told herself, but she knew people. She had friends in this town, people who'd want to help if she just asked.

Cecily had gone over to Samantha's—Muriel wasn't sure for what, but it most likely had something to do with the festival. So the house was hers.

A couple of weeks ago she'd have taken advantage of that time alone to look through photo albums or sleep or simply cry. She'd cried enough tears in the past few weeks to make the Wenatchee River flood. Nights were the worst. She felt her loss acutely when she climbed into bed and no strong arms reached out to hold her. Trying to fill up that big bed all by herself reminded her how utterly adrift she was.

But with the daylight hours, more pressing concerns took precedence. If they couldn't save the company she wouldn't have to worry about being alone in her big bed or this house. The house would be gone, like the company her grandmother had founded.

There was no time for moping. She grabbed the phone. She couldn't run a business, but she knew how to get donations. She'd made these kinds of calls raising money for the food bank when she and a couple of friends at Icicle Falls Community Church first started it years ago. It was time to make some calls again, this time for some personal loans.

She'd begin with Del Stone. If he was as interested in her sober as he was drunk, then maybe he'd like to put his money where his mouth was and help her out.

Seventeen

Expect the unexpected. This way you'll always
be ready for company and prepared for problems.
—Muriel Sterling, *Knowing Who You Are:*
One Woman's Journey

Samantha had gotten in touch with her inner Cecily and
kept quiet about her traitorous romantic exploits after
the Mr. Dreamy kickoff, and Cecily left her on Saturday assuming she was hungover and worried about the
business. No lie there. She was. That pathetic makeout
session with Blake was merely the cherry on top of a
big cupcake made of poop.

Friday had been torture and Saturday had been exhausting. After meeting with Cecily on Saturday, she'd
made the rounds of all the restaurants, wheeling and
dealing and talking up the festival, encouraging them
to come up with special recipes featuring Sweet Dreams
chocolates. She'd visited shops, glad-handing and flattering fence sitters and offering free chocolate right and
left. With all her bribes and promises, she'd spent a fortune. *Way to ignore your bottom line,* she scolded herself.

What bottom line? How could you have a bottom line
when you were a flatliner?

By Sunday she needed stress relief. She decided to
hide out in her condo.

"That's the last thing I want to do," she said when

Cass called and suggested an afternoon hike on Lost Bride Trail. Well, there were other things she'd like to have done, like rob a bank (and she knew just the one), but she was better off hiding at home.

"Come on," Cass urged. "The sun is out and the sky is blue. How often do we get that in winter? You don't want to sit inside and grow fat on your hips."

Actually, yes, she did.

"And you might see the lost bride," Cass teased.

Locals always looked for the ghost of the lost bride. According to legend, back in the 1860s a farmer named Joshua Cane got himself a mail-order bride. He quickly became the envy of every man within a fifty-mile radius because his bride, Rebecca, was beautiful. In fact, she was so beautiful that Joshua had a hard time keeping her to himself. She fell in love with his younger brother, Gideon, a gold prospector. Townspeople witnessed fights in the saloon and threats were exchanged. Then one day Rebecca went missing. So did Gideon. Speculation abounded. The two had run off. Joshua had murdered them both and buried the remains somewhere in the mountains. Joshua murdered his brother and left Rebecca on the mountain to starve. Sometimes people would swear they saw her over by Icicle Falls. After the town spinster saw her right before the new Methodist minister proposed, it became a lucky thing to catch sight of the lost bride's ghost flitting behind the waters of the falls. If a woman saw the ghost of Rebecca Cane, it meant she would soon be married. Naturally, the falls became a favorite destination for couples on the verge of engagement.

Samantha wasn't on the verge of anything except maybe a nervous breakdown. "No chance of that," she said.

"You never know," Cass said.

"You could see her, too," Samantha teased back.

"That'd be the day. But I think Dani's got hopes. So come keep us company. You need to think about something besides the festival."

Samantha reluctantly agreed and went to find her hiking boots. What the heck. If she sat around all day she'd probably drive herself insane worrying about the festival, not to mention the fate of Sweet Dreams.

An hour later they were making their way up the trail that ran alongside Icicle Creek. The air was fresh as only mountain air can be and they could hear the thunder of the falls in the distance. In spite of the blue sky and sun they could see their breath as they walked, and the trail was muddy from the recent showers of sleet and wet snow that refused to stick. It sucked at their shoes as they walked.

"Gosh, it's wet," Samantha said, dodging an icy puddle.

"I hope we don't have a rockslide," Danielle muttered.

"Bite your tongue," her mother said. "That's all we don't need. Anyway, the sun will help dry things out."

That was fine with Samantha. If they couldn't have a foot of snow, they could at least have a little taste of sunshine.

They made it to the falls without mishap, in spite of the slippery trail, and the view of white water lunging over the jagged mountain precipice was well worth the walk. "Look," Danielle cried. "A rainbow in the water!"

If only there was a pot of gold at the end of it…

"Is that all you see?" Cass asked her.

Danielle blushed. "That's all."

"It doesn't get much better than a rainbow," Samantha said, gazing at the rushing water. Then she caught a fleeting glimpse of something else. A person? She took a few steps closer and strained to see. *Was* that a person? Good heavens, it was! "There's someone in back of the falls," she said, pointing. "On that ledge. See her?"

Cass looked where she was pointing. "See what?"

"That's dangerous. She could slip." And bounce off the jagged rocks on her way down into the creek. "Hello!" Samantha called.

"Who are you calling? There's no one there," Cass said.

"Yes, there is." Samantha frowned at her. "Don't you see her? She's right…" But now there was no one. "Well, that's odd. I could've sworn I saw someone."

"The lost bride," Danielle gasped. "You saw the lost bride!"

"That's just a legend," Samantha said.

"But you saw her," Danielle insisted.

"And you know what that means, don't you?" Cass asked.

Samantha gave a snort. "It had better mean the festival will be a huge success."

According to the ad they'd taken out in the *Mountain Sun,* it was going to be stellar. Samantha stopped at the Safeway on the way home and purchased a paper. She stepped out of the flow of traffic and opened the paper to the full-page ad, which featured their calendar of events. Celebrate Icicle Falls' First Annual Chocolate Festival proclaimed the banner at the top. Oh, how she hoped it would be the first of many.

Lila Ward walked by and grudgingly wished her a good-morning, then added, "That's going to be a zoo."

"I sure hope so," Samantha responded.

With a disgusted huff, Lila walked on.

Samantha went home and celebrated by trying a glass

of white wine from the Sleeping Lady Winery that Ed had given her a while back. After a couple of sips she opted for cocoa instead. She raised her mug to Nibs, who was regarding her from one of the kitchen chairs. "Here's to success." Maybe seeing the lost bride would bring her luck.

That night she slept like a stone, dead to the world, and awoke the next morning refreshed. She had to meet with Lizzy, the bookkeeper, today and that would not be fun. She'd already pared her spending down to the bone but they were going to have to get out the knife and pare some more.

Still, she felt hopeful. The festival would be a success. They'd make a chunk of money and with that she'd find a way to bargain for time. Or she'd do…something. Something good was going to come of this, she'd make sure of it.

She was still smiling when she entered the office.

Elena didn't smile back at her. "You haven't seen today's paper?"

Cold fingers of dread squeezed her heart. "What's in the paper?" What could possibly have happened between yesterday and this morning?

Elena said nothing, simply handed it over.

That was what had happened. "A rockslide," Samantha said weakly.

"Right on Highway 2."

The highway that tourists traveled and the main road into town. It was now January 30. The festival was less than two weeks away.

Still, that was plenty of time. "D.O.T will get it cleaned up in a few days," Samantha assured herself.

Elena looked doubtful but said nothing.

Other people had plenty to say, though. Samantha's

mailbox overflowed with panicked emails and the phone rang off the hook all morning. Finally, Ed called an emergency committee meeting at his wine shop where they could drown their sorrows in cabernet sauvignon and try to think of a way to salvage the mess. Of course, as the instigator of this, they'd all be looking to Samantha for a solution. As if she had one.

She needed…no chocolate, she told herself firmly. Except she was out of fingernails. She left her office and stopped by the shop to get a salted caramel.

Heidi didn't say anything as she raided the display behind the glass, just looked at her sadly. Samantha took another caramel for the road.

She was just going out the door when she met Darla Stone, Del's middle-aged sister, and Hildy Johnson.

Both women were notorious sugar addicts. By all rights, they should've been regular customers but Samantha knew for a fact that they both preferred a cheap high to the good stuff and always stocked up whenever candy bars were on sale at the grocery store. So what were they doing here?

"Good morning, ladies," she said, trying to sound happy to see them. She *should* be happy. Even though they weren't her favorite people they were still customers.

Darla offered her a sympathetic smile and then turned to Hildy. "Look at the brave face she's putting on."

Samantha stared at them in confusion. "Excuse me?"

Darla patted her arm. "Oh, we know, honey. I think it's wonderful how supportive you girls are of your mother, but sometimes you just have to throw in the towel, especially now with this rockslide closing the highway."

"I assume you're already marking down your candy?" Hildy added.

"Marking down my candy?" Samantha repeated. "I don't understand—"

"There's no need to pretend with us. Del talked to your poor mother."

Samantha's heart stopped. "What did my mother say?"

"Well, only that you're about to go out of business," Darla said. "She was hoping Del could help, but his money is all tied up. I told him the best thing we can do is buy up your chocolate, which I'm sure you're marking down. I mean, that *is* what you do when you're going out of business, isn't it?"

This, after all her hard work trying to keep her employees from panicking—her blood turned to molten lava in less than a second. "I don't know what exactly my mother said to Del, but whatever it was, she's mistaken. We are not closing our doors. And we're certainly not having a fire sale."

Darla's pudgy face grew pink. "Oh, well," she stammered. "I just thought…" The words trailed off and the pink turned red.

"I know what you thought," Samantha said. *Okay, don't go any further. Get in touch with your inner Cecily.* "Yes, we've had a few challenges after losing my stepfather but let me repeat—Sweet Dreams is not ready to close its doors. We're an important part of this town's economy. Surely you ladies wouldn't want to see us go under."

"Oh, no, of course not," Darla said.

Samantha smiled at her. "I didn't think so, and I appreciate that you've come to show your support and shop with us." She opened the front door so they had no choice but to go in. "We all support one another in this town, don't we?" she added, now turning her attention to Hildy. "My family's been filling their prescriptions at your drugstore ever since you first opened."

Hildy got the hint. She pressed her lips firmly together and followed Darla into the gift shop.

Savoring the small moment of one-upsmanship, Samantha poked her head in the door and called to Heidi, "Give these ladies ten percent off. As our thanks for being such loyal customers," she told the women. The irony would no doubt escape them but if not, she hoped it made them distinctly uncomfortable and spurred them to spend appropriately.

Fuming, she hurried over to Ed's via the Riverfront Park, opting to avoid the more public streets. It was a beautiful path, playing peekaboo with the river between fir and pine trees and all manner of shrubs and bushes. Some of it was muddy and an icy drizzle did its part to make sure those spots remained that way, but she kept walking.

The weather matched her mood perfectly. First the highway closure and now her mother. What in the name of Godiva had Mom been thinking, talking to Del Stone of all people? Del, whose sister was one of the biggest gossips in all of Icicle Falls? Had her mother been thinking at all? Probably not.

"Crap," she muttered with every step. "Crap, crap, crap, crap, crap!" Her family was going to be the death of her—if Mother Nature didn't do her in first. She marched on, sourly taking in the sodden landscape that had shed most of its sparse snowfall. What a crappy year it had been. And what a crappy new year it was starting out to be! Why couldn't something, *anything,* go right?

She could feel tears stinging her eyes and fiercely

blinked them back. No way was she letting this damned rockslide take her down. No way, no way, no way.

She remembered Trevor Brown, waiting in the wings to absorb Sweet Dreams into his company, and Blake Preston and his gang of bank thugs doing all they could to truss her up like a Thanksgiving turkey and deliver her on a platter. She wanted to run away.

With Blake.

Where had that come from? She wouldn't run away with him if it was the end of the world and he was driving the last working car out of town. And if he and his cronies thought she was just going to lie down and die because of a minor inconvenience like a few rocks on the road, they could think again. She set her jaw and quickened her pace.

She was almost at the footbridge when she caught sight of other people, teenage people, people who should be in school. Instead, they were hanging out here in the park, smoking cigarettes. Samantha frowned in disgust. She'd never tried smoking, never had any desire to. It was an expensive habit that made your clothes smell and shortened your life, so she couldn't understand why anyone would want to suck on the nasty things. But people did all the time. And that was their business, she told herself.

But then she got a couple of steps closer and recognized one of the kids. The girl with the short hair dyed jet-black tipped with red and wearing jeans and a ratty jacket was Cass's fourteen-year-old daughter, Amber. Cass had been worried about her. It looked like Cass had been right to worry.

Samantha hesitated. What to do? Did she pretend she didn't see? Did she say something? Oh, for heaven's sake, did she even need to ask? She marched over to where Amber and another girl stood with two pimply faced gangly boys.

One of the boys had just given Amber a cigarette and she had it halfway to her mouth when she saw Samantha. Her eyes got saucer-big at the sight of her mother's friend and the cigarette instantly went behind her back.

"No point hiding it," Samantha said. "I saw."

The taller of the two boys eyed her with hostility. "Who are you?"

"I'm someone who doesn't have to be in school," Samantha said, whipping her cell phone out of her pocket. "And you have one minute to turn your tail around and get back there before I call and tell your principal you're all cutting class."

The boy raised his chin. "You don't know us."

"Nope, but I know her and I bet it won't be hard for your teachers to figure out who's missing."

The boy hunched inside his coat and stalked off, flipping the old one-finger salute at Samantha as he left. She flipped him right back. The other boy and girl followed, keeping their fingers to themselves, settling instead for shooting her dirty looks as they went. She almost laughed. Like that sample of sullenness was supposed to bother her? She was doing battle with a rockslide and chocolate vultures. A little teenage anger was nothing more than comic relief.

Amber lingered. "Are you going to tell my mom?" she asked in a small voice.

"Should I?"

Amber shook her head vigorously, making the little hoops in her row of earrings rattle.

"You're smoking."

"I was just going to try it."

"And fill your lungs full of tar and nicotine and end

up getting hooked and wrecking your health. And your looks. Amber, have you ever noticed how many wrinkles women who smoke have? All around their mouths. It's really ugly."

Amber shrugged like she didn't care.

Samantha tried another approach. "You know how much your mom loves you? Can you imagine how unhappy you'd make her if you took up a habit that can wreck your health? And where would you get the money to pay for those cigarettes? They're not cheap. Oh, of course," she said, snapping her fingers. "Those terrific friends of yours would help you get the money, probably by shoplifting. It's hard to shoplift in Icicle Falls, though. Everybody knows everybody. You'd get caught for sure. They send you to jail for that."

Amber bit her lip. She looked like she was going to cry. "Please, Sam, don't tell Mom."

Maybe she'd scared the girl enough, at least for now. But for good measure she decided to add some positive reinforcement. "If you want an addiction, try chocolate. It won't make your clothes stink and it's got endorphins to help you feel good. Come by the shop after school and I'll have a box waiting for you."

Amber's face lit up. "Really?"

"Really. And if you bring up your grades by next report card, I'll give you a two-pound box."

Now Amber was practically jumping up and down. "Oh, wow, thanks. And you won't tell my mom?"

"I didn't say that."

"I promise I won't even touch a cigarette."

"If you do your mom will find out. She'll smell it on you."

"So please don't tell her," Amber begged.

"I'll think about it," Samantha hedged. "Just like I

hope you'll think about the kind of people you want to hang out with. You're old enough to know the difference between a winner and a loser. Which one do you want to see when you look in the mirror?"

Amber dropped her gaze and mumbled, "A winner."

"A lot of us think you're a pretty cool kid," Samantha said. "I hope we're not wrong."

Amber nodded. Then, figuring the lecture was over, she turned and fled toward town and, hopefully, school.

If ever there was a walking ad for birth control, it was a teenager. Yes, Samantha had a business to save but she'd take that over raising a teenager any day.

Oh, but she had her mother, which was almost as bad. And dealing with Mom would have to be the next order of business after she finished with the festival committee.

She found them huddled around the oak table in the private room at D'Vine Wines. The cheery Italian mural on the wall behind them, the cheese and crackers, the open bottle of wine and the glasses—it could have been a party except for the long faces.

"What are we going to do?" Olivia moaned.

"We're going to continue with our plans," Samantha said. "The Department of Transportation will have that mess cleared away in plenty of time for the festival."

"Have you seen it?" Ed asked.

"Well, no."

"It's huge," he said.

Just like the headache she was fighting. "It'll be okay," she insisted.

Annemarie shook her head and pointed to the ugly headline in the newspaper. Rockslide Danger on Highway 2: Governor Urges Travelers to Stay Home. The reporter might as well have added Governor Kills Chocolate Festival. "I've had six cancellations in the past hour," she said.

"This is it for our festival," Cecily said, pushing away her glass untouched. "So what's the plan now?" she asked Samantha.

Everyone was looking at her expectantly. "Okay, here's what we do." *We panic!* That was hardly a productive option. "We keep moving forward," she said again. "Cecily, call D.O.T. and see if you can find out when they think this will be cleared. Then we'll take out another ad in the Seattle paper, full page." She looked apologetically at Ed. "I'll figure out a way to pay for it, Ed." *Right. How? With chocolate?*

"Good idea," Annemarie approved.

"And, Cecily, try to get hold of the producer for *Northwest Now* again. We've got a great story angle. Town versus rockslide. Or something like that."

Cecily nodded, making notes in her tablet.

"Anything else?" Olivia asked. "Surely there's something else we can do."

"Yeah," Samantha said. "We pray like crazy.

Eighteen

When a woman is in trouble, that's when she
learns who her true friends are.
　　　　　—Muriel Sterling, *Knowing Who You Are:*
　　　　　　　　　　　　　　　One Woman's Journey

Motherhood was the world's hardest job and being a
mother to grown daughters was right up there with trying to turn straw into gold. Now, once again, it would
appear that Muriel had made a poor choice.

"Mom, you can't tell people we're in trouble," Samantha scolded over the phone. "Perception is everything."

"I'm sorry," Muriel said. "I just thought I could get a
few people who might have some money to help us out."

It had seemed like a good idea at the time. Her first
and only call had been to Del and she'd realized almost
immediately that it hadn't been a good idea. He'd offered to help her come up with a solution, which seemed
encouraging. But then she'd heard his bigmouthed sister talking in the background and knew Darla was over
there and decided she'd better pull back from this plan
until she'd considered all the possible ramifications. Of
course, she'd pulled back too late. She'd known even before she hung up that Del would spill the cocoa beans.
Darla knew all her brother's business and, sure enough,
now she knew the Sterlings' business and Samantha
was not happy.

"Mom, please, don't try to help. I can't afford to have

people like Darla coming in and panicking our employees all over again. And we don't need the whole town thinking we're going under when we're trying to boost business."

"I understand," Muriel said. She was close to tears and it was hard to keep her voice steady.

Samantha softened her tone. "Look, I appreciate your efforts, I really do, especially after everything you've been through. But if you can just stick to the creative end of things I'll keep working on the money angle. Okay?"

"Okay," Muriel said. "And I'm sorry this created more problems for you, especially with the rockslide to deal with." She wasn't so ignorant that she didn't understand what this fresh trouble could do to her daughter's festival and, consequently, their business. And here she was, adding to the problem rather than helping. So much for motherly good intentions.

"Don't worry. We'll find a way around it," Samantha said, and her tone of voice dared fate to go ahead and keep messing with her.

Her eldest was nothing if not efficient, but the deck was certainly stacked against her.

They said their I-love-yous and goodbyes and Muriel sat staring out the living room window at the mountains, hemmed in by gray skies, contemplating the disaster that currently passed for her life. Most parents, if they lived long enough, became something of a burden to their children but she was too young to be this big a burden.

So, she asked herself, *what are you going to do about it?*

She was going to quit being so ignorant. She called Mountain Escape Books.

"Isn't this rockslide business awful?" Pat greeted her. "It's certainly not helping our festival."

Or our company, thought Muriel.

"But you probably didn't call to talk about that."

She certainly hadn't. If she started talking about the rockslide and the festival, that could lead to other topics that were verboten. "I need a good money book. Or two. Have you got some kind of *Money Management for Dummies* book I can buy?"

"Personal finance? Or business?"

"Personal." After her faux pas she'd be lucky if her daughter ever let her cross the threshold of Sweet Dreams.

"I'll see what I can find," Pat promised. "Do you want me to bring it to dinner tomorrow?"

"No, I'll come by this afternoon," Muriel said. The way her life was going she couldn't afford to wait even another day.

Samantha had just finished talking another worried B and B owner down from the ledge when Elena buzzed her on the intercom. "You've got a visitor—Amber Wilkes."

Samantha had set aside a box of candy for Amber but hadn't been sure Amber would take her up on her offer, since it meant coming by the shop and possibly having to face her again. *Never underestimate the power of chocolate,* she thought.

"Send her in." Hopefully, Amber was just stopping by to thank her and not to draw her into any teenage drama. She already had enough drama in her life.

A moment later the door to her office opened and Amber entered, clutching a box of Sweet Dreams salted caramels to her chest and looking back over her shoulder as if expecting…what? Her mother? The chocolate police coming to see if she'd paid for that candy?

"I, um, wanted to thank you for this," she said.

That wasn't all she wanted. With her uneasiness and sudden shyness, Amber was the picture of a teenage girl with something sitting uncomfortably on her mind.

But Samantha didn't ask what. Instead, she simply said, "You're welcome."

Amber gnawed on her lower lip. Yep, here it came. "Um, what did you decide about telling my mom? You're not going to, are you?"

Would Cass thank her for keeping this from her? Probably not. But Samantha couldn't help remembering an incident from her own middle-school years.

Straight arrow that she was, she'd still made one bad slip, given in to peer pressure and snitched a pair of earrings from Gilded Lily's. She'd been a lousy thief and Lily Swan had caught her and called her mother. It had been mortifying enough to be caught by the glamorous former model who had recently moved to town and opened her shop, but then to see the look of disappointment on Mom's face—that had been the worst moment of her young life. Mom had made sure she paid her debt to society, farming her out for a summer of afternoon weeding in Ms. Swan's flower beds. That hadn't been fun, but it had sure beat having to live with the humiliation of Mom telling Dad.

"Please don't tell Dad," Samantha had begged, horrified at the idea of her adored father, who'd called her Princess, changing her nickname to Scumbag or Sticky Fingers. The idea of sinking so low in his estimation had been more than she could bear and Mom had sensed it.

"If you're never going to do it again, I won't tell him," Mom had said.

Now she said the same thing to Amber. The girl was

already on her mother's doo-doo list. Did Samantha need to give Cass another reason to be unhappy with the kid?

Relief flooded Amber's face, washing the worry lines from her brow. "Thank you," she breathed.

"But you'd better keep your end of the bargain," Samantha said sternly, "or I'll rat you out in a heartbeat."

"Don't worry, I will. You rock," she gushed, then turned and practically danced out of the office.

Rock...rockslide. Ugh. Samantha decided it was time to go home and have a pity party.

Her condo was a nice place for a party, with walls painted a warm brown, photographs of lupines and lady's slippers Samantha had taken on her mountain hikes, framed and hung over the electric fireplace.

And the welcome committee was ready and waiting. Nibs was always glad to see someone who could master the mysteries of the cat-food can.

"You're lucky," she told him as she scooped food into his bowl. "You have someone to take care of you. No worries, no stress." What would that be like?

If she gave up the fight, she'd have no worries and no stress, either.

Except her mother would end up a bag lady and she'd go down in the family history books as the one who lost the company—generations of work and enthusiasm and creativity gone. *Poof.*

"How could this happen to a nice girl like me?"

Nibs didn't answer. He was too busy eating.

She turned off her cell phone and threw it in her junk drawer. Then she went to bed and lay there, staring at the ceiling. Bad idea. Her mind was whirling so fast she nearly gave herself bed spin. She got up and left the bedroom.

What to do, what to do? She paced the condo but no answer came.

She finally grabbed the chocolate seconds she'd brought home and parked on the living room couch in front of the TV and turned on the news like a good little masochist.

"A hard blow for the town of Icicle Falls this week," Erin Knowle, newscast chick, was saying. "With a rockslide across Highway 2 and the governor warning people to avoid the pass, their chocolate festival is in danger of being canceled. This, coming on top of the weather, is a double blow for the small town that caters to winter sports enthusiasts. Highway 2 is currently closed, so if you need to go over the pass, use an alternate route."

"Oh, by all means," Samantha shouted at the woman, throwing a chocolate at the TV.

Erin's partner in misery put in his two bits. "We've had unusually warm weather and light rainfall here in the Pacific Northwest this year, haven't we, Erin?"

"Yes," said Erin, all prim and perfect in her power suit and her perfect world where bad news only happened to other people, "and that's translated into very little snow in the mountains. And now these unusually warm temperatures have spelled disaster for ski areas like Snoqualmie Falls and Crystal Mountain and, of course, Icicle Falls, whose economy depends on good winter weather."

Samantha hurled another chunk of chocolate at the TV.

You're being childish, she told herself. And wasting chocolate. She walked over to where the candies had landed, picked them up and put both pieces in her mouth. Then, mature adult that she was, she sat on the floor and wailed.

She was just hitting her stride when someone knocked on her door. Oh, no. Who had heard her? She choked back a sob and sat perfectly still, hoping whoever it was would go away.

A muffled voice called, "Are you okay in there?"

Lila Ward. She was coming to pour salt on the wound. The drapes were closed but Samantha felt foolish and pathetic for having been caught sitting here on her living room floor crying. She held her breath and willed the woman to give up and go away.

But, like Samantha's problems, Lila stuck around. Another knock. "Samantha?"

"Shit," Samantha muttered. She took a swipe at her cheeks and went to answer the door.

She opened it to find Lila standing there holding a box of tissue. "I heard you and thought you could use this."

The unexpected kindness started the tears rising to flood level again and Samantha's throat constricted. All she could do was take the box and nod.

Lila cleared her throat. "Well, I'll be going. If you need anything I'm downstairs."

She needed the pass cleared. She needed the governor to shut up. She needed a ton of free publicity. And she needed people to come to the festival and spend a fortune. But she hugged that box of tissues as if it were a gift from heaven.

She managed to choke out a thank-you. Then after Lila left she shut her door, returned to the couch and made use of the tissues.

By the time Cecily knocked on her door, she had a mountain of used tissues on the coffee table and a headache. But she was dry-eyed and resigned to her fate. Was this how people felt just before they drowned? Did some voice inside them whisper, *Give up and die?*

"Are you all right?" Cecily asked, taking in the mess on the coffee table.

Samantha heaved a sigh. "I will be." At some point in her life, maybe ten years from now. Or twenty.

She went back to the couch. Her sister followed her and snagged a chocolate. "I'm sorry you had to get hit with all this."

That made two of them. If she'd just had a little more time, if she could've made a go of the festival. If, if, if. "I give up." *I'm sorry, Great-grandma. I really am.*

"Don't give up, Sam." Cecily held a piece of chocolate to Samantha's mouth. "Open."

Samantha obliged and her sister popped the candy in. It soured in her mouth and she spat it into a tissue. She couldn't eat this stuff anymore. "It's not just us. The whole town was counting on this. The B and Bs have lost bookings right and left."

"I'm sure they'll be able to hang on till summer when the hikers and river rafters come," Cecily said.

"That's longer than we can hang on." Suddenly drowning in a vat of chocolate looked pretty darned good. Samantha fell back against the couch cushions. "What's going to happen to Mom?"

"She'll be fine. She just got a royalty check."

Mom wasn't exactly a household name. It couldn't have been for much. "How much?" Samantha asked.

Cecily shrugged. "I didn't see it, but she says it should tide her over for a month."

Samantha shook her head. "How would she even know? She has no idea what's going on with her finances." She never had. Their mother's brain was not wired for math.

"Yeah," Cecily agreed. "But she should be able to figure out how to make a house payment and pay the power bill."

"I hope so." Samantha rubbed her aching head. Mom was going down the financial tubes. And without Sweet Dreams, so were all their employees. "If I lose the company—"

"You'll go on to start another," Cecily said. "That's what successful people do. They encounter a roadblock and they find another route. But let's not worry about that yet. I came to tell you some great news. D.O.T. should have the road open by Thursday." Her cell phone rang. "Bailey," she announced before answering. Then, "Yes, we're here. Yes, she's fine. Well, sort of." A moment later Cecily held out the phone to Samantha. "She wants to talk to you."

How many family members does it take to pull a girl back from the brink of despair? Samantha took the phone.

"I've been so worried about you," Bailey said. "You weren't answering your cell."

"I turned it off." The last thing she'd wanted was to talk to anyone in her time of misery. Or so she'd thought. But having her sisters here was like wrapping herself in a down comforter on a cold evening. It didn't make the night any less cold but you *felt* warmer.

"I heard about the slide and I figured you might be upset," Bailey said.

Now there was an understatement.

"Don't worry, Sammy. Everything will work out. D.O.T. will get it cleaned up."

Samantha sighed. "Thanks to the governor and the media, people will be too scared to drive the pass."

"Not if they hear that everything's been cleaned up.

We just have to get the word out," Bailey said as if that was the simplest thing in the world.

"Bailey," Samantha began.

"I know you can fix this."

"I'm not God," Samantha said irritably.

"You sure acted like it when we were growing up," Bailey retorted. "Remember how we got lost in the woods that time we went camping with Daddy and Grandpa? You found the way back."

"We weren't that far from camp."

"We aren't that far now," Bailey said.

If only she was right…

When Cecily left, Samantha still had no solution to her problems and no guarantee that things were going to turn out well, but she'd recovered her fighting spirit. She got on her computer and began to spread the news via Facebook and Twitter. "Highway 2 rockslide will be cleaned up." There had to be something to this power of positive thinking stuff. "The Icicle Falls chocolate festival is still a go. The rocks won't get you but the chocolate will. Come eat chocolate and go to heaven."

Okay. There. She didn't know if she'd accomplished much with that flurry of activity but she sure felt better.

"I think it's going to take a while to master everything in that book you chose for me," Muriel confessed to Pat as the LAMs gathered for dinner at Zelda's. "I'm afraid managing money is all a terrifying mystery to me." She almost added, *I wish Waldo was still alive.* But Waldo hadn't been much smarter about money than she was.

"You'll get the hang of it," Olivia assured her. "Oh, look, they've added huckleberry cheesecake to the dessert menu."

"You told me you were dieting," Dot said.

"I am. I'm cutting back," Olivia said. "But not on our dinner nights. It's my one night out."

Dot shook her head. "Pathetic."

"Well, at least I don't smoke," Olivia shot back.

"Okay, okay. Point taken," Dot conceded.

"Anyway, I need cheesecake for comfort," Olivia said. "I had two more cancellations today, even though I told them the highway would be clear by next week."

"People are spooked. The media did a pretty good job of scaring them," Dot said in disgust.

Her daughter was right, Muriel thought miserably. Perception was everything.

"We can't control the media or the mountain," Pat told them. "All we can do now is hope. So let's talk about some things we *can* control." She turned to Muriel. "Besides being financially challenged, how are you doing?"

Her daughter was ready to throw her off a mountaintop, she still cried herself to sleep at night and she was probably going to lose her house. "I've been better," she confessed.

"You'll come around," Pat said.

"Don't worry. We'll get you through," added Dot.

She sincerely hoped so, because she wasn't doing such a good job of getting herself through.

The following night Del stopped by, offering to take her to dinner and help her find a solution to her financial problems.

"Thank you, Del, but I think I'm going to just try and deal with this on my own," she told him. That way there'd be no chance of betraying business secrets.

"Nonsense," he said heartily. "Everyone needs a shoulder to cry on once in a while. I've got a nice quiet corner table reserved over at Schwangau."

"Well…" She hesitated.

"Come on," he urged. "You've got to eat, right?"

Yes, but not with Del. Between making passes at her and leaking information to his sister he'd hardly proved himself trustworthy.

"I think the two of us can get your finances all sorted out," he said.

Getting *anything* sorted out would be a blessing, and it was only dinner. She'd make sure they didn't talk about the business, but maybe he could advise her on what to do with the house. "All right," she decided. This time she'd sit across from him. That should keep her legs out of range.

They'd barely placed their orders before she knew she'd made a mistake. Over his martini Del proceeded to pump her about the business and predict that the chocolate festival would be a flop. "Not enough time. Very poor planning. And now, with the rockslide…"

"The Department of Transportation will have that cleaned up before the week is over," she protested.

"Too late. The damage is done. People won't come. But even if they did, it wouldn't be enough to save your company. I'm sorry to have to be the one to tell you that, Muriel, but it's true."

"My daughter is saving the company," she said huffily. Too bad she hadn't told herself that before starting her desperate phone campaign.

"And that's why you called me asking for a loan?" he scoffed.

"I called asking for a loan because I need to make my house payments." That wasn't a lie, not really. She'd be okay this month, thanks to the small check she'd received, but after that she was in big trouble.

Now he looked shocked. "Waldo had life insurance, didn't he?"

The horror of her situation brought tears to her eyes. She bit her lip.

"Oh, no. Well, he had investments, right?"

Once upon a time. He'd also had some sort of pension, but she'd discovered that the pension stopped when Waldo's heart did. She shook her head.

"Muriel, this is terrible." Del reached across the table and took her hand. "But don't worry, we'll figure something out."

"I just need to get over this rough patch," she said, extricating it. If he could lend her a couple thousand she'd be fine. She could give most of it to Samantha.

"Of course you do," he said comfortingly. "I understand. A woman has…needs."

Needs? Oh, no. Not those kinds of needs. "Del, you've misunderstood—"

He patted her arm. "You don't have to be ashamed, Muriel. You're only human."

And Del Stone was subhuman, and proof that charm and character didn't always go hand in hand.

"After dinner, let's go back to my place. I've got a Chablis I know you'll love."

Pass number one, she could excuse. He'd been drunk. Pass number two, there was no excuse. "Del Stone, my husband has been gone less than a month. What are you thinking?" Silly question. It was obvious.

"Nothing," he insisted. "I just thought you needed comforting."

"I don't," she snapped. "I need money. And now I need to go home." She started scooting out of the booth.

"But we just ordered."

"I'm sure you can eat your meal and mine."

"Muriel, don't leave," he pleaded.

"I'm afraid I'm not hungry anymore," she said, and left.

She marched from the restaurant and down the street. Of all the nerve! What was it about widows that made men think they could just waltz in and take advantage like that?

It took half a block for her to acknowledge that she herself was part of the problem. She'd been the one to call Del, hoping she could persuade him to help bail her out. What was he supposed to think except that she was a lost, lonely widow?

She was. Her heart hurt. And now so did her feet, thanks to these ridiculous heels that pinched her toes. Still, there were no taxis in a town the size of Icicle Falls. She would be limping home.

She was halfway there when a car cruised up beside her. She turned to inform Del that she wasn't getting into his car, only to discover that the car wasn't Del's. It was a conservative black Lexus and Arnie, her old friend from the bank, sat behind the wheel, looking at her with concern.

He rolled down the window and called, "Do you need a lift?"

She nodded and gratefully got in.

"I was just on my way home from the grocery store when I saw you," he explained.

"Well, thank you for stopping," she said. "You saved my life. My feet are killing me."

Arnie wasn't the handsomest man on the planet. He was thin and his hair was doing a disappearing act. But he had a beautiful heart and he knew shoes. "Those are nice," he observed, "but not exactly walking shoes."

"I hadn't intended to walk," she said. She removed

one of the offending heels and rubbed her aching toes. "I left a dinner engagement early."

Arnie didn't ask questions. He merely nodded as if that was the most normal behavior in the world. "How are you doing these days, Muriel? I haven't seen you since the memorial."

Samantha had told her not to talk about the business but surely that didn't include Arnie. He knew about their loan. But did he know they were behind? Maybe not. Maybe she shouldn't say anything. "I'm managing," she lied. She didn't have to tell him that she was managing to ruin everything she touched.

He looked over at her and frowned. "All right. Now, tell me how you're really doing."

A tear slid down her cheek. "Awful. Waldo didn't keep up the payments on his life insurance, I'm upside down on the house…" She stopped herself there. What she'd already shared was depressing enough.

"Oh, Muriel," he said sadly.

She sounded pathetic. How humiliating! "I'll work things out."

"I have a little money set aside."

Oh, no. She wasn't going down that road again.

"I couldn't ask it of you, but thank you for being such a good friend."

He wanted to be more. He'd wanted to be more well before Waldo came along. She supposed if she'd married Arnie she would never have had to worry about money. He was gainfully employed, now working as a claims adjustor for an insurance company in Wenatchee, and he could balance a checkbook. Still, that was no guarantee of stability. A man could lose his health and his mental faculties, leaving both his wife and his checkbook vulnerable. There really was only one person a woman could depend on—herself. It was time she learned that lesson.

"Isn't that what friends are for, to help?" he countered.

"I appreciate the offer, but I think I'm going to have to figure out how to fix my problems without borrowing from anyone. I could use some advice, though."

"I'll be happy to do that," he said. "And if you do find yourself in a pinch, don't hesitate to call."

She was already in a pinch.

That will change, she told herself. Life was always changing, sometimes for the better, sometimes for the worse. As bad as things were now, they had no way to go but up.

Samantha and Cass sat at Bavarian Brews, fortifying themselves with caffeine. "I swear I'm going to end up in a straitjacket if my daughter has anything to do with it," Cass said.

Oh, no. Had Amber already broken her promise to reform? Samantha suddenly felt like an accomplice to a crime. Maybe she should have told Cass. If she were a mother, would she want a friend keeping this kind of information from her?

"What's she done?" Samantha asked cautiously.

"Cut class," Cass said in disgust.

"I can think of worse things," Samantha said. Smoking. Shoplifting. Failing to tell a friend you'd caught her kid sampling coffin nails.

"I know." Cass nodded. "I cut a couple of classes in my day. It's the kids she was with. I don't like who she's hanging out with these days."

Samantha didn't, either.

"God knows what she'll do next. By the way, she

came home with a box of your chocolates. She says you gave them to her."

"I did," Samantha said, and hoped Cass wouldn't ask why.

"Why? What was that about?"

"Call it a bribe."

Cass took a sip of her mocha. "A bribe, huh?"

"Well, you were worried about her grades, weren't you? Chocolate can be a powerful motivator."

"There's more to this than you're telling me, isn't there?" Cass was studying her as if looking for the hole in her story, and that made her squirm.

"A little," she admitted, "and I guess I should have asked you before I gave her that chocolate."

"No. I trust your judgment."

That should have been a comfort but it only added to the weight of responsibility on Samantha's shoulders. She should have ratted out Amber. She still could.

But then she remembered the look of relief on the girl's face when she promised to give her a break. Everyone deserved a second chance, especially erring daughters who wanted to shine in their mothers' eyes.

"We all need a mentor, I guess," Cass said, "and sometimes a second mom. And I've got to admit I've been so crazy with the business, I haven't given her as much attention as I should." She shook her head. "Ever since she spent Christmas with her dad she's been a handful." Cass set aside her half-finished mocha and frowned. "Sometimes I want to run away from my life."

Samantha could more than identify with that. "Living isn't for sissies."

Cass grinned. "Thank God for friends, that's all I can say. And thanks for being a friend to my daughter."

"Any daughter of yours is a friend of mine," Samantha quipped.

But a certain fourteen-year-old had better watch her step. Samantha had enough stress in her life. She wasn't about to let Amber add to it.

Be glad you didn't have children, she told herself. Imagine having kid problems on top of her business woes. She'd have gone completely insane.

Or maybe not if she had a husband to help stave off the insanity, a big man with broad football shoulders to cry on.

Where had *that* come from? Once again she had to boot the image of Blake Preston out of her mind. *Get out and stay out!*

He left but she could hear him saying in an Arnold Schwarzenegger accent, "I'll be back."

The permits finally surfaced from the sea of red tape at city hall. It was a sign, Samantha told herself. The permits were in place and the rockslide would be history. Now they just needed visitors.

If you have it they will come. At least she hoped so. "Let's push forward aggressively," she told her festival committee. "We need to get every service club and church signed up for a booth, as well as the restaurants. That will bring out our people and the ones from nearby towns. Who has a list of all our local artists and crafters?"

"We've got one on file over at the Chamber office," Ed replied.

"Great," Samantha said. "I think, instead of emailing, we should make phone calls. It will be more personal that way and easier to get a commitment."

"Oh, my," Olivia said weakly. "I'm already busy with

the tea, although if this mess doesn't get cleaned up I don't know who'll come."

"I'm not good at that sort of thing," Annemarie Huber said.

Ed shrugged. "Sorry, Samantha. The virus I had really took it out of me. I can email you the list of contacts but that's about all I've got the energy for."

After doing whatever he'd done to nudge the permits along, Ed was off the hook. Still, some of the others could pitch in. She looked hopefully at Heinrich.

He shook his head. "We have several arrangements to do for Frank Reinhold's funeral and I have two birthdays. And I'm busy planning decorations for the ball. I won't have time to make so many calls."

Where was everyone's team spirit? Well, never mind. She'd rather make all the calls herself. That way she'd be sure they got done. "Fine, I'll do it," she said.

"I'll help," Cecily told her.

What would she have done without her sister? She smiled gratefully at Cecily, then asked briskly, "Okay, what else do we need to cover?"

"Publicity," Cecily said. "I've sent out press releases to the papers both on this side of the mountains and in Seattle saying that the slide will be cleared in plenty of time, and I've called and left messages for the producer of *Northwest Now*. But I haven't heard back."

"We need to take out more ads," Samantha said.

"Are we sure the highway will be cleared this week?" Annemarie fretted.

"It will," Samantha assured her. That road would be cleared even if she had to get out there with a borrowed truck and haul away boulders with her bare hands.

"How much can I spend?" Cecily asked. "I checked

and it's not going to be cheap to run an ad in a Sunday paper in Seattle."

"My goodness, that's steep compared to our Icicle Falls paper," Olivia said after Cecily quoted prices.

"But think how many people will see it," Samantha countered. "We have to spend something. Much as we all love free publicity—" except when it involved embarrassing situations "—papers are more interested in printing bad news than good. If it bleeds it leads."

"We can't afford a fortune in advertising," Annemarie cautioned. "Not after all the money we've already spent."

But if they didn't get the word out, they wouldn't have any visitors. All this would wind up being for nothing. "One ad? Can we do one ad?" Samantha pushed.

Ed turned to Cecily. "Get me all the information. We'll see what we can do. And meanwhile, keep trying to get hold of that TV producer. Now, *there* would be some great publicity."

As long as no one told Bill Will that TV people were in town they'd be fine.

The meeting broke up and Samantha reminded Ed to send her the list of artists.

"Will do," he said. "Then I'm going to go home and crash with a good book."

No surprise there. He was Pat's best customer. "I hope you feel better soon," she said. "And I don't know what you did to get those permits through, but thanks."

He shook his head. "I'd love to take credit but I didn't do a damned thing. I went home and hit the sack."

"Oh. Well."

Ed smiled. "The wheels of progress move slowly in our city hall sometimes, but they do move."

Still, getting those permits had begun to feel like the impossible dream. So what had happened?

Who cared? They'd finally sailed across the sea of red tape and that was all that mattered. She was just grateful to whatever good fairy had helped with the crossing.

Now, if they could get people to come…

Nineteen

Every successful person encounters roadblocks, but when your family is with you, you can always find an alternate road to success.
—Muriel Sterling, *When Family Matters*

The Department of Transportation had the rockslide cleaned up by Thursday but the damage had been done. Most of the people who had booked rooms at the town's B and Bs had canceled, and no one was calling in with fresh reservations.

"Our poor town," Olivia lamented to Blake when she came in to draw money out of her savings. "First no snowpack and now this. You know, I was booked solid until this happened. Now I'm down to one couple. And Annemarie is in the same boat. So are Gerhardt and Ingrid over at Gerhardt's Gasthaus. Samantha is trying to let people know we're still having the festival, and her sister made I don't know how many calls to newspapers and even that Northwest TV show, but she hasn't had any success. And at this late date who will come?"

With the festival less than two weeks away, it didn't look promising for the Sterlings or the town. Restaurants, B and Bs, stores—everyone was paying the price for this travel scare. But the ones Blake was most concerned about were the Sterlings. One Sterling in particular.

Samantha Sterling couldn't seem to catch a break.

Could he catch one for her? He didn't know if he could succeed where she and her sister had failed but he was willing to try. Heck, he owed it to them and his other bank customers to enter the publicity fray.

The next morning he was up and out the door by 4:00 a.m., headed for Seattle. Sometimes phone calls weren't enough. Sometimes it took a little face time to make things happen.

"Have you seen the Seattle paper, *chica?*" Elena greeted Samantha when she came to the office on Friday.

Samantha didn't care if she ever saw another newspaper again. But Elena was smiling, so it couldn't be bad news.

"Look," she said, holding it out. "It's on page two but that's okay."

Samantha took the paper. The words in big print above the article made her eyes pop. D.O.T. Clears Up Pass in Time for Town's Festival. "Oh, my gosh," she gasped. Free publicity—it was a miracle!

It appears chocolate-lovers will be able to get over the pass to enjoy the chocolate festival scheduled to take place in Icicle Falls the weekend before Valentine's Day, after all, thanks to the Department of Transportation crews working overtime. A major rockslide recently made it a challenge for travelers going over the pass via Highway 2, but D.O.T officials say the pass is once more clear for travel. "We're open for business," says Ed York, Icicle Falls resident and owner of D'Vine Wines. Ed's business is one of many participating in the upcoming festival.

"Not bad, eh?" Elena said again.

Ed must have contacted the paper. Go, Ed!

Samantha's lips tugged upward. What was that unusual movement? Oh, yes, a smile, the first one she'd managed in days, and it felt fabulous.

She went into her office and started emailing. The clock was ticking and she had a festival to promote. Thank God.

She was in the middle of putting a tweet on Twitter when Elena buzzed her. "The producer of *Northwest Now* is on line two and wants to know if you'll do an interview about the company and how you got the idea for the festival."

Would she!

On Monday it was lights, camera, action as the film crew from *Northwest Now* hit town. Samantha had asked Mom and Cecily to join her, partly for family solidarity, partly as an olive branch to Mom. She'd been pretty hard on her mother the past month, and considering how sweet Mom had been it grated on her conscience. This seemed like one way Samantha could make that up to her.

So now here they sat in the gift shop on soda fountain chairs borrowed from Cass's bakery with piles of chocolate boxes for a backdrop, lights and cables everywhere, about to talk to Kiki Long, host of *Northwest Now*. Kiki looked impressive in her red suit but she couldn't hold a candle to Cecily, who was pretty in a pink cashmere sweater and dress jeans, or Mom, who was wearing a pencil skirt and cream-colored silk blouse accented with gold jewelry. Samantha had opted for her favorite embroidered green jacket over a white blouse and jeans—Icicle Falls business casual. She still could hardly believe that their luck had turned and this was happening.

Now, if she just didn't blow the interview. She'd never been on TV and her deodorant was working overtime.

"Don't look at the camera," Janice, the producer, instructed them. "Just make eye contact with Kiki."

Samantha nodded and swallowed in an effort to hydrate her dry throat.

"And smile," Janice added, giving her arm a pat. "This is supposed to be fun."

Yes, fun. Relax. She glanced over at her mother. Mom was as serene as the *Mona Lisa*. Of course, she'd done this sort of thing before. She'd had a radio interview with a Seattle station when her last book came out.

She smiled encouragingly at Samantha and Cecily and said, "Think how proud your Great-grandma Rose would have been."

That made Samantha smile. *Yes, Great-grandma, we're still hanging in there fighting.*

The camera started rolling and Kiki kicked off the interview by sampling a lemon-white-chocolate truffle. Her reaction was worth a fortune in advertising dollars. Her eyes widened and she actually groaned. "Oh, my God, this is amazing," she said, fanning herself in typical dramatic Kiki fashion.

"That's actually my mother's recipe," Samantha said. Before she channeled her creativity into writing, Mom had contributed a recipe or two. Unlike her eldest daughter, who was obviously recipe-challenged.

"So tell me about your company," Kiki began. "Is it true that your great-grandmother, who started it, literally dreamed your first recipes?"

And with that they were off. Mom was charming, Cecily was beautiful and Samantha couldn't stop smiling. What woman, seeing their cute pink boxes and bonbons wrapped in gold foil and secured to little satin pillows with magenta bows, wouldn't want to visit the gift shop or go online and order Sweet Dreams Chocolates? They talked about the company, about Icicle Falls and, of course, the festival.

"What made you decide to host a chocolate festival?" Kiki asked.

Desperation. "Well, who doesn't like chocolate?" Samantha quipped.

"Not only do we make the world's best chocolate here in Icicle Falls, but we also have beautiful scenery, great shops and restaurants, and wonderful people," Cecily added.

There was the perfect sound bite, thought Samantha. Why hadn't she come up with that? Her sister had a real gift for marketing.

"I agree with you," Kiki said. "And your candy is incredible. So, Samantha, you're the head of the company, right?"

"Yes, she is," Mom said.

Deep inside Samantha, something tight and hard that she'd been carrying around for a long time broke and shattered.

"Have *you* dreamed up any new recipes for Sweet Dreams?" Kiki asked Samantha.

What? Of all the questions in all the world, the woman had to go and ask that one? Panic seized Samantha by the vocal cords and she sat frozen in her seat.

Mom stepped in. "Every company needs both dreamers and doers. Samantha is a doer. Thanks to her, our company is going to be around for many years."

Samantha couldn't have been more overwhelmed if the president of the United States had pinned a medal on her. Tears sprang to her eyes and she found herself squeezing her mother's hand.

"Let's hope so," Kiki said. "And all you chocolate-lovers and sweethearts looking for a great getaway this weekend before Valentine's Day, Icicle Falls is the place to be."

And that was it, the end of the segment.

"Perfect," Janice said.

It was time to shake hands, thank everyone and make sure they got complimentary chocolate. The crew packed up their gear and Cecily escorted Kiki and Janice over to Schwangau for lunch, which would be on Sweet Dreams, of course.

Samantha caught her mother's arm. "Mom, thanks. For what you said."

"Oh, sweetie," her mother said, "I should be thanking you."

"For what? Being so angry?"

Mom sighed. "Sweetheart, I don't blame you. I know I mishandled things with Waldo." She hesitated and bit her lip.

"Mom, what is it?" Samantha pressed, now anxious to fully clear the air between them.

Her mother sighed. "About Waldo."

Samantha could feel herself stiffen, bracing for a lecture. *You should have been nicer to him. He loved you.*

Go ahead and say it, she thought. *I deserve it.*

"He wasn't well."

Of course he wasn't well. He died. "What does that mean exactly?"

"He had something called Lewy body disease."

Ice-cold shock smacked Samantha in the face. "Lewy… What is that?"

"It's a brain deterioration similar to Alzheimer's," Mom said wearily.

"So some of the strange things he was doing…" Of

course, that explained why his decisions went from incompetent to disastrous. "How long?" How long had they known? Samantha felt sick.

Her mother shrugged. "Several months at least. It started with what we thought was restless legs. He was having trouble sleeping. I got him vitamins. They didn't help. Then he fell on the deck. But it was slippery that day, so we didn't think anything of it."

Samantha remembered that fall. She also remembered hoping it would keep him out of the office and her hair for a few days. *Rotten daughter of the year.*

"He started forgetting things—"

Like the quarterly taxes.

"—and getting confused. But other times he was fine. We kidded ourselves, saying he was having senior moments, but by October I knew we were dealing with something more. We didn't get the final diagnosis until December. The doctor had ordered a brain scan." Mom stopped, pressing her lips together while she got control of her emotions and then continued, "The only way to be completely positive it was Lewy body would've been with an autopsy but I couldn't do that to him. Anyway, the brain scan told us enough."

Their so-called getaway to Seattle right after Thanksgiving hadn't been a getaway at all. They'd been off seeing doctors, enduring a battery of tests, all alone with no emotional support.

Samantha was going to throw up. Or cry. Or both. "Why didn't you tell us?" she croaked.

"We didn't want to spoil everyone's Christmas. And you had your hands full at work with holiday orders."

And fighting with Waldo. Fuming over the penalty Uncle Sam had slapped on them because they'd been late with their quarterly taxes. Creating a scene in his office when she learned he hadn't been able to make the payment on their loan in December. Tattling to Mom.

"Mom, I…" Her throat closed up and she just stood there in the middle of the shop like a big, dumb boulder. All those bizarre purchases he'd made, the paranoia, the increasingly inept decision-making, the financial tangle. Why hadn't she figured out that Waldo's problem was medical?

Because she'd been too busy with the business and with being angry. Now Waldo was up with the angels, practicing his golf putt. When it was her time they'd probably lock the pearly gates and tell her to go look for a hotter climate farther south. Heck, they wouldn't have to tell her. She'd go voluntarily. Why didn't life have a rewind button?

Now she saw something new in her mother's expression that made her feel even worse. Regret. "I should have told you as soon as I suspected," she said to Samantha. "Obviously it was affecting his ability to run the company."

Obviously. Samantha should have felt exonerated to hear her mother say this—she'd known all along he wasn't fit to run the company—but all she felt was sad. Here her mother and stepfather had been grappling with life-and-death issues and she'd been having hissy fits because he bought cases of bottled water. "Mom, I'm so sorry. I wish I'd known."

"And I wish I'd encouraged Waldo to do something else."

That made two of them. Poor Waldo had fancied himself a savvy businessman but he'd been out of his depth from the beginning. Still, she could have worked with him, helped him more. If she'd tried harder could she have averted disaster? She'd never know.

"I want you to know that after we found out what was wrong, he was going to step aside," Mom said. "We talked about it right before he died. You should have been in charge of the company all along. It was your heritage."

There it was, out in the open at last, the source of Samantha's anger. Waldo, who'd been the perfect happy ending for her mother, the perfect stepdad, had slipped in and stolen her birthright and Mom had gone along with it. Samantha had been saddled with anger over that ever since, and no matter how she'd tried to hide it or ignore it, the nasty emotion had ridden her hard. But it was time to buck off the saddle. This was baggage she didn't need to carry anymore.

"Can you forgive me for my poor choices?" Mom asked, tears in her eyes.

So many emotions crowded Samantha's throat, all she could manage was, "Oh, Mom." And as they hugged she could feel the anger sliding off her.

"I'll make it up to you," Mom whispered.

"Mom, there's nothing to make up." Not now. She was the one who had the making up to do, for her bad attitude, her lack of understanding, her resentment of a man she had genuinely cared for once.

Her mother gave her a watery smile and anchored a lock of stray hair behind Samantha's ear. "If anyone can pull us out of this, you can. Remember your favorite story when you were little?"

"The Little Engine That Could." Mom still had the book tucked away somewhere, saving it for future grandchildren.

"You've always had such confidence," Mom said, "and I'm confident it will stand us in good stead now. We have sweet things to deliver and you're the engine that will take us where we need to go. You have the drive and determination to do it."

Samantha hoped so. With the highway open again and all the great free publicity maybe, just maybe, she had a chance.

Twenty

You can, indeed, mix love and business, and wind
up with something wonderful.
—Muriel Sterling, *Mixing Business with Pleasure:
How to Successfully Balance Business and Love*

"Pat, I can't thank you enough for helping me," Muriel said as they worked their way through the piles of paperwork, bills and bank statements on Waldo's desk.

It had all felt so overwhelming, like the money book she'd gotten from Pat. Tax deductions, refinancing, mortgage rates, compound interest (she was supposed to understand that chart? Really?)—it made her eyes glaze over. She didn't speak this language. This was…math! The book had served a purpose, though. Only a couple of pages of reading was all it took to put her to sleep at night. Better than a sleeping pill.

But that wasn't exactly helping get her financial house in order. An SOS call had brought Pat over, armed with her calculator, and now the two women were about to do battle with the bills.

"I have no idea how I'm going to make what I have stretch," Muriel confessed. "All these bills." She shook her head. "This is humiliating. I'm an idiot savant. The only thing I can do is write."

Why, oh, why hadn't she persisted in taking a more active role in the money-managing process when Stephen was alive? Or even Waldo. After Stephen's death she should have dug in and handled everything.

But there'd been so much to handle—mountains of paperwork to fill out, bills to sort through. She'd bounced checks right and left. Arnie had come over many a night to go over her bank account and straighten out the latest mess, trying to explain where she'd gone wrong. *Here, Muriel. Just make out this check to P.U.D. 1 for ninety-two dollars.*

She was still bouncing checks when she met Waldo and had been happy to let him take over. *Don't you worry, honey. I'll take care of the bills. You just write.* Looking back now, she realized she'd been like a person who couldn't read, never mastering the skill she needed but instead always finding ways to work around her deficiency.

"You'll get the hang of this," Pat assured her. "For now let's work with what you've got and see how we're going to divvy it up."

Two hours later they had Muriel's expenses listed on a spreadsheet. What was going out was definitely more than what was coming in. Even Muriel could see that. She'd have to sell Waldo's Beemer before it got repossessed, and the house would have to go on the market immediately. No surprise there. Still, she'd hoped for a little more time to get her feet under her.

"You probably won't come out with much," Pat said, "but you should wind up with enough to tide you over until you can finish your next book."

Would there ever be another book?

Putting the house on the market was a big enough emotional hurdle for the moment. One step at a time, she told herself as she called Mountain Meadows Real Estate to set up an appointment with a Realtor.

The conversation was encouraging and after she hung up she felt she was moving in the right direction. Now she had a plan and a spreadsheet, and that was encouraging. She felt as if she could master anything. *Ah, Stephen, you never thought I could do this, but it looks like I can.*

And if she could cope with the unpleasant chore of money management she could certainly cope with helping to put on a chocolate festival. *Bring it on.*

Bailey arrived at Sea-Tac Airport the Wednesday morning before festival weekend, lugging two suitcases and her carry-on. "I'm here, let the games begin!" she declared, falling into Samantha's arms. Literally. Not watching where she was going, she tripped over a fellow passenger's carry-on.

"And so is half your house," Samantha observed, righting her.

"It's all stuff for the dinner and the tea, Sammy," she said, pushing her chestnut curls out of her face. "I found all kinds of decorations at the dollar store. I know we haven't been able to draw from the business, but can you maybe reimburse me? I'm a little short on cash till my next catering job."

Bailey had been "a little short on cash" since she was twelve. Like Mom, she was math-challenged. Samantha was already dreading the bill. Even at the dollar store she suspected her sister could rack up the dollars.

"Give me the receipt and we'll reimburse you," Samantha said as she took a bag. Somehow. With everything they'd had to buy for the various events, expenses were mounting and at this rate she'd be paying Bailey in foil-wrapped chocolate coins.

"I can hardly wait to see," Cecily said, taking the other bag.

That left Bailey with just her carry-on and free to link an arm through her big sister's. "This is going to be so much fun."

Fun, that was the code by which Bailey lived. Even starting her catering business had been more play than work, with Dad generously bankrolling her. Samantha wasn't jealous, though. She wouldn't trade her experiences at Sweet Dreams for anything. She'd worked her way up from selling goodies in the shop to building the company, and that was something to take pride in.

"It will be fun," Cecily agreed, "now that the crisis is averted," she added, referring to the rockslide.

Well, one crisis, anyway. They still needed money. But thanks to a new ad in the Seattle paper encouraging travelers to brave the pass and the *Northwest Now* TV segment, it looked like they were going to override the earlier panic. Reservations were starting to come in at the B and Bs once more and shop owners were feeling hopeful. The whole town had worked hard to pull this together in record time and visitors were bound to fall in love with Icicle Falls and, of course, Sweet Dreams Chocolates.

Still, Samantha wouldn't rest easy until the weekend was over. She felt like a juggler, trying to keep a dozen flaming torches in the air, all while doing an Irish jig on a high wire. In heels. She'd chewed her fingernails down to the nubs and gained six pounds due to her chocolate consumption, but if the festival was a success, it would be worth every moment of stress and every extra pound.

"I've got the best dessert recipe for the chocolate dinner," Bailey bragged. "Chocolate truffle trifle, using our chocolates, of course."

"That sounds decadent," Cecily said. "It'll be a miracle if we don't all die from a chocolate overdose this weekend."

Samantha could identify with that. She was already halfway there. Was there such a thing as Chocoholics Anonymous? If so, she was going to have to join it.

"Oh, and I have more good news, the best news of all," Bailey continued.

"You found a millionaire who wants to give us money," Samantha cracked. *If only.*

"Almost as good. I catered this baby shower on Sunday and you'll never guess who I met."

"Mimi LeGrande," Samantha said, piling on the sarcasm. Cecily had managed to get the name of Mimi's producer, but her emails had gone unanswered.

"I met the cousin of her producer," Bailey crowed. "I told her I'd bring her some samples after the festival."

Samantha stared at her baby sister, hardly able to believe her ears.

"Oh, my gosh," Cecily gushed. "Way to go, sis!"

"You can say that again," Samantha said.

Going the friend-of-a-friend route was always a long shot, but this was one well worth taking. The festival was a go and now they had a possible in with Mimi LeGrande. Mom always said, "Every good thing comes to she who waits." It looked like Mom was right.

They drove away from the airport, Bailey still chattering happily, Samantha watching the road and seeing a future filled with success.

It was nice to see their mother taking an interest in life again, Cecily thought as she went to the office to check the goody boxes for the Mr. Dreamy contest. She had left Mom and Bailey talking recipes; they'd been so engrossed they barely noticed her departure. Yes, there was still sadness in her mother's eyes and she often slipped away to bed early, but that was understandable considering how fresh her grief was. In fact, considering everything she'd gone through, it was amazing to Cecily that she could cope at all.

What would it be like to have two men who were devoted to you and lose both? Cecily couldn't imagine. She couldn't imagine having a good man, period.

They were out there; she'd matched up a few in her brief career as a matchmaker. But they sure seemed to be few and far between.

She got to Sweet Dreams just as Luke Goodman was approaching from the other end of the street. Here was one of the good ones, a man fortress.

"Hey, there, we've got your gift boxes ready," he greeted her. "Want to see?"

"That's why I'm here," she replied, and followed him into the warehouse. Walking behind Luke Goodman was like walking behind a wall. A woman could feel safe with a man like him.

Did she know any woman who'd be a match?

You're not in the business anymore, she reminded herself.

Still, old habits died hard. Maybe Bailey? Except, good as he'd be for her, Cecily couldn't see her little sister with this man. Bailey was still a kid herself and Luke already had one child to raise.

"I wish you'd come by about an hour earlier. I could have used your help shopping," he said.

"Oh? For what?"

"A dress," he replied, deadpan.

"Probably hard to find one in your size."

He grinned. "For Serena. I had to give my expert

opinion. Mom took her to Gilded Lily's to get one for the tea and they had it narrowed down to two."

Shopping, one of the fun aspects of having a little girl. Little girls, babies—Cecily became suddenly aware of a *tick-tick-tick* at the back of her brain.

She quickly took a mental hammer to the culprit. A ticking biological clock wasn't a good enough reason enough to jump into a relationship. Not these days. Biology and culture didn't always mate well; the high divorce rate was proof of that. It seemed people rarely got together with the idea of staying together anymore.

Even Icicle Falls wasn't immune to the big D. She thought of Cass Wilkes and Charlene Albach, both great women who should've been living in Happily-Ever-After Land. And she'd heard rumors that her old pal Ella O'Brien, who ran her mother's shop, Gilded Lily's, was having problems. She hoped the rumors weren't true.

Ella and Jake had been high school sweethearts, her first successful match, in fact. Ella hadn't said anything when they'd gone to lunch a couple of weeks back. Still, they'd been out of touch for the past five years and that probably wasn't information you blurted out the first time you saw an old friend, especially the old friend who got you together with your husband.

Cecily and Luke were in the warehouse now. She grinned at the sight of all the inventory building up. This weekend the town would experience a veritable avalanche of chocolate. Cecily shivered, as much from cold as excitement, and rubbed her arms. He took off his leather jacket and draped it over her shoulders— more perfect-man points for Luke Goodman—then led her to where several cartons stood stacked in a corner.

He opened one and took out a little pink box wrapped in gold ribbon and sealed with the gold medallion bearing the company logo, a slumbering quarter moon with long, girlie eyelashes and a smile. The box was what they called a four-seater, holding four different chocolates: salted caramel, a white-chocolate-lemon-cream truffle, a dark chocolate truffle with chocolate ganache filling and a mint chocolate—four of their most popular flavors.

He handed it over for her to inspect. "Perfect," she said.

"I guess you're going to have a crowd at your pageant," he said, looking at the cartons.

"We're sold out," she said proudly. Samantha had balked at the idea, and now Cecily took secret delight in proving that her big sister didn't know everything. Everyone she'd talked to was excited about the event. Actually, everyone was excited about the whole festival and she was really enjoying the anticipatory buzz that had taken over the town. Promoting chocolate was considerably more fun than finding matches for unappreciative customers.

"These should be a hit," he predicted as she returned the box to the case. "Let me know how they go over."

"You're not going to come and see for yourself?" she asked. "It should be quite a show."

"Not interested. My mom's trying to convince me to go to the ball, though. Support the company."

"You should, Prince Charming. You might find a princess there."

He leaned against the wall and looked at her speculatively. "Think so?"

Oh, dear. Now she'd just led him on. "Well, you never know," she said lightly. "I might put on my matchmaker's hat one more time and see if I can find her for you."

"Is that how it worked for Prince Charming?" he countered.

"Well, in a way, if you count the fairy godmother."

He shook his head. "She just provided the clothes and the ride. The magic was up to them. Kind of like real life."

Cecily pointed an accusing finger at him. "You're a romantic."

He shrugged. "Nothing wrong with that. I believe in magic."

She'd believed she had, too, but the magic never lasted.

"Anyway, you never know what can happen at a ball. If you keep an open mind," he added, giving her nose a playful tap.

"I'll remember," she said.

As she left the warehouse for the office, she realized she was feeling all warm and happy inside, as if some of that magic they'd talked about had slipped into Luke's finger when he touched her. *He is a nice man,* she told herself. And what woman in her right mind didn't want a nice man?

Up in the office she found Jonathan Templar getting ready to leave.

"This man deserves a medal," Elena said. "He has saved us once again."

Their hard-drive hero pushed his glasses up his nose. "Slight exaggeration."

"No, no. It is no exaggeration, believe me," Elena said. "You are the king of the computer."

"That's me," he said with a smile as he zipped his jacket.

"So why are you here, *chica?*" Elena asked Cecily.

"I have to do a little work on the Mr. Dreamy contest," Cecily said.

That produced a frown on Jonathan's face. He hid it quickly but not quickly enough.

"I don't think Jonathan approves of our contest," Cecily teased.

"Hey, if it's bringing in money," he said diplomatically.

"But it's beneath you, right?"

"I'm not exactly Mr. Dreamy material," he said.

"Oh, I don't know," Elena said, looking him over. "Lose the glasses, go to the gym a little. You have potential. Doesn't he?"

"Absolutely," Cecily agreed.

Now Jonathan's face was turning red. "Uh, I've gotta get going. You guys have a good day." And with that he was out the door.

"Poor Jonathan," Cecily said. "We embarrassed him."

"He needs a better self-image," Elena said. "You should find someone for him."

"I'm not doing that anymore," Cecily told her. "Anyway, there's only one woman he wants, and that's Lisa Castle."

Elena gave a snort of disgust. "That one. He'll never get her. Why do so many men want women who don't even see them?"

"Misplaced loyalty? Insanity? Who knows? It's another one of love's mysteries." And why were so many women attracted to the wrong kind of man? If she could solve that mystery, her own love life would take off.

With a sigh, she sat down at the spare office desk and got to work finalizing details for the Mr. Dreamy contest. That done, she went on to check her email.

Before they'd left to pick up Bailey, she'd sent notices to all the Mr. Dreamy contestants, reminding them of the walk-through scheduled for that night at Festival Hall. Most of them had responded cheerfully.

Have the crown ready, Bill Will had written. And how about going kayaking with me when I win?

Good old Bill, the picture of confidence. But his competition was going to be stiff. There were some great-looking guys entered.

A picture of Todd Black popped into her mind. With his swarthy pirate face he was probably a shoo-in. Talk about a hypocrite—entering the contest at the last minute after mocking her so thoroughly. The prize package had obviously been too sweet to resist.

And speak of the devil. Here was an email from the black pirate himself. I didn't enter this.

She typed back. Really? I have your picture and entry form right here at the office. You barely made the deadline.

A moment later the phone rang. "Todd Black on line one for you," Elena alerted her.

"Okay, you've had your fun," he said, without giving Cecily time to say hello.

Luke had left her feeling warm and happy. Just talking to Todd made her feel like she'd swallowed a lit sparkler. "Someone entered you in our contest," she said, dousing the sparkler with the firm reminder that Todd Black was a cynical turkey. "Nice picture, by the way. It makes you look like a real ski pro."

"I am."

"Great choice, then."

"I didn't send it," he growled.

"Who did, then?" she asked. "One of your girl-friends?"

"How the hell should I know? It was up on my Facebook page. Anybody could've printed it. Probably my bartender's idea of a sick joke."

So her contest was a sick joke. "Some joke. He paid the twenty-five-dollar entry fee."

"Keep the money, but un-enter me. I'm not parading around in my boxers in front of a bunch of horny women."

"Fine," she said. "No one wants to see you in your boxers, anyway." She flashed on an image of Todd Black in a pair of boxers decorated with valentine hearts. He wasn't a walking wall like Luke but he was all male and she could envision those rock-hard abs and beautifully sculpted pecs with maybe a smattering of dark hair. There were no sparklers in her chest now. Oh, no. Those had been replaced with bottle rockets.

"I can think of a few women," he said. "I do give private shows," he added silkily.

Another bottle rocket went off. "Thanks for sharing. If I meet any brainless bimbos I'll send them your way."

"Ha, ha," he said, and hung up.

"Oh, very original," she said to the dial tone. She hung up a little more forcefully than necessary and realized Elena was over at her desk wearing a know-it-all expression. "What?" Cecily demanded.

"Nada," Elena said airily.

"Nada is right," Cecily muttered. Todd Black was a big *nada*.

Was it hot in here?

Twenty-One

Sometimes the more preposterous the idea, the greater the success.

> —Muriel Sterling, *Mixing Business with Pleasure: How to Successfully Balance Business and Love*

Chocolate Festival, Schedule of Events

FRIDAY EVENING:

5:00–7:30 p.m.: Chocolate Walk, sponsored by Sweet Dreams Chocolate Company

Participants can enjoy special chocolate drinks and desserts, along with a treat from Sweet Dreams Chocolate Company.

Participating restaurants: Zelda's, Schwangau, Der Spaniard, Italian Alps Pizza

8:00 p.m.: Festival Hall, Ceremony to crown Mr. Dreamy, sponsored by Sweet Dreams Chocolate Company

SATURDAY

8:00 a.m.: Lost Bride Trail guided hike, sponsored by the Alpiners Hiking Club

Get out in the great outdoors and hear the legend of the lost bride.

9:00 a.m.–11:00 a.m.: Lovers' Breakfast, served at the Breakfast Haus

10:00 a.m.–3:00 p.m.: Street Fair

Enjoy the food and craft booths and meet our local artisans. And be sure to stop by the Sweet Dreams

booth to purchase your "chocolate survival kit" and meet Mr. Dreamy, who will be there from 10:00 a.m. until noon.

11:00 a.m.: The Romance of Flowers, at Lupine Floral

Learn the language of flowers, get tips on how to make your floral arrangement last and put your name in a draw to win a lupine lovers' bouquet.

1:00 p.m.: Sweet Dreams Chocolate Company Tour

Come see how we make our fabulous chocolates and get your picture taken with Mr. Dreamy.

2:00 p.m.: Chocolate High Tea with Mr. Dreamy at Icicle Creek Lodge, sponsored by the Gingerbread Haus and Sweet Dreams Chocolate Company. For reservations, call Icicle Creek Lodge

5:00 p.m.: Wine and Chocolate Tasting at D'Vine Wines

Sample dessert wines made by local wineries along with locally made Sweet Dreams Chocolates.

6:30 p.m.: Sweet Dreams dinner at Zelda's, sponsored by Sweet Dreams Chocolate Company and Zelda's restaurant

Tickets are available at Zelda's and must be purchased in advance. Seating is limited so make your reservations early!

8:00 p.m.: Sweet Dreams Masked Ball at Festival Hall, sponsored by Sweet Dreams Chocolate Company

Tickets may be purchased at the Sweet Dreams Gift Shop or at the door.

SUNDAY

10:00 a.m.–2:00 p.m.: Town Treasure Hunt

Visit our local merchants and find bargains on all kinds of treasures. Several stores are the location for valuable prize packages, which will be awarded randomly to shoppers throughout the day.

Prizes: Dinner for two at Ludwig's. One night free lodging at the Icicle Creek Lodge. A bottle of Riesling from D'Vine Wines. One free trip down the Wenatchee River with Adventure Outfitters. A coupon for one free small gingerbread house shipped anywhere within the continental U.S. from Gingerbread Haus. A snow globe from Kringle Mart (valued at fifty dollars). A box of chocolates from Sweet Dreams Chocolate Company. One hat, courtesy of the Mad Hatter Novelty Hat Company. A one-hundred-dollar gift card for Sleeping Lady Salon and Spa. A twenty-five-dollar gift certificate for Mountain Escape Bookstore. **We Hope You'll Enjoy our First Annual Chocolate Festival!**

Preparations were going forward at warp speed now.

The decorating committee, headed up by Heinrich and Kevin, had outdone itself, hanging baskets overflowing with artificial pink and white flowers from storefront roof overhangs and festooning trees with strings of red and pink heart-shaped lights. Restaurants were offering lovers' dinners and the town chefs had knocked themselves out creating recipes featuring Sweet Dreams chocolates. With the exception of Johnson's Drugs, every shop in town was participating in a treasure hunt, which would lead visitors from store to store in search of bargains and prizes. Heinrich and Kevin had been creating special chocolate-lovers' floral arrangements over at Lupine Floral, incorporating Sweet Dreams candy, and were going all out on flowers for the chocolate ball, while Ed York was offering a wine-and-chocolate tasting on Saturday evening before the chocolate dinner at Zelda's, which was sold out.

Not to be outdone, the social and service clubs had gotten into the act. The Alpiners Hiking Club was conducting guided hikes up Lost Bride Trail. The Rotary Club was sponsoring the Lovers' Breakfast at the Breakfast Haus, with proceeds to go to the food bank. The town churches were providing free taxi service for any celebrants who drank a little too much wine with their chocolate, and every artist, club and youth group within a ten-mile radius was going to be manning a booth of some kind, giving visitors a chance to buy everything from chainsaw carvings to elephant ears. Samantha was especially excited about the booth Bavarian Brews was running. All their hot drinks would come topped with whipped cream and a Sweet Dreams chocolate.

Excitement was growing all over town, much of it focused on the Mr. Dreamy contest.

"I'm sure my Brandon is going to win," Olivia predicted when Samantha stopped by to see how preparations were going for the chocolate tea.

"Are you coming to cheer him on?" Samantha asked, not making any promises. If she'd had her way, Brandon wouldn't have been allowed to compete. Talk about waving temptation right under Bailey's nose.

"Oh, I'll be there," Olivia said. "All the LAMs are going. To support your mother," Olivia added. Samantha couldn't help grinning, and Olivia's pudgy cheeks turned pink. "Well, and to admire all the good-looking men."

"Olivia, you are a cougar," Samantha teased, making the color in the older woman's cheeks deepen to magenta.

"There are some things a woman never loses an appreciation for, and one of them is chocolate. I'm sure you can guess the other," Olivia said.

"I think I can," Samantha said. And she had to admit that her sisters had been on to something. Tacky as this whole Mr. Dreamy contest seemed, it was a hit, and a moneymaker. And the more moneymakers they had, the better.

"Everyone's talking about the pageant, you know. Well, the whole festival, actually," Olivia said. "It's all going to be so much fun. Everyone's going to be there."

Spending money. Samantha smiled at the thought of being able to walk into the bank on Monday with a big, fat check. *Take that, Blake Preston.*

"Brown wants to come up and check out the chocolate festival," Darren said to Blake. "I told him you'd be happy to show him around, take him out to lunch."

Happy? In what parallel universe? "Sorry," Blake said shortly. "I'm afraid I can't help you. I won't be around on Saturday." He'd had plans to hang out at the street fair, buy a ton of stuff at the Sweet Dreams booth, but not now.

"You won't?" Darren sounded surprised. "Not very good public relations."

"Probably not very good public relations to be seen with the guy who wants to take our client's business, either," Blake retorted.

"Now, listen here, Preston," Darren began.

Blake cut him off. "Sorry, Darren. You're on your own."

"Well, what am I supposed to do with Brown?" Darren demanded.

"Hey, it's a nice drive," Blake said. "And if you decide you want to do dinner, try Zelda's. They make a great steak."

Darren was still sputtering threats when Blake hung up. He wouldn't follow through on any of them, though, and they both knew it. Blake was doing a good job here and bringing in new business from neighboring towns. He was an excellent bank manager. But he wasn't a good whipping boy and, after that disastrous visit to the factory, he was done letting Darren bully him into unethical behavior. Darren could damn well drive up here with his pet pig, let Trevor Brown drool over Samantha's company and eat bratwurst to his heart's content. Blake hoped he choked on one.

By late Friday afternoon the town was full of tourists, intrepid explorers going from shop to shop, filling bags with merchandise. And that night Festival Hall was packed with women of all ages. There was probably enough estrogen to hot-flash the entire forest to cinders and there was certainly enough perfume in the air to send anyone with an allergy right to the new medical center. The noise level was on a par with a convention of geese.

"I'd say you've got a hit on your hands," Cass said as the judges took their places at the judges' table.

"I'd say we've got a potential riot on our hands," Samantha said, and wondered who was doing crowd control, since half the police force were contestants. Across the hall she saw Dot's daughter, Tilda, tall and impressive in her uniform, standing at the back, frowning.

Like her mother, Tilda was tough as a turtle's shell.

Nobody messed with her and if Tilda stopped you for speeding there was no point in trying to talk your way out of a ticket. But even Tilda might have a problem controlling this crowd. High on chocolate and hormones, they were ready to party hearty. The men would be lucky if these women didn't rip their shirts right off them.

Oh, yeah. They were removing their shirts voluntarily.

The contest theme music started ("It's Raining Men") and the crowd went wild. Bailey came out on stage wearing a white tux she'd picked up on sale in a tuxedo rental shop and had altered, along with three-inch heels that threatened disaster. With her curves and chestnut hair she looked like Betty Boop 2.0.

The music died down and she spoke into her handheld mike. "Welcome everyone to the Sweet Dreams first annual Mr. Dreamy competition. Are you ready for a good time?"

The audience responded with a wall of sound. Samantha glanced over to where Cecily and Mom sat. Mom was smiling her Miss Manners smile, ever the lady, even though Samantha suspected inwardly she was cringing and wondering how she'd gotten roped into this nonsense. Cecily looked smug. Well, she was allowed. This would go down as a big success and a nice moneymaker.

"Okay, then," Bailey was saying up onstage. "Meet your men!"

The music started again and the herd of beefcake paraded across the stage, some of them seeming more comfortable than others. Of course, Bill Will had to stop and do a Mr. Universe pose, which produced squeals of delight.

This really was tacky. Samantha sighed and resigned herself to a long evening.

The evening proved more entertaining than she'd expected. There was no talent competition but Cecily and Bailey had come up with other ways for the men to show off, including a tug-of-war contest that took place in the center aisle between the seats, as well as a "sweet talker" pickup line competition where the men got points for originality and sincerity.

Bill Will scored high with "I just had my thrill of the day. I saw you." But Joe Coyote stole the heart of both the judges and the audience when he said, "I'm not real good at pickup lines so I guess all I can tell you is what I said when I first met Lauren—'I know every guy here wants you for keeps but would you give me a chance and go out with me?'" That was rewarded with a collective sigh.

The final round of competition required each man to explain why he should be the next Mr. Dreamy.

Brandon Wallace had a cocky comeback when Bailey asked him that all-important question. "Because once I've kissed you, you won't be able to dream of anything else."

Samantha didn't like the way he looked at her baby sister when he said that. Wasn't it time for Brandon Wallace, ski bum, to run away from home?

Cecily leaned over and whispered, "I should have gotten someone else to MC."

No kidding. Bailey and Brandon were only a year apart in age. When she was a kid she'd had a terrible crush on him and had given him her treasured rock collection. When they were in high school she'd given him her virginity. After high school he'd moved on to bigger game but the damage had been done. Bailey's heart was locked up and Brandon still held the key.

Samantha could see her sister blush even down where

she sat. Bailey kept her cool. "That's a pretty big promise," she said. "Are you sure you can live up to it?"

In response, he moved closer. "Want a demonstration?"

Of course, the audience did. "Yes, yes, yes!"

"Well, I'm not the judge," Bailey said, trying to step away.

She stepped a little too quickly, though, and lost her balance. The crowd let out a gasp of pleasure as he caught her and said, "Put in a good word for me." Then he dipped her dramatically and laid a kiss on her that was hot enough to melt the contents of all those little pink boxes they'd handed out at the door. A collective sigh rose from the audience and Samantha growled.

Once he released Bailey she stood there in a stupor, forgetting her MC duties.

No one seemed to notice. Half the women in the room were in a stupor, too.

"Oh, my," his embarrassed mother said faintly.

That broke the spell and the women came back to life, tittering and clapping.

Olivia didn't know all the details of Bailey and Brandon's past (a good thing for all concerned) but she did know enough to be embarrassed. Her wild boy wasn't, however. In fact, he didn't seem in any hurry to leave. He covered the mike with one hand and leaned over and whispered something in Bailey's ear.

She frowned at him and moved away, reclaiming the mike and her dignity. "Thanks, Brandon," she said, dismissing him. "And now we're down to the final contestant. Joe Coyote."

Joe limped out on stage, and Lauren and the rest of her posse hooted and clapped. Even though an accident on the job had taken him out of construction, he'd kept his construction-worker body. Caramel-colored skin and midnight-black hair added to his charm. From a distance it was hard to see the scar that marred an otherwise pleasant face.

"So, Joe, why should you be our first Mr. Dreamy?" Bailey greeted him.

He shrugged. "I don't know that I should."

"Yes, you should!" Lauren called from three rows back, and her friends all clapped.

"If you don't think you should be our first Mr. Dreamy, then why did you enter?" Bailey asked.

Some of the men had been lured by the prizes or they'd entered on a dare or, like poor Joe, who resembled a deer that had wandered into a hunter's campsite, because their girlfriends had suckered them into it.

"Well, Lauren asked me to," he said, looking over to where she sat, "and I'd do anything for her."

Sentimental sighs rose from the audience. Then clapping. And then Joe got a standing O.

"There's our Mr. Dreamy," Cass said.

Obviously.

Mr. Dreamy was duly crowned and the two runners-up, Enrico Vargas, one of Icicle Falls' finest, and Brandon Wallace, ski bum, each received a free month at Bruisers Fitness Center—rather a joke, considering the fact that both men were already members. The contest over, attendees and contestants mingled and slowly drifted out of the hall to take the party over to Zelda's or Italian Alps Pizza. Or, in the case of many of the couples, somewhere more private.

"I'd say this is definitely going to become a yearly tradition," Cass said, complimenting Samantha.

"We just might make it one," Samantha agreed. If everything else turned out to be as successful and as popular this weekend, she was going to be a happy woman.

"Anybody want to go get pizza?" Cass asked.

"Yes," Cecily said. "I'm starving."

What else was new? How her sister kept from weighing two hundred pounds was a mystery to Samantha.

"Are you up for getting some pizza?" Cecily asked Mom.

"I don't think so. You girls go on and have a good time."

Mom's smile was looking strained now. How silly this must all seem after grappling with death and loss.

"You sure?" Cass asked.

"Yes, I'm sure," Mom said. "I'll see you later." She kissed her daughters and gave Cass a hug, then slipped past the remaining celebrants and out the door.

The three women stood watching her. "It can't be easy, what she's going through," Cass said sadly. "Divorce, death, somehow we always end up alone."

"Not always." Cecily frowned. "You shouldn't close yourself off. I've got a feeling—"

Cass held up a hand. "Oh, no. I've heard about your feelings. I'll pass, thanks."

Cecily made a face and Samantha couldn't help chuckling. "You're not in the business anymore, remember?"

"Yes, and now I remember why," Cecily said. "I'll go get Bailey."

"Good idea." Bailey was talking with a couple of women but Brandon Wallace was moving toward her like a shark toward a pair of tempting legs dangling in the water. She was relieved to see Cecily sweep their little sister away. Safe from Jaws, for the moment, anyway.

The pizza place was already filling up when they arrived. The aroma of garlic and oregano and tomato sauce that greeted Samantha had her taste buds clamoring for instant gratification. She distracted herself by looking around to see who was there. She waved at a few people she knew while waiting to place her order, then began threading her way through the crowd to their table. She was halfway there when she realized who was at the table next to theirs.

Oh, come on. Yes, Icicle Falls was a small town but really, did she have to keep running into Blake the Snake everywhere she went?

Twenty-Two

*A woman can go through life just fine denying
some things (like the fact that she's aging or that
she's gained weight), but she won't have a life
worth living if she denies love.*

—Muriel Sterling, *Knowing Who You Are:
One Woman's Journey*

Why hadn't she seen Blake when she first came in?
Then she could have gone right back out. *I'll just walk
past and pretend I don't see him,* Samantha decided.
Which was, of course, ridiculous since she'd have to be
blind not to. There he sat, big as life, sharing a pizza with
Jimmy Robinson, the produce manager from Safeway,
and Tennessee transplant Bubba Swank, who owned Big
Brats, a favorite lunch haunt of both locals and tourists.

Still, the last thing she wanted was to talk to him.
She was almost at his table and picking up her pace, de-
termined to speed right past, when he called her name.
Okay, so she would be blind *and* deaf.

But was that smart business? This man's bank held
the note on her company. It was in her best interests to
remove her porcupine suit and play nice, something she
should have done from the beginning. Ugh.

He stood politely, a wall of muscle hiding under jeans
and a sweater. If he'd been up onstage in Festival Hall
tonight, she'd have seen him without his shirt.

You don't care about seeing him out of his shirt, she reminded herself, *you just want him out of your hair.*

She said a well-mannered hello to his pals, wished all three of them *bon appétit* and was ready to move on.

Before she could, Blake said, "I hear your contest was a success. Congratulations."

She donned a smile even Cecily the diplomat couldn't top. It wasn't an easy fit. "Thanks. I'm sure all our other events will do as well. We've already brought in a big chunk of money and I expect to make a lot more before the weekend is over."

It probably wouldn't be enough to pay off what they owed, but surely it would be enough to melt his hard heart and convince him and his evil boss to work with her. After all, wasn't that what business was about, people working together? Banks worked with Donald Trump all the time and he was the king of credit.

"I hope you make a fortune," Blake said.

She raised a skeptical eyebrow. "Do you? Really?"

"Of course. Believe me, I don't like the position we're in any more than you do."

"Well, that's comforting to know," she said, and moved away. *Hypocrite.*

"That looked like a fairly calm encounter," Cecily commented as she sat down at the table.

"It was," Samantha said. "I can be diplomatic." Sort of.

"I wouldn't mind having diplomatic relations with him," Cass said.

Cecily shook her head in mock disgust. "Dirty old woman."

Cass shrugged. "What can I say? Seeing all that beefcake tonight gave me an appetite."

"I bet Cecily could find you someone," said Bailey, who'd missed their earlier conversation.

"I really don't want a someone," Cass said. "I already have enough aggravation just dealing with my ex-someone."

"But don't you get lonely?" Bailey asked. "Don't you ever feel the urge to merge?"

"Yes, but all I have to do to lose it is think about Mason," Cass replied.

The conversation turned in a new direction, but Samantha was still stuck on the corner of Urge and Merge. What would it be like to meet Blake Preston on that corner?

Oh, no. Not going there. Not now, not ever.

Downtown Icicle Falls on Saturday was a mob scene, with people spilling out of shops and restaurants and perusing vendor booths. Children darted through the crowd, clutching elephant ears and cotton candy. Lots of people clustered around the Bavarian Brews booth, which was selling hot chocolate and doing a brisk business, and Cass's booth was selling out of cookie jewelry and cupcakes.

But Cecily was happy to see that the busiest booth of all was the Street Dreams one. Celebrants were lined up to purchase white-chocolate-dipped apples, chocolate mint candy bars and their little pink four-seater boxes of chocolate heaven. And of course, to meet Mr. Dreamy, who was posing for pictures, mostly with middle-aged women.

Joe appeared about as comfortable as a man buying tampons for his wife when one woman asked him to pretend he was feeding her a chocolate, but he obliged. Of course, that opened the floodgates of inspiration and soon Joe was kissing wrinkled cheeks and picking up women and posing like he was a caped superhero about to fly off with them while the cameras snapped.

Cecily watched him struggle to lift one portly customer. Poor Joe. She hoped he didn't get a hernia. And if he did, she hoped he wouldn't send the medical bills to Sweet Dreams. Samantha would kill her.

Samantha didn't look ready to kill anybody today, though. She was smiling, chatting up the customers as she took their money.

She and Bailey were running the booth for the morning shift, along with Elena, who had offered to pitch in. Cecily and Mom would take over in the afternoon while Bailey took charge of the chocolate tea at Olivia's B and B. Then, that evening, they'd all be at the chocolate dinner and ball.

Samantha had seen her now and waved, and Cecily went to the side of the booth to check in.

"How does the hall look?" Samantha asked.

"Gorgeous, I can hardly imagine how stunning it's going to be once all the candles are lit."

"So it's all done?"

"Almost. Mom's gone home and I just left Kevin putting the final touches on the centerpieces."

"Great."

Bailey handed white-chocolate apples to two teenage girls. "Enjoy," she told them. They didn't waste time replying, just bit into their apples and wandered off. "Awesome, isn't it?" she said to Cecily, indicating the milling crowd.

Cecily nodded. "I'd say we've got a hit on our hands."

"We're going to need more apples," Bailey said.

"I can't believe we're almost out. Guess we should've doubled production on those yesterday." Samantha looked speculatively at Cecily and Cecily knew what was coming. "Can you get some more apples and run over to the kitchen and make another three dozen?"

Cecily had hoped to take a few minutes to check out the booths before coming on duty, but she nodded and said, "No problem." This was an all-hands-on-deck weekend, after all.

"I can help," said a deep voice behind her.

She turned to see Luke Goodman standing there with his daughter. Little Serena was bundled up in leggings and a skirt topped with a pink parka with faux-fur trim. She looked like a cross between a snow baby and the Sugar Plum Fairy. In short, she looked adorable. Her dad didn't look so bad himself in his jeans, flannel shirt and winter jacket.

"Hi," Cecily said. "Are you having fun?" she asked Serena.

The child nodded. "We're getting chocolate apples, and I'm going to a tea."

"That does sound like fun."

"And my daddy's going to a ball," Serena continued. "He's going to meet a princess."

Luke's cheeks turned russet. "You never know."

"Moonlight and magic," Cecily quipped.

"So would you like some help with those apples?" he asked.

Unlike her type-A older sister and high-energy baby sister, Cecily enjoyed stopping to breathe once in a while, and having some assistance in the Sweet Dreams kitchen would have been nice. But she didn't want to pull Luke away from his daughter, and she didn't want to give him the wrong idea that she was interested in being anything more than friends. Cozy kitchen time together could become a recipe for hurt feelings. Better to keep him at a distance.

"That's okay, thanks. I can manage," she said. "You guys have fun."

"Let's get our apples, Daddy," Serena said, tugging on his arm, the equivalent of a puppy trying to tow a mountain.

The mountain allowed himself to be moved but as he fished out his wallet he asked, "How about saving me a dance tonight?"

It would have been rude to refuse. "Okay," she said.

He was such a nice man. She should have been dying to dance with him. What was wrong with her?

She was still pondering the question when she walked into the Safeway produce department in search of Granny Smith apples. Surely if she gave him half a chance, Luke could hit her zing-o-meter. He was probably a wonderful kisser. He'd been married, after all, had a child, had to know what turned a woman on.

It had been way too long since anyone had turned her on.

A male arm reached right out of her imagination and around her, brushing hers in the process and hitting the old zing-o-meter, sending it soaring. *Whoa, what was that?*

Todd Black!

"Need some apples." He held one up for her to see.

"You could have said something. I'd have moved." What was he doing here, intruding on her thoughts, playing with her zing-o-meter?

"I would have, but you were so intent on fondling the apples I hated to interrupt."

Okay, it was official now. Todd Black was the most irritating man in Icicle Falls. She began randomly snatching apples and stuffing them in her produce bag. "Well, I'll hurry up and get out of the way. It's obvious you're anxious to have a turn."

"Oh, no. I can wait. I'm a big believer in ladies first."

"I doubt that," she retorted.

"A little cranky, are we?" he teased. "Is all the stress of the festival getting to you?"

"No." Naturally, that had to come out all snippy-sounding.

"You sure? 'Cause you look stressed. There's no stress over at my place and we'll be open all night."

"Well, thanks for the offer," she said, putting the apples in her cart, "but I'll be at the chocolate ball tonight."

"And anyone who's anyone will be there," he finished cynically.

"You could say that," she said pleasantly, refusing to rise to the bait.

"Well, Cinderella, don't lose anything," he said. He grabbed another apple and took a bite.

"You haven't paid for that," she pointed out.

"Play now, pay later." He brought the apple to her mouth. "Go on. You know you want to."

She'd had enough of his smart mouth. "Bite me," her evil twin snapped.

"Anywhere you like," he said as she wheeled her cart away.

Samantha was on an endorphin high as she and her sisters made their way to the chocolate dinner at Zelda's. Only an hour ago she'd dropped off a big chunk of cash in the night depository. They'd made a nice bundle on the Mr. Dreamy pageant and their chocolate booth had been a huge success and so had been the tea, according to Bailey.

"What's not to like about white-chocolate-lavender scones and chocolate-dipped strawberries?" Bailey had said.

Indeed.

Now it was just the sisters. Mom had worked at the booth and gone to the tea, but she'd sent them off to the dinner and ball without her, claiming exhaustion. Samantha knew it was more a case of preferring to be home with her memories than going out and watching other couples dancing.

Their schedule was too tight for them to go home and change after dinner, so they were all in their evening wear. Samantha felt ridiculously overdressed. "We look like prommies," she said as they emerged from Cecily's car in front of the restaurant.

"We look great," Bailey corrected her.

Bailey was in borrowed finery, wearing a faux-fur coat over a creamy off-the-shoulder number with satin roses that she'd accented with Mom's pearls. Cecily was elegant in a midnight-blue designer gown she'd found at a consignment store in L.A. Samantha's gown was a green taffeta creation with a black netting underskirt that made her feel like the reincarnation of Scarlett O'Hara. Her sisters had insisted on paying for it and she'd given in and accepted when Cecily's old friend Ella had refused to accept her credit card. "Sorry, Samantha, but your sisters win."

"That's rare," Cecily had joked. "This is a moment to go down in history."

Talk about a moment to go down in history, Samantha thought as they entered the restaurant. This was one she would remember for years to come.

Many of the other diners were also dressed to the nines, obviously ready for a night of dancing. Samantha felt a swell of pride as she looked around and saw the place packed with familiar faces, all smiling and enjoying the success of their festival. They'd set out to do the impossible and they'd succeeded.

"I love your dress," said a woman who was in line in front of them, waiting to be seated.

"Thanks," Samantha murmured.

"All your dresses," the woman went on, taking them in. "Are you going to that chocolate ball I heard about?"

"As a matter of fact, we are," Bailey said cheerfully.

"Wow," said the woman. "You people really know how to do things right."

Samantha thanked her and filed that comment away to share with her fellow Chamber of Commerce members when this was all over.

"Be sure to tell your friends," Bailey said.

"Oh, I will," the woman promised. "You're going to do this next year, aren't you?"

"Absolutely," Samantha said confidently. They'd had to scramble to find their footing, but she knew, deep down, that they were firmly on the road to success now.

"You guys look great," Charley greeted them. "Now I wish I'd gotten a ticket."

"We can smuggle you in," Cecily offered.

Charley shook her head. "I don't want to risk meeting Prince Charming. I hope you all do, though."

Bailey stuck out a foot to reveal a rhinestone-studded clear acrylic heel. "I'm ready. I've got my glass slipper."

Samantha just hoped she wasn't planning on giving it (or anything else) to Brandon Wallace. If she could have picked someone for her sister she'd have selected his older brother, Eric, who was steady as a rock and dependable. Of course, he'd have bored Bailey to tears.

What was with them? Why couldn't the Sterling sisters manage to get it right when it came to men?

She let Charley lead her sisters to their table, a favorite corner booth by the stone fireplace, while she set out to make the rounds among the diners. As the face of Sweet Dreams, Samantha knew she had to say hello to all the people who had anted up for this event. She didn't mind doing that at all. She was happy to see everyone who was here.

Well, almost everyone. What had brought Blake Preston out? Since when did he care about chocolate or Sweet Dreams? There he sat at a table with his grandmother, his mother and a woman Samantha was pretty sure she recognized as his sister. Mr. Genial Host, whooping it up at what he hoped was her last supper.

They were going to pull out of this, and once they did they would pull their account from his First Bank of the Heartless before he could say, "Your money or your business."

She started at the farthest end of the restaurant from where he sat, greeting Lily Swan and her daughter, Ella.

Lily looked like she'd just stepped out of the pages of *Vogue*. She wore a strapless black gown and her perfectly dyed blond hair had been swept up to show off her long, Audrey Hepburn neck. Around that neck hung a pink gold chain from which a single diamond dangled—tasteful but expensive, like the woman wearing it. Lily was somewhere in her fifties but she looked forty. She still, after all these years, intimidated Samantha just a little, maybe because Samantha suspected that, deep down, Lily still saw her as the sneaky kid who'd lifted a pair of earrings from her when she was new in town and just setting up shop.

"You look ravishing tonight, Samantha," she said in her aloof Lily Swan voice.

"It's all thanks to the gown," Samantha said. "Your daughter has great taste, Mrs. Swan." And a generous heart. Ella had given Bailey and Cecily enough of a discount to save her from a guilt overload over their sisterly gesture of kindness.

"She does have good taste. In clothes," Lily said. Samantha sensed a double meaning in there somewhere. Ah, mother-daughter relationships. They were complicated.

Samantha smiled at Ella. "You can say that again. Where's Jake?"

"He's got a gig in Wenatchee," Ella said.

Jake was a struggling musician so a gig was a good thing as far as Samantha could tell, but Lily let out a long-suffering sigh and Ella frowned.

Okay, time to move along. Samantha wished them *bon appétit* and stepped away. Next stop: Pat and Ed.

He was distinguished in his tux and she was wearing an amber gown that looked vintage, possibly something she'd had for years. Samantha hoped when she got to be Pat's age she could still fit into this gown. Maybe she could—if she stopped sampling so much of her company's product.

Ed saluted her with his wineglass. "Great idea, Samantha. This is going to be quite a night."

Yes, it was. "I hope it's not too soon to pronounce our festival a success," she said.

Pat nodded. "No other word for it. I haven't seen Zelda's this packed in ages. I think we've even got some out-of-towners with us tonight."

Samantha looked around the room. "Oh, I know we do." Surely these visitors would tell their friends and next year even more people would come, snow or no snow.

As her gaze skimmed the room, she suddenly became aware that she was being watched. Like nails to a magnet, her attention was drawn to the table where Blake sat holding court—and taking in every inch of her, like some horny adolescent lounging on a street corner. She told herself he was a jerk and a Scrooge and the sudden flash of heat searing through her had nothing to do with attraction. It was simply warm in here.

Seeing that she'd caught him watching, he gave her a quick wave. She waved in return and then turned her back.

She stopped at six more tables and then there was no avoiding it. She had to visit his. He stood as she approached and she managed a smile—polite on the rocks.

It should have turned him into a giant ice sculpture but it didn't. "You look lovely tonight," he said to her.

And you look like a snake in a suit. "Thank you," she murmured.

"I'm sure you know my grandmother, Janice, but have you ever met my mother and sister?"

Poor them, related to him. "Thanks for coming," she said after he'd finished the introductions.

"Oh, we wouldn't have missed this for the world," Janice said.

Janice Lind was one of those women who were the heartbeat of the town. She volunteered at the food bank and every year her cake won the prize in the annual Raise the Roof bake-off that raised funds to maintain historic town buildings.

Their families hadn't moved in the same circles, but they'd seen each other around for years, and Janice often purchased chocolates to give away at Christmas. Now here she was with her grandson, the very man who had put the noose around Samantha's neck. She couldn't know what a foul bastard he was.

If she doesn't, that means he isn't broadcasting your misery all over town, Samantha told herself. That was something, certainly more than she could say for Del Stone.

"Thank you," she said to Janice. She couldn't help turning to Blake. "I'm surprised to see you here. After all, you're a busy man." Hadn't Pissy informed her of that?

"I want to do my part," he said.

"Oh, you're already doing so much," Samantha said. Then before he could reply, she excused herself and returned to her table. She wouldn't be able to eat a thing now. Blake Preston had stolen her appetite.

"She's a lovely girl," Gram observed as Samantha made her way back to the table where her sisters were sitting.

Lovely didn't begin to describe her.

"I don't think you have to tell Blake that," his sister teased.

He shot a look across the table that plainly said, *Shut up or else.*

That mouth of Tess's—she'd spent their entire childhood torturing him with it, either tattling on him or harassing him. Even though they were grown up now, little sister still liked to get in the occasional dig. Of course, if he ever needed anything she'd be there for him in a second and he for her.

Now it was as if she realized she'd shone a spotlight on something he didn't want the matchmaking women in his life to see. So, just when hopeful curiosity was dawning in his mother's eyes, she did her part to throw them off the scent, saying, "Any man with eyes can see how pretty Samantha Sterling is." Then, she couldn't resist adding, "If you like redheads."

He did. *Thank you, sis.* She had just spared him from getting prodded with a million questions. Samantha's business problems were not for public consumption, so it would be difficult to explain that, in spite of how much he wanted things to be different, circumstances had made him her archenemy.

Still, when it came to the possibility of a wife and more grandchildren, his mother was a romantic bloodhound. "You should ask her out," she said.

"She's a bank customer," Blake said, hoping that would close the subject.

"Half the town is a bank customer," Gram scoffed.

"I'm not that into her," Blake lied.

"Here comes our salad," Tess said. "This should be interesting. I've never had salad with chocolate mint leaves in it before."

That put Mom and Gram onto a new conversational track, thank God. Another thing to be thankful for— none of them were going to the ball. If he got an opportunity to dance with Samantha he wouldn't have to worry that they'd spot him with her. He was having a hard enough time convincing her he wasn't the devil incarnate. He didn't need his family coaching him from the sidelines or singing his praises. He could fight his own romantic battles.

Except this wasn't a battle. It was World War III. He scowled at his salad. Chocolate mint leaves, ugh. Way to ruin a salad. In fact, way to ruin a dinner. There wasn't much here he'd be able to eat, but he'd come anyway, determined to show his support.

* * *

"You are going to love this dinner," Bailey predicted once Samantha had rejoined them.

"I'm dying to try that chocolate pasta," Cecily said.

Samantha doubted she was going to enjoy anything now that Blake Preston had ruined her appetite.

Once the food arrived, though, it was a different story. Every course provided a new sensation for her taste buds. "This is wonderful," she told Bailey, who had planned the menu with Charley.

Bailey preened. "Wait till you taste dessert."

She hoped she had room. At the rate she was going, dessert on top of everything else could make her evening gown explode right off her.

Just before dessert, diners got an unexpected treat as a man knelt in front of a young woman and opened a small, black velvet box to reveal a diamond ring.

The woman's hand flew to her mouth and she nodded and all the other diners applauded.

"That's so sweet," Bailey gushed. "Are they locals? I don't recognize them."

"I don't think so," Samantha said.

"I'm going to go find out," Bailey announced.

"Bailey Sterling, girl detective," Samantha said, shaking her head as their sister swirled off.

"Well, he did propose in public," Cecily pointed out. "They're probably excited to share it with someone."

Sure enough. Bailey had barely introduced herself when the three fell into an animated conversation, and Bailey was buzzing with excitement when she returned to the table.

"They're from Seattle," she reported. "They came up just for the festival. How cool is that? And guess what?"

"They want you to be a bridesmaid," Samantha said.

Bailey frowned at her. "Very funny."

"What?" Cecily asked, playing along.

"She saw the lost bride. They went on one of those guided hikes and she actually saw the bride."

"That's just a legend," Samantha said dismissively.

"But she saw the bride and now she's engaged," Bailey insisted as if that settled everything.

"It's a fun story, but that's all," Samantha said. If it worked, she'd have had the perfect man proposing to her tonight, preferably one with lots of money.

Bailey sighed. "Sammy, sometimes you are a real doo-doo dump truck."

Fortunately, their dessert came and Bailey got distracted and the subject of the lost bride was abandoned.

But Samantha was now stuck with a vision of some faceless man (who looked like a tackling dummy in a suit—Blake Preston, aack!) slipping a fat diamond on her finger. *Some things are better than chocolate.*

No! Get out of my head.

But leave the chocolate.

Twenty-Three

The most wonderful thing about love is the mystery and surprise of it.
—Muriel Sterling, *Knowing Who You Are:*
One Woman's Journey

Cecily had seen the work in progress as her mother and Kevin and Heinrich created their gala event setting and been impressed by her mother's creativity, but seeing the finished product when she and her sisters entered Festival Hall made her jaw drop. The place had been transformed from an empty hall to a ballroom fit for a queen. White and gold ceiling drapes set the tone for elegance and, from all the tables along the side of the hall, magenta votive candles cast light on globe vases filled to overflowing with white roses. The chairs at the tables had been draped with silk grapevines. Votives and vines adorned the punch table, too. In strategic corners of the room, tall floor vases held branches and white flowers. The stage was a swirl of fabric and more floor vases and flowers, hiding the disk jockey, and a few people were already on the floor slow-dancing to music that seemed to float at her from all directions—Nat King Cole and his daughter, Natalie, crooning "Unforgettable."

Like this night would be for her sister, she hoped. Samantha had just donned her mask, a black-and-gold carnival mask Cecily had found for her in L.A. that let her hazel eyes peer out mysteriously. And she was grinning from ear to ear.

Samantha had worked so hard to make this weekend happen she deserved to savor the moment of success. Cecily couldn't shake the nasty feeling that the festival wasn't going to save them but she wasn't about to mention that to her sister. There was no sense in depressing her. She was out of fingernails to chew.

Bailey put on her mask and immediately skittered off to see an old friend and Samantha got waylaid by Ed York (hard to mistake that tall, skinny bod), so Cecily was left on her own to wander the edges of the hall, taking in the sights and sounds. For the next half hour she watched as eager dancers flooded in the door. How many tickets had they sold? Were they going to have more people in here than the room could hold? If they did, she hoped Fire Chief Berg didn't notice. He'd purchased a ticket so he was probably here somewhere.

Now the music had picked up to something a little faster, "Somebody Like You" by Keith Urban. Bill Will came up to her, all duded up in a cowboy shirt with pearl buttons and his best black jeans. He'd exchanged his cowboy hat for some goofy evil court-jester mask with a skull for a face.

"How about a dance?" he asked.

She barely had time to say, "Sure," before he swept her off into a fast country two-step.

What he lacked in grace, Bill Will made up for in enthusiasm, nearly taking out any dancers who happened to be in his path as they made their way around the floor. Maybe this wasn't such a good idea.

Then he stepped on her gown and she felt a rip. This really hadn't been a good idea.

"Shit," he muttered. "Gosh, I'm sorry, Cec—I mean, mystery lady. Damn."

She patted his arm. "It's okay, Mr. Jester. It could happen to anyone."

"Not to me. But hey, I'm used to dancing with girls wearing shorter dresses."

She just bet he was. "I think I've got a safety pin in my purse." Thankfully, she'd come prepared.

He nodded, making the pointed ends of his jester mask bob like big puppy ears, and she left him, probably with a beet-red face. There was another advantage of a masked ball. No one could see your embarrassment.

She managed to repair the gown with a couple of safety pins and went back to the perimeter of the party. It was safer to watch. Just as Bryan Adams began singing "When You Love Someone," she became aware of a large man in a *Phantom of the Opera*–style mask approaching. Luke.

"How's the dress?" he asked.

"Have you been watching me?" she teased.

"Busted. It's a slow dance. I promise not to make the rip bigger."

He held out a hand. It would have been rude not to take it so she did and let him lead her onto the floor. He put an arm around her, drew her gently to him and started them swaying. She felt the needle move on the zing-o-meter. Well, dancing this close to a hard male body, she'd have to be dead not to feel anything.

"You know, you're enough to take away a man's breath," he said.

"Luke, I'm not here looking for anything. After the festival…" What? She'd be gone. There wasn't anything here for her.

He smiled. He had a nice smile. "I wasn't looking for anything when I met my wife."

Oh, boy. She didn't like the way this conversation was going. "You're a nice man, Luke."

"So, I've been told. You looking for a bad boy, Cecily, is that it?"

"I told you, I'm not looking for anything."

He rubbed a hand up her back, sending a slow warmth pouring through her. "Does that mean you're not open to stumbling onto something good?"

"I…" Why was her mouth suddenly dry? "We wouldn't be a match."

He nodded slowly. "You know about those things, of course."

"I do," she said defensively.

"Tell you what. Let's make a deal. I won't push you but if you decide to stick around, you give me a chance to change your mind. Fair enough?"

"Not fair to you."

"I can deal with it," he said easily.

He pulled her just the slightest bit closer, making her very conscious of the fact that he was a male and she was a female. Then he put them into a slow spin and she was aware of her gown flaring out, of a strong arm around her, keeping her from falling backward, of the glimmer of candlelight and the soft wash of a love song. And a little voice whispered, *You could come home to stay.*

Samantha saw him moving toward her from clear across the room. He wore a black tux and a Venetian mask that covered his whole face. Of course, there was no disguising that big, football-player body. He didn't look like a banker as he walked toward her—more like James Bond on steroids—and the sequins in the mask glinted in the candlelight. She didn't want to dance with him. Yes, she did. No, she didn't.

You have to be polite, she told herself, settling the issue, so she stood there and tried to calm the ridiculous fluttering in her chest. "Hello, Blake," she greeted him.

He shook his head. "This is a masked ball, remember? Nobody knows anybody. I'm just a man who wants to dance with the most beautiful woman here."

Garth Brooks started crooning "To Make You Feel My Love" and before she could say anything more, Blake had hooked an arm around her and pulled her against him, turning her insides to lava. *Some things are better than chocolate.* Oh, jeez.

Keep your mind on business. "The ball is a great success."

"I don't want to talk about the ball," he said, his voice low. "I don't want to talk about anything. I just want to feel you."

She could certainly feel him and he felt good, all muscle and male energy. She was going to go limp and slide down into a puddle here on the floor. *Get a grip, Samantha.*

That wasn't hard to do when she remembered the position she was in with the bank. "Nicely said, considering the fact that you're about to put me out of business."

"I'm not your enemy, Samantha, no matter what you think."

She looked up at him. "Really? You could have fooled me."

He heaved a sigh. "Believe me, I don't like this situation."

"Neither do I," she said, drawing back to put some distance between them.

"Just for tonight, just for this one dance, let's forget about business," he said softly.

Forget about her family heritage, her future and all the people depending on her simply because he was dancing with her. What did he think she was? She knew what *he* was. The fire inside her went out with a hiss. "You really have your nerve. I'm about to lose everything and you expect me just to waltz around the floor in a daze with you."

"Samantha."

"That's not a Lone Ranger mask you're wearing and I can't be a hypocrite and dance with you," she said.

In fact, she couldn't stay here and enjoy herself now. Every smile she managed would be fake. The song wasn't finished yet, but she pulled out of his arms and left the dance floor, anyway. The room was a kaleidoscope of color and beauty but all she saw was her future, dark and looming. She snatched her coat from the table where she'd put it and ran from the hall, the day's successes now nothing but ashes in her mouth.

She speed-walked back to her condo, drawing inquisitive stares from tourists. No wonder. She looked like a lost prom queen.

She was all the way home before she remembered that she'd never told her sisters she was leaving. Eventually, they'd realize she was missing and look for her, so she called Cecily's cell and left a message that she wasn't feeling well. Then she got out of her ball garb and into her jammies and went straight to bed, where Nibs was happy to join her.

"What am I going to do?" she asked as she scratched his chin.

Sadly, Nibs had no solution.

She slept little that night, mostly lay awake thinking

of all the people on her payroll, all the families who'd put their faith in Sweet Dreams. Had Blake really meant what he said? If he wasn't her enemy, then couldn't he be her ally? That thought brought her full circle to her original hope. Surely if she paid a big chunk on that bank loan he'd find a way to extend it.

It was a slim hope but it was the only one she had, the only solution her exhausted brain could come up with. She got up in time to see the sun rise over the mountains in a wash of orange and gold. A new day.

She made herself some oatmeal and then took a shower and felt better, so much better that she went out for an early-morning run along the Riverfront Park path. The morning was crisp and clear, a perfect day. Coming home she heard Gerhardt Geissel blowing his alpen horn over at Gerhardt's Gasthaus, his normal weekend ritual. Later in the morning, the church bells would ring at Icicle Falls Community Church, calling residents to prayer. By the time the bells rang, she'd be working the Sweet Dreams booth, praying like crazy that they'd sell a fortune in chocolate.

Her cell phone rang at nine. Cecily. "I called to see how you're doing. Are you still sick?"

"I'm fine now." And determined once more. After all, what other choice did she have? Quitting wasn't an option.

"You sure? 'Cause Mom and Bailey and I can work the booth if you don't feel well."

"No, I'll be there," Samantha said. "How was the ball last night?"

"A raging success."

"I hope Bailey didn't go wandering off with Brandon Wallace." She should have stayed to watch over her sister.

"She didn't wander off with anyone. Anyway, too many other men were keeping her busy on the dance floor for him to have much access to her."

"That's a good thing," Samantha said. "And how about you? How many men did you dance with?"

"I lost count."

"Anyone in particular?" Samantha had seen how Luke Goodman looked at her sister. Cecily would be a fool to pass him up. Of course, when it came to her love life, Cecily had no sense. Why was it a woman couldn't ever see what was right in front of her face?

"No," Cecily said airily. And then, before Samantha could pry further, she added, "So, Mom says she'll meet you at the booth at ten. I'll show up at one with Bailey." End of conversation.

"Okay," Samantha said, taking the hint. She didn't know why she was poking around in her sister's business, anyway. She had enough on her hands with her own.

She drank a cup of coffee and then walked out the door. Center Street was already full of people, many of them wearing crazy Cat in the Hat stovepipe hats and other creative headgear from the Mad Hatter. She passed young families, groups of girlfriends obviously enjoying a girls' weekend and couples strolling hand in hand. The ice rink was doing a brisk business, too, with lots of children and teenagers skating in wild circles around the more sedate older people. This was how Icicle Falls was supposed to look, and she'd helped make it happen.

She was smiling by the time she got to the Sweet Dreams booth, and she kept the smile all morning as she and her mother took money and handed out chocolate bliss. The crowds continued to swell.

"I think there are more people here today than there

were yesterday," Bailey said when she and Cecily showed up to take over the booth.

"The more, the better," Samantha said. "We're low on inventory. I'll run over to the shop and get it."

What a wonderful errand to be running—off to get more chocolates so they could sell more and make more. Oh, yes, there was hope. There was always hope. Never give up, never give in.

She was halfway down the street when she spotted him. Her smile fell off and her heart plummeted into her boots. This was how Little Red Riding Hood felt when she stood by her granny's bedside and realized that the granny with the big teeth wasn't really Granny. *The better to eat you with, my dear.* Trevor Brown strolled along the street with the other bank snake, what's-his-name, hands in his pockets, surveying the whole party like a king observing his subjects. Of course he was up here spying, probably figuring he'd organize a festival, too, once he owned her company.

Well, he wasn't going to own it. She'd blow it up before she let that cheap candy maker get his greedy paws on it. Jaw set, she marched to the warehouse and grabbed a case of their salted caramels and one of their sampler boxes, as well as the last of their four-seaters. Then she set the whole mess on a dolly and made her way back to the booth.

And there he was, right in front of it, chatting up her baby sister.

She narrowed her eyes and entered the booth to stand next to Bailey. "Mr. Brown, what brings you up here?" As if she didn't know.

He smiled at her. "Just thought I'd check it out. You've done a great job of pulling this festival together."

"Thank you," she said stiffly. "I couldn't have done

it without the rest of the town. We all pull together in Icicle Falls."

"Do you?"

She raised her chin a notch. "Yes, we do." Now she shifted her gaze to Blake's boss. "That's how we've always worked here."

"That so?" he said. "Well, let's try some of your chocolate. What do you recommend?"

That you go jump in the river.

"They're all delicious," Bailey said, clueless that she was talking to the enemy. "Try the salted caramels. They're sweet but they have a bite."

"Actually, I think we're out," Samantha said coldly.

"No, we're not, Sammy," Bailey said. "You're just in time, though," she informed the men, "because we are running low."

"How much?" Trevor Brown asked.

As if he couldn't tell. It was listed on the sign hanging behind them.

Bailey told him and he passed her the money.

"I'll take one, too," said his evil companion.

I hope you choke on it, Samantha thought as Bailey gave a caramel to him, too. "We make the best chocolate in the state," she insisted. "One taste should be enough to show you what a good investment we are. For the bank," she added. *Not you, Trevor Brown.*

"Pretty good," said Bank Snake #2.

Pretty good? That was all he had to say? Pathetic.

"You make a good candy," Trevor told her.

Better than yours. Samantha stretched her lips as far as they would go, which was about half a smile.

Now Trevor was studying the rest of their candy. "Lavender fudge, huh? Interesting."

Okay, enough was enough. "I'm sure you want to go

visit the other booths," Samantha said before he could continue his candy espionage. "Enjoy the festival." She turned her back on them. "Bailey, can you unload those cases?"

Bailey sent her a funny look but said, "Okay."

"Give her a hand, Cec," Samantha asked Cecily. *There. Get the message, you vultures? Get lost!*

They moved away, like wolves just waiting for the campers' fire to die down. Samantha suddenly felt sick.

"Who were those guys?" Bailey asked in a low voice as they unpacked the cases.

"The older one is Trevor Brown."

Bailey's brows knit. "Trevor…"

"From Madame C's Chocolates."

Bailey gasped. "We just gave candy to Madame C? Yikes! Who was the other guy?"

"A big bank mucky-muck."

"Bigger than Blake Preston?"

"Blake is his lapdog."

Bailey hung her head. "And here I was, talking away to them like they were nice. Gosh, I'm a dope."

Cecily patted her arm. "You didn't know."

"But now you do," Samantha said. "If they come back, tell them we're sold out."

"Or that we don't serve their kind here." Bailey produced a wicked grin. "We're prejudiced against creeps."

And creeps they were. Their very presence in town gave Samantha the willies, so instead of wandering around and visiting with various pals from the Chamber of Commerce, she went to the office to hide out.

She had plenty to do there, but no amount of work could take her mind off her troubles. They stayed right there at her desk with her and that night they went to bed with her, crowding her mind as she squeezed her eyes shut and tried to sleep. Finally, after two mugs of warm milk (yuck!) she drifted off.

She slept soundly for a while, but then she entered the gates of dreamland and found herself running down Center Street. It was deserted except for her and two men—Trevor Brown and his thug from the bank, and they had guns aimed at her.

"You may as well stop running, Samantha," Trevor shouted. "We're going to get your business one way or another."

"No," she cried, and kept on racing down the cobbled street. She turned the corner onto Mountain Vale, where her condo was, and dashed up the steps to her door. The men were on her heels but somewhere along the way they'd morphed into big, slobbering wolves and they were growling. She slammed the door in their faces. "You'll never get me!"

She stumbled into her kitchen, which was unusually well stocked, and started pulling out ingredients. She got down her double boiler from the cupboard and stood staring at it. "What am I doing?" she asked herself.

"You're saving your company," a soft female voice said. "And I'm going to help you."

Lo and behold, there was a ghost dancing at her elbow. The woman was young, with chestnut-brown hair and vintage clothes, and Samantha recognized her from one of the pictures that hung on the Sweet Dreams office wall. *Great-grandma Rose.*

"I hope that's good quality," Great-grandma said, pointing to the block of white chocolate Samantha had set on her counter.

"Of course it is," Samantha said. "You know we only use the best ingredients."

Great-grandma nodded in approval. "Now, get out the rose water and let's get to work."

And so they did.

And when Samantha awoke she blinked in amazement. It was a first, a wonderful miraculous first! She had just dreamed up new recipes for Sweet Dreams. And she remembered them. A miracle!

She threw off the covers and ran to her computer to get everything down before the details drifted away from her. Then she checked the time. It was only eight, but lucky for her Safeway opened at eight.

She didn't bother to dress, just threw on a coat over her pajamas, slipped her feet into boots and dashed out the door to get cream and butter. No wolves waiting outside for her on this bright, beautiful morning. Only opportunity.

Twenty-Four

Family is the one blessing we sometimes forget
to count.

—Muriel Sterling, *When Family Matters*

By midmorning Samantha had three new confections
to add to the Sweet Dreams catalog. She was buzzing
and not just from sugar. *She'd done it*. She'd actually
done it, dreamed up a new candy exactly like Great-
grandma Rose.

Her cell phone rang. It was Cecily. "I just made a
fat deposit."

Fat was right. The number Cecily gave her was impressively high. Not high enough to pay off the bank,
but surely high enough to impress Blake and his band
of vultures. Oh, what a great morning!

"And I just made three new candies," Samantha
crowed.

"Seriously?"

"Seriously. I'll get a shower, then meet you at Mom's
and we can all try them."

"I'll tell Bailey. She was about to go to Olivia's for
tea."

A chance to drool over Brandon. Samantha had called
in the nick of time.

She carefully packed up samples of her new creations,
then remembered to call the office and tell Elena she'd
come in after lunch.

"You'd better," Elena said. "So many people have called this morning to talk about the festival. My ear hurts and I am getting no work done."

"You're a gem. Have I told you that recently?"

"No, but this I already know," Elena said, and Samantha could hear the smile in her voice.

"Go help yourself to some caramels and take a break," Samantha offered. "Oh, wait. Save your taste buds. I'll bring you something new when I come in."

"New?" Elena was intrigued now.

"We have new recipes," Samantha announced proudly. And maybe even one that would put them on the map.

"Why are you wasting time talking on the phone? Hurry up and get here."

Samantha smiled as she ended the call. Oh, yes, she could build some buzz with this.

At the house, her sisters and mother were waiting eagerly. "Oh, my gosh, this is so exciting," Bailey said as Samantha opened the little box.

"They're lovely," Mom said reverently.

Yes, they were. White-and-dark-chocolate truffles topped with a delicate pink rosebud. "First I give you the chocolate rose," said Samantha.

They all took one and she watched as her family bit into them. Cecily's eyes widened in surprise. "This is incredible."

"Oh," Bailey moaned. "I'm having a chocolate orgasm."

Mom frowned at her, then turned to Samantha. "It's lovely, a wonderful tribute to your great-grandmother."

"It was the least I could do," Samantha said, and told them about her dream.

"Wow," breathed Bailey. "That is so awesome. What's this one?" she asked, pointing to another candy.

"Cleanse your palettes," Samantha reminded them, producing a baguette.

The next goody paired milk chocolate and lavender. "This is lovely, too," Mom approved.

The final treat in the trio was yet another floral, and all three of the Sterling women gave it a resounding thumbs-up. "We've got a winner," Cecily said. "Three winners. We could put these in a pretty floral box and call it the chocolate garden."

"Oh, I love that!" Bailey cried. She snapped her fingers. "I need to give these to Caroline. The minute she tastes one, she'll want Mimi's producer to try them."

"Mimi LeGrande?" Mom asked.

"Bailey met someone who knows her producer," Cecily explained.

"Oh, my goodness," Mom said faintly.

It was their last chance to pull out of the red. And the clock was ticking. Samantha had no intention of waiting around for the alarm to go off. "We need to get you on a flight right away," she said, and went up to Mom's upstairs office to make arrangements.

"I'll go pack," Bailey said.

They got Bailey out on a late-afternoon flight and while Cecily ran her to the airport, Samantha went to the bank to hand-deliver a check to Blake. It wasn't for the full amount they owed, of course, but it made a sizable dent.

"Very impressive," he said when he looked at it.

"Does it impress you enough to convince you to bend the rules? We're on the verge of getting a spot on a big show on the Food Network."

Lying wasn't a good business principle, but Samantha

decided she wasn't so much lying as making a prediction. If they got themselves featured on *All Things Chocolate,* they were golden. And why shouldn't they? Bailey had an in with the producer's cousin. The chocolates were incredible. Mimi LeGrande would be all over this.

Blake let out a sigh and looked at her steadily. "I told you, I'm on your side, and believe me, I've argued your case. But there are some things I can't control, and this is one of them."

"It's a poor way to do business," she informed him.

His jaw tightened. "It's the way I have to do business. I'm locked in, Samantha. I don't own this bank. I only work for it."

As its henchman. "How do you sleep nights?" she asked in disgust.

"These days? Not so well."

"That's a comfort."

He frowned and shook his head. "Look, there's got to be some way we can get the bank out of this. Isn't there some family member who can help you?"

"You're kidding, right?" she said bitterly. What family member would that be? Her mother, who was upside down on her house and had no life insurance money? Her sisters, who were nearly as broke as she was? Maybe Uncle Ralph, Dad's older brother who was off in the Florida Keys, living on retirement and working part-time on a fishing boat. *How dumb do you think I am?* "If I knew someone with that kind of money I wouldn't have come to the bank in the first place." She could feel her eyes filling with tears and blinked furiously to drive them away.

Blake took a deep breath. "I can barely imagine what you're going through right now, but I want you to consider something."

She was already considering something—how wrong this all was.

"Let's say when you got back to your office one of your employees came to you and told you she's about to lose her house. She owes three months' rent and she asks you to pay it. What do you do?"

"I give her the money to pay it, of course," Samantha snapped, in no mood for a business parable.

"Do you?" Blake countered. "But you have no money. It's not in your power to help her."

"Then I…" Samantha stumbled to a stop. What *would* she do?

"Would you take money from your struggling company, jeopardize your other employees?" Blake pressed.

He didn't have to say any more. She got the point. She dropped her gaze, trying to hide the tears that were escaping in spite of her effort to hold them back.

"Samantha," he said softly, and reached across his desk to lay a hand on her arm.

Here she was in enemy territory, and yet that big hand felt comforting. Pathetic.

"Don't think this isn't tearing me up inside," he said.

Then why can't you help me? She didn't voice the thought. He'd just told her why. He had obligations of his own, other people to answer to, other people depending on him. It wasn't his job to save her and clean up her mess. She'd known that all along, deep down, where she didn't want to look.

She should say…something. But it was hard to talk around the lump in her throat so she simply nodded.

"I wish I could help," he said. "If anyone deserves a break it's you. If I owned the bank we'd be having a very different conversation."

She stood wearily. "We still have sixteen days."

He stood, too. "Anything can happen in sixteen days."

Yes, she thought as she walked out of the bank. Anything could.

And something would, she told herself, determined to be positive. They'd get their eleventh-hour rescue. Bailey's new friend would pass on the chocolates and Mimi LeGrande would love them. How could she not? Samantha's dream had been a sign and a gift. They were going to pull out of this.

On that upbeat note she went to the office to catch up on calls and prepare for success.

Blake stared unseeing at his computer screen. He wished he'd told Samantha about the things he'd done behind the scenes to try and help her. Then maybe he wouldn't have felt so useless when he looked into those big tear-filled eyes.

Except he'd probably have come off as an incompetent braggart. So what if he'd moved things along for the permits? Big deal that he'd gone to Seattle and done some schmoozing with the paper and that producer. None of it had paid her loan. He was all talk and no action.

"I hate being impotent," he muttered.

He heard a nervous cough and the rustling of papers and turned to see his secretary, Sheri.

"I know a good doctor," she said, her cheeks pink.

Great, just great.

"Que bonita!" Elena exclaimed when Samantha gave her a sample. Elena tasted the chocolate rose truffle and closed her eyes in ecstasy. "Ah, *chica,* this is going to sell like crazy."

"That would be fine with me," Samantha said. All they needed was a nod from Mimi LeGrande. And how could they *not* get it once she tasted those chocolates?

Samantha went into her office, sat down at her desk and looked over at the family pictures on the wall. "We're going to make it, everyone," she assured them. Then she booted up her computer and got to work.

She was still there when Bailey called.

"Oh, Sammy," her sister wailed.

This was not the way to announce good news. Samantha's stomach tensed.

"I'm so sorry."

"Sorry about what? What's happened?"

"The…the…candy," Bailey sobbed.

Oh, no. Samantha braced herself. "What happened to the candy?"

"I—I… Ohhhh."

Shit. "You what?" Samantha prompted. Did she really want to hear the gory details?

"I dropped them."

"You…dropped them." Surely one or two had survived. "Well, brush them off and—"

"And they got run over."

"They what?" Samantha asked weakly.

"I was on my way to baggage claim and showing them to this nice older man I met and, well, I just don't know how they fell."

With her sister the klutz it wasn't hard to imagine.

"Anyway, they kind of skidded across the floor and before I could get them…" Bailey started wailing again.

"It's okay," Samantha lied. "What exactly happened?"

"You know those carts they drive people around the airport with?"

Samantha was glad she was sitting down. "One of them ran over the chocolates," she said dully.

"Squashed them flat. Oh, Sammy, I'm so sorry."

"It's okay," Samantha said even though it wasn't remotely okay.

"Send down another box," Bailey begged. "I promise I won't drop it."

Samantha heaved a pained sigh. If you wanted anything done you had to do it yourself. "Never mind. I'm coming down," she decided. "And we're skipping the middleman. Find out where Mimi LeGrande eats. We're bringing her chocolate for dessert."

"Okay," Bailey said, and sniffed. "Sammy, I really am sorry."

"I know you are," Samantha said, and thought, *Never send a girl to do a woman's job.*

She had barely ended the call when Cecily's ringtone started.

"What are you, psychic?" Samantha answered.

"Are you okay?"

"Bailey called you?" She couldn't have already. They'd hardly finished their conversation.

"Yes."

And then it dawned on Samantha. "She called you first."

"She was afraid to tell you."

Afraid of her big, bad sister. "Am I that much of an ogre?"

"No," Cecily said. "But she felt so bad."

"It's not her fault really," Samantha said. "I should have gone myself."

"No. You were right to delegate."

"Not on something this important." And not to Bailey.

"You can't do everything yourself. You need people in your corner."

To sit on you when you're down.

"What's our next move?" Cecily asked.

"My next move. I'm making a fresh batch of candy and taking it down tomorrow." Another hit on her poor credit card, but a girl had to do what a girl had to do.

"Do you want me to go with you?"

"No. I appreciate the offer, but I'm fine on my own." The last thing she needed was any more help.

"Okay. By the way, I ran into Emily Brookes."

Pissy's underling. What did that have to do with anything? "And?"

"Well, remember how those permits for the festival suddenly came through? You'll never guess who was behind it."

"Pissy," Samantha cracked. That would be the day.

"Blake Preston."

Samantha nearly dropped the phone.

"After I learned that, I got to thinking and I did a little poking around, made a couple of calls," Cecily continued. "Remember how I was getting no response from the producer of *Northwest Now?* Well, guess who went over to Seattle and tracked her down and talked to her in person."

Not… "Blake?"

"Yep. He was also behind that article in the Seattle paper."

"Oh," Samantha said weakly.

"Yeah, oh," Cecily said. "I saw when you left the ball."

Oh, boy. Here came a well-deserved lecture from her sister the matchmaker. "I didn't feel good," Samantha lied. That was nothing compared to how she felt now. Shame coated her heart.

"Maybe you felt more than you wanted," Cecily countered. "Anyway, I thought you ought to know."

Samantha said goodbye and sat at her desk, staring out the window at the gray sky. The weatherman was forecasting heavy snowfall for the following afternoon. Finally. She'd be long over the pass and at the airport by the time it hit, but first she'd have to stop by the bank to deliver a peace offering.

People weren't all good or all bad. Blake was no cartoon villain, but he'd made a great scapegoat. So had Waldo. She'd sure made a habit of blaming other people for her problems—ironic considering the fact that she liked to manage everything and everyone.

She pushed away from her desk with a sigh. Tomorrow was Valentine's Day. *Oh, Cupid, please be kind to me. I could use some help.*

It wasn't easy going into the bank the following day feeling like a fool who had to eat an entire humble pie, but Samantha did it, anyway. Blake saw her coming. He ran a hand along his shirt collar like a man preparing for something unpleasant—hardly surprising in light of their previous encounters.

She sat down across from him and pushed a box of her newest creations across his desk. "I need to thank you."

He looked at her warily. "For what?"

"I just learned about some of the things you've been doing behind the scenes. I'm sorry I was so awful to you."

He shrugged. "I'm sorry I couldn't do more."

"You did a lot. You could have said something."

"Would it have made a difference?"

As in, could they have gone out, become an item? If they'd slept together would it still have been like sleeping with the enemy? "I don't know," she said honestly. In the end his bank still wanted to swallow her company. She wasn't sure she could get around that.

He nodded slowly.

"That's our newest product," she said, indicating the box. "It's pretty amazing stuff."

"I'm sure it is," he said.

"I'm off to L.A. to see Mimi LeGrande."

He gave her a look that asked, *Who is that?*

"She's the host of *All Things Chocolate,* the show on the Food Network that I mentioned yesterday. I don't have to tell you what that'll do for our business if she features us."

"I hope it does great things for you," he said.

She smiled at him. "I believe you do," she said, and stood.

He stood, too. "Good luck. And happy Valentine's Day."

Oh, yeah. That.

"Let me walk you out."

Once they were outside the bank and at her car, he said, "Maybe, when you get back, we could—"

She shook her head before he could even finish the sentence. "I'm sorry, I can't. Not until I know my company's safe."

He nodded. "I understand."

She was tempted to add, *But I want to. I wish you were a plumber or a carpenter, anything but my banker.* Instead, she got in her car and drove away.

Blake went back into the bank and sat down heavily at his desk. Samantha's gift mocked him. Chocolate, just what he always never wanted. He'd been getting a lot of things he didn't want ever since he came back to Icicle Falls—stress, aggravation, headaches and rebuffs from the woman whose life he was helping to ruin.

Damn it all, he didn't *want* to ruin her life. He wanted to be part of it. He could hardly concentrate as he reviewed George Tuttle's loan application, and he had a hard time putting on his bank-PR-guy face when he took Del Stone and Ed York to lunch at Zelda's. When their waitress suggested they try the new chocolate truffle trifle that had been a hit over the weekend and was now on the menu, he felt as if his heart would crack.

After lunch his grandmother stopped by and he gave her the chocolates. At least someone would enjoy them. Gram was free of both allergies and guilt.

"Lovely," she said. "I'll take them to my book club meeting tonight. They're bound to be a hit. Everyone loves Sweet Dreams chocolates."

She sounded like a commercial. *Everyone loves Sweet Dreams chocolates.* Which meant no one would love him when he called in their note—and he'd be at the head of that line.

At six he went to Bruisers to work off his frustration, running the treadmill until the sweat poured off him. The anger, however, remained. He did a round with the punching bag but even that didn't help. He didn't want to punch something. He wanted to punch someone, namely that prick Darren Short. He went another round, envisioning Darren's smug face at the top of the bag. *Now you know how it feels to be sucker punched. You did as much to the Sterlings.*

Blake was good and tired by the time he got done but he didn't feel any better. Samantha Sterling was going to go down the tubes unless somebody came to her rescue. She needed a hero.

He remembered how, as a kid, he'd envisioned himself all grown up with a superhero's muscles (and a cape, of course), flying off to save people about to be taken down by bad guys or rushing to the rescue in the Batmobile.

All he had was a vintage Camero and a business suit, but he needed to find a way to be the hero he'd always wanted to be. Before it was too late.

Twenty-Five

There's nothing a woman can't accomplish if she
sets her mind to it.

> —Muriel Sterling, *Knowing Who You Are:*
> *One Woman's Journey*

"Muriel, thanks for letting me have an exclusive. I
know we can sell this place," Nenita Einhausen from
Mountain Meadows Real Estate said. "I can already
think of a couple of families who might be interested."

"Even this time of year?" Muriel asked. "I didn't
think people would be looking before spring." Not that
she could afford to wait until spring.

"Spring is right around the corner," Nenita said. "And
I have a family who's anxious to get out of the city and
live in a small town. This would be perfect for them."

It would be perfect for anyone. It had been perfect
for her and Waldo.

Letting go was hard. Her life was picking up speed
like a roller coaster running through a house of horrors.
Waldo's death, the troubles with the business, now losing her house—she hoped this nasty ride would level
out soon.

"We don't need to do too much to stage it," Nenita
continued. She set her cup on the coffee table and began
walking around inspecting everything, a skinny little
bundle of energy in a black suit. "I'm sure you remember what we did when we sold the other house. We'll

have to take down some of the family pictures, put away a few of those knickknacks."

Muriel's family memories and beloved treasures. Who didn't like Hummel figurines, for heaven's sake?

This wasn't coming as news; she'd done it before. But when she'd put her other house up for sale she'd had Waldo. She'd been saying goodbye to a place filled with wonderful memories but she'd been moving on to make new ones. This time she was just moving.

"And…oh." Nenita stopped to take in the fireplace and the urn with Waldo's ashes sitting on the hearth. "Is that— Are those…?"

Muriel nodded. "Yes, that's Waldo." Her sweet, wonderful husband.

"Well, I know how much you loved him but maybe you could, er, find somewhere else to keep him. Just while we're showing the house," Nenita added quickly.

"Where would you have me put him, in storage?" Muriel asked with some asperity. But she knew Nenita was right. Encountering Waldo's remains would be off-putting to potential buyers. "I'm sorry. That was rude. I'll find someplace more private for him."

"I'm sure he'd understand."

Muriel picked up the urn and clutched it to her. Poor Waldo. Poor, poor Waldo. "I'll bring him to the cemetery." She hadn't been ready to do that yet, but she hadn't been ready to sell her house, either. Some things a woman had to do, ready or not.

"Good idea," Nenita said. "I'll get some photos of the outside of the house. Meanwhile, why don't you take down a few pictures and start a fire in the fireplace. That will give us a nice shot of the living room. The kitchen looks great as it is. I'll get a shot of that, too. Oh, and the bedrooms."

It was a good thing Muriel had made the bed.

"I'll put this up on the site tomorrow and it will be in the multiple listings by the end of the week. I'm positive we'll get a lot of interest," she said as she fished her camera out of her purse.

A lot of interest. That's what you want, Muriel reminded herself. Soon the house would listen to a new family's laughter, some other woman's pies would cool on the kitchen counter, another woman's Christmas tree would sit in the corner by the window next year. That was how life went.

Moving can be an adventure, she told herself, and hoped she knew what she was talking about.

Samantha was off to save the company and Mom was recovering from her meeting with the real estate agent by going out to dinner with friends. Cecily had the night off and was at loose ends. They'd finally gotten snow during the afternoon and since she hadn't enjoyed a stroll in the snow since she moved to L.A. she decided some outdoor exercise was in order.

She borrowed a pair of boots from Mom's closet and set out to enjoy the crisp, cold air that came with new-fallen snow. With mountain slopes right in her backyard, Cecily had skied since she was three. She loved the feel of the wind in her face when she whooshed downhill and she liked the beauty of cross-country skiing. But she also enjoyed a quiet walk once in a while, and after the craziness of the festival it was nice to have some downtime.

The houses she passed reminded her of Kinkade paintings, all snugged in by snow with lights spilling out from inside, where families ate their dinners or watched TV. Downtown looked like something out of a fairy tale with its Bavarian-style buildings all iced with snow. A few lazy flakes danced to the ground, spotlighted by the old-fashioned lampposts. She ambled on aimlessly, enjoying the quiet.

But suddenly it wasn't so quiet. Fierce barking shocked her out of her reverie and she realized she was on the edge of town. And she had a welcoming committee. From out of nowhere a pit bull came running toward her, barking fiercely. Cecily had been bitten by a dog as a child, and she'd never gotten over her distrust. This approaching animal inspired more than distrust. Terror made her freeze in her tracks as it ran up to her, spilling over with doggy animosity. The dog stopped, too, and put on a real show, slavering and snarling.

A mere parking lot away was sanctuary, Todd Black's Man Cave. If she could get to it. But she couldn't. She was glued to the snowy ground. And all the while the beast stood there, feeding on her fear. It was dinnertime. He was probably hungry. No-o-o. She could feel her heart banging around in her rib cage.

"Elmo!" a sharp voice called. A moment later a man came into sight. He was wearing a parka over jeans and combat boots. "Elmo, damn it, heel."

The dog gave Cecily a goodbye growl and trotted over to its master.

"Sorry, lady, he got out of the truck," the man said.

Cecily could barely hear him past the ringing in her ears. Little bells. Sleigh bells? She felt light-headed. Next thing she knew she was falling and she couldn't seem to stop herself. Hey, who put out the lights?

Now she was in the dark and the little bells were still ringing. She was vaguely aware of male voices and strong arms picking her up. She could hear other voices and music, Gretchen Wilson singing "Here for the Party." Was this a party? When were the lights going to come back on?

She could feel herself being stretched out on a couch and a familiar voice saying, "Get me some 7-Up."

Slowly the light began to return and a face swam into view. Todd Black?

He grinned. "Welcome back."

"Where's the dog?" she asked weakly.

"Back in Sam's truck. By the way, he's really sorry."

"That thing almost ate me for dinner," Cecily said, struggling to sit up.

Todd gently pushed her down. "Why don't you give yourself a minute?" Another man appeared with a pop can. "Come on, dude. Where's the glass?" Todd said with a frown.

"Oh. Sorry," the guy said, and disappeared.

"So what were you doing out in my neck of the woods?" asked Todd. "Coming by for a drink?"

Now she did sit up. "No." Oh, that made her head spin.

"I told you not to do that," he said, easing her down again.

The close contact tickled her nose with a hint of aftershave and just plain old musky male. That is not a turn-on, she told herself firmly. She tried to ignore the man sitting next to her and instead took in her surroundings. The room wasn't big, but big enough to hold an old desk with a laptop computer on it and a sturdy chair behind it, a filing cabinet and this beat-up leather couch she was on. A library lamp on the desk and faint light wandering in from a nearby streetlight were only enough to leave their corner of the room in semidarkness.

The other man, Todd's bartender, had returned with

a glass filled with ice. Todd took it, popped the top on the can and poured in the soda. "Here," he said, holding it out to her. "This should help."

"Thanks," she murmured. It did. The bartender slipped out of the room, quiet as a shadow, and she laid her head back against the sofa pillow.

"So, I hear your festival was a big success," Todd said.

"Yes, it was."

"Bill Will said he danced with you at the ball."

Cecily found herself smiling at the memory of that disastrous dance.

Todd frowned. "He can't have been that great a dancer."

"I didn't say he was."

"I won a dance contest once."

"No way," she scoffed.

He nodded. "Oh, yeah. I had a girlfriend who was into it."

She couldn't resist asking, "What kind of dancing?" *Dirty?*

"Salsa. Ever salsa dance?" He took a slug out of what remained in the pop can. Now why was that sexy?

She'd wanted to—had meant to—take lessons. "I've been busy doing other things," she said, and realized she sounded prissy.

"You'd like it." He looked at her from under slightly lowered lids. It was an intimate gaze, fitting with the dimly lit room. "But tango is the best, almost like having sex on the dance floor."

"Well, I'll have to try it sometime." Her mouth suddenly felt dry and she drank a sip of her pop.

The music out in the bar had softened, some sort of love song. She needed to get home.

He leaned over, his mouth so close that his breath raced around her ear. "I could show you now."

She turned her head and that brought them nearly mouth to mouth. "Um."

Aack! What was she doing here like a fish about to chomp on a lure? Todd Black was not her type. Well, okay, he *was* her type, but that was the problem. She needed to change her taste in men.

She moved her lips out of range and swung her legs over the side of the beat-up leather couch. "I don't think so. I've had about all the excitement I can stand for one day."

He gave a snort. "Okay. I'll take you home."

"I can walk."

"Hoping to see Elmo again?"

"Take me home."

He grinned. "Thought so."

First that little chat in his dark office, now the intimacy of his car—she should have taken her chances with Elmo and walked. This close proximity was giving her the jitters.

"So, the festival's over now, everyone's made a pot of money. What next?" he said. "Are you off to L.A. to match up lonely hearts?"

There was a depressing prospect. She didn't bother to reply.

"Small towns aren't so bad, you know. Lots of interesting people wind up in small towns. Guys who can dance, for instance."

"A lot of guys can dance," she said dampeningly.

"Not like me."

She turned from staring out the car window to take in that perfect square chin and that cocky expression. "How many girls have you danced with?"

"Enough." He grinned at her again. "You do like to… dance, don't you?"

"I've danced some."

"Why are you in such a hurry to leave Icicle Falls?"

"It's time."

"Yeah, I guess small towns can be a little scary. You get close to people fast in a place like this. Easier to hide in the big city."

"What is that supposed to mean?"

"Nothing."

"Oh, brother," she said in disgust. "You know what else small towns offer? Amateur shrinks and men who are bored and need a new skirt to chase."

"Oh? And which one of those am I?"

"Both," she said. They were on her street now. "Thanks for the ride. You can let me out here."

The LAMs had much to discuss at dinner, the chocolate festival being the main topic of conversation. All agreed it was a smashing success and Muriel received kudos for the fabulous decorations at both the ball and the tea.

"You've got a gift for that creative stuff," said Dot. "But tell us, how are you coming with mastering your finances?"

"Well," Muriel said, "I think I'm making progress thanks to Pat. I'm sure you were shocked by how ignorant I was."

"Not at all." Pat shook her head. "It's understandable, considering the fact that you were never the one handling the finances."

"I let Duncan handle our finances when we were first married," Dot said. "He went out for dog food one day and came home with a truck we couldn't afford, and that was the end of that. Afterward he got an allowance. The man was hopeless when it came to money."

The blood drained from Muriel's face as she had a sudden vision of her hopeless self going out and doing something equally dumb.

"You'll be fine," Pat said reassuringly.

"I hope so," Muriel said. "We put all my bills on a spreadsheet so I can go through and check them off as I pay them every month," she told the others. "So I'm organized, but I need money. I got a small royalty check, thank God, so I could make my house payment this month, but I know I can't go on like this. Nenita was just over. I'm going to put my house up for sale."

"Oh, no," Olivia protested. "You and Waldo loved that house."

"No, Waldo loved that house. It was going to be ours together, but without him there's no need to stay."

"If you can sell the house and get out from under, it'll be great," Pat said.

She appeared so well-put-together sitting there in her jeans and crisp white blouse topped with a forest-green blazer and scarf. Pat had seemed to float easily into widowhood, like a butterfly landing on a down comforter.

Muriel, on the other hand, had been like a bug on the windshield. But whose fault was that? She'd happily let someone else run her financial life. She'd never worried about where the money came from or where it went. That big cosmic windshield had been heading toward her for a long time. It really was a miracle she hadn't hit it before now.

"If only I'd paid more attention to money," she lamented.

"If shit didn't happen there'd be no need for toilets," Dot said.

Olivia wrinkled her nose. "What is that supposed to mean?"

"It means stuff's going to happen," Dot said. "You can't be prepared for everything. I don't care what the Boy Scouts say."

"Will you have enough money left after you sell the house to buy another?" Olivia asked Muriel.

She'd be broke. She shook her head. "I'll find some place to rent." At least she hoped she would.

"We don't have very many rentals here in town," Dot said.

"You could have a room at my place," Olivia offered.

Muriel had never thought she'd be down to one room until she was an old woman in a nursing home. But she'd also never envisioned herself practically penniless. Even with selling her house she'd be on a tight budget. If she'd spent the money her first husband had left her more wisely instead of dribbling it away with Waldo, she wouldn't be in this position now. Still, she had time to make changes that would improve her life. She'd take that room. It beat having to become a burden to any of her daughters, none of whom was really in a position to help her.

This was the beauty of having friends. They saved you from so much humiliation. "Thank you," she murmured.

"I have another idea," Pat said slowly. "You could rent the cottage."

"Your little guest house? But you use that for tourists," Muriel objected.

"It's empty half the year. I'd love a full-time tenant. Let me know if you need it. I'll give you a deal," Pat added with a smile. "It's small but you can't beat the view."

A lovely little vineyard with a mountain for a backdrop—the view would more than make up for the size of the place. And while it wouldn't be as big as her house, it was more than a room. Muriel felt as if a weight had been lifted from her. Selling the house would be hard, but she could do it. For the first time in her life she'd be living on her own and learning to stand on her own two feet. And that was a lesson well worth some discomfort.

"And meanwhile, tell me if you need money," Dot said.

What was it Muriel hadn't liked about Dot? She couldn't remember. "Thank you. Thank you, all of you."

Dot shrugged. "No need for thanks," she said. "LAMs stick together."

As the evening rolled on and the women shared their problems and their dreams, she couldn't help feeling that she had, somehow, turned a very big corner. She would be fine, if not immediately, eventually.

She wished she could say the same for the family company. That mess was her fault, too. What, oh, what was she going to do about that? She spent the rest of the evening only half listening to the conversation as she pondered this question. By dessert she'd come to the conclusion that there was nothing she could do—other than pray that Samantha succeeded in tracking down Mimi LeGrande.

Los Angeles. People lived here on purpose? Samantha thought as Bailey threaded her secondhand VW Bug in and out of traffic on their way down the freeway from LAX. "It's like being in an ant farm," she said, looking around.

"Yes, but it's warm," Bailey said.

"Warm and smoggy." Exactly like it had been the

last time she visited her sisters. What did they see in this place?

"But it's exciting, full of movie stars and swimming pools and palm trees. And there's the ocean, too."

It was just as smoggy and crowded there as it was everywhere else, in Samantha's opinion. And the traffic—how did her sister sit through this without gnawing off her arm? She didn't care how many palm trees they had here. She'd take her small mountain town and clean air over this mess any day. And it was nice to have four seasons. How long could a person look at palm trees without getting bored, anyway?

"There is one thing it's missing," Bailey said.

Only one? "What's that?"

"My family." Bailey sighed. "Sometimes I wonder why I came all the way down here."

"You listened to Mitzi and Bitzy," Samantha said. Bailey had been friends with the twins since grade school and when they decided to move to L.A. and become stars they'd painted a picture of glamour and success she couldn't resist. So far, neither sister was a star. One had landed a bit part in a B-movie. The other was waiting tables.

Bailey made a face. "You never liked them."

"Because they're airheads." Sheesh.

Bailey dropped the subject of Mitzi and Bitzy, instead saying, "It's still fun here, but I hate only getting to see you and Mom a couple times a year. Oh, well," she went on before Samantha could suggest she pack it in and come home, "when I'm a famous celebrity chef I'll fly you guys down whenever you want."

Which would be never. "And you can fly up to see us," Samantha said. If she was still in Icicle Falls. If she didn't have to move cross-country for a new job. The idea made her heart contract and she took a firm grip on the carton with the ice-packed box of candy sitting in her lap. There had been no taking this box out to show anyone.

"Absolutely," Bailey said. "Meanwhile, I've got great friends to keep me company."

Like Mitzi and Bitzy, the two most self-centered creatures on the planet? "Friends can't take the place of family. Family loves you no matter what." *Thank God*.

That got Bailey nibbling her lower lip as she zipped from lane to lane.

It was all Samantha could do not to cry, "Watch out!" and grab the wheel. Jeez, these people all drove like maniacs. Of course, that wouldn't bother her so much if *she* was driving. "Bailey! They're braking up ahead."

Bailey, who had been tailgating the red Corvette in front of her so closely the two vehicles could have mated, eased up on the gas. "I really am sorry about dropping the candy, Sammy."

"That could have happened to anyone," Samantha said. Especially Bailey, but her heart had been in the right place and Samantha wasn't about to make her feel any worse than she already did.

"But it didn't. It happened to me," Bailey said miserably. "I so wanted to be there for you, Sammy."

"You were," Samantha assured her. "And you still are, and I appreciate it."

Funny how she'd always had it in her head that her family needed her. Now, remembering the past few weeks, she realized that door swung both ways. Mom's kindness and creativity, Cecily's hard work, Bailey's unwavering confidence in her—they'd been a source of strength, a silent wind pushing her forward. She owed them all a debt of gratitude.

* * *

The next day they went to Spoonie's, the latest up-scale addition to restaurant row in Los Angeles. It featured soups, homemade breads and, for dessert, all manner of exotic ice cream flavors. Decor was simple and sweet. Wind chimes using vintage sterling spoons dangled from the ceiling, and spoon collections hung on the walls. Tables were covered with linen tablecloths and adorned with little vases holding silk daisies—a little bit of old-fashioned in a sophisticated city. The place was packed and even with reservations they got stuck at a table right by the kitchen. Bailey had to scoot her chair in close to the table to avoid getting hit when the kitchen door swung open.

Still, in all that crowd it wasn't hard to spot Mimi Le-Grande, a gamine, fortysomething woman with short, dark hair. There she sat, resplendent in jeans, a black sweater and her trademark gorgeous jewelry, talking with a man who could be either her producer or significant other. Samantha looked at Mimi's necklace, which consisted of pink and black pearls and crystals (probably Swarovski) and practically drooled. Or maybe she was just salivating over all that opportunity waiting across the room, sipping coffee.

"Good thing we got here when we did," Samantha said to Bailey. "Any later and we might have missed them."

"They're eating lunch kind of early." Bailey checked her phone. "It's only a little after noon."

Their waiter had come up to tell them about the specials when Bailey pointed and said, "Oh, my gosh. They're leaving. Quick!" She jumped up and pushed back her chair just as another waiter emerged from the kitchen bearing a large tray with a soup tureen and several bowls and, being Bailey, managed to bump into the tray.

Like a juggler balancing plates, the waiter wobbled to the side, trying to keep everything from sliding south.

He might have succeeded if Bailey hadn't reached out to help him steady the tray. "I'm so sorry," she said.

"I've got it." He tried to move out of range as everything slipped and slid.

"Look out!" their waiter called.

But it was too late. Yet another waiter came out of the kitchen with another tray laden with soup. The two servers did a millisecond do-si-do and then everything went to the floor with an impressive crash. And there stood Bailey, gaping in horror at the whole mess while Samantha sat on her side of the table, her whole face sizzling with mortification.

From across the room Mimi and her companion looked on with mild interest as they moved away from their table. *Ah, the peons are at it again.*

Oh, boy. This was not the way to influence a chocolate mover and shaker.

But it was the only way Samantha had. She took a deep breath, left Hurricane Bailey to deal with the disaster and hurried after Mimi.

She caught up to her at the door. "Ms. LeGrande!"

The woman turned and arched an eyebrow. *Do I know you?*

"It looks like you didn't have dessert," Samantha said. "My name is Samantha Sterling and my family owns Sweet Dreams Chocolates and I'd love to give you a complimentary sample." She held out the box, all wrapped in pink ribbon, giving Mimi no choice (if she had any manners at all) but to take it.

Mimi took the box. "Sweet Dreams?"

Obviously, she'd never heard of them.

"Our company is in Icicle Falls, Washington. We're named Sweet Dreams because my great-grandmother, who founded it, literally dreamed the first recipes."

That almost made Mimi smile. "Really."

"These are our newest truffles. I hope I'm following in my great-grandmother's footsteps. I discovered the recipes in a dream just the other night and I think you'll like them. We're calling this our chocolate garden."

Now Mimi was intrigued. To Samantha's surprise and delight, she stepped over to the reception area, found an empty chair and sat down with the box.

Samantha held her breath as Mimi selected one and took a delicate bite. Then both eyebrows arched. "What on earth is that flavor? I swear it tastes like rose water."

Samantha nodded. "Actually, it is."

"Try one, Miles," Mimi offered the box to her companion, who was standing next to her.

The man took one and popped it in his mouth. And smiled. "Very nice."

"And you say these came to you in a dream," Mimi asked.

Samantha nodded.

"And where is your company again?"

Samantha launched into a spiel that would have made both her great-grandmother and her fellow Chamber of Commerce members proud. If the woman didn't want to come to Icicle Falls and check them out after this, there was something seriously wrong with her.

"This is intriguing," Mimi said. "Have you got a business card?"

Yes, yes, yes! "I do." Samantha calmly, like a true business professional, produced one while on the inside she was doing the Snoopy dance.

She returned to the table to find the waiters cleaning up the mess while Bailey sat there looking like a child who'd been sent to the principal's office. But when she saw Samantha she beamed. "She loved them, right? I can tell by the way you're smiling."

"She asked for my business card."

Bailey jumped up to high-five her with an enthusiastic, "Yes!" just as another waiter came out the door with a laden tray.

As it went flying, Samantha said, "I think we'd better go eat somewhere else."

Mimi LeGrande's producer, Miles, called Samantha the next day as she was waiting for her plane to Seattle. Mimi would like to do a segment on them the following week. Would Monday be all right?

More than all right. Samantha hardly needed the plane to fly home.

Once more it was lights, camera, action, as Mimi's crew hit town to film.

Cecily had put together a huge gift basket, which Mimi accepted as her due with only a minimum of thanks. Mom's faint frown of disapproval was barely noticeable. Not that Mimi would have noticed, anyway. She was too busy looking around the gift shop. "Small," she pronounced it, "but charming."

Okay, they could live with charming.

After the filming, Mimi and Miles went off to lunch at Schwangau, leaving Samantha and her mother and sister in shock.

"Did I hear him right?" Cecily asked faintly.

Samantha nodded. It was all she could manage since her throat was choked with tears. The show wouldn't air until May. Her mind closed the door on the happy vision she'd entertained of orders (and money) flooding in. Oh, orders would flood in after the show aired, but it would be too late to help her family. The new owner of Sweet Dreams would reap the benefits of her hard work.

This was a dark day for the Sterlings, indeed. There went their last hope for keeping their company from floating down the River of No Return.

The thought of Sweet Dreams Chocolates winding up in the hands of Trevor Brown, the king of cheap chocolate, made Samantha want to throw up.

So, what are you going to do about it?

Good question. She went to the office and locked herself in to eat truffles and think.

Twenty-Six

Love makes heroes of us all.
—Muriel Sterling, *Mixing Business with Pleasure:*
How to Successfully Balance Business and Love

"**I** wish you weren't leaving, sweetie," Mom said as Cecily pulled her carry-on from the trunk of Mom's car.

"It's time. There's nothing left here for me to do," Cecily said.

She wished there was, but the chocolate festival was over, they'd finally lost the battle to keep the company and that was her cue to ride off into the sunset. Yesterday they'd pulled their hopes off life support. There was nothing more she could do for her sister now. They were out of options.

"Are you sure you have to go?" Luke had asked when she stopped by Sweet Dreams to say goodbye to everyone. He'd walked her outside. Although her mother was waiting at the curb, the car engine idling, and people were passing on the street, it had felt like it was just the two of them standing here.

"I've got my ticket," she'd said.

"You don't have to use it."

"I have a life back in California." Consisting of an ex-boyfriend who still tried to hit her up for money and a business she'd shut down. Some life.

"Overpriced real estate and shallow people?"

"You can find that anywhere." And they weren't all shallow. She'd met some great people in the City of Angels.

"Not here," he'd said. "Look, Cec, I know you made it pretty clear that you weren't interested in starting anything, but I think we could be good together."

Luke needed a woman who would appreciate him, not a woman with a foolish heart who was constantly falling for bad boys, not a woman who was fed up with love and men. "I've got to go," she'd said, and backed away. "Take care, Luke."

"He's a nice man," Mom had said as they drove off down the slushy street.

"Yes, he is."

"He's going to make some woman a wonderful husband."

"Yes, he is. I wish I knew someone for him."

"I do."

It had been impossible to misinterpret that motherly expression. "Not me."

"Why not? You're a lovely woman, he's a wonderful man."

"There's just no chemistry," Cecily had said with a shrug. Well, maybe a little, but not enough.

"Maybe you haven't spent enough time in the lab together. Feelings can grow."

So she'd heard.

"After the big city, Icicle Falls must feel ridiculously small, but the people who live in it all have big hearts. I think it did you good to get away, but maybe it would do you even more good to come back."

Cecily hadn't said anything to that and Mom let the subject drop. Their conversation turned to other topics as they drove over the pass, but her mother's words lingered at the back of her mind.

Once she was in L.A. she'd pack up and sell her condo. And then what? She had no idea. What did she want to be when she grew up? And where did she want to be?

She wanted to be in Icicle Falls. She hadn't realized how much she'd missed the place until she'd returned and gotten involved.

Everyone says you can't go home, she reminded herself as her plane touched down in sunny California. But she wanted to. Wanted to indulge her creativity and spend time with her mother, wanted to start her mornings with lattes from Bavarian Brews or stop by Gingerbread Haus to sample Cass's cookies.

The plane finally taxied to a stop and cell phones went on all around her. The whole plane buzzed as people told loved ones they'd arrived safely, took their luggage off the racks and began to jostle their way off the plane. Everyone had somewhere to go, someone waiting for them, and she felt oddly alone in that crowd.

She couldn't help remembering the fun she'd had planning the Mr. Dreamy contest, of the nice people she'd met while working at Zelda's. (What was so wrong with being a restaurant hostess, anyway?) She remembered that dance with Luke at the ball. And, unbidden, Todd Black's smirking pirate face came to mind.

Here she was in a big, exciting city and all she could think about was a small town nestled in the mountains. But there was nothing for her to do there, no real way to make a living and build a future.

Just get on with your life, she told herself as she picked up her luggage from baggage claim.

* * *

Just get on with your life, Samantha told herself as she hung up the phone. Tears sprang to her eyes. *Sorry, Great-grandma. I tried, I really did.*

At least it looked as if her company might end up in good hands. If the Elegance Chocolates people liked what they saw when they came up on Friday.

What was not to like? They were getting a fabulous company at a bargain price. Yes, the past year had been a bit of a mess, but she'd sent them the financials for the past five. Anyone with a head for business could see this was a temporary blip.

She'd been assured her people would be able to keep their jobs. The only one out of a job would be her. She could hardly stand to think of someone else coming in and taking over Sweet Dreams but that was exactly what would happen. After a brief transition period, she'd be history. The Elegance executives would, naturally, want to move in their own person to run the company. She knew that without even asking. *A new broom sweeps clean. Out with the old, in with the new.*

She'd never thought of herself as old before, but in this instance that was exactly what she was. *You did the right thing,* she reminded herself. If Elegance took over the company, all would end well. Yes, Sweet Dreams would be no more, but their chocolates would live on and her employees would still have jobs. That was what mattered. As for her, she'd do…something.

And speaking of that, what would she do if, after seeing it, the Elegance people decided they didn't want her company? She felt sick.

Elena buzzed her. "Blake Preston is here to see you."

That didn't make her feel any better. This was how it

felt to be dying in the desert with the vultures circling. *Well, we're not dead yet.* She set her jaw. "Send him in."

He entered her office like a man on a mission. "Blake, I don't know what you're doing here but I still own this company till the end of the month," she said.

He smiled at that. "Till the end of the month and beyond," he corrected her, and laid a check on her desk.

"What's this?"

"It's about keeping a family company where it belongs—with the family who started it."

She felt like Alice after she'd tumbled down the rabbit hole. "I don't understand."

"Merry Christmas early, or happy Valentine's Day late. Or whatever you want to call it," Blake said, and nudged the check closer to her.

She picked it up and stared at it. What in the name of— "A personal check?"

"All you have to do is endorse it and deposit it. I'll expect you in tomorrow." He turned to leave.

"Wait." She jumped up from her desk and ran to him. "But where did you get this kind of money?"

"Does it matter?"

"I need to know," she insisted. How on earth had he come up with it?

"Let's just say I used my bank connections," he said.

Her brows knit. "What do you mean?" Suspicion turned to horrified understanding. "Tell me you didn't take out a loan."

He shrugged. "Even bank managers can qualify for employee loans. I should have thought of it sooner. My only excuse is that there was no way I could come up with what you needed at first, so this wasn't even an option. But after you left for California I got thinking and realized that, thanks to the festival, we were down to a number I could manage."

It was still a huge amount and a huge commitment, and she couldn't, with a clear conscience, let him make that kind of sacrifice. "I can't accept this," she said, holding out the check.

"Why not?" The look in his eyes lit those sparklers inside her.

"It's too much."

"Yeah? You're saying your company isn't worth saving?"

"I'm already saving it. I'm going to sell it to Elegance."

He nodded, apparently thinking that over. "I assume they make good chocolate."

"Fabulous," she said, struggling to keep her voice even.

"Is that what you want, Samantha?" he asked softly.

"Of course it's not what I want," she cried, "but I can't just take money from you."

"Can you take a personal loan from a friend?"

How she needed a friend! She bit her lip.

He took a step closer. "From a friend who would maybe, someday, like to be more?"

"I…don't know." Were there conditions that came along with this loan? Would he want to run her company? Expect her to sleep with him? Hmm. Would that last condition be so bad?

"There are no strings attached," he said as if reading her mind. "I think you can rebuild this company and that will be good for the whole town. If you're uncomfortable with doing this on just a handshake we can draw up a contract. Either way, that money is yours. I went into banking to help people, and there's no one I'd rather help more."

"I can't believe I'm hearing this," she said. She had to be dreaming. Where was Great-grandma Rose with more recipes?

"I told you, Samantha, I'm not your enemy."

Her mind was a Tilt-a-Whirl, sending thoughts zooming in all directions. She'd tried so hard to keep this company, run down every blind alley she could find, and in the end her solution was as simple as someone unexpected coming through for her? How could that be? "I don't know what to say."

"How about thank you?" he teased.

"Thank you," she said, and burst into tears.

He gathered her in his arms and she felt his lips brush the top of her head. How wonderful it was to be held by her archenemy. *Make that former archenemy,* she corrected herself.

"There is one more thing you could say," he murmured.

"What?"

"That you'll go out with me."

Now she was crying and laughing. "I might have some free evenings on my calendar."

They sealed the deal with a kiss, a big juicy, melt-your-panties kiss. Oh, yes, there *was* something better than chocolate and Blake had just given her a very nice sample of it.

He suddenly turned serious. "I do have a confession to make."

Uh-oh. Samantha braced herself. "What's that?"

"I'm allergic to chocolate."

She gaped at him. "Those chocolates I brought you?"

"My gram's book club loved 'em. Everybody loves Sweet Dreams chocolates."

"Except you." How ironic.

He grinned. "That's okay. I'm more interested in the woman who makes them."

And to prove it, he kissed her again.

"So when do you think you might be open to that date?" he said after they'd come up for air.

"Oh, maybe as soon as I call Mom and my sisters and tell them the good news," she said with a grin.

She called Cecily first. Her sister was happy for her but didn't sound all that surprised. "I just had a feeling," she said.

"What else have you got a feeling about?" Samantha asked, smiling at Blake.

"Well, I've got a strong feeling that Blake is still there with you. Am I right?"

"Oh, yeah. By the way, we're going to be pretty busy rebuilding the company and I could use help with the marketing and advertising. I know you've got a life down there but I'd love to have you back here. I don't suppose I could talk you into coming home?"

"I don't suppose you could keep me away," Cecily replied.

Oh, yes, life was looking good.

Samantha and Blake celebrated by going to dinner at Zelda's. "Are you having dessert?" Maria asked.

Samantha smiled at Blake. "Yes, but not here."

Maria, no fool, cracked, "Let me guess. You're going someplace for chocolate kisses?"

"Something much better," Samantha said with a grin.

* * *

Muriel was walking on Lost Bride Trail with both her husbands. "It looks like Sweet Dreams will be around for a long time," she told them. "Samantha saved it."

"That takes a load off my mind," Waldo said.

"Mine, too," Stephen agreed. "The only thing that would please me even more is to know that she's found someone who can make her happy."

"I think she has," Muriel said.

He smiled. "I'm glad to hear it." He looked up the path. "We have to go now. Will you be all right?"

She smiled at both of them. "Yes, I will. You two go on ahead. I'll be fine here."

They both kissed her and then walked up the path. She stood watching until a mountain mist swallowed them.

She awoke to find herself alone in her bed, morning sunlight filling her bedroom. She smiled, then threw off the covers. It was a new day.

May had arrived and the countryside was lush and green with vineyards come back to life and blossoming fruit trees. This particular Saturday was a perfect day for a hike, all blue sky and sunshine.

Blue skies or no, Samantha had planned to get caught up on her laundry and maybe clean her apartment. And she said as much to Blake when he suggested a hike. Cleaning had never sat high on her priority list but these days, between running Sweet Dreams and spending her free hours with Blake, it never happened. If she didn't do something soon, her condo was going to be condemned by the board of health.

"Come on, babe. On a day like this, that stuff can wait."

When he put it that way... "I'll get my camera," she said.

Two hours later they were on Lost Bride Trail, the sun warm on their shoulders, the thunder of the falls promising a stunning view right around the bend. Normally it wasn't a two-hour hike to the falls—unless you stopped frequently to take pictures. Or kiss.

"I remember hiking up here when I was a Boy Scout," Blake said. "I guess I've come full circle."

"Only without the boys," Samantha said.

"I like girls better." And to prove it he drew her to him.

As always, contact with that big, football-player body of his set off a thousand sparklers inside her.

He smiled down at her. "Have I told you recently how amazing you are?"

"Oh, you're only saying that 'cause it's true," she quipped.

"Yeah? How do you know I'm not just saying it to protect my investment?"

The answer to that was easy. The hungry glint in his eyes betrayed him.

He touched his lips to hers and threaded his fingers through her hair and that ended the joking. They got serious.

After a long delay they finally made it to the falls. "Look at that," she said. "Gorgeous."

"I'll say," he agreed.

She turned to see he wasn't admiring the falls at all, and that glint was back in his eyes, promising another lengthy delay before they started back down the trail.

"Here," he said, "give me the camera. I'll take your picture."

She handed it over.

"Pretend you're searching for the lost bride," he said.

"Oh, that's B.S." She'd seen the lost bride and...well, here she was with Blake. Still.

"Come on, be a sport," he coaxed.

"Oh, all right." She turned and shaded her eyes as if she were, indeed, searching.

And that was when she saw the figure of a woman flitting behind the waters. The hairs on her neck stood on end and she gasped.

"That's perfect," Blake said. "Got it."

She turned back to him, wide-eyed. "Did you get her?"

"Get who?" he asked, puzzled "Oh, yeah. Ha, ha."

"No. Really. She's right there." Samantha followed the direction of her pointing finger and saw...nothing. "She was there. I saw her." She took the camera and flipped back to the shot. There was only one woman in it, one crazy woman.

Now Blake was staring at her earnestly. "Did you see her?"

Well, that was the power of suggestion for you. She shook her head and blew off the legend of the lost bride with a flick of her hand. "Nah. It must have been a shadow."

Or a promise of things to come.

Epilogue: Dreams Coming True

The much-anticipated episode of *All Things Chocolate* aired on the Food Network the following week. The Sterlings had a viewing party, squeezing as many friends as possible into Muriel's new digs—Pat's charming little cottage overlooking Ed York's vineyard.

"I must say—and I don't say this very often—these chocolates are to die for," said Mimi LeGrande, holding up one of Samantha's new creations. "But I think I can guarantee you'll die with a smile on your face."

Everyone applauded as she put in a plug for visiting the Sweet Dreams shop and Icicle Falls.

"You did it, Sammy," Bailey said. "You saved us."

"No," Samantha corrected her. "We all did it."

"Thank God," Ed murmured. "And this." He waved a hand in the direction of the TV. "This should bring in a ton of orders."

"And visitors," Olivia added. "I bet we'll have twice as many people at the chocolate festival next year," she predicted gleefully.

"Let's not rush our festivals," Ed told her. "We still have an Oktoberfest to put together."

With Mom and Cecily involved, Samantha suspected it would be spectacular.

Her sister had jumped into community life with both feet when she moved back, volunteering at the food bank and getting herself (and Mom) on a committee to plan future festivals—a real benefit to the town. She was also a benefit to Sweet Dreams and was doing a great job of promoting the company.

In addition to the festival planning, Mom was writing a new book, a cookbook titled *A Chocolate Lover's Sweet Dream,* but that didn't stop her from coming into the office a couple of times a week to assist Cecily with marketing.

Curled up on the sofa next to Blake, looking around at all the people who meant so much to her and thinking about how they'd all helped one another through a difficult time, Samantha felt almost overwhelmed with gratitude. Waldo would have loved this party, she thought with a smile. *Everything worked out, Waldo. You're off the hook.*

Blake gave her a kiss that promised fireworks when they were alone, then went to the kitchen counter where the champagne was sitting to freshen their glasses. That done, he turned and cleared his throat. "While we're celebrating, I have a very important question to ask Samantha."

"Like when am I going to pay back the money?" she joked.

He returned to the couch and held out a champagne glass. "Like how about making me a silent partner?" At the bottom of the glass something bright and sparkly winked at her.

"Oh, my gosh, it's a ring!" Bailey cried.

"I knew you were a match all along," Cecily crowed.

Samantha was the only one of the sisters who was speechless. She stared at the glass and the diamond in it. Then she stared at Blake. Her company was safe, the future was looking good for Icicle Falls once more, and now the most wonderful man in the world was asking her to marry him. Great-grandma Rose couldn't have dreamed up anything better than this.

"I know I can never properly appreciate your chocolate, but I sure do appreciate you. Samantha Sterling, I'm crazy in love with you. Will you marry me?"

"Yes!" She kissed him and everyone applauded.

While she fished out the ring and slipped it on her finger, her mother and sisters circulated among the guests, making sure everyone's champagne glass was filled.

Once that was accomplished Ed York raised his glass. "A toast. Here's to a sweet future for both of you."

"I'll toast to that," Blake said, and kissed his bride-to-be.

Samantha closed her eyes and savored the moment. No chocolate could compare to Blake's kisses. Like Waldo said, did it get any better than this?

With the man she'd chosen, she was sure it would.

* * * * *

Recipes from the Sterlings

If you're ever in Icicle Falls we hope you'll come visit
Sweet Dreams. Meanwhile, enjoy trying some of our
favorite chocolate recipes.
Samantha Sterling

THE CHOCOLATE ROSE
WHITE CHOCOLATE TRUFFLE

(Our friend Sheila Roberts tried to make this and failed
miserably, but her pal Doreen Geidel came through and
saved the day. Doreen, you're a real chocolatier!)
Yield: 48 candies

Ingredients:
2 14-oz bags of vanilla candy disks,
such as Wilton's Candy Melts
(one for your ganache filling,
the other for the outside coating)
1 cup heavy cream
½–¾ tsp rose water
(Start conservatively. You can always add more.)

Directions:
For ganache, put one bag of candy disks in a large, shallow dish. Bring cream slowly to a light boil, then pour
over disks and keep stirring until they all melt. When
the ganache is warm, it is very creamy. You can thicken
it by whisking it and then putting it in the refrigerator.
This may take a couple of hours, which gives you time to
go do something else (like read a Sheila Roberts book).

After your ganache is cooled and firm, form it into
small, candy-size balls. Place them on parchment or wax
paper. Melt the second bag of disks in a double boiler,
then dip each ball in the melted white chocolate. Once
they've set, store them in a cool place.

BAILEY'S CHOCOLATE TRUFFLE TRIFLE

Serves 8

Ingredients:
*1 regular size (10.75 oz) frozen pound cake
such as Sara Lee
½ cup raspberry liqueur (Although you can also make
this without the liqueur and it will taste great.)
1 cup raspberry jam
1 package instant white-chocolate pudding mix
2 cups whole milk
1 pint fresh raspberries
½ pint heavy cream
1 tsp vanilla
1 Tbsp sugar (Optional—use this if you like your
whipped cream sweetened.)
1 cup coarsely chopped dark chocolate truffles*

Directions:
Cut pound cake into slices, then cut the slices into thirds.
Line the bottom of a trifle bowl (or any large cut-glass
bowl) with half the slices. Sprinkle with half the liqueur.
Next spread on half the jam. Mix the pudding and milk
until thick and layer half of that over the jam. Add half
the raspberries and half the cut-up truffles. Repeat the
process, using what's left of the ingredients. Add vanilla
and sugar to the cream and whip it until stiff, then frost
the top of the trifle.

ICICLE FALLS MOOSE MUNCH

(This one is courtesy of our friend Dee Dee Giordano.)
Yield: anywhere from 24 to 36, depending on what size
you make them

Ingredients:
2 cups Cap'n Crunch peanut butter cereal
2 cups broken pretzel sticks
2 cups roasted peanuts
1 bag of vanilla or chocolate candy disks such as Wilton's Candy Melts

Directions:
Mix the first three ingredients together. Then melt the
disks in the microwave until completely melted. Pour
over the mixed ingredients. Working fast, so the chocolate doesn't set up, drop by spoonfuls onto wax paper.
If the chocolate sets before you can spoon them all out
microwave for several seconds to reheat chocolate and
continue spooning.

WHITE LAVENDER FUDGE

Yield: 9 to a dozen (You can make more or less, depending on how big you want your pieces of fudge.)

Ingredients:
2 cups granulated cane sugar
1 cup half-and-half
1 Tbsp light corn syrup
½ tsp salt
1 Tbsp butter
¾ tsp lavender (You can add more but try this
small amount first. Like rose water,
lavender is powerful stuff!)

Directions:
Butter the sides of a heavy 2-quart saucepan. (This prevents grains of sugar from clinging to the sides of the pan and forming unwanted crystals when the fudge starts to bubble.) In it combine the sugar, half-and-half, corn syrup and salt. Cook over medium heat, stirring constantly until the sugar dissolves and the mixture comes to a boil. Then cook to soft-ball stage. Immediately remove from heat and cool to lukewarm without stirring. Then add butter and lavender and beat vigorously until mixture becomes very thick and starts to lose its gloss. (Good exercise!) Spread in a buttered 9 x 5 x 3 (or 9 x 9) inch pan. Score into squares while warm. Cut when cool and firm. Store in a cool place. (If you can keep it long enough to store. Good luck with that!)
Note: If you cook this for too long and too high you will

wind up with caramels—not a bad thing, either, but we thought we should warn you.

To extend the life of your fudge you can store it in the refrigerator. Line an airtight container with wax paper and put wax paper between the layers of fudge so the pieces won't stick to the container or one another. You should be able to store it for up to three weeks this way. Before serving allow it to remain in the container until it returns to room temperature.

BEAR DROPPINGS

(This is courtesy of our friend Carol Hostetter.)
Yield: 24

Ingredients:
2 cups milk chocolate chips
1 Tbsp shortening
½ cup raisins
½ cup slivered almonds
(You can substitute walnuts if you wish.)

Directions:
In a double boiler over simmering water, melt the chocolate chips and shortening, stirring until smooth. Remove from heat; stir in raisins and almonds. Drop by tablespoonfuls onto waxed paper. Chill until ready to serve.

$7.99 U.S./$9.99 CAN.

- ✂

REQUEST YOUR FREE BOOKS!

2 FREE NOVELS
FROM THE ROMANCE COLLECTION
PLUS 2 FREE GIFTS!

YES! Please send me 2 FREE novels from the Romance Collection and my 2 FREE gifts (gifts are worth about $10). After receiving them, if I don't wish to receive any more books, I can return the shipping statement marked "cancel." If I don't cancel, I will receive 4 brand-new novels every month and be billed just $6.49 per book in the U.S. or $6.99 per book in Canada. That's a savings of at least 19% off the cover price. It's quite a bargain! Shipping and handling is just 50¢ per book in the U.S. and 75¢ per book in Canada.* I understand that accepting the 2 free books and gifts places me under no obligation to buy anything. I can always return a shipment and cancel at any time. Even if I never buy another book, the two free books and gifts are mine to keep forever.

194/394 MDN GH4D

Name	(PLEASE PRINT)
Address	Apt. #
City	State/Prov.	Zip/Postal Code

Signature (if under 18, a parent or guardian must sign)

Mail to the **Reader Service**:
IN U.S.A.: P.O. Box 1867, Buffalo, NY 14240-1867
IN CANADA: P.O. Box 609, Fort Erie, Ontario L2A 5X3

Want to try two free books from another line?
Call 1-800-873-8635 or visit www.ReaderService.com.

* Terms and prices subject to change without notice. Prices do not include applicable taxes. Sales tax applicable in N.Y. Canadian residents will be charged applicable taxes. Offer not valid in Quebec. This offer is limited to one order per household. Not valid for current subscribers to the Romance Collection or the Romance/Suspense Collection. All orders subject to credit approval. Credit or debit balances in a customer's account(s) may be offset by any other outstanding balance owed by or to the customer. Please allow 4 to 6 weeks for delivery. Offer available while quantities last.

Your Privacy—The Reader Service is committed to protecting your privacy. Our Privacy Policy is available online at www.ReaderService.com or upon request from the Reader Service.

We make a portion of our mailing list available to reputable third parties that offer products we believe may interest you. If you prefer that we not exchange your name with third parties, or if you wish to clarify or modify your communication preferences, please visit us at www.ReaderService.com/consumerschoice or write to us at Reader Service Preference Service, P.O. Box 9062, Buffalo, NY 14240-9062. Include your complete name and address.

ROM15